EDITORIAL PRAISE]
IND

“A well-written thriller with a superb hook.”
- Wayne Brookes, Associate Publisher, Pan Macmillan

"I ended up reading it in two sittings! I thought this was a perfectly paced thriller, brilliantly commercial and with such a clever and high concept premise.”
- Sam Eades, Fiction Publisher, Orion

“The writing and plotting were really pacy and engaging, and it reminded me of TM Logan.”
- Joel Richardson, Publisher for Crime, Michael Joseph

Readers are enjoying The Honesty Index:

‘I have just finished reading The Honesty Index. Every time I had to leave the book I couldn't get back to it quick enough. This has to be a winner. I loved it.’

‘I really enjoyed it. It kept me engaged and entertained until the very end.’

‘I really, really enjoyed it. I felt immersed in the plot from the first page and the tension didn't let up.’

‘What a great story. I thoroughly enjoyed it.’

‘Thoroughly enjoyable, fast-paced narrative kept me hooked into the small hours.’

BOOKS BY NJ BARKER

AVAILABLE FROM AMAZON

STANDALONE THRILLERS:

The Honesty Index.

The Genius Club, available in early 2024.

THE KENNEDY LOGAN THRILLERS:

The Catastrophe Test, the introductory short story.

The Moral Authority, book one in the series.

Book two, available in 2024.

THE HONESTY INDEX

READY TO PLAY?

NJ BARKER

For my family

"Honesty is the first chapter in the book of wisdom."

— THOMAS JEFFERSON

PROLOGUE

S*uburban London, April 2009*

THE SEVEN TEENAGERS were sitting on logs that formed a circle around the fire. A glitterball moon spun in the night sky to the ambient lo-fi techno soundtrack of the nightingale song. Around them, silhouettes of trees lurked in the shadows.

Trent Ryder shoved his hands deep into his donkey jacket pockets and flexed his fingers to warm them. The party was winding down and the fire had dulled to an amber glow. He looked at the packet of cigarettes Paddy was holding out. With sandy brown hair and freckles and eyes to match, Paddy was the kind of kid that parents found easy to like but hard to trust.

Trent didn't really like cigarettes but he accepted the offer because he had an audience. He blew out the smoke, turned and locked eyes with Lila Jain: Bollywood princess meets home counties girl-next-door. Flawless skin, radiant smile and not even a blush of make-up. Her crimson down jacket was zipped up to the neck; her breath hung in frosty clouds, her eyes reflecting the firelight.

He held her gaze for a fraction too long. He would have carried on forever but she turned away – which was a bad sign. But she was smiling. Which was a good sign.

Trent had suggested to her earlier that they do some exploring, but she'd just laughed. First at him, because he was being suggestive. And then she'd laughed with him, because he was funny. *Good-looking, with a great sense of humour. Keen explorer. Contact Trent if you're looking for love.*

Trent sighed and watched the smoke spiral up to greet the stars as he sat flanked by Nicholas Samson and Lila. between the devil and heaven on earth, wondering how many more minutes of this bonfire to Samson's vanity he could take.

The six of them had known each other for years but they'd agreed to give the new kid a chance. It was Samson's birthday, after all. But the evening hadn't been easy. Samson was academically precocious, already a school year ahead of his age, which maybe didn't help.

Copper, sitting on the other side of Samson, had tried to engage him in conversation but after each question the silences had lengthened. Trent imagined Mrs Samson insisting on the birthday party to help her son to make some friends. *They just need to get to know you, Nicky darling. The real you. The completely freaky, wide-eyed nutjob that Mummy loves so dearly.* Well, maybe not those precise words. But Nicholas Samson had cornered them all in the lunch queue two fateful weeks earlier and once Copper had said yes, the others didn't have the heart to decline. Although the idea of leaving Copper to fly solo at Samson's birthday party had been almost funny enough to swing the balance.

They still had an hour before Paddy's father was due to

pick them up in his battered old Volvo Estate. Trent could think of plenty of ways he'd like to pass the time with Lila but none of them involved smoking. He was about to stub the cigarette out when he caught her glancing at him. He took another puff – cool, nonchalant – and gave her a wink. She shook her head gently in response, her dark bobbed hair swaying in front of her smile.

Samson had led the group of friends to the clearing by torchlight, then left the light switched off by his feet. Trent was peering into the shadows trying to count the shades of grey, when a shaft of torchlight illuminated Nicholas Samson's face, making his skin look pale and unworldly. The fire spat out a bright orange spark which sizzled on the dry ground.

'It's time,' Nicholas said. His voice was pure gargled gravel, like he thought he was auditioning for a voice-over in a horror film trailer.

Lila covered her mouth with her hand, shoulders twitching. Dub, on the other side of the fire, caught Trent's eye. Maybe Samson thought edgy was the way to go. Boy, had he read that wrong. But he could still recover it with a joke.

'Everyone has to reveal a secret,' Samson continued. 'And we all swear to keep it. Forever.' His words would have been a good effort, if only Samson hadn't been deadly serious.

'Jesus, Samson,' laughed Paddy, 'this isn't the Blair Witch Project.' His voice was louder than normal. He'd rolled off his log and was lying back on the grass, propped up on his elbows. His round face was glowing, his eyes unfocused. The six pack of lager he'd smuggled into the party was now safely hidden in his bloodstream, the empty cans kicked under a hedge at the end of the garden.

Secret. Trent folded his arms. Despite the warmth of his coat across his shoulders, there was a knot gathering in his stomach. But there was no way that he'd be revealing his secret. Not here. And not to Nicholas Samson.

'I think it sounds like fun,' said Oli. You could tell she meant it. Fun was her personal stamp of endorsement. *He's so much fun. They're all really fun.* When she was sure everyone was looking at her, she flicked her blonde hair and slowly tilted her head until she caught the perfect angle for the freeze frame.

'You go first, then, Olivia.' Samson was still shining the torch up at his own face because, he was so, you know, fun, fun, fun.

Oli took a moment to arrange herself as if she were on the cover of a magazine and started to talk. 'Well, my favourite sixteenth birthday present last year ... was the sex.'

Trent tuned her out. Not in an 'I'm so bored, I'm too cool to follow the rule' sort of way. But because his mind had flashed back to the fire. Memories clawed for his attention. He blinked and shuffled forward, pushing those thoughts away. Before he knew it, Oli had finished and Paddy was sitting up and talking, clearly having warmed to the idea of sharing secrets.

Trent chewed on his thumb, his teeth biting into the fleshy pad until he could feel the resistance of the bone underneath. Samson's secrets game was just that. A game. And the others already knew about the fire a year ago. Even Samson would know, although Trent had never told him directly. He didn't have to. Trent could rely on others to do that. *He doesn't like to talk about it but I should tell you, so you don't, you know, say something by accident.* So they all knew about the fire, about how his parents and younger brother had died and that only he and his sister had survived. But that was all they knew.

Trent shook his head. Just because Samson said they were

going to reveal a secret didn't mean he *had* to say anything. He could just keep quiet, even if that looked odd, as though he had something to hide.

He could hear the birdsong. More insistent than before. Everyone was laughing, Paddy the loudest. Paddy dialled everything up to eleven. A few of the group clapped as he finished his confession, although Trent had heard the story of Paddy's father interrupting his son's 'private bedroom activity' several times before.

And then Dub was talking. Dub was so thin, as if he only ate one square meal a day, but as tall as if he ate four. His expression matched his tone. Serious.

'... and I didn't know what to do. Whoever it was, they were face down on the grass next to the river. I was sure they were dead.'

The laughter froze and died. Anxious glances shot around the circle and Lila blew out air from her cheeks. A ripple of wind pulsed the fire, which glowed a deep red; its dying breath.

'Jesus, Dub. What did you do?' asked Oli, her eyes movie star wide.

'I ran home and told my dad. I reckon we were back to the riverbank within ten minutes.' Dub was staring at the floor, shaking his head. The others leant in. 'But there was no one there. I checked all the local news sites for weeks. I was sure there'd be a report of a body being found somewhere, but nothing.'

Paddy slapped Dub on the back. 'Maybe it was a ghost. I remember reading about a girl who was murdered down by the river, forty years ago. She's come back to haunt you.' He raised his hands over his head and rolled his eyes back. 'I'm coming for you, Andrew Dubnyk.' His voice was a high-pitched wail. 'I'm watching you.' Paddy's laugh triggered the others. Even Dub managed a grin.

Copper was next up. Copper by name and copper by hair colour, although the hair came first. Trent couldn't imagine *she* would have any earth-shattering secrets. The only rule-books she hadn't read were the ones she'd written. Fifteen years old but already middle-aged.

'I discovered my father's stash of porn mags at the bottom of his cupboard,' she said with the confidence of a teacher setting lines. Write it out one hundred times.

'Copper.' Paddy's mouth was wide open. 'No way. I don't believe it. Does he know?' He was clutching his stomach.

'Of course not. I'm hardly going to tell him, am I? So, that's my secret.' A flicker of a smile. 'Well, my dad's secret.' She turned to Samson, who was next in the circle.

Trent needed to decide on what he was going to say. Paddy and Copper had opted for humour. Samson was still talking and Trent forced himself to tune in.

'... and it was all over Facebook. So my mum decided I had to move school. And that's why you are now lucky enough to have me in your lives.'

He flicked the torch off and back on again, his expression blank. There was something weirdly staged about the whole thing. Samson had suggested the game and it had sounded spontaneous but Trent wondered whether he'd planned it just to be the centre of attention.

Trent scanned his friends' faces, looking for a clue as to what Samson had just said. Lila wore a Mona-Lisa smile, Copper was frowning, and he caught Dub raising an eyebrow at Paddy. Trent frowned. His desire to know the secret wrestled against his reluctance to admit he hadn't been paying attention. He cleared his throat. 'Sorry. I didn't catch the beginning of that. What was all over Facebook?'

Samson flipped the torch down until it was shining directly into Trent's eyes.

Trent blinked and turned away. 'Jesus. What was that for?'

'You must be punished for not listening to the secrets.' Samson's voice was hollow.

Trent shook his head. He could only take so much, and Samson's capacity for playing the oddball appeared endless. Although it was possible that he wasn't acting at all.

Lila leant towards Trent. 'His dad was accused of election fraud and a group of vigilantes targeted him. A mob turned up at the family home.'

'Blimey.' Trent said. Everyone was staring at him. Why were they expecting him to provide a more detailed reaction? It took a few further seconds of silence before he realised they were waiting to hear his secret. A few seconds in which he locked away his emotions. He couldn't share those, because if he started he wouldn't be able to stop. He glanced at Lila, whose turn followed his.

He started to speak. 'You all know about the fire.' *The* fire. That was enough. The others looked as if they had turned to stone.

Lila rested her hand on his arm. 'You don't have to talk about that night, Trent,' she said. 'This whole thing is just a bit of fun.'

Trent cleared his throat and continued. 'Which is why,' he smiled, 'I'm not going to talk about that.' Lila punched his arm and he saw Paddy's shoulders drop. 'My secret is,' he looked at each of them in turn, 'I have no secrets.'

'Boo.' Paddy's foghorn of derision was magnified by his hands cupped around his mouth.

'I think I'd better take my turn.' Lila was looking at Trent. He shrugged at her and felt the spotlight swing away from him and towards Lila. The natural order of things restored.

Trent sunk back into the moonlight shadows. It was only a game. Not just that. It was Nicholas Samson's game. There was no reason to share anything of consequence. No reason at all.

Lila leant forward, looked around the circle of friends, and smiled. She spoke in a conspiratorial whisper. 'Okay, guys. Here's my secret.' She shot Trent one quick, intense glance, then looked back at the others. What had that meant?

Trent's brain scrambled to make some sense of how he was feeling. And then he heard her words.

'I have a massive crush on someone.' Her hair fell across her face so he could no longer see her expression. Did she mean *him*? Was she going to announce it here? Lila brushed her hair back again. All eyes were on her – especially his.

'I love it. A real secret,' Paddy shouted. He pointed at Oli. 'Countdown please, Olivia.'

'Five, four...'

Lila laughed. Paddy began clapping in time with Oli's chanting. Trent held his breath.

'Three, two, one.'

'I'm not going to tell you his name,' Lila said, grinning. Trent let out a slow breath. Lila tucked a strand of hair behind her ear. 'But I will say that he's older than me.'

Trent's world tilted. He was four months younger than Lila. He scratched his nose. Were the others looking at him? He forced himself to grin and prayed that someone else would say something.

'No, no, no,' Samson said, raking his fingers through his hair. He rocked backwards and forwards. 'That's not...' He screwed his face up, struggling to find the words. Trent didn't understand why Samson was upset. But now their host was on his feet, his pointing hand sweeping round the circle of friends. '*None* of you are taking this seriously. I don't *care* about your superficial lives. Give me something *real*.'

Trent glanced at Paddy just in time to catch the eye roll.

Samson was still going. 'I told you about something important.' There was a tremor in his voice. 'Something that changed my life. And you...' He shook his head.

Copper stood up and rested her hand on Samson's shoulder. 'We were just having fun, Nicholas.'

He shrugged her off. 'I don't care about fun.'

Oli was blinking, no doubt trying to digest a worldview so opposed to her own. Trent was caught between laughing at the whole ridiculous charade and trying to process Lila's announcement when Samson leant back and screamed into the night sky.

They all stared at him. It must have lasted ten seconds. When he finally lowered his face Trent could see tears in Samson's eyes. What the hell?

'You're supposed to be my friends.' Samson's voice cracked as he wiped his face. 'And friends trust each other with secrets.' He turned away from them and started walking back towards the house.

Trent risked a glance at Lila. He'd thought that the two of them had something special. But it seemed he'd been wrong. His thoughts were interrupted by Samson shouting back towards them.

Trent tried but failed to translate the guttural rage into words. He looked at Lila. 'What did he say?' he asked.

Lila was frowning. 'He said, *you should have trusted me*.'

The group stood in silence and watched Nicholas Samson walk, all alone, back to his house.

NINE YEARS LATER

1

SUNDAY 1:53PM

Trent hadn't liked Nicholas Samson when he was alive but hey, why not change the habit of a lifetime? Trent's habit. Samson's lifetime.

And besides, the others would be there, and they were all very much alive. Trent had come to see them, and one of them in particular. It had been seven years since they'd all left school and their group had splintered, some to university, some to work and one, *the* one, had moved to the US.

So, here he was, standing on the street outside the Samsons' gated family home, smoking a cigarette, thinking about Lila Jain, and wondering whether, after all these years, he would still ...

She appeared around the corner and paused as she spotted him. Even though she was maybe a hundred metres away he wondered whether she could hear his heart thumping against his chest.

So, that would be a yes. Even now.

He watched her walk towards him and seven years warped into a handful of days. She wasn't seventeen any longer, but the years hadn't dimmed the light. The changes were subtle. Her bob was a degree or two more angled, and her complexion now reflected the Californian climate with hints of sun, sea, and sand.

Their relationship has shifted, too. Over a year ago, he'd stopped replying to her messages. Which meant he was unsure how she would greet him. He swallowed.

'Hi, Trent,' she said with the approximation of a smile.

'Hi, Lila.' He dropped his cigarette to the floor and crushed it with his foot. Lila had once told him that she didn't like smoking but she liked *him* smoking. That thought had mainlined its way into his memory banks the second she'd said it, and when he'd woken up that morning he'd known it would be the first time he would smoke a cigarette for over five years.

She shaped for a hug. Which was more than Trent could've hoped for. And as the warmth flooded through him, and he felt her hands rubbing his back, he wished that they were anywhere but there. Going anywhere but into Nicholas Samson's family home. Doing anything other than attending his wake.

Trent stood back, and ran his hand through his hair. 'I'm surprised you came back for this.'

She scrunched her nose. 'I didn't feel as though I could say no. His mother emailed me a couple of times.'

'Yeah, me too.' He shuffled on the spot. In truth, every communication with Mrs Samson had been awkward. 'It's odd to be invited, isn't it? I don't know about you but I didn't have anything to do with Samson after we left school.'

'Just the odd message, social media post, that kind of thing.' Lila's years in the US had rounded out her accent. Just a little. A change so subtle that you wouldn't notice it unless you had spent your formative years falling asleep with her voice beckoning you into your dreams. 'I feel guilty now that I didn't make more of an effort.'

'Well, he never messaged me, so the invitation from his mother was a complete surprise.'

'Didn't he send you his annual newsletter?' Lila's eyes widened slightly.

Trent rolled his eyes. 'Yeah.' He'd forgotten about that. He scratched his chin. When had he received the last one? He wasn't sure. 'I opened it but I never read it all. I don't know why he bothered sending it to me.'

Lila nodded. 'I always had the feeling that we meant more to him than...' She trailed off.

'...he meant to us. Yeah, me too.' He paused. Shrugged. 'I guess we do our duty. And then get out of there.' He glanced towards the house.

Lila shivered. 'You're right though,' she said. 'It is weird. Why do you think we've been invited?'

'I guess he told his mother that we were his friends,' Trent said.

'You're supposed to be my friends.' Lila said it as if she was quoting a line from a cult film.

'What?' Trent said. That phrase sounded familiar.

'That's what Samson said, at his birthday party.'

'Wow.' Memories clawed their way into Trent's mind. The acrid smoke of the bonfire. The flickering pale light of the torch. The emotional hide and seek of the game of secrets. And Samson, his face smudged with tears. 'I'd forgotten that.'

Lila looked distant for a moment. 'Well, there's something else that's strange. Everyone who was there that night has been invited to the wake. And I haven't heard of anyone else from school being invited.'

Trent raised his eyebrows. 'Really?' Lila held his gaze but didn't reply. 'That's actually creepy.' Trent blew out a deep breath. Why would Samson leave his mother instructions to invite the old gang to his wake?

'Maybe it's not that weird. He didn't really know anyone else,' Lila said, tucking a strand of hair behind her ear. 'Are you still in touch with the others?'

She placed a gentle stress on the word *others*. Trent couldn't tell whether she meant other than Samson, or other than her.

'Yeah,' he replied. It was only partially true. He had sporadic evenings of drinks and cards with Paddy, calls with Dub on and off, but hardly any contact at all with Copper over the last year. He'd not seen much of Olivia either but there'd been a weird day a couple of years ago where she'd insisted on meeting up with him, and only him. They went to the theatre together followed by a meal out. Trent had spent the whole time expecting some grand revelation, but it had never come. Instead, they'd both suffered through four hours of slightly awkward interaction before an even more awkward parting of the ways. They'd only swapped messages since then.

But Paddy had emailed them all after receiving the unexpected message from Samson's mother telling them that Nicholas had died from cancer and inviting them to the wake. Paddy had agitated for them all to attend and Trent had been in the mood for a reunion. Life was busy but he'd decided he needed to make more time for his old friends.

'How about you?' be asked. So casual it hurt. Almost as if he wasn't fishing to find out whether she was still in contact with her ex-boyfriend.

'I saw Oli, Paddy, and Copper a couple of days ago.'

Interesting. She'd been back from the US for at least a few days but she hadn't told him. Which was totally as expected, but also hurt like a hangover after heaven's closing down party. He silently noted that she'd made no mention of Dub.

Trent turned towards the gate. He had no clear recollection of the house itself. On that night, nine years ago, everything important had happened in the woodlands and in his soul.

'I thought there'd be someone here to meet us.' He peered through the bars of the gate before giving it a gentle push, the metal cold to his touch. He stepped backwards as it swung open. 'Huh, okay. There we go.' He gestured to Lila. 'After you.'

They walked through the gate, which closed automatically behind them, and along the path to the steps that rose to the front door of the house. It was definitely a period house – which period, Trent wasn't sure. Edwardian felt like a safe bet if he was pushed. And it wasn't hard to imagine it going for a few million quid. The front door was open and he could hear voices from inside. One, in particular, that had a subtle Canadian twang.

'Sounds like Dub is here,' he said, watching Lila.

She nodded but said nothing. Total shutdown. Then she pointed towards the steps that led up to the house. 'Well, shall we?'

Trent nodded and waited for Lila to lead the way. He wanted the cover. He wasn't wired for crowds of strangers so that was his strategy; hang back before you hang out. He'd let Lila break the ice, then all he need do was navigate the freezing cold currents and try not to capsize.

2

SUNDAY 2:06PM

Trent and Lila headed through the hall into a spacious kitchen bathed in sunlight. The granite worktops and gleaming chrome appliances twinned with pale green walls gave it a contemporary feel. There was no one else in the room and the sound of chatter floated in from the garden. Trent followed Lila as she walked out the open French doors and began to weave through the crowd of suits and cocktail dresses. Trent's conviction that smart jeans were the very definition of the casual dress code specified in the invitation began to waver under the weight of popular opinion.

He scanned the crowd, looking for his friends and, true to form, heard Olivia Pearson before he saw her.

'Lila,' Oli swept Lila up in a hug. It may only have been two days since they last saw each other, but Oli always loved an audience.

Lila was nearly a foot shorter than Oli and had to perch on tiptoe to receive her embrace. 'Hey. Good to see you, again.'

Trent held back. Partly because that was what he always

turned to see Mrs. Samson standing at the side of the garden under a cherry tree, holding a piece of paper. Trent nodded his silent thanks to the barman as he took the drinks and followed his tall friend back to the others.

Mrs Samson started to speak. 'Firstly, thank you all so much for coming. It means so much. And I know it would mean everything to Nicky that you are all here. Every single one of you was so important to him.' Trent and Paddy shared a glance. 'You all know how much he loved computers. And he showed a real talent for programming.' She smiled. 'Not that I understood any of it.' Polite laughter. 'He inherited that ability from his father.' She hesitated, and the hand holding her cards wavered. 'Nicky and his father were very close.' Her voice cracked. 'I'm not sure he ever totally got over Christopher's death.' She paused and took a sip of water. 'At least now, they are together again.'

Trent's mouth was dry. He hadn't known that Nicholas had lost his father. Poor guy. He raised his eyebrows at Dub who, almost imperceptibly, shook his head. Trent studied Mrs Samson, wondering where she found the strength to go on. The end of the eulogy was met with clapping and the general resumption of conversation.

Trent found himself staring at the back of Lila's head, at her hair, dark and glossy. Now he'd seen her again, after so long, he knew he had to explain his reasons for not responding to her messages. Whatever happened next, he at least owed her that much.

Lila turned to face the group. 'Why don't we all go down to the park when this finishes?'

Trent balled his hands, his nails digging into his palms. The park. In the years after the fire, when he and his sister, Pen, were living with their aunt, they often went there and sat on the swings and talked. He'd only been back sporadically, and he hadn't been to the park with his mates since the summer after their A-levels. The park still reminded him of a time he'd rather forget.

Paddy clapped his hands together. 'Great idea. We can get some cider and party like it's two thousand and eleven all over again.'

Oli looked up from her phone. 'I won't be able to stay for long.'

Same old Oli, Trent thought. 'You've got a date?' he asked.

But Oli shook her head. 'No. Just got some stuff I need to sort out.'

Trent shot a look at Oli. Perhaps they were all growing up after all.

'Well, I vote we head off now,' Dub said. There was a murmur of agreement from the group.

'I need to use the toilet.' Trent started walking towards the house, calling over his shoulder to his friends as he went. 'Don't go without me.' He edged past a group of guests and went inside the house to find Mrs Samson standing alone in the kitchen.

'Oh, I'm sorry,' Trent said. 'I was looking for the toilet.'

Mrs Samson pointed down the hall. 'Last door on your right.' Trent mumbled his thanks and started to walk away when she spoke again. 'It's Trent Ryder isn't it?'

He turned back. 'Yes, that's right.'

She nodded. Trent wanted to leave but he felt as if his feet were glued to the floor. 'I don't think we ever met properly. Nicky was quite private about his friends.' Trent managed a nod. 'But he left notes on all of you.' Trent swallowed but said nothing. *Left notes on all of you.* A shiver fingertipped down his back. 'Nicky liked to plan everything. He loved detail. He arranged all of this.' She waved her hand towards the people chatting in the garden. 'Ironic given that he's not here to enjoy it himself.'

What the hell was Trent supposed to say to that? He cleared his throat and went with, 'Yes, I guess so.'

'Now, what was it that he wrote about you? There was one phrase in particular that was intriguing.' She momentarily closed her eyes. Trent's palms were sweating. Samson had written about him. About *everyone* it appeared. 'Oh, yes, that's right. You're the man with no secrets.'

Trent did a double take. 'I'm sorry, what?'

'*Trent Ryder claims to have no secrets.*' She smiled.

Trent tried to read her. She'd pronounced each word with exquisite care, as though reading from her son's script. She hadn't put any stress on the word *claims* but Trent heard Samson's meaning loud and clear. All those years ago, Samson hadn't believed him.

'Nicky was very interested in you all.' She frowned. 'Although I don't recall him saying much about you all when he was at school. You must have seen more of him over the last few years, to be that close.' Trent opened his mouth to speak but no words would come. 'Oh dear. I'm making you uncomfortable. I guess I've had more practice than most at dealing with grief, what with Christopher, and now, Nicky. I find it helps to talk.'

'I'm sorry.' Trent bowed his head, wishing he could teleport to anywhere else on earth.

Mrs Samson nodded. 'Well, thank you for coming, Trent,' she said.

'Of course.' Trent walked down the hallway, forcing himself not to look back.

. . .

TRENT STRODE UP to his friends. He glanced around. Mrs Samson was well out of earshot.

'You'll never guess what Samson's mum just told me,' Trent said.

'We were invited by mistake?' Paddy deadpanned.

'Ha. No.' Trent dropped his voice. 'He wrote notes on us all.'

'What?' Lila was the first to react but a ripple of surprise travelled through the group. They all shuffled slightly closer together.

'Yeah. And, get this. She told me he'd written *Trent Ryder claims to have no secrets.* She was very precise so I think it's an exact quote.'

'Jesus. That *is* creepy,' Dub said.

'That's what you said at his birthday bonfire,' Frances said. 'When you were asked to share a secret.' Her fingers tapped against her mouth. 'His mother said he'd written that down?'

'Yeah.' Trent glanced down the garden again. Mrs Samson was engrossed in conversation with an elderly couple. 'And the way she said it made it sound like there was more than that.'

'About you?' Oli asked.

'About all of us,' Trent replied.

Paddy was pulling at his ear. 'I vote that we make our excuses and get out of here.'

'That's the best idea I've heard all day,' Oli said. 'But we should say goodbye to Mrs Samson.'

'Bagsy not me,' said Trent.

'Let's all go together. I'll do the talking,' Frances said, already starting to move. 'Come on. Follow me.'

3

SUNDAY 6:14PM

The gang drifted along to the park. They turned off the road through the avenue of trees and made their way along the side of the cricket pitch where a couple of young lads were recreating the Ashes in the fading light.

'That whole thing was pretty weird.' Oli scraped her hair back as if to put it into a ponytail before releasing it. 'I wish I hadn't gone.'

Trent was thinking the same thing. He'd gone mainly because Lila was going, but his conversation with Samson's mother had spooked him.

'Let's talk about something else,' Lila said, right on cue.

Frances laughed. 'Well, last time we were here, Paddy was so drunk he fell off the seesaw.'

'Only because Trent jumped off it when I wasn't looking.' Paddy's words were slightly slurred, and he gave Trent a nudge with his shoulder. Then he stumbled, grabbing Trent to keep himself from falling over.

'I wasn't anywhere near it. No one was,' Trent protested. He waited until Paddy was more or less stable on his own two feet before releasing his grip on him. Paddy had clearly been knocking back the free booze. 'You were sitting at one end, with your feet on the ground and you were shouting at the other end which had, and I need to really stress this point, no one sitting on it.'

The others were laughing. Even Paddy was smiling.

'It's gone.' Dub pointed to where the seesaw had been.

Trent didn't need to look. He'd noticed the change when he was last there. 'They pulled it out couple of years ago.' He paused for effect. 'Health and safety concerns, apparently.'

Two things happened at once: Paddy hit him on the arm, and Lila broke into a run. Brushing off the punch, Trent sprinted after her. He drew level with her when they closed in on the two swings. One red, the other yellow. At least that hadn't changed.

He edged past her in the last few strides and claimed red. Because history mattered. Lila sat on the yellow swing, smiling. She took two steps back and one swing forward. The others sauntered over, Paddy slightly off the pace, looking at his phone.

Trent felt his phone buzz in his pocket. Simultaneously he heard buzzes and chimes from the others' phones.

Paddy was grinning. 'Did you get it, too? The message.'

'What are you talking about?' Lila was digging into her pocket.

'Check your phones. All of you.'

Trent's shoulders tingled as he looked at his phone screen.

Welcome Hayden Road leavers of 2011.

'What the hell's this?' Trent asked. There was a link underneath the message. The text was from an unknown number, but it referenced their school, and the year they'd all left.

'I'm going in,' Paddy said.

'It's spam, Paddy,' Frances said.

'It says Hayden Road.' He hiccupped before continuing. 'Leavers of 2011. That's us. Come on. Bit of nostalgia.' Paddy's enthusiasm was a return to his old form; always up for trying something new.

'Yeah, I think it's spam too,' said Dub who was leaning on the swing's A-frame and giving it a run for its money, 'Don't be an idiot, Paddy. Just ignore it.'

'You would say that,' Paddy said. It was like being back in the playground. Paddy following the smoke signals to the bike sheds whilst Dub scoured the timetable for the next available revision class. Then without a word Paddy lunged towards Dub, and snatched his phone from his hand.

'Paddy, don't you dare.' But Dub was too slow. Paddy had already put five yards between them, his wobbly legs moving surprisingly fast.

Dub took off after Paddy, his giant strides eating up the ground. A few seconds later, he launched himself through the air. The impact of his tackle sent both their mobile phones bouncing across the grass. Dub pushed Paddy's face down into the ground before reaching over to pick up his phone.

'Jesus, Paddy. It's downloading something.' He jabbed at his screen, muttering under his breath. 'If this doesn't work...'

Paddy brushed the dirt off his trousers before picking up his own phone.

'Well, I'm not clicking on it,' Frances said.

'What's it doing, Dub?' Trent asked.

Dub was walking back towards the others whilst Paddy stayed standing, swaying slightly on the firm ground, a few yards away. Trent peered over Dub's shoulder. An icon had appeared, a black oriental symbol inside a blood red square. It no doubt meant something; Trent just had no clue what.

'Any ideas?' he asked.

'It's an app,' Paddy shouted.

'I know that, genius. I meant the symbol.' Trent looked at Frances. 'Is it Japanese?'

Frances took the phone from Dub. 'Yes,' she said. 'It's hard to translate into English though.'

'I thought you did Japanese for your degree?' Trent said.

'I did psychology for my degree,' Frances replied. 'My Japanese is self-taught. Um ... this ... it means honesty ... and – value?'

'Honesty value?' Trent was caught between disappointment and relief. At least it didn't mean death, or something else sinister.

'Wait. Actually, this is better. Honesty Index.' Frances nodded with a degree of self-congratulation and handed the phone back to Dub.

Trent let his mind stretch around the phrase. Honesty Index. He shifted on his feet and glanced at the others.

'Hurry up you lot,' said Paddy. 'You haven't got to the fun part yet.' He was hopping around, barely able to contain his glee. 'Oh, this looks incredible.'

Dub's sigh was heavy. Oli and Lila had also gathered round him, huddling up with Trent and Frances. They watched on in silence as he clicked on the icon and waited.

Trent peered at the screen. He was looking at some sort of web page. A page which appeared to give access to mines of data. Very ... *specific* data.

'Bloody hell, Dub. That looks like your life history.' Trent's eyes flicked to take in the different headings. Dub's name at the centre and then a series of paragraphs of text, with certain key words highlighted. The headings covered an expansive range of topics: *Mortgage Application*, *Personal Text Exchanges*, *Religion*, *Family Tree*. For a second Trent imagined his own name at the centre. He felt a tightness at his temples, the flickering of a distant flame. He swallowed hard and then Dub's name was back.

'Yup,' said Paddy, staggering back over towards the group. 'It's the Dub database.'

Dub had gone very quiet which wasn't unusual in itself. Easy to spot, hard to hear would be his epitaph. 'This isn't funny, guys,' he said. 'Paddy, you're a moron.'

Paddy's foot was tapping as if playing a bass drum. 'Come on, I'm sure it'll just be a laugh. Why don't we find out what it's about. If it's dodgy we'll just switch out and forget about it.'

Oli spoke next. 'Do you think Samson's done a belated yearbook?' She scowled. 'He's dead. How bad can it be?'

'That's the spirit, Oli' Paddy said.

'You're buying us replacements,' Trent poked Paddy in the chest, 'if this ends up bricking our phones,' Trent replied.

Lila spoke next. 'Okay, I'm in too.'

'You're all insane.' Frances shook her head, but she stayed looking over Trent's shoulder.

'Right. Let's get started then.' Trent clicked on the heading on the top left of the screen – Personal Text Exchanges, hoping to see something with Dub's old girlfriend: Lila Jain. Nothing happened. With a shrug he clicked on a different heading. Again, nothing. Either the pages weren't there, or he simply wasn't allowed to access them. 'My links don't seem to work,' he said.

'Jesus,' said Dub. 'This is my old school report. How the hell did it get hold of that?'

Trent's screen shimmered and then he too was looking at a scan of what seemed to be A4 paper. There was a grid, subject names down the left-hand side and teachers' comments in the larger boxes on the right. At the foot of the pager were comments, a couple of lines each, which went across the entire page, signed by the Head of Year, and the Head of Sixth Form.

Trent scanned the text. Maybe this was going to be fun after all.

Andrew has worked hard throughout the year. He is a quiet boy but appears well liked. His attitude is generally positive and I wish Andrew all the best for the future.

'No great shocks,' said Oli.

Trent lifted his head. 'Well, you say that, but I never knew Dub was well liked.' Cue laughter.

'Hey, have you all got a countdown on your screen?' Paddy asked.

At the top right hand of his screen, a small digital clock was ticking down by the second. 'Yeah. Five minutes and counting. I've no idea what we're meant to do though.' Trent blinked. 'Oh, wait. There's a message at the bottom. *Waiting for player.*'

'Mine has a different message.' Dub's voice was wavering. 'And there's a button to press.' His eyes were wide.

'What does it say?' Trent asked.

Dub was pale. He stared at Trent. 'Ready to play?'

4

MANIFESTO EXTRACT 1

They must all play. It will end only when the final truth is revealed.

PLAYER

PLAYER_LIST ='TRENT RYDER'
'Olivia Pearson'
'Patrick Wilding'
'Lila Jain'
'Frances Churchill'
'Andrew Dubnyk'

SELECT PLAYERI

. . .

PLAYERI= rank.choice(Player_List)

COMPILE DATA_SET (PLAYERI)

5

SUNDAY 6:53PM

'I'm not doing this.' Dub turned off his phone. He was breathing hard. 'I don't know what you're trying to do. Assuming it's one of you. Maybe it's *all* of you. But it's not funny.' He stuffed his phone into his trouser pocket before turning to Paddy and jabbing his finger at his friend's face. 'I *told* you not to click on the link. You can be such a dick sometimes, Paddy. Everything's such a laugh to you, isn't it?' And with that he spun round and started to stride away.

'Dub,' Trent called after him.

But Dub didn't answer and he didn't look back. He kept going until he'd turned the corner and was out of sight.

Trent looked at this screen. It was black with a red digital countdown in the top right corner. There was a new line of text beneath *Waiting for player* which read *If the player refuses to play, the truth will be revealed when the countdown reaches zero.*

The digital timer hit 1:47.

'Christ, what's he so uptight about?' Paddy slurred his words as he waved a hand in the general direction Dub had taken.

'How would you like it, Paddy?' Frances murmured. She'd always been the grown-up in the playground. 'Actually scratch that. Dub isn't like you. He's never liked being the centre of attention.'

'The whole thing *is* very creepy,' said Oli.

Lila was motionless, and then she shivered and hugged herself, still looking at where Dub had disappeared from view. Trent watched her. Was she waiting to see if he would come back? And just what *was* the relationship between the two of them now?

The sun had sunk low in the sky and a dull drizzle was starting to set in. Trent cleared his throat, unsure what to say. He scratched his fingernails against his thumb and glanced at Oli's phone. The display was the same as his. The countdown. And the ultimatum.

'Forty seconds left,' Paddy said, in a mock sinister voice. Trent turned away, swallowing the urge to giggle, and saw Dub walk back into the park. He stopped at the entrance, his face illuminated by the soft light of his phone.

The timer was still counting down. Which presumably meant that Dub hadn't pressed the button. What the hell would happen if he didn't? Or if he did for that matter? Trent's hand gripped the phone tightly as he watched the timer click down towards zero.

Three, two, one.

Trent jolted as a sequence of alerts punched into the silence. There was a new message: a notification from a newly created chat group. The title was the same Japanese symbol. Trent realised he was holding his breath as his finger hovered over the screen. A message popped up into the group chat:

Sometimes people don't want to hear the truth because they don't want their illusions destroyed.

What did that mean? Trent thought it sounded like a quote from a six-form philosopher.

'It's Nietzsche,' said Frances, her voice rock steady. *Close enough.* She looked at Trent. 'My degree did help with that one.'

Trent felt a slight tremor in his arms as a video clip appeared in the group chat created by the app, a red circle spinning as it uploaded. Then it shifted upwards as a second video started to load. And then another. And another. Six videos in total. Waiting to be viewed.

Trent stared at the freeze frames. There were glimpse of skin and contorted faces.

'Jesus Christ,' Paddy said with a half-gasp-half-laugh. 'Is that –'

Paddy's question was met by a gasp – a real one this time – from Lila. Her hand was over her mouth and her eyes were locked onto her phone screen. Deciding quickly that he didn't want to watch – not now, anyway – Trent closed his own phone down and put it away.

Lila wouldn't meet his eyes. In fact, she didn't look up at all as she cleared her throat. 'It's Dub. That bastard.'

'It is. I think he's in all of them,' Paddy said. 'Looks like a different women in each one. Jesus. Sex tapes.'

Yes, that's what it had looked like to Trent, too.

'Explains why he was so keen to leave.' Oli said the words carefully.

Trent was turning it over in his mind. You thought you knew someone and then boom, six sex tapes. He looked over to where Dub had been standing but his friend had disappeared once more. Had Dub walked away because he'd known what was coming? Surely not – though he might have guessed. Obviously Dub had known that the videos existed, but he wouldn't have chosen to share them. Which left the question, how could anyone else have gained access to the now not-so-private recordings?

Trent looked over to Lila, sure that she was thinking exactly the same as him. Someone had found these videos online somewhere. Which meant that Dub must have posted them somewhere. A website or a chatroom, maybe.

He froze. Videos of Dub and women having sex. Lila's reaction. Oh, God. No wonder she was horrified. Was there a video of her out there? Was she one of the women on these recordings?

She couldn't be. Lila looked irritated but not distraught. If she'd seen herself on one of those videos, surely she would have totally flipped. He was glad he hadn't watched, but now self-generated graphic images of Lila and Dub seared into his cortex. He balled his hands, his fingernails digging into his palms. He forced his hands open and tried the same with his mind. Don't rush to judgement. This wasn't about him. Think of Lila.

'Are any of them you, Lila?' Paddy asked, rushing in where a fool feared to tread.

Time stretched before Lila shook her head. Trent's stomach unknotted.

'Who the hell managed to get hold of these?' Oli asked.

'And why post them to us all?' Lila added.

'Someone's clearly upset with Dub,' Paddy said. The temperature was dropping with the sun and the air frosted as he spoke. Paddy wrapped his arms around his torso.

'I hope that's what it is,' Trent said. Because another possibility had edged its way into his mind.

Oli looked up from scrolling through the videos. 'Why?' Naivety set to the max.

Trent wasn't going to spell it out, but Frances picked up the baton.

'Because if it wasn't just about Dub, then one of us is going to be next,' she said.

Give that girl a cigar.

6

SUNDAY 7:10PM

Trent heard the teenagers before he saw them. They spilled into the park, a couple of lads jostling each other; two girls singing and dancing as they walked. They all looked impossibly young and Trent wondered when that had happened, the changing of the guard. The youths slowed down as they spotted Trent and his friends hanging out in the playground. Perhaps it wasn't Trent's red swing any longer.

Darkness had fallen quickly and the chill in the air stung Trent's face. He shuddered and pushed his hands into his coat pockets. The observation that the game might work its way around the group had caused them to fall silent in anticipation of act two. They flicked glances at each other, furtive looks squeezing out the earlier laughter. Paddy, in particular, had performed a full one-eighty. The easy banter had evaporated, and he was muttering to himself as he paced around.

Trent pulled his phone back out. The group was still open, the six videos paused. He closed the chat. The Honesty Index icon was still visible. He stared at it for a few seconds and then switched his phone off.

'It has to be something Samson arranged,' Frances said.

Lila shrugged, but Oli was nodding. 'It's the only thing that makes sense.' She paused. 'It's a bit sick, though. Creating something like that and sending it to us at his wake.'

'And why?' Trent said. The initial shock of Dub's videotapes had given way to a sense of puzzlement. If it was Samson who'd wanted to embarrass Dub, why wait, and why go to such lengths?

'Did Samson have anything against Dub?' Oli asked.

Paddy scratched his head. 'I don't think Dub ever really upset anyone.' He glanced at Trent, and then immediately at Lila. 'It's hard to think that he did anything that would make someone, even Samson, release those videos as retaliation.'

'And how did he even get hold of them?' Frances asked. Which Trent had to admit, was another excellent question.

'Do you really think that this game is going to come after all of us,' Lila said.

Frances shrugged. 'I have no idea. It's got to be a possibility though.'

'Jesus.' Paddy was blinking rapidly, as if trying to sober himself up. His face was gaunt and Trent was once again struck by how much weight Paddy had lost. What could be behind that? Could this game possibly know something about Paddy? Perhaps something that was stressing out his friend.

Paddy was wiping his hand over his face. 'You think it might do something similar with all of us?'

Trent began to imagine his own round. What could the game know about him? He shuddered.

'I'm just going to delete the app. Try and forget about it,' Oli said.

'I don't think that will stop it,' Frances replied. Everyone else turned to look at her. 'Dub didn't play.' She paused, as if her response was explanation enough.

'I don't follow,' Paddy said. For once he was speaking for the others, too.

Frances sighed. 'Dub didn't play. And the truth was revealed in any event. Which is exactly what the game said would happen.'

'What do you think would've happened if Dub had played?' Paddy asked. His voice was strained.

Frances shrugged. 'I don't know. Maybe there would've been a way to keep his videos secret.'

'What was that quote, again?' Trent asked. 'The one that was in the group chat. The one you said was Nietzsche.'

'*People don't want to hear the truth because they don't want their illusions destroyed*,' Frances recited from memory.

'Yeah. What does that even mean?'

'I think it means that we prefer to believe what we prefer to be true,' Frances replied.

'Blimey. That's good, Frances,' Oli said.

'It's another quote. The other Frances.' A pause. 'Francis Bacon.'

'So, the game's telling us to face up to the truth?' Lila asked.

'Maybe,' Frances said. 'Again, I don't *know*. I'm simply guessing.'

'I can't get my head round this.' Oli shook her head. 'Jesus, why did you have to download it, Paddy?' For once, Paddy didn't offer a retort, he merely hung his head. But Oli wasn't finished. '*And* it was your suggestion that we all came to the wake in the first place. What a great idea that turned out to be.'

'I'm sorry,' Paddy mumbled. 'I wanted...' He trailed off before trying again. 'I wanted to see you all. I've been...' He swallowed. Hard. 'Let's just say things haven't been easy the last few months.'

Trent exchanged a glance with Oli. It didn't seem as though Paddy was going to elaborate. 'How about we go to the pub,' Trent said. 'Talk it through over a pint or two.'

Frances checked her watch. 'I can't I'm afraid. I need to get home to the kids,' she said. 'Sorry.'

Olivia was busy typing on her phone and didn't even look up as she spoke. 'I'm going to head home, too. I don't really want to, though. This has freaked me out and the thought of being alone in my flat isn't great.'

It was unusual for Oli to pass up a night out. 'Are you sure you can't you stay for a drink?' Trent asked. 'Sort everything out another night?'

Oli shook her head, her teeth biting down on her lip. Trent had never seen Oli like that. She'd always been carefree, yet right then she looked troubled. 'I really can't,' she said.

'That's fair enough,' Trent said. 'How about you guys?' He looked at Lila and Paddy.

Lila replied first. 'I don't fancy a pub. The flat I'm renting is only a ten-minute walk from here. We could go there?'

A rented flat? She hadn't mentioned that before. So it was definitely more than just a flying visit, Trent thought.

'Not me,' said Paddy. He sighed and buried his face in his hands before gently slapping his cheeks. 'I need to sober up. I've got work tomorrow.'

Which was the most accounting manual response Trent had ever heard from Paddy. He was usually the last to leave. Now, Trent saw him glancing at the kids making their way over and scratching his forehead. His friend's sense of mischief when the first text arrived had given them a glimpse of the old Paddy, but it had since vanished. Now he looked as if he'd rather be anywhere but here.

'I'll give you a call soon, Paddy,' Trent said.

'Just me and you then, Trent,' said Lila, as they started to drift towards the park gates. The anticipation twisted in Trent's stomach. The main road beyond shimmered as the street lamps tried to burn through the mist. 'You okay with that?'

'As long as you've got something to drink,' he replied. *Or even if you haven't.*

The others said their goodbyes when they reached the tube station, the reunion vibe of the early afternoon totally shredded by the game. Trent watched them disappear down the escalator, Paddy, Oli, and Frances standing single file to the right looking to all the world as if they were total strangers to each other.

Trent and Lila made their way down the street with the drizzle of rain blurring the neon signs above the tightly bunched shops. The smell of fat and vinegar drifted across the road.

'It's not much further,' Lila said, ducking under an umbrella being carried by a woman walking in the opposite direction. A few yards ahead of them a group of lads stood on the corner, sharing their chips, and throwing out menacing looks. Trent pulled his jacket tighter around him then, glancing at Lila, he slung his arm around her shoulder and steered her firmly but casually over to the other pavement. Maybe he really was growing up. Five years earlier he wouldn't have had the confidence to do that. The gang seemed to lose interest, looking down the road for another target. Maybe he was being unfair; it could be their regular homework discussion meeting.

Lila leant in towards Trent and he caught the scent of apple-blossom. 'Thanks for keeping me company,' she said.

'No worries. It would be good to have a proper chat. It's been a while.'

'And whose fault is that?' Her laughter smoothed over the truth of her words. Just. 'My place is over here.'

She released herself from Trent's embrace and led him to a ground floor entrance. She punched in a security code as he stared up at the block of flats. They looked like the type of properties designed to drag up local house prices, slightly out of place and a touch too modern. Neither of them spoke as they travelled up in the lift, along the corridor and then, with the silence beginning to feel like a third person, into Lila's flat.

7

SUNDAY 7:28PM

Trent slipped off his jacket and hung it up on the rack just inside the door. Different venue, same old routine. Back when they were school age, they'd been in and out of each other's houses almost daily. Even after Dubgate broke, they still spent much of their spare time together. Dub seemed to accept that that was how it was and Trent had been grateful that they hadn't had to deal with that rivalry. At least, not from Dub's quarter. But ... maybe Dub had been more jealous than he'd seemed. Where did this secret sex-taping come from? And who knew when it had started?

He followed Lila into the living room. There were two sofas covered in bright orange fabric either side of a rustic looking coffee-table which was pragmatically decorated with an empty coffee cup, a wine glass, and a laptop. But the striking thing about the room was the artwork: one whole wall was covered in Escher prints.

Lila caught him staring. 'Airbnb.'

Trent nodded as if it made sense. 'Do your parents still live in London?'

Lila shrugged. 'They moved to India a few years ago. You know it was always Dad's dream. I guess once it was clear I wasn't staying in England they had the chance to go.' She picked up the empty glass and mug. 'Wine?' she asked as she headed towards the kitchen.

'Perfect. Thanks.'

Trent watched her leave the room then pulled out his phone and navigated to the video clips. He studied the freeze frames. The first one was in black and white and was indoors. Trent scrolled down. The second still clearly showed an outdoor location. From Arthouse to risqué. And it was in glorious multicolour. He'd scrolled again. And again. None of the first four women looked anything like Lila.

She appeared holding two wine glasses in one hand and a bottle in the other, and set the bottle on the table. Trent switched off his phone and waited for her to pour his drink. They clinked glasses and Lila slumped onto one of the sofas.

'Are you okay?' Trent asked, immediately feeling that it was an inappropriate question. 'I mean, obviously you're not okay.' He lowered himself into the other sofa.

Lila twisted a stand of her hair around her finger then leaned forward and clicked on her laptop. Music drifted out of the speakers, and she lowered the volume until it was quiet enough to talk over.

'I keep thinking,' she said, 'did he video me? I know it's selfish but that's my main reaction. You're lucky, you don't have to deal with that.'

'Well, I haven't watched all six videos yet.' He caught her look. 'Too soon?'

'Yeah,' she said, 'too soon,' but she stopped twisting her hair and her shoulders relaxed.

'Do you think that's the end of it, for Dub, I mean?' he asked. 'Someone's gone to the lengths of sending us the videos, but so what? Is it really so bad for him – even if we were all to cut him off, would he really care? What's the point of it all?'

'I don't know.' Lila reached over and picked up her laptop. She started to type.

'What are you doing?'

'Just trying to see if I can find out anything about Dub. Perhaps this whole thing has been set up to get some sort of revenge on him. Maybe there's been something posted on social media.'

Trent stood up and walked around behind her so he could see over her shoulder. As he bent down to rest his arms on the top of the sofa he caught again the soft scent of her perfume. He tried to focus as she flicked through Facebook, Instagram, and Twitter.

'Nothing,' she said, typing in the Google search bar. Trent tried reading the results she was scrolling through but the perfume was winning, pulling his thoughts away. The playlist fell silent in between songs, and all Trent could hear was Lila's breathing.

'There's nothing here either.' Lila's words snapped him back into the room. 'A few links to some journo articles he's written.'

'Anything that's likely to have upset anyone?' Trent asked.

'There's nothing obvious that I can see. Perhaps it was an ex-girlfriend.'

'Now there's a thought.'

The words spun through the air. Lila turned towards Trent. Their faces were an inch apart and time stretched. And then Lila was sitting forward, pouring more wine. He walked back around the sofa and sat down next to her.

Lila relaxed back, tucking her feet underneath her. 'It wasn't me, Trent,' she said. 'Dub and I split up years ago.'

Trent nodded. 'I know. I guess we may never find out who wanted to humiliate him. Or why.'

'I think he's done a good enough job humiliating himself.' Lila rested her head against the arm of the sofa, cradling her glass. A retreat – from him? It was subtle but it was definitely there.

Trent glanced at his phone, closed the group chat, and stared at the red and black icon for the Honesty Index. Then he held his finger down on it until it shimmered and a small cross appeared over the corner. He clicked on delete.

The icon had vanished. Gone but not forgotten.

Lila was looking over his shoulder.

And then the icon reappeared, the white circle quickly filling up to show that it had finished downloading. There was a buzz accompanying a new group message.

You can try to delete the app but you can't erase history. And even if you aren't watching, the world will see the true you.

'Jesus,' whispered Lila. Her hand sought out his, and she gripped it tightly.

'Yeah. That's not good.' Trent locked his screen, and placed his phone on the table. Lila was staring at the floor. 'Are you okay?'

She looked up and shrugged. 'I don't know.' She nodded towards Trent's phone. 'I guess that means that it isn't over.'

Trent was thinking the same thing. Either the game wasn't finished with Dub, or someone else was in its sights. Whichever it was, it wasn't good.

8

SUNDAY 7:44PM

'I don't want to think about that game anymore,' Lila said. 'Can we talk about something else?' She took another mouthful of wine and nudged Trent with her knee. 'I thought you wanted to talk about us.'

Trent nodded. It would be good to think about something different. He shuffled forward as he edged towards the questions that he really wanted to ask. So, as a starter for ten.

'How long are you back for?' he asked. 'From the US, I mean.'

'I don't know. I feel as though I need to make some decisions.' She spoke evenly.

'Decisions about what?'

Lila sighed. 'Where to live. What I want from life. It's like... I feel as though I've spent most of my life feeling trapped.' Trent didn't speak. 'And I'm only now growing up. Twenty-six.' She shook her head. 'Finally facing the world, ready to make better decisions.' The happiness had gone and Trent couldn't quite name what he saw in its place.

'You think you've made bad decisions?' He smiled. 'I mean, I can certainly think of some.'

'Ha. Well, yes. I ran away. I think maybe that was a mistake.'

Trent balled his hands. 'Why did you leave?'

There was a pause before Lila responded. 'My parents, mainly. They thought it would be best.'

Trent nodded and looked at the pictures on the wall. Not because he loved the art, but because he didn't want to look at Lila.

'Trent?' He could tell from her tone. Here it comes. Buckle up. He glanced at Lila and immediately had to turn away. There was a softness in her expression that could break him if he let it. 'Why didn't you reply? Why did you cut me off?' He could sense that she was scanning his face.

Trent had rehearsed this conversation so many times. He'd finally settled on a direct three-word answer. 'I met someone.'

Lila frowned. 'And?'

Trent dropped his head. Of course it wasn't an answer, it was just the beginning of one. The truth, the whole truth and nothing but the truth, was much more involved. 'She read some of our messages.' He could still remember Becky's glare. And the start of her inquisition. Who *exactly* is Lila? He tried a smile. 'The cross examination didn't go well.'

'But our messages weren't—'

'I know, I know. But she gave me an ultimatum.' He still couldn't meet Lila's gaze. Not because he was lying about the ultimatum, but because he'd accepted it.

'Are the two of you still together?' Lila leant forward and poured herself more wine. 'Does she know you're here with me now?'

'It only lasted a couple of months.' He knew the moment he replied that he'd made it worse. 'I'm sorry,' he said, to pre-empt the obvious next question.

She half-smiled at him. He wanted to explain. There was so much more to talk about. Because his subsequent silence was all about him, and nothing much to do with his transitory girlfriend. He wanted to explain that he hadn't contacted Lila because he was trying to protect himself. Because he was confused. And hurt.

She sipped her wine, seemingly in no hurry to reply. And then she shivered. 'Tonight really freaked me out. Are you scared?'

Trent scratched his head. The change in conversation hadn't lasted long. Perhaps Lila hadn't enjoyed the walk down memory lane. Or maybe, like him, she was finding it hard to shake off the game.

'I wouldn't say scared but it was creepy. Someone's gone to an enormous amount of effort to set this thing up.'

Lila shuffled forward on the sofa. 'The chat group is just the six of us, right.' Trent saw her purse her lips which meant that Lila had a theory. 'I can't see how, or why, it would be Samson.' A pause. 'You don't think it's Paddy, do you? He was the first to click on the link and he's always liked a practical joke. And, like Oli said, he was *very* keen for us all to go to the wake.'

'Well, if it is, he did a pretty good job of acting it out. Did you see his reaction? I've never seen him like that.'

'Maybe it was guilt. Realised he'd gone too far,' Lila said.

'Maybe.'

Lila looked distant for a moment. 'If it's not a joke I think we should go to the police.'

Trent had been thinking about that. 'I'm not sure that they'd be interested. Perhaps we should wait to see if anything else happens. Dub can go to the police if he wants to.'

Lila drained the last of the wine from her glass and placed

it on the table with an end of the evening type flourish. 'Well, it's been a long day, and it's late.' Trent counted silently whilst Lila stood up and held out her hand to him. He reached out and allowed her to pull him up. 'You can stay over if you want.' And there it was.

She let go of his hand as soon as he was standing. No pressure. Literally hands off. He didn't look at her. Couldn't. Didn't want to see whether *the* offer was there or not.

He cleared his throat. 'Thanks. I'd better...' Better what? No, not now. Not when he felt like this. 'I'd better head home.'

Lila was nodding.

The vibration of his phone in his pocket tickled his leg. What *had* Lila meant? Surely she just meant stay over. Nothing more. He pulled out his phone.

'What's wrong,' Lila asked, her eyes dark with concern.

Trent's grip on his phone tightened. There was a notification on the game icon. The number one, white in a red circle, hovering over the top right corner of the icon. He looked at Lila. Then he tapped on the icon.

'It's a message from the game,' he said, swallowing hard.

Lila was swiping at her own phone, frowning. 'I haven't been sent anything.'

Trent was looking at the chat history. Above the group chat with Dub's videos was a new thread. This message had been sent just to him, rather than the whole group.

'There's just a link.' He forced out a breath and clicked again.

'Jesus, Trent, wait,' Lila said.

But Trent was already staring at the photos that it had revealed. Pictures that were of an altogether different nature to the Dub videos. The first image was of a circular, silver medal with a crowned effigy of the Queen. The ribbon it hung from was coloured with three equal stripes, dark blue either side of pearl grey with a narrow pink stripe defining the centre line.

The second photo showed the flip side and Trent read the words 'The Queen's Gallantry Medal' inscribed on the medal, flanked by laurel sprigs.

He looked up at Lila, his eyes wide. She placed her own phone on the table as he handed her his phone. There was a slight tremor in her hand as she took it from him.

'What does this mean? What's going on?' She shook her head. 'Why would someone send you this? I don't understand.'

Trent tried to focus, to pull his thoughts away from the medal and from Lila. 'Can I use your bathroom?'

'Sure. First door on the left,' Lila said pointing out towards the hallway. 'Are you okay?'

Trent nodded and headed out the room, blinking rapidly until he was inside the bathroom. He turned on the taps and filled the basin before pushing his face into the water. The cold numbed his skin as he held his breath, his eyes closed. After a few seconds, he lifted his head, letting the drops run down his neck before raking the remaining surface water into his hair. He stood there for a minute with his eyes closed, trying to still his mind. He needed to be able to think clearly. Only three people knew of the significance of the Queen's Gallantry Medal. Trent, Penny, and their father's sister, Aunt Josephine.

When he walked back into the living room, Lila's hand was over her mouth. His phone was still in her hand and she was staring at it.

'You've just received another message.' Her voice was strangled. He grabbed his phone from her hand, his heart rate accelerating as he focused on the screen.

The new message had appeared above the link to the medal. Another communication for Trent's eyes only. He read it.

Don't you want to know the truth about the fire?

He jerked his head back up. He could feel pressure building in his chest. The game was teasing him. What the hell did it mean? It still didn't seem like it was the start of his round. There was no message asking whether he was ready to play. There was no countdown.

He reread the message and shivered. The game had found Dub's private videos. There'd also been a whole store of data about Dub that they'd only been given a glimpse of. And now the game was targeting him. Until these two messages he'd been leaning towards the jilted girlfriend theory. Perhaps with some bizarre connection to Samson. But this changed everything.

'And you haven't received anything?' he asked.

'No,' Lila replied.

'Can you check again?'

Lila picked her phone up from the table and tapped on the screen. She shook her head. 'Nothing. Sorry. The last thing I have is the group chat.' She twisted her hand to show him her screen.

Trent nodded. He could hear the rain now, coming down hard.

Don't you want to know the truth about the fire?

The message reverberated through his head. He still couldn't think clearly. He needed to be able to process what was happening. Or at least try to. And he needed to speak with Pen. He moved towards the front door.

'I should go,' he said.

'Why don't you stay?' Lila asked. 'At least for a while.'

He slipped on his coat, but Lila took him by the arm.

'Please stay, Trent. I know you're upset. But if it knows about the fire–'

'Everyone knows about the fire,' Trent shot back. But nobody knows about the medal, he thought.

Lila took a half-step back.

'I'm sorry,' he said. 'This thing's got me on edge.' He paused. 'But the fire was reported in the news. It's not a secret.' But even as he said it out loud, his mind was racing. His parents had argued that night, and Aunt Jo's posthumous application for a gallantry medal for his father had been denied. With no specific reason given.

'I guess so,' Lila said, her voice quiet but unsure.

'I'm sorry, but I need to go,' Trent said. 'I'm going to try and find out who's behind this thing.'

She half-smiled. 'Okay.' Then she pulled his coat tight across his chest and put her fingertips on his cheek. Another wave of perfume floated over him as she rose up on her tiptoes and kissed his other cheek. And as she stepped back there was something, definitely something, in her eyes. He wasn't sure, but it might have been fear.

'Thanks for the wine,' Trent said. 'It's been great to see you again.'

He soaked up one last look, then turned and headed out into the rain.

9

SUNDAY, 10:15PM

Paddy drained the last of the beer from his glass. His hand was still shaking but the extra three pints at his local had helped unwind the tension in his shoulders. Instinct had kicked in when he'd seen the message to join the game. He'd clicked without hesitation. A throwback to his old life.

But that bridge to the past had shattered when he'd seen Dub's videos. Not that he cared about the sex tapes. Provided it was all consensual, his main reaction to them was jealousy. He laughed to himself. Dub was a dark horse. Maybe if Paddy had spent all those extra hours studying, he too would have a sex-life worth documenting.

No, it hadn't been the tapes that gripped his heart and yanked him back to the present. It was Frances' comment. *One of us is going to be next.* Those words struck at his core. Just replaying them made him feel queasy.

Because a few weeks ago he'd made *the decision*. A decision that meant people were looking for him. People who would hurt him if they found him. Because no one likes a grass.

He snatched up the pint glass, turned his back to the room full of pub regulars to try for some privacy, and gagged. With the glass pressed against his chin, he slid of his stool and shuffled towards the toilets. He barged the door open with his shoulder, sucking in air. Only a few more yards. He scanned the bathroom. Thank God, there was no one else there. He slammed the pint glass down onto of the cistern as he doubled over and heaved his guts into the porcelain bowl. Tears stung his face as the recycled beer dripped double his face. He reached for toilet paper, wiped his mouth, and flushed. He clenched and unclenched his fists. Once. Twice. Then he forced himself to stand upright, blew out a breath, and walked towards the basin.

He could taste the bile. He cupped his hands under the tap and drank some water, swilling it round his mouth before spitting it out. He ran his hands over his face, savouring the temporary coldness of his skin. He caught his reflection in the mirror. He hardly recognised himself. Just above his head someone had scrawled 'You suck' in black marker pen. If the hat fits, he thought.

Paddy flinched as the door opened. Still looking in the mirror, he watched a man walk in. His heart rate jacked up as he looked at the man's face. Paddy didn't recognise him, although that didn't mean that the other guy didn't know him. But the man didn't react, just lurched towards the urinal behind Paddy.

Paddy's shoulders dropped and he closed his eyes. His life had changed the moment after he made the call to the tip-line to report his client of suspected fraud. He'd expected to feel relief, a lifting of the weight he'd been carrying throughout the weeks he'd been wrestling with the decision of what to do. But it hadn't turned out like that. Ever since he'd been a nervous wreck. The other day, he'd come close to having a panic attack in the work lift. Just because the only other guy in it with him had stared at him for a little too long.

And now, the game. Someone was playing with them. Whoever it was might think that they were being amusing. Just harmless fun. Maybe they didn't know that Paddy had a secret that he wanted to keep buried. A secret that could cost him his life. He shuddered. He wasn't being melodramatic, that was just a calm evaluation of that facts.

A quick shuffling of feet made Paddy open his eyes. The new arrival was lurching towards him. Paddy spun round, his hands up protecting his face. His chest suddenly felt as though it was in a vice. The other man thrust out a hand and aimed for the wall. His open palm caught the tiled surface and although he was standing at a precarious angle, he was upright. Just about. He looked as if he'd been drinking since midday. He could barely stand up, let alone threaten Paddy.

'You okay, mate?' Paddy asked.

'Never better.' The guy balled his hand and held it out in front of his chest. Paddy took a step back, away from the basin. Jesus, what was going on? 'Divorced today.' The man waved his fist in celebration. 'See. A free man.' He pushed himself up and took an unsteady step towards the sink.

'Congratulations,' Paddy said, already walking towards the door.

He kept going, out the bathroom and through the pub until he was outside, the rush of the cold night air stinging his face. He paused outside the pub and pulled out his phone. His mouth was dry as he checked to see whether there was anything else from the game. The icon was still on his screen, but there were no new notifications. There was a text message from his mother, asking him to call. He typed a reply.

I'm fine, Mum. Don't worry about me. Will call when I can. X

Paddy scanned the road. He preferred bustling streets. Plenty of people meant it was unlikely someone would try and jump him. Next best was nobody at all. But right then it was quiet but not deserted, just a handful of people out and about, which was the worst of all worlds.

He stood at the pedestrian crossing, waiting for the green light, keeping a paranoid eye on the woman walking along the pavement. The lights changed and he started the walk home, his legs slightly unsteady.

Drinking probably wasn't a clever response. But what else could he do? It wasn't as if he could talk to anyone. He'd considered confiding in Trent. They'd been close at school, and still got on well, even if they'd seen less of each other in recent months.

But Trent had always thought of himself as a martyr. Or at least, Paddy felt that he acted as a martyr. To be fair, the man's brother had died in a fire, along with his parents. That was tough. Probably as tough as it gets. And yet, if Paddy was being blunt, and several pints in he wasn't able to stop himself, it didn't have to define him. Not everything could be reduced to that one event. Christ, Trent had even fallen out with Lila over the fire. He'd never said as much, not directly, but Paddy was sure that that's what had happened. Because everything was always about the fire, which never left any space for anyone else. So, Paddy could tell Trent about his problems, his very real, very current problems. But he just wasn't sure his friend would listen.

10

SUNDAY, 10:45PM

Olivia slid down to the floor, her back pressed against her front door. She clutched her phone in front of her, blinking away the tears. The app was open and she was looking at the group chat. She'd watched a few seconds of each video. Dub was such an idiot. How could he have let someone have access to those videos? And if the game had those, what else would it have? She shuddered and opened Facebook.

The first three posts on her feed were all from Vince. She'd friended him a few years ago. Both in real life and on Facebook. He'd been interested in her, she was sure of that. But nothing had ever happened between them. For all his confident views on politics and socioeconomics, he'd never plucked up the courage to make a move. Which had suited Oli. She'd been swept along by his rhetoric, his friends – the *movement* as he somewhat grandly called them. But now she scrolled past his posts without reading them. Brexit. Immigration. Taxes. Still beating the same drum.

The next post was a dog playing in the sea, bemused and delighted by the waves. Pure timeline cleanse. After rewatching the video three times, Oli touched her profile photo – a picture of her holding a green glow stick and dancing on a table from years ago - and her own page appeared. A photo of the sea and the words 'Amazing to think that 71% of the Earth's surface is water.' She'd enjoyed the day she'd taken that photo, standing on the beach, staring at the sea. She smiled as The Cure compilation album of the same name crept into her head. Being a Goth had been another short-lived phase. Add it to list with raver and hippy. Even Vince had been a phase. She always moved on.

Olivia tapped on the three-lined menu button in the bottom-right corner of the screen. Two seconds later she selected Delete Account. She worked methodically through her other social media accounts, deleting them all.

But she knew nothing was ever gone. Just ask Dub. Someone somewhere could drag everything back if they wanted to. And if they knew what they were looking for.

She let out a deep sigh. It was the best she could do. But she had a nagging feeling that it wouldn't be enough.

11

MANIFESTO EXTRACT 2

The medal will trigger the memory of his father. It will be only a matter of time before he searches on his father's name.

Trigger for release of image 012 and message 012 to Trent Ryder

If search_term = 'David Simon Ryder' then exe.data012

12

SUNDAY,11:31PM

Trent stood on the tube with his back pushed against the column next to the doors. His body rocked with motion of the train. He peered at the Wikipedia entry pulled up on his phone. It was years since he'd last looked at it.

The Queen's Gallantry Medal is a United Kingdom decoration awarded for exemplary acts of bravery by civilians, and by members of the Armed Forces "not in the face of the enemy", where the services were not so outstanding as to merit the George Cross or the George Medal, but above the level required for the Queen's Commendation for Bravery.

The taunting question from the game seared through his brain.

Don't you want to know the truth about the fire?

It started with a scratching sensation in his skull and when the thought fully formed his knees buckled and he reached out for the bright yellow post to steady himself. He repositioned his feet and leant his weight into the glass partition as the train started to bounce him around. He shook his head. How could someone else have discovered that Trent's father was rejected for a posthumously nominated award? Surely rejections weren't made public.

His chest was tight as he typed out a name in Google.

David Simon Ryder.

He hit the search button and held his breath for the 0.62 seconds it took for 6.3 million hits to return. The first hit was a story about the fire. He knew the text word for word, and he knew there was no mention of the medal. He scanned the page of results. Most of them were about the wrong David Ryder. A couple more were about the fire. None of them referenced the Queen's Gallantry Medal.

He was only vaguely aware of the train slowing as it glided into the station. The world had dimmed and he forced his eyes wide open to try and bring it back into focus. An alarm beeped to signal the imminent closure of the doors and he lurched towards them, squeezing through just before they slammed shut behind him. He staggered onto the platform, gasping for air.

'Out the way, mate.' A suited office worker running the other way shoved him sideways.

'Sorry.' Trent shuffled up the stairs and out into the night. He looked around at his surroundings, blinking until they crystalised into a familiar location. He'd rushed off the tube a station too soon for home. His phone buzzed and sweat beaded between his shoulder blades. He raised his hand to see that the game had sent another message. He opened his chat thread to reveal a screenshot of a what appeared to be a Government webpage. Even before he read the detail, he knew it was about the Gallantry medal. He swallowed down the bile rising in his throat and forced himself to read.

How to recommend someone for a gallantry award

. . .

Email the Honours and Appointments Secretariat.

You'll need to write a detailed description explaining why you're recommending them. Include the person's:

- name
- date of birth
- address

Give as many details as possible about what happened. This will make your application more likely to be considered. Include:

- location
- date
- any emergency or official services that were there.

Honours and Appointments Secretariat\honours@cabinetoffice.gov.uk

After you recommend someone for a gallantry award

All recommendations will be assessed by the George Cross Committee, which makes recommendations to the Queen, who awards the honour.

And below the screenshot was another message from the game.

Not all recommendations result in an honour being awarded.

Trent's head was spinning. He blew out a deep breath as he fumbled with his phone to navigate away from the app and to dial his sister's number. It was late but this was important. When he heard Pen's voicemail message kick in he hit the end call button and fired off a text.

Need to speak urgently. Will come over to you first thing tomorrow.

He heard the swoosh as the text was sent and then added a postscript.

I'm fine. Nothing to worry about. It's about Dad.

He stared at his last message. His breathing was ragged. He buried his phone in his pocket and started walking home. The walk would give him time to think, and hopefully calm him down. But his mind was racing, already pulling him back into the past. A past he'd done his best to bury.

LIKE MOST OF the nights for the past ten years, Trent dreamt of his brother.

Typically, in those dreams, Trent was fifteen, his age when Freddy had died. But that night he was older. Which was weird because Freddy was still five.

Frozen in age forever, not by cryogenics, but by fire.

His chubby face was covered with soot, smudged where he'd rubbed his hands over his face.

Freddy was trying to get his older brother's attention, which was difficult because Trent was talking with Lila. 'Trent, Trent,' Freddy was calling out, pulling on Trent's arm.

Trent twisted away from Lila. His little brother was dressed in his Mario and Luigi pyjamas – Yoshi must have been in the wash.

'Look.' Freddy pointed to his chest, to the medal. A silver

effigy, a blue and grey ribbon. Freddy's smile could have powered the world.

Trent reached forward, felt the cold metal in his hand, ran his finger over the profile of his father.

'Where did you get this, Freddy?' he asked.

And then he swore, jerking his hand away from the metal. There was a hiss as the medal fell back against Freddy's chest, and a spark spat towards Trent. Then Freddy was screaming, his body a ball of flame.

Trent sat upright in bed. Soaked through. Gasping for air.

13

MONDAY, 7:50AM

Trent only slept for a few hours after making it home from Lila's flat but he dragged himself out of bed early to climb onto his motorbike and set off to see Pen. She hadn't replied to his texts the night before or answered her phone when he'd called before leaving his house, but then she was usually early to bed on a school night and liked her lie-ins. Or maybe she'd invited her boyfriend over, and she hadn't had time to check her messages.

His twenty-three-year-old sister often drove him nuts. She was impulsive and loud. The extravert to his introvert. The yin to his yang. Which might have explained why she seemed to have fallen for Bobby. Bobby was the same age as Trent, had no regular job, little money, and an opinion on everything. Trent had tried hard to like him but was increasingly coming to the view that he might not ever make it to the summit of that particular mountain, instead having to settle at the lower ridge which signified mere acceptance.

But he loved his sister. No matter how painful Pen could

be at times, Trent would always look out for her. But right then, he needed her help.

He rang on the doorbell and waited. She was a lodger in a house which was a quick scooter ride away from the secondary school where her pupils were giving her an education of their own design. Being a trainee teacher was tough but then, so was Pen. She would teach them to dot their i's and cross their t's whilst trying to stop them from dropping e's.

The house was a starter home although the family who owned it were already mid-way through life. They treated Pen as if she was one of their own, which meant that she did what she liked and they shouted at her, but it seemed to work okay for all involved and she had been living there for nearly nine months now.

The door was opened by Mr. Holland, shouter-in-chief, half-dressed in corduroy slippers and a pair of smart trousers with a yellowing dressing gown on top. Quite the look. He turned towards the stairs and bellowed, 'Pen, visitor!' Then he shuffled down the hallway, hopefully to finish dressing, leaving Trent to close the door and make his way upstairs.

As Trent reached the top floor, Pen shot out through the door and brought herself to a shuddering halt, catapulting her sense of disappointment right into him. 'Oh, it's you,' she said, looking nonplussed. If her expression hadn't given her away, the flatline greeting would've done the trick.

Unlike Mr Francis, Pen was dressed and then some. A short, floaty blue dress, yellow tights, and bright white trainers. Not what Trent's teachers used to wear but hey, times changed. She had switched her hair colour again. Still dyed, but back to a less *un*natural colour for her. Trent wasn't sure what the fashion magazines would call it, but in his book, it was blue.

'Hi. Did you get my text?' he said.

They stood on the landing for a few seconds, Pen blinking as if trying to wake up her brain. 'No, my battery was dead. I charged it overnight but I haven't checked it this morning. I've only just got up.'

'Have you got time for a quick breakfast before work?'

'Shit.' She scratched her head. 'I've agreed to meet Bobby this morning. Sorry.'

Trent clenched and then released his hands. 'Sorry, give me a minute to cancel Bobby, or sorry but I'm going for breakfast with Bobby?'

The hesitation as she shifted her weight before reaching to adjust one of her shoes told him everything he needed to know. 'You're really rejecting me for Bobby G? After I came all this way.'

'Don't call him that, you know I hate it.' Of course he did – that was why he had used it. But Trent could hear the warmth returning to her voice.

'You told me *all* his mates call him Bobby G,' he said, knowing she'd hate that, too, because she'd made it very clear that she'd never call him that herself. He decided to change tack. 'I really need to speak to you, Pen.'

'You're impossible.' She was shaking her head but smiling. 'I've got ten minutes. Come on in.'

Pen walked back into the room, leaving her door open for him to follow. He looked round her one-room universe. Green flowery duvet falling halfway off the bed, iPad set up as her TV, yoga mat rolled up and leaning against one side of her desk, and an acoustic guitar on the other.

One thing particularly caught his eye: Mr Dop It. As always, it yanked him right back to when, aged thirteen and ten, Trent and Pen were left alone together after learning that their parents and their little brother had died. They'd been sitting in the spare room at their aunt's house, two beds squashed into a study along with a cardboard box containing those few toys that had been recovered from the fire. Pen had pulled out Mr Dop It, a soft, orange stuffed elephant with multicoloured patches sewn on to it. One of Freddy's favourites, it had been named by their father after a trunk-tied elephant from a bedtime story who repeatedly tried to say, 'stop it.' That night, Pen had placed the elephant on the shelf in their room, nestling between the clock and the bible.

Now Pen followed Trent's gaze and something passed between them. A silent renewal of their family contract. Mr Dop It looked on. That was his role in these things. No one needed to call him out; everyone always knew he was there. The toy elephant in the room.

'Come on, nine minutes left now,' Pen said slumping onto her bed. 'What's going on?'

Trent moved a small stack of marking aside and reclined against Pen's desk. He couldn't really blame her for choosing Bobby over him; she was beyond the first blush of a fling and into the serious relationship stage, so he was prepared to make allowances. But right then he needed to focus.

'I was sent an anonymous message last night,' he said. Pen reached for her wide rimmed glasses and slipped them on, blinking as she stared at him. 'It was a photo of the Queen's Gallantry Medal.' Penny's eyes stretched wide. 'And here's the kicker.' Pen leant forward into his words. 'Whoever sent the message has linked it to the fire.'

Penny's head swivelled as she tried to get her words out. 'The fire? But how would ... how would anyone know?'

Trent felt the tightness inside him ratchet up. Pen was as mystified as he was. He waited until she'd managed to collect herself. 'You haven't mentioned it to anyone?' he asked.

She shook her head. 'No. I've never said a word about it since Aunt Josephine told us her application had been rejected.'

Trent nodded. 'There was a separate message saying that not all recommendations result in an award being made.' He paused. 'Someone knows that Dad was nominated. And they know he was rejected. And I think...' He raked his hands through his hair.

'What?' Pen asked.

Trent sighed. 'I think maybe whoever this is, somehow, and I have no idea how, they know the reason it was denied.'

Pen's eyes widened. 'But *we* don't even know the reason.'

'I know,' Trent said. 'Maybe it's some sick joke.' He paused again. 'I could contact the relevant department and try asking for the details. Perhaps they would release that to next of kin.' Pen was looking at him intently and he knew she was thinking the same thought as him. 'I know. If they wouldn't tell his sister, why would they tell his son.' He shrugged.

'Aunt Jo specifically told us that she wasn't given a reason. Nothing more than he didn't meet the criteria.' Pen stood up and massaged her temples. 'This is unbelievable. Maybe Aunt Jo does know but didn't want to tell us.' She sighed. 'I don't know either.'

Trent had his phone out and was scrolling through his address book. He clicked on Aunt Jo and hit the call button. He'd contacted her when he decided to go to Samson's wake, planning to call in beforehand, but she'd said she would be out of town on a holiday with friends. But this was important. Holiday or not, he was going to at least try to reach her. He lifted the phone to his ear and turned to Pen. 'She's on another cruise. God knows where she is and what time it is for her.'

Pen shuffled closer to Trent waiting for the call to connect.

'Voicemail,' he said as the default recorded voice clicked in. He nodded as she mouthed at him to leave a message. He took a breath and waited for the beep. 'Hi, Aunt Jo. It's Trent and Pen. We need to speak to you.' Pen was gesticulating at him, encouraging him to say more. 'It's about Dad,' he added. 'It's important. I'm sorry to bother you on your holiday but please can you call me or Pen back when you pick this up. Thanks, Aunt Jo. Bye.'

'TRENT?' Pen had been looking out the window but now turned back to face her brother. 'Who the hell could have sent you that message?'

He considered giving the long answer but in the end it came to the same conclusion as the short answer. 'I don't know.'

'It just came out the blue?'

'No. Well, yes and no. A bunch of my old school friends, we all received this invitation headed up Hayden Road leavers. Paddy clicked on it first. It downloaded this app.' He cleared his throat. 'It appears to have certain information about us all.'

'Bloody hell. Can't you track the number? Find them that way.'

'I hope so. I'm going to try.' He saw Penny glance at her watch. His minutes were counting down. 'One more thing, Pen. I wanted to finalise our arrangements for the anniversary.'

Her gaze flicked away from his – just for a moment, but it was there. They'd been together on the same day of the year, from ten in the morning, just the two of them, every year since it had happened. Surely she couldn't have forgotten.

Pen stared at the floor, her usually pale cheeks flushed. 'Shit. That's Saturday isn't it?' She was shaking her head, lost in thought. 'It's just ...' She took a sharp breath. 'That Saturday is our six-month anniversary. Bobby has made all these plans. He's put so much thought and effort into it already. I'm really sorry. I can't believe that I didn't clock the date.' Trent didn't trust himself to speak. She paused and nodded to herself. 'I'll talk to him,' she said in a rush. 'See what we can do.'

Trent nodded. Just about. The doorbell rang. Ding, dong. Time's up.

'I guess that'll be the Bobster,' he said, forcing the jollity into his voice.

Pen stuck her tongue out at him. 'You're so not funny.' She started to walk out of her room, looking relieved to have an excuse, but Trent caught her hand.

'Please try, Pen. I know you're excited. And I'm happy for you. I am. It's just–'

'I know. Of course I will.' She smiled as she squeezed past him.

Trent followed his sister downstairs for what he expected would be the briefest of interactions with Bobby G.

'Hey, by the way, guess who's back?' He had almost forgotten to share the news.

'Tupac? Elvis?'

'In town, I meant. Not from the dead.' A beat. 'Lila.'

Pen's hand froze on the latch of the front door. Trent could see a distorted Bobby through the glass. Pen turned to him. 'And how do you feel about that?' For a moment it was as though she was older than him, but he shook the feeling off.

'It's as if she's never been away.' Trent indicated the shape on the doorstep.

Pen pulled the latch. 'I love Lila, you know I do. I just don't understand where it went wrong between you two. You were so close before she left. I'd love to catch up with her whilst she's here.'

Trent tensed. He'd never told Pen that Lila had tried to stay in touch and that it was him who'd cut the cord. Pen stepped back as she swung the door open.

'It's complicated,' Trent said, but Pen didn't hear because Bobby had swept her into a hug and was spinning her round.

Trent waited for her feet to come back down to earth, taking Bobby in. Tall, thin and balsa wood pale, he was wearing drainpipe jeans, a Strokes' *Is This It?* t-shirt and a leather jacket two sizes too large for him. Which no doubt made it the perfect fit. His buzzcut hair was a ladybird red and Trent wondered if it'd been inspired by a matchstick.

Trent sighed. At least he should try. For Pen. 'Hey Bobby. Good to see you.' He held out his hand and was rewarded with a barely perceptible nod. Trent withdrew his hand. Trying could be so trying.

Bobby slung his arm around Pen's shoulders. 'Hey, Penilicious, let's chow.' New York City cool.

The couple walked down the drive, and Pen shot Trent a toothpaste-advert smile back over her shoulder. Trent grinned back, happy to see his sister riding her relationship wave; but hoping that she knew how to surf.

'Hey, pal.'

The voice came from inside the house and Trent turned to see Mr Holland waving at him. He'd lost the robe but was sporting a smart pair of red braces over his bare torso. Trent grinned. New York City, bow down to Campden Town keeping it real.

'You're letting the heat out.'

Trent apologised and closed the front door behind him, stepping onto the pavement. He'd be early if he headed to work now but he could do with some extra credit in the bank. Because he needed to ask his boss for a favour.

14

MONDAY, 11:12AM

Andrew Dubnyk lowered himself into the chair under his boss's gaze, glad to be sitting down. He hadn't eaten since the videos had been shared the previous night. Somehow he'd made it into work and managed to get through the morning. But if anyone were to ask him what he'd worked on, he wouldn't be able to answer. The whole morning had been a blur. He'd written maybe twenty words of an article; he wasn't confident that even those would survive his editor.

When he'd been called in to see Helen, it had almost been a relief. It took him away from his article, and chatting to Helen was easy. He just needed to listen, nod, and then do what he'd been asked to do.

'You look like hell,' she said. As an opening gambit, such bluntness wasn't her usual style. She paused and looked at him before turning to cross the room. Helen liked to walk and talk, even if the other person was seated.

'Sorry,' he said, talking as much to the floor as to her. 'I had a bad night.'

She nodded, but didn't immediately reply. Adrenaline

jolted through his body. Did she know about the videos? There was something about her expression. Her lips were pursed, a slight furrow on her forehead. She even stopped walking. 'This isn't easy, Andrew.'

He swallowed, and tried to keep his breathing steady, even as his pulse kicked up.

'We've received a complaint.' She started moving again. 'Against you.'

'A complaint?' He was conscious how weak it sounded to simply repeat the word.

'We're suspending you on full pay until we have conducted an investigation.' She reached the window and pivoted back round.

'I...' He closed his eyes. Tried to think.

'You should gather your things together and go home. We'll be in touch.'

It would be too much of a coincidence for it not to be related to the videos. Should he say anything? Helen leant on the table. The meeting was clearly over.

'I don't know.' He stopped. Shook his head. Tried again. 'I haven't done anything wrong.' A touch of belligerence in his voice, but that was fair enough. 'Who's made the allegation?' he pressed. He could hear some strength returning to his voice. 'What am I meant to have done?'

'I'm afraid I can't go into that, Andrew. Not yet. We've been sent some material. We'll be in touch as soon as we can.'

Dub pushed himself out of the chair. 'I haven't done anything wrong.' He forced himself to meet Helen's eyes. Conscious that he now towered over her he took a slight step backwards.

'I hear you, Andrew.' He couldn't read her expression. 'You shouldn't have any contact with anyone from work until you hear from us. I imagine that'll be in the next couple of days.' Her phone started to ring and she hesitated. 'Look, I understand this is difficult for you. We'll work diligently and a fast as we reasonably can. We'll be in touch.'

She reached for her phone, her hand hovering over it, and waited whilst he walked out of the room.

Dub didn't speak to anyone as he stuffed his personal belongings into a canvas bag and left the office. He decided to walk home, needing space and time to clear his mind.

It had to be the videos. But what did they have to do with his work?

He quickened his step. If anyone had shared those videos with his work, they were the ones who'd broken the law. He was on the path that led to his flat and he looked up at his front window on the second floor. He froze. There was a man moving around in his bedroom. Dub lived alone, and he hadn't invited anyone round. He broke into a run. Whoever it was had chosen the wrong day to break into his property.

15

MONDAY, 11:46PM

People often laughed when Trent told them that he'd quit as a trainee solicitor to become a personal assistant but he'd worked for Tina for nearly three years now and he loved it. He'd joined just as her software business was really beginning to take off and she'd taken him along for the ride. Even if his role in some meetings wasn't much more than to pour coffee and take the notes, he was always in the room. But today he needed her help, he just had to pick his moment.

Trent was staring at his phone. Every time there had been a notification his hand had twitched but, so far at least, there'd been no more messages from the game but also no reply from his aunt.

'Any chance you might do some work today, Trent?'

He hadn't heard Tina leave her office or walk over to his desk. She was wearing blue jeans and a red long-sleeved t-shirt and she had twisted her blonde hair into a bun secured with what looked for all the world like a pencil. Her software company CEO vibe was completed by her large framed, round glasses and a look that said don't bother trying to impress me.

'Um, sorry.' He screen-locked his phone and placed it on the desk next to his keyboard.

'Everything okay?'

It was one of the things that Trent loved about his job. He was lucky to have a boss who genuinely cared about him beyond his ability to do things for her. Even so, he'd never asked her for help, not directly. 'I might need a favour.'

Her eyes narrowed and she pushed a loose strand of hair back behind her ear. 'It's not more money, right? You're three months early for that conversation.' The corners of her mouth twitched.

'No, it's not money.' I don't know what it is, he almost added. Trent cleared his throat. 'I wouldn't ordinarily ask but I ... I find myself in ... an unusual situation.'

'Go on.' Her expression was impassive.

'It's nothing to worry about but I've been receiving some messages through an app and I would like to find out more about who's sending them.' He held out both palms towards her. 'No, it isn't a dating app.' He tilted his head. 'It's more like a stalking app.'

'You say potato.' Trent smiled but he could see that Tina was weighing things up. 'You'd like one of my tech guys to take a look?' Straight to the point.

'That would be great, if you don't mind.'

'Actually, I have a better idea.' Tina pulled out her phone. 'I'm going to give you a contact. She's the best there is and she'll do this for nothing. Partly because she loves this stuff and partly because she owes me. Get in touch and tell her I'd like her to help you.'

Trent tapped on his own phone to accept the virtual business card and studied the details that Tina had provided. 'Dylan? Unusual name for a woman.'

'She's an unusual woman. Super bright. I keep trying to convince her to come and work for me.' Tina was now looking at her phone, ready to move on to other things. 'Just don't expect to make friends with her. She doesn't really do friends.'

'Thanks, Tina,' he said replacing his phone on the desk and visibly turning his attention to his work. At that moment his phone vibrated and he snatched it back up. It was a text from Pen.

Lila and I are going for lunch, today. 1pm. Free to join us? X

Tina was still standing next to him, watching. 'If you've got something going on then why don't you take a couple of days holiday? You're not much use to me in this state anyway.'

Trent tried to push sex, lies, and the friends you make to the back of his mind. He sat up straight in his chair and pulled the keyboard towards him. 'Sorry. I've been a bit distracted, but I'll try–'

'Trent,' Tina interjected. 'It's fine, really. I'm not testing your loyalty. It's a quiet week, there's nothing that can't wait and you've got some holiday. Take some time.'

Trent recognised an executive order when he heard one and, in truth, he could do with the time to investigate the game. The more he considered it, the more sense it made. He nodded decisively. 'Thank you,' he said, turning towards Tina, but his boss was already walking back to her office.

16

MONDAY, 1:10PM

Trent told the waitress his name and followed her as she led the way towards the back of the restaurant where he caught sight of Pen and Lila sitting together on the same side of a table. They were each holding a glass of red wine, their elbows on the blue checked tablecloth, Pen talking and Lila nodding and laughing.

Visually they couldn't be more different; Lila was short with dark hair and olive-coloured skin, while Pen was tall, with blue dye enhancing her natural blonde hair colour, and a skin tone that relied on a constant layer of factor fifty. They had known each other nearly their whole lives and yet Trent wondered whether this was the first time they had formally arranged to spend time together. Before, any time together was accidental or as a result of Trent and Lila's plans, although no less friendly for that. He walked over to the table and pulled back a chair, saying 'Don't feel the need to wait for me.'

'We didn't,' said Lila, topping up both Pen's glass and then her own before she emptied the last of the bottle in Trent's glass. Thimbleful would be an exaggeration.

'I've got the afternoon off. And anyway, wine helps with the marking,' Pen said, giggling before stopping a passing waitress to request another bottle.

'How long have you two been here?' he asked.

'Pen was here before me,' said Lila. 'I was pretty much on time. We've just been catching up on each other's love life.'

'Glad I was late.' He glanced at them both. 'You want me to leave again, or have you finished?'

Lila smiled. 'I think you're safe to stay.' She turned to face Pen. 'Although I want to hear much more about Bobby. He sounds intriguing.'

The waitress returned with the wine and filled up Trent's glass. 'A toast,' he said, lifting his glass.

'To Bobby,' Lila replied immediately.

Trent was slow to join in the chorus and he saw Lila catch the look that Pen shot at him.

'Ah,' Lila said. 'I'm sensing that maybe your big brother doesn't approve of Bobby.'

Pen raised her glass and her eyebrows at the same time.

'Bobby's fine.' He kept his voice neutral.

Lila leaned in towards Pen and whispered. 'Is he like this with all your boyfriends?' Trent looked at the two of them. 'What's not to like, Trent? From what I've heard,' Lila dropped her voice, 'from a source that I trust *implicitly,* he's good looking, clever, thoughtful and romantic.'

'Bobby's arranged this whole day for us to be together,' Pen said. She turned to Lila. 'It's our six-month anniversary.' She seemed to imbue those five words with the persuasive power of the Socratic method. 'But it's the day that Trent and I always spend together. Because it's the anniversary...' She hung her head rather than finish the sentence.

Of the day the fire killed our parents and our beloved baby brother, Freddy.

That's what she didn't say. But everyone heard it loud and clear. Lila and Trent exchanged a glance. He wasn't sure but he thought he saw her wink.

'Why do I feel like I've just walked into a minefield? Sorry, guys.' Concern was shining from Lila's face.

'It's not your fault, Lila. It's no one's fault.' Pen paused. Trent bit down on his lip as his sister continued speaking.

'Bobby's so excited. He's booked somewhere for us to stay overnight. It's a surprise venue.' The excitement in her voice clawed at Trent.

'Have you told him? Bobby, I mean.' Lila spoke gently, reaching out to take Pen's hand. His sister looked as though she was at a tipping point. 'I know, it's not my place, Pen, but he sounds like a nice guy. I'm sure he'd understand if you pushed dinner back by a day. Or even if you made it a late dinner and an overnight stay. That way you could do both.'

Trent dropped his eyes to study the tablecloth. Anywhere but Pen. He placed his hands together to ensure they didn't shake.

'I can–' Pen blew out a lung-full of air. 'I'm sorry. Thinking of Freddy always makes me emotional. Even now.' She seemed to be gathering herself. 'Of course I'll tell him.'

Tension flooded out of Trent's body. He stretched out his hand to rest it on his sister's. 'Thanks Pen.'

She nodded at him and glanced at their arms resting on the table. 'It looks like we're holding a séance,' she said removing her hands and turning to face Lila. 'I'm starving. Let's order some food, and whilst we wait, I want to hear all about California.'

THE LUNCH HAD BEEN a success with the three of them reminiscing about their own time at school with Pen bringing things up to date with stories of her own students. Trent had just pushed away the board with the last unclaimed chunk of cheese when he felt his phone vibrate in his pocket. Which was enough for his heart rate to kick up a level.

He unlocked his phone and his eyes locked onto the icon with the red background with the black Japanese symbol. He had a new message.

Don't you want to know why?

He raised his head. Lila was laughing at Pen's latest tail of student embarrassment but Pen's eyes were fixed on him, her forehead creased. 'What is it? You look worried.'

Trent glanced at Lila and then back at his sister. 'I've had another message.'

Lila gasped and hurriedly reached into her bag to grab her own phone. She was blinking rapidly. He saw her swipe down to refresh.

'I haven't received anything,' she said, frowning.

He scratched his forehead and then he pushed his chair back. 'I'm sorry. I need to go.' He pulled out thirty pounds from his wallet and dropped it on the table. 'Let me know if I owe more.' He leaned over and kissed each of them on the cheek. 'Sorry,' he said again. He could feel pressure building in his chest.

'Trent, hold on. What did it say?' Pen was standing up and reaching out towards him.

'It said, don't you want to know why?' The words caught in his throat.

Pen's hand flew to cover her mouth.

He started to walk away. 'I'm sorry. I just need to...' He didn't know how to finish so he turned his back on them both and started to weave his way through the restaurant.

'Call me,' he heard Pen shout after him.

He gave her a thumbs up but without looking back. His

surroundings blurred and he stumbled out of the way of a waiter coming the other way. Then he was outside. He raised his hands to pull down on the skin under his eyes before rubbing around the sockets. Then he put his head down to walk back to where he had left his motor bike.

He flicked back to the message as he strode along the pavement.

Don't you want to know why?

Yes. Yes. Please, yes.

He studied the app. Yet again there was no message asking him whether he was ready to play. Again, no countdown. Was this all part of the build-up? The appetiser before the main course.

He engaged pedestrian autopilot. So many people, all of them seemingly walking in the opposite direction to him. He increased his pace. He recalled the last time he'd asked Aunt Jo, perhaps a couple of years ago, but her answer had been the same as always. *We weren't told any details. What's important is that your dad was hugely respected. He was a good man.*

Her answer had made him angry at the time. Why didn't she want to know the truth? What reason could there be to deny the award of the medal? On the face of it, his father's actions were as heroic as many others whose bravery had been publicly celebrated with an award of the medal. Was he the only one who cared?

But Pen had nudged him and shot him a warning look and with that he had left it alone. He'd watched Jo, his father's sister, tear up as she chewed her food in silence. Perhaps if he'd believed she knew more he would have pushed harder but he was confident she knew no more than she'd told them.

But now it seemed that someone knew more. And Trent needed to find them if he was going to uncover the truth.

The woman in front of him stopped without warning, captivated by something on her phone. He knew that feeling. He swerved around her.

His motorbike was just ahead of him now, he'd be home before too long.

17

MONDAY, 4:03PM

It was four o'clock in the afternoon when Trent arrived home. The light was fading fast and the rain was steadily ratcheting up its tempo. He opened his garage door and wheeled his motorbike inside. Then he picked up a chamois cloth to wipe off the worst of the rain.

He'd bought his house not long after starting his job with Tina. Everything of his parents had been split evenly between him and Pen, but for years he hadn't wanted to touch any of it, even when he was old enough to do so. He'd hated what it represented. But one day that changed. After denial, anger, bargaining, depression, and acceptance came the final stage of grief: spending. He wanted the money gone. There'd been enough inheritance for him to put down a decent deposit on the semi-detached, three-bedroom house.

He'd worried that he'd feel the same way about the house as he did about the money. After all, he'd simply swapped one for the other. It still surprised him how quickly the bricks and mortar shell had grown from a building into his home. And he was at peace with that.

Once inside, he grabbed a clean towel from the

cupboard. He was heading towards the bathroom when his phone buzzed again. He rubbed his head. Then there was another buzz from his phone. There was a metallic taste in his mouth as he unlocked the screen. The hairs at the nape of his neck lifted as the flash of colours announced the game. Black and red. A cold shiver tracked down his spine. This time it was a message to the whole group.

You've seen what happens when you don't play. Your only hope is to face up to the truth.

Trent leant against the wall. Dub hadn't played; he'd waited for the timer to count down to zero and then his videos had been released. But what would've happened if he'd played? Trent's breathing was fast and shallow. He closed his eyes and sucked in a deep breath. *One, two, three–*. His eyes sprang open as the chime of his front doorbell stopped the count.

Trent wasn't in the mood for visitors. He threw the towel over the side of the banister and made his way towards his front door, facial expression set to unwelcoming. The defining characteristic of the shape he saw through the frosted glass was size.

He slipped on the security chain and opened the door just an inch or two to find Dub peering at him through the narrow opening. His hair and clothes were wet from the rain and, even odder, he was wearing a rucksack and carried two suitcases.

'Hi, Dub,' Trent said, his reflex greeting kicking in fractionally faster than his memory of the videos.

Dub eased the rucksack off his back and steadied it on the doorstep, rubbing his shoulders. 'That's better. Look, mate, I need a massive favour.' Dub was scowling, his irritation six foot high and rising.

Trent pressed the door to unclip the silver chain, then eased the door open and stood back. 'What's happened?'

Dub ran his hand over his face. 'I've been suspended from work and when I got home I found I'd been served with an eviction notice by my landlord.'

That explained the rucksack and the suitcases. 'Jesus, why?'

Dub shrugged. 'Those videos, I guess.' He glanced at the floor and then back at Trent. 'One of them was filmed at work.' His grin was an homage to sheep. 'And another featured the Landlord's sister.'

Trent raised his eyebrows. 'His sister?'

'Yeah. She came round to do some decorating. Asked me to help clean out her paint pots. What was I supposed to do?' His eyes twinkled.

Trent shook his head and helped lift Dub's bags into the hall, then led him into the kitchen. It was the one room he'd decorated himself. He'd attempted to give the room some sophistication by painting the cupboards bright red but he'd had only managed to emulate the look of a children's soft play area. Without the fun of a ball pit. He cast around and, unable to locate the wisdom of Solomon, started making a pot of coffee.

'Tell me what happened,' he asked.

'Okay. I went into work, today, as normal. My editor called me in, just before lunchtime, which never happens. She shut the door and told me she was suspending me whilst they investigated certain material that had been sent to them.' Certain material. Only one guess allowed.

'Did those women know they were being filmed?' Trent asked. He hadn't meant to be so direct, but it was probably best to get it out there.

Dub's eyes blazed. 'Jesus, Trent. Of course they did.' Dub

raked his fingers through his hair. 'I normally find people online.' A four-word philosophy that was unlikely to lead to anything but trouble. 'We are all consenting adults who want to be filmed having sex. We share the videos with each other but no one else.'

Trent let out a deep breath as he turned off the beeping pot and poured two mugs of coffee. He held one out to Dub.

'Thanks,' said Dub before lowering himself onto one of the kitchen chairs.

'Sorry,' Trent said, sitting down opposite him. 'I shouldn't have asked. I know you better than that. Tell me what happened with your flat?'

'Pretty much what I told you. When I arrived home my landlord was in the flat. Bastard had just let himself in without so much as a call. Told me he wanted me out of the flat. Right there and then.'

'Surely he can't do that. You're entitled to some notice.'

Dub took a sip of coffee. 'I haven't got a lease, mate. I just pay weekly rent.' He peered at Trent. 'So, will you put me up? I can pay you. You were saying yesterday that you had a spare room and finding a place to rent at short notice is a nightmare.'

Trent recalled mentioning his house but the open-ended offer of half board to anyone who needed it eluded him. He took another sip, a slow sip, of coffee. 'Who do you think sent those videos?'

'They were private.' It was a whisper, made harder to hear by Dub burying his face into his hands.

Trent bit his lip. 'Well, someone sent them to all of us,' he said, 'and, I'm guessing, your work and your landlord. Perhaps someone doesn't like you very much.'

He was thinking as he spoke. Surely whoever was behind this wouldn't include themselves. And yet, if it was an angry ex-girlfriend, they might well have made their own video with Dub. Maybe that's how they knew about them.

Tiredness crept through Trent's body and he stifled a yawn. He'd already made up his mind. Dub may not be nominated for role model of the year but he hadn't done anything wrong. 'The spare room is on the left at the top of the stairs. The bathroom is next to it.'

'Great.' Dub pushed himself up. 'Thanks, mate. I appreciate it. Alright if I take a shower?'

'Sure.' Trent scratched his head and called out as Dub headed out of the room. 'Dub? Once you've unpacked, come back down will you?'

18

MANIFESTO EXTRACT 3

fter their round, they will think it is over. It won't be. The follow up messages must make that clear.

#Time lapse message to Player1

#Time to send: Round1 + 24:00

Background colour: Black

Font colour: Red

Text:

. . .

Six videos have been released. I have not yet released the final video. Or more accurately, the first video. You will have one chance to tell the truth. Only if you do that will the remaining video be permanently deleted.

19

MONDAY, 4:19PM

Trent heard Dub turn off the shower so he guessed he would be down soon. And when Dub appeared he would face Trent's cross-examination. Starting with whether there was a missing video.

Five minutes later, the kitchen door creaked open. Trent pushed his phone over the worktop towards Dub. 'Look at the videos. We were sent six. Tell me who's missing.'

Dub reacted in slow motion, reaching out and picking up the phone before sitting down and methodically scrolling through, mumbling to himself. He looked at Trent, his eyes foggy. 'There isn't another video.' Dub's delivery was matter of fact.

Trent pushed on. 'Whoever sent those needed to know about them. They were private so the most likely answer to that is that it's someone who's in a video with you. But they wouldn't send their own video. So, I figure that there's a missing video.'

Maybe Dub needed another coffee to kick start his brain or maybe he just needed time to think but whatever it was he was struggling to formulate an answer. Trent could see him mentally ticking off names on the list before nodding to himself. Dub stared into space as he spoke. 'There's no missing video. There were only six. Those six.'

'Are you sure?' Trent asked. Dub's denial wasn't convincing. He wouldn't meet Trent's gaze.

'I was there, and I'm telling you, there were only six,' Dub said with a shrug.

But his tone and his manner were off. He was too casual, and he hadn't engaged with the theory that the most likely suspect was one of the woman Dub had filmed. 'I don't believe you.'

'I can't help that, mate,' Dub batted back.

'I'll check it myself if I have to. I'll start by speaking with your work and trying to identify them one by one.'

'Yeah right,' Dub said with a dry laugh. 'You're not going to do that, and they wouldn't know anyway.' Dub's eyes clouded. 'Why do you care so much, mate? Can't you just leave me alone?'

It was a fair question. Trent probably could have done that, if the same person who posted the videos hadn't also sent him a message about his father. He stared at his friend. Dub was holding back something. He rubbed his chin and waited until, after a few seconds, Dub pushed back his chair and let out a deep sigh.

'Okay, look, you're right. It's an ex-colleague and it got a bit messy.' He tipped his head back and stretched his neck. 'She's an investigative journalist. She used to work for the online paper.'

'A work colleague?' Trent asked. That meant someone who was skilled in the art of tracking down information and he assumed that whatever caused the mess it would be enough motivation to want to humiliate Dub. 'So she could be behind getting you suspended from work.'

'Yeah,' Dub said but he was shaking his head. As if he was trying to wake himself from a nightmare. He scratched his nose. 'There's more. She's the one that originally told me about the flat. You couldn't make it up,' he said, almost to himself. 'Mate, my landlord was her boyfriend.'

'That makes sense, I guess,' Trent said.

A disgruntled ex-girlfriend set on revenge, a dish best served filmed and posted on social media. Trent frowned. Except why would she message Trent about the medal? He wasn't about to share details of his messages with Dub. For one thing, he didn't yet fully trust Dub. And secondly, he certainly didn't want to talk about the medal. He gave Dub another push. 'Why don't you contact her? Address this thing head on.'

Dub nodded but without conviction.

Trent stood and placed his cup in the sink. He couldn't shake the feeling that Dub was still lying about something. When Trent had refused to accept his first answer, he'd come up with option two, but it seemed a little too neat. And Dub had now confessed to sleeping with the landlord's sister, as well as his girlfriend.

Trent needed a way to check Dub's story. A plan began to form in his mind. He'd need to be careful because Dub was already in enough trouble. He'd refused to play the game and it had released his videos, videos that had already put his job at risk and lost him his flat. And if Dub was lying about the missing video then all bets were off.

Tomorrow Trent would make an early morning call to find Dub's landlord. And then he'd discover whether or Dub was telling the truth. If he was, then they'd find the person behind the Honesty Index. The person who claimed to know the truth about Trent's father.

But tonight he needed to call Dylan Steele. 'You can stay here for a few days until you get back on your feet,' he said.

'Thanks, mate. I appreciate it,' Dub said.

Trent nodded whilst walking out of the kitchen. 'Help yourself to food. I need to make a call.'

20

MONDAY, 6:35PM

The game appeared to be using sophisticated technology and yet Trent's own tech know-how was pretty limited. Luckily he had Tina's number one transfer target to call for help. He punched in the number for Dylan Steele. The phone rang twice and then he heard a voice.

'This is Dylan. Who's this?'

Well, how do you do, too. He kicked his voice into gear. 'My name is Trent Ryder. Tina Holmes gave me your number. She said you could help me.'

'Trent Ryder. Is that your real name? It sounds like a superhero alter ego.' Her speech was flat with no obvious trace of an accent. When AI took over the world it would sound like Dylan.

'I can neither confirm nor deny that I am a superhero.' Thirty seconds in and Trent was miles off his script.

'Why not?'

'You don't do humour then?' Tina had warned him that Dylan was unusual. 'Never mind, Tina said that you're the best.'

'I'm Wonder Woman and Iron Man rolled into one.' Deadpan, but funny. Which was unexpected. 'I've got your details now so we can drop the small talk.'

He absorbed the body blow of what she'd just said. *I've got your details now*. What the hell?

'What do you need help with?' she asked.

Decision time. 'I actually have two issues I could do with help on.' He used to work with a policy guy who would have called that 'floating a trial balloon.'

'Tina only referred to one.'

Tina had clearly told Dylan to expect his call. That had to help. 'So...' The balloon was still rising.

'So, pick one.'

Bang. The balloon was history. Trent was quiet.

'Take your time, Trent Ryder.'

'Sorry. I was thinking.'

'I would have thought you might've done your thinking before calling me. This isn't a philosophy chat-line.'

Time to close his eyes and jump. 'I want to find out the truth about my father,' he said. This time there was no immediate come back. 'Hello, Dylan? Are you still there?'

'What if the truth isn't actually what you're looking for?'

Not the response that Trent was expecting. 'I thought this wasn't a philosophy chat-line,' he responded, but thinking, isn't that one hell of a question.

'Touché.' A beat. 'You want to give me any more to go on? Or is that it?' Trent heard Dylan tapping on a keyboard.

'Wait, don't hang up.' There was a pause. Hopefully she was still listening. 'Someone has messaged me with some information about my dad. It's an app that me and some friends, downloaded. It seems to have information on a couple of us at least. Maybe all of us.'

'What are you going to do if you find out who's behind it?'

So many questions. 'I don't know.'

Dylan's sigh was audible. 'Can you bring your phone to me? Outside Tottenham Court Road tube station. Tomorrow night. Eleven thirty.'

'Erm, okay. Yes.' Trent wasn't at all sure he wanted to hand his phone over to a complete stranger, but Tina had said that Dylan was the best, and he trusted Tina. 'How will I know who you are?'

'I'll be the woman who comes up to you and asks you for your phone. From that point on, it's all on you.' She had a clarity of thought and expression that was simultaneously impressive and annoying.

'Okay, but how will you know who I am?' Trent liked to be clear on all the basics.

'I'm looking at photos of you right now. Provided you haven't signed up to a witness protection programme in the last couple of years, I'll recognise you.'

'No, I look like I always have.'

'Never mind.'

What did that mean? But he didn't have time to ask. The line was already dead.

PEN ANSWERED on the phone on the second ring.

'Hey, Trent. What's up?'

'I wanted to apologise for running off.'

'Have you made any progress?'

'Not yet, but I'm hopeful. I've got someone lined up to look at my phone. If we're lucky we'll get an answer soon.'

'I hope so. I don't like the idea of there being someone out there who knows more about Dad than we do.'

'I know.' Trent used the silence to build himself up to the second reason he was calling his sister. He swallowed. 'I also wanted to call to say, thank you. About ... well, you know.' He couldn't bring himself to say why he was calling. The words were too painful. Even now.

A pause. 'You're thinking about Freddy?' A lump caught in Trent's throat. But Pen knew him well enough to know that his silence meant that she was right. She was well versed in Trent's late-night calls. 'You want to talk about him?' she asked.

'I do.' His voice was scratchy.

'Okay. Well, let's think.' Pen seemed to have an almost inexhaustible supply of Freddy stories. Which was just as well, considering how often Trent made her dig one up. 'Remember when they tried to teach him tennis at school? He'd spin round between each point?'

'Each shot,' Trent corrected.

'Yeah, right. A full three-sixty. Bam, another spin, bam.'

Trent could practically hear his sister's smile. 'Do you think he ever won? At tennis.'

'What, God, no. Never.' Pen was laughing now. 'The balls went everywhere but where they were meant to.'

'Yeah, he was pretty bad at tennis.' Trent blinked. Again and again. 'I miss him so much, Pen.'

'I know, bro. Me too.' Perhaps she was closing her eyes. 'Me too.'

21

MONDAY, 10:57PM

Dub stood in front of the bed, everything laid out on the duvet before him and his backpack and two suitcases lying empty on the floor. His phone was on the bedside table. He'd switched it off after reading the latest message from the game.

The follow up message to him from the game hadn't been explicit, but it had hinted strongly enough. The truth was that there had been another video. The *first* video. One that he never wanted anyone to see.

He'd read and reread the message from the game.

Six videos have been released. I have not yet released the final video. Or more accurately, the first video. You will have one chance to tell the truth. Only if you do that will the remaining video be permanently deleted.

But the game couldn't have it because it had been wiped. And he'd smashed up the disc just to be sure no one could recover it. He recalled his delight at the moment he realised that he'd be able to get the recording back. The leverage he'd needed had fallen into his lap after an evening at the pub. At first, he'd merely been intrigued. And then it became clear that the amorous couple had spent the night together, and he suddenly had the ammunition to ensure that the video would never see the light of day.

I have not yet released the final video.

It had to be a bluff; that recording was dead and buried. And there was no way that the other person in the recording would have told anyone, or be the one behind the game.

Dub scratched his chin. Trent had been fixated on a missing video, but it'd been clear that he thought it was a similar video to the six that had been released. He massaged his palms over his eye sockets. It had been gut instinct not to answer honestly when Trent asked him about the missing video. But when it became clear that Trent wasn't going to let it go, he decided on a bit of misdirection. Anything to buy him some time. He'd been pleased with how easily that had come out, and his mate had bought it. Well, it made sense, didn't it. An ex-girlfriend, the link to the landlord. Yeah, that was sweet.

Dub carefully selected some clothes and folded them tightly before placing them in his backpack. Why had Trent pushed him so hard? The thought that'd been circling in his brain came into focus. He didn't want to believe it, but he couldn't rule out that Trent was behind this whole thing.

There had always been an underlying tension between Trent and Dub. Well, ever since Dub and Lila had got together. They never really talked about that. Dub had accepted that Lila and Trent's relationship had some sort of 'special status.' He'd been pretty sure that nothing physical had happened between them whilst he was with Lila, but it was almost worse than that. *Beyond* that. Sort of spiritual. Something Dub couldn't or wouldn't understand. He realised he was clenching his fists and relaxed his hands. That narrative had mostly come from Lila. And Dub had been happy to roll with it. It wasn't like Lila Jain was ever going to be the great love of his life.

But that wasn't the case for Trent. You didn't need to spend much time around him to know that two things shaped him. One was the fire that killed his family. And the other was Lila Jain. And perhaps Trent had never got over either of them.

The backpack was already nearly half-full. He needed to be more ruthless. He pulled out everything he'd packed so far and threw it back on the duvet to begin thinning out the clothes. He didn't have a plan as to where to go, but if the game shared the final video with his friends, or worse, with the police. He felt pressure on his chest.

Dub shook his head. He couldn't think about it. He just had to be ready to disappear.

22

TUESDAY 7:47AM

Trent was going old school. To find the truth, you had to go and talk to real people. And if Dub was telling the truth then his landlord could be his witness. Trent was on edge. He didn't like the fact that he was going behind Dub's back, but he'd been presented with an impossible position. He'd asked Dub straight out, and he hadn't been convinced by the answer.

He set off from home early that morning, figuring his best chance to catch anyone would be before the morning commute. He chained his motorbike to the lamppost and unzipped his leather jacket, letting the cold morning air flood around his body. Helmet tucked under his arm, he waited for a gap in the pre-rush hour traffic rolling along the main road.

He slipped out in front of a cautiously driven Royal Mail van and jogged over towards an archway on the far side of the road. Within a few minutes he had climbed the stairs to the first floor and was standing outside the front door to Dub's old flat. He rang the bell. If there was no one in he'd be back to square one but the door creaked open and a young woman wearing a pale blue dressing gown and her hair in a ponytail stood blinking in the doorway. Her face was weathered and her expression still waking up.

'Who are you?' she asked, covering a yawn with her hand.

'Oh, sorry.' Trent took a step back as if to reappraise which flat he'd called on. 'I think I've got the right house. My friend lives here. Are you and him ...' He hung the words in the air as if unsure how to phase his question delicately.

'I moved in yesterday. The previous guy left in a hurry.' She yawned again. 'Worked out well for me, though.'

'Really? Right.' He scratched his head and sighed, trying to channel crushed by disappointment. 'Don't suppose he left a forwarding address?'

'No. Sorry.' She started to push the door closed.

'How about your landlord?' Trent said, as if the idea had just come to him. 'He might know.'

The door slowed. 'I guess so. Wait there.' The door clicked shut and then a few minutes later the woman re-appeared and handed him a scrap of paper. 'I've written his details on the back.' She looked as if she was trying to push her face into a smile but gave up and simply nodded at him.

Trent squeezed out a thank you before he was facing the door once again. Walking away, he started punching the digits into his phone.

'Yeah?' The call had connected without ringing. Clearly this was a man in a hurry.

'Hi. I'm looking to rent a flat. A mate of mine used to rent from you. He gave me your number. Andrew Dubnyk.'

The landlord went off like a grenade. 'He's got a flaming cheek. Mate of yours, yeah? Made a video of you too, has he? Pervert. Using *my* flat for pornos.' The man had no filter, which suited Trent down to the ground.

'Erm, well, he thought the flat might still be available.' Keeping his voice level.

'It's already gone. Glad to be shot of him.'

Trent could feel the conversation dipping for the finish line. 'For what it's worth, I know he's sorry about what happened with your girlfriend.' Trent was nearly back to his bike and he reached into his pocket for the key to unlock it from the lamppost, his phone still clamped to his ear.

'What?' The landlord pumped up the volume.

'He's sorry. About your girlfriend.' Trent heard the landlord take a sharp intake of breath.

'What the hell are you talking about? Girlfriend? I've been married for thirty-four years, mate.'

'I'm sorry, I–'

'The wife's already got me in the doghouse. I don't need no stories about me playing away from home. Now, sod off.'

Trent had never met the guy but he was sure that he was telling the truth – he didn't have a girlfriend. Which meant that Dub had lied about the final video. And if he'd lied about that, he could be lying about everything else, too.

23

TUESDAY, 8:15AM

'I thought we were friends,' Oli said. She rested her elbows on the table and clamped her hands together. The café was busy with the early-morning rush. Customers squeezing in breakfast before work or after school drop off.

'We are,' Lila replied, blowing on her coffee to cool it down.

But the truth was that apart from one brief flurry of messages a while back, Lila had hardly heard from Oli whilst since Lila left for the US. Until the last few days, during which Oli had practically been stalking her. Emails, texts, phone calls. It was as if Oli was desperate to meet up. And then, that morning, she'd doorstepped Lila and insisted they go for breakfast at the local café. Lila hadn't even given Oli her UK address. Maybe she'd got it from Trent.

And now she had dropped the bombshell. She wanted a loan.

'Well, it doesn't feel much like it, right now.' Oli was scowling.

'I just haven't got that sort of money, hon. I would help

you, if I could, but I used my savings to pay for this trip over.' Oli was asking for a *lot* of money. 'What about the bank of Mum and Dad?'

Oli shook her head. The tension in her shoulders suggested that whatever she needed the money for, it wasn't something her parents would be happy to help with. 'Can't you at least lend me something. A grand?' Which was much less than the five thousand she'd started with, but was still a staggering amount of money. And Oli suggested it with the breezy ease of asking to borrow a dress.

Lila lowered her gaze. 'I'm sorry.' She cleared her throat. 'What's this about, Oli? What do you need the money for?'

Oli turned and looked out of the café's window. 'I've made some bad decisions. People I've met. Things I've done that I regret.'

'Do you owe someone the money?'

'No. Nothing like that.' Oli shuffled on her chair. 'I can't tell you what it's for.'

'Can't or won't?' Lila asked. She hadn't expected Oli to confide in her. They'd never been especially close. They operated in very different ways. Oli operated a revolving door policy to relationships – at least she had when she was in the sixth form, whereas Lila had always been very particular.

Oli sighed. 'You won't lend me anything, anyway, so there's no need to tell you.' She turned back to face her friend. Lila had never seen Oli cry but there were tears in her eyes.

'I'm sorry,' she said. 'I didn't mean to upset you.'

Oli sniffed and dabbed a tissue at her eyes. 'It's not you.' She took a moment to compose herself. 'It's my parents. I'm worried about how they'll react.'

'To what?' Lila asked gently.

'I can't afford to live without help from them.' Which, Lila noted, wasn't an answer to her question.

'Couldn't you move back in with them?' Lila tried to keep up with her friend's flow of thoughts. 'At least for a while.'

Oli had dried her tears. She managed a smile. 'Yeah, I don't think that's going to be an option.' Lila waited. 'One way or another, I can't risk them finding out.'

'Are you worried about the game?' Lila asked.

'No.' Oli shot the response back. 'Well, I mean. Sure. It's going to have a go at all of us, isn't it. It would look very suspicious if it didn't.' Lila studied her friend. She seemed distant for a minute as if considering that thought for the first time. 'Too suspicious,' she added, having thought about it. 'Well, look. I'm sorry for asking for money. I wouldn't have done it if I had another option.' She pushed her chair back and stood up. 'Thanks for breakfast.'

She waved her fingers at Lila and blew her a rapid volley of air kisses. And with that, she swept out of the café, leaving Lila staring at the bill that was sitting unpaid on the table.

24

MANIFESTO EXTRACT 4

My guess is that player 1 will refuse to play. They won't have any evidence that I know everything.

But player 2?

That will be very different.

They'll know what will happen if they also refuse to play. But just to push them a little further, I will send them a message three hours before their round starts.

#TIME LAPSE MESSAGE to Player 2

#TIME TO SEND: Round[Player_2] - 03:00

BACKGROUND COLOUR: Black

FONT COLOUR: Red

. . .

TEXT:

YOUR TRUTHS WILL BE REVEALED today. One way or another. What will happen when your friends and family know about your mystery man?

25

TUESDAY 9:44AM

Trent heard their voices as he turned his motorbike into his road. Oli, modelling a red dress with a denim bag slung over her shoulder with casual calculation, was standing in his drive. Dub, barefoot but dressed in jeans and a polo shirt, filled the front doorway and Oli was sounding off at him like a firecracker. Trent parked on the drive and spotted his neighbour peering out of her kitchen window. It was usually a quiet area and an altercation like this would almost certainly mean that Trent's name was being inked on the agenda for the next Neighbourhood Watch meeting.

'It doesn't make any sense.' Dub's arms were in front of him, as if pleading for some explanation. 'Didn't you think it might be important to tell me before now?'

'No. You got what you wanted.' Oli was standing her ground. 'What difference does it make.'

Trent caught Dub's eye as he rolled the motorbike onto the drive, but his friend immediately focussed back on Oli. 'I'm not listening to anymore of this,' Dub shouted before shaking his head at Trent and turning to go back inside the house.

Trent hit the button on his key fob to open the garage doors. He hoped the few minutes he took to park his bike would give the two of them time to calm down. He walked back out to the drive and motioned to Oli. 'Oli, please go inside.' He could do without this argument full stop, but if it was going to happen, he'd rather that it took place outside of the public eye.

Oli spun and jabbed her finger at Trent. 'How could you let him in your house? That pervert. He's disgusting.' The word pervert seemed to echo up and down the close. So much for keeping things low key.

'Let's talk about it inside.' He gestured towards the front door.

Oli crossed her arms and jutted her chin. 'You'll have to make me.'

'I'm not going to make you do anything.' Trent walked round her. 'But I'm going in.'

'Going to record some porn are you?' Her voice had a touch of hysteria but also enough volume to make Trent glance over once more towards his neighbour's window.

He could hear Dub moving around in the kitchen and he thought back to how he'd felt when Dub had appeared on his doorstep. Hadn't he acted the same way as Oli? Only a little quieter and with a lot less snark. He sighed before he turned around and sat down on the step only a few feet from where Oli was standing. 'What were you arguing about, anyway?'

She glared at him and then looked away. Trent waited. 'I thought you were going inside.' But the heat in her voice was cooling.

'Dub's monopolising the TV.'

Oli laughed. 'That's not funny.'

But it was progress and if Trent could just get her talking she might graduate to listening. One way or another he needed her to calm down. To go inside or to leave discretely. And he had to aim for the former because he couldn't imagine Oli leaving quietly.

'What was he upset about?' he asked. He dropped his voice to a whisper and waited whilst Oli wrapped the loose folds of her dress around her legs and sat down on the step next to him.

'Honestly, I don't know. He was ranting at me,' she said.

Trent could smell her perfume and he felt her hair brush against his shoulder but the world didn't stop turning and Cupid didn't give him a nudge in the ribs. 'He told me that everything was consensual. They all knew what they were doing. They all agreed to share the videos.'

Oli's nose twitched. Perhaps she was conducting her own smell test. 'You really thought they might not be?' She turned to look at him.

Trent sighed. 'No, I guess not,' he replied.

Her response surprised him. He'd assume she was upset about the videos. If he turned to face her now their noses would touch, so he stared at the ground in front of him. Oli loved personal space so much that she seemed to like to experience other people's as much as her own. Why did she need to be so close? He leaned backwards, propping himself up on his arms.

'Why are you here, Oli?' he asked.

She shook her hair and stretched her neck from side to side. Then she twisted, arching over him. Her front teeth bit into her bottom lip. 'I was going to ask you a favour. But not whilst he's here.' She nodded her head towards the house.

A favour? Surely she didn't need somewhere to stay, too?

'Is everything okay?' Which seemed like a fair enough question.

Oli lowered her head towards him and Trent flinched as she whispered in his ear. 'No. Everything is not okay.'

Her words chiselled into his veins. 'Why don't you come in, Oli? Let me speak to Dub first and I'll ask him to give us some space.'

He could sense that she was wavering. She must really need that favour. He swivelled out from beneath her and stood up to lead the way. 'C'mon. Come and have a drink.' He held out his hand and after a pause she reached out and allowed him to pull her up, her hand cool in his. 'You can wait in the living room. Give me a minute and I'll go and speak with Dub.'

Oli nodded. Her anger seemed to have abated. At least, for now. Dub was pacing up and down in the kitchen.

'Who the hell does she think she is? Like she's so morally superior to the rest of us.' He reached the wall and spun around without drawing a breath. 'Her? Olivia Pearson. Or all people. Give me a freaking break.'

Dub had a point but Trent wasn't going to waste time debating it. He wanted to talk to Dub about the game. And why he was lying about the missing video. His friend was still muttering about Oli as Trent tried to bring some order to his thoughts. He'd been planning to challenge Dub but hadn't counted on the complexity of having Oli as part of the conversation. If he waited until they were all in the same room there was no telling what might happen. It had to be there and then.

'Dub,' he said sharply enough to break up the under-the-breath rant. 'Have you spoken with your ex-girlfriend yet?'

Dub was so deep into his character analysis of Oli that he stopped walking and blinked repeatedly before responding.

'Not yet, mate. Give me a chance. Anyway, I was going to message her first. See how she reacts. Take it from there.'

'No time like the present,' said Trent.

'Yeah.' Dub shuffled on the spot. 'I guess.' He stared at Trent, his jaw set.

'Do it now.' Trent wondered what his friend would do. After all, it's hard to contact someone who doesn't exist but Dub was rising to the challenge. He watched as Dub typed on his phone and hit the screen with a flourish.

'Done,' Dub said.

'Good.' Who the hell had Dub just messaged? He'd have to follow up later. 'Now, I'm going to go and speak with Oli. I think it's best if you keep away for the moment,' Trent said.

Dub's phone beeped before he could reply and a flash of confusion clouded his face. Trent assumed the alert was a reply to Dub from whoever he'd messaged but Trent's phone was also flashing with a notification. His stomach was a tight knot as he saw the red and black icon – one new notification waiting for him. Taking a deep breath, Trent tapped to read the message.

A chime sounded as Trent's phone screen filled with the red and black motif. Trent's shoulders were tight. A subtle sign that his mind wanted him to turn away. And yet he was locked on. This time the app opened as it had done for Dub's round. And then he was looking at another database. A collage of photographs; Pinterest for the devil. He scanned the information before he saw the name. All he knew for sure was that it wasn't his round.

And then he focused on the name of the friend typed in the centre of the collage. The friend who would be faced with the decision: to play or not to play.

Olivia Pearson.

26

TUESDAY 10:12AM

Trent shivered. He glanced at Dub. 'Is your message from –'

'Yes.' Dub's voice was hollow. Any sense of relief that the game was moving on was buried deeply in his own pain. 'It's chosen Oli.'

Trent tried to make sense of it. One picture showed a group of people, including Oli, sitting in a pub. There must be something significant about it but he didn't know what he was looking for. He peered at the faces more closely but he didn't recognise any of the other people. Squeezed next to it, and framed on the other side by a picture of a ballot box, was a copy of a newspaper report of a traffic accident. Across the bottom was a police line-up; five men wearing trench coats over jeans, the numbers one through five pinned onto their jackets. And the name Olivia Pearson was sheltering in the eye of the storm.

Trent's throat was dry and his head started to thump. The picture changed and he was looking at an extract from Oli's school report. So far, so chillingly familiar.

Olivia is a conscientious student. She is punctual with her homework and performed solidly in her mock exams. On occasion she is too easily distracted.

Trent started to walk towards Oli who was still in the living room. Now she'd be facing her choice, staring at the invitation, deciding what she would do. He froze in the doorway. The five-minute red digital countdown in the top right of Trent's screen had begun and the message: *waiting for player*.

He sensed Dub stop behind him but his attention was on Oli. She was standing in the centre of the room, holding her phone in her outstretched arm. Eyes front, steely calm, s if ready to swat this game out of her path.

Her words from earlier echoed in Trent's mind.

No. Everything is not okay.

Trent heard the strain in Dub's whisper as the screen shimmered. 'Jesus. She's playing.'

A quote filled the screen.

You must have chaos within you to give birth to a dancing star.

There had been a similar cryptic quote at the end of the countdown to Dub's round but from here on everything would be different. Trent felt the urge to call out to Oli but he didn't know what to say to help.

She was impassive. Oli had always wanted the world to be watching her but she can't ever have imagined a performance like this. The screen morphed into the black background. Then red text began to appear.

Have you ever blackmailed someone?

What the hell? Starting with a bang. Trent felt Dub tense behind him. Oli's shoulders stiffened but she stretched out her hand and clicked on the screen. Trent forced out a breath. What was her answer? He couldn't see. His mind scrambled back to the photographs trying to find a fit but another question was already appearing.

Have you ever shoplifted?

Oli didn't hesitate before tapping her screen. Trent knew the answer to that was yes. They all knew it.

'My battery died,' Dub said. Oli shot him a look as he moved to watch over Trent's shoulder. The cursor blinked waiting before the third question unfurled.

Have you ever attended a meeting of the English Defence League?

Jesus. It was only a question but surely there was no smoke without fire. Trent had never heard Oli express a political view. He guessed that she wasn't a natural liberal but he hadn't expected this. He shook his head. The meeting in the pub. Had that been the clue; the warning to Oli that the game knew? She must have given her answer because already the next question was waiting.

Have you ever asked someone to admit to your traffic offence?

Trent watched Oli as she again answered immediately. How did the game know any of this stuff? It had access to school reports, photos and who knew what else. But did it really know the answers to these questions? Then it hit him. Oli didn't drive. Which didn't mean that she couldn't have committed a traffic offence, but surely made it unlikely. Perhaps some of the questions were simply playing the odds.

But it did have Dub's videos. That, at least, hadn't been a game of bluff and bluster. It knew what he had done, it had the evidence and it had released it.

Trent let out a slow breath. He had no idea how Oli was answering but unless the answer to everything was no, her life was about to get bumpy. Her parents had high standards. She'd been grounded for acts that Trent had thought were normal teenage behaviours. God only knew how they'd react if any of these allegations were true. Another question appeared and Trent bit down on his lip.

Have you ever slept with a married man?

His brain had barely processed the question when the screen turned black. For a second he thought it had switched off and his eyes darted between Oli and Dub but then a bright red line burned from the centre of the screen to the top. The line started to scan round in a circle, the red line leaving a ghost image behind it that faded away after a few seconds. He stood transfixed, watching the radar sweep through three circuits. He could feel his heart thumping against his chest, and his mouth was dry. *Jesus Christ. What was this thing?*

Oli tapped on her phone. Her jaw was set and her eyes were switched to stone cold.

The radar disappeared. Trent couldn't even hear Dub's breathing as more red text appeared.

HONESTY INDEX

100%

No dishonest answers.

Oli had answered truthfully.

'What? What does that mean?' Dub was shouting. Oli had played the game and told the truth. She'd done what the game had asked her to do, but none of them knew what would happen next.

Oli lifted her face and stared at the two of them. Was there a hint of moral superiority when she looked at Dub? Triumph maybe, a sense that she had beaten the game. Trent wasn't sure but if there was, he couldn't find it within himself to blame her for that.

The screen flickered and displayed the five questions once more. It took a second for Trent to take in the difference. Now they each had single word answers.

Have you ever blackmailed someone?Yes

Have you ever shoplifted?Yes

Have you ever attended a meeting of the English Defence League?Yes

Have you ever asked someone to admit to your traffic offence?No

Have you ever slept with a married man?Yes

Oli's *eyes* hardened. For a second she looked as though she was about to say something to Dub but then she swept her bag over her shoulder and brushed past him, saying nothing, but with her head held high.

The screen turned black, and a notification appeared. There was a new message on the group chat.

Honest answers will not be shared more widely. The only people who will know these truths are all of you. You are the judge and jury. What decisions you each make are for you alone.

And then the text faded away like a secret chalk marking on a pavement being washed off by the rain and Trent was staring again at a black screen. Seconds later he heard the click of his front door closing.

27

MANIFESTO EXTRACT 5

When the player tells the truth, they will feel relief.

They will hide away their darkest secret in the belief that I have missed it.

Thirty minutes after the end of their round, I will let them know that they are wrong.

#Time lapse message 1 to Olivia Pearson

#Time to send: Round[Olivia_Pearson] + 00:30

Background colour: Black

Font colour: Red

Text:

I know all about your first love.

#Time lapse message 2 to Olivia Pearson

#Time to send: Round[Olivia_Pearson] + 00:31

Background colour: Black

Font colour: Red

Text:

You will have one chance to tell the truth. Only if you do that will the information be permanently deleted.

28

TUESDAY 10:40AM

Trent watched through the window as Oli walked down the road. She didn't turn back and she didn't look at her phone. It was impossible to process everything that had happened and even if he could, what would he do? The game had left them as the arbiters of Oli's behaviour. Was that the choice that it was giving them? Tell the whole world or tell your friends.

'God,' Dub was shaking his head. 'Married men and blackmail. Jesus. And what the hell is English Defence League?'

Trent was still trying to process what had just happened. 'Far-right political group. Anti-Islam.'

'Wow. I had no idea.' Dub pushed out a deep breath. 'About any of it.'

'The game doesn't pull any punches,' Trent replied.

'I can second that,' Dub said. 'But at least Oli's secrets have only been shared with us.' He paused, clearly replaying his round in his head. 'I should've played.'

Trent shrugged. He didn't have an answer to that. 'I need a coffee.' He walked back into the kitchen.

Dub followed him and plugged his phone in to recharge. There was an immediate beep as soon as it turned back on.

'I just got a WhatsApp from Paddy,' Dub said and then he whistled.

'What?' asked Trent, filling the kettle.

'Paddy lent Oli money. Just this morning. Before she came here.'

'What?' Trent's mind was spinning. Oli's favour must have been to ask Trent for money.

'Guess how much?' Dub asked. But he didn't wait for a response. 'Ten grand.' He paused. 'Money must be good in the accountancy business.'

Yeah, but not that good, thought Trent. Where the hell had Paddy got that sort of spare cash from? And why did Oli need money? She had a steady job working in her parent's family business.

'Paddy said he's going to message the group,' Dub said. Trent pulled out his phone just as Paddy's group message arrived. He was relieved that this incoming message was via WhatsApp rather than The Honesty Index.

I know there might be a good explanation for what just happened Oli but we need to talk. Right now.

Another message flashed up.

Olivia Pearson left.

Trent scrolled down his screen. The same message appeared next to every chat group that he was in with Olivia. 'Wow,' he said. 'She's cancelling herself.'

It didn't look as though Paddy would be getting his money back any time soon but right then Trent realised that it was Oli who he felt sorry for. Was that just? He didn't know. His estimation of Oli had shifted. Down and to the right. But her quiet acceptance as she'd left had almost broken him. She had been revealed. No, that wasn't right. She had revealed herself, her true self. But she hadn't argued, she hadn't shown defiance. Surely there was something to be admired in that.

'Can you believe it?' Dub asked. There was a sense of satisfaction in his voice.

Dub had always been the serious one. Seriously tall. Seriously serious. But Trent hadn't seen him seriously bitter before. He checked himself. Was that what it was? Or was it simply relief that the spotlight had moved on?

'This may be a strange question, Dub, but does your old girlfriend know Oli?'

Dub shook his head. 'My what? Oh, my ex.' He lowered himself onto a chair. 'No, I don't think so.'

Trent watched his friend closely whilst drumming his fingers on the worktop. 'Because whoever leaked your videos, and I'd thought it was your ex, has also done some serious digging into Oli's life.'

Dub shrugged. 'I guess they could've met.' It was a casual answer. Too casual.

Two could play that game. Trent brushed at his shirt as he spoke. 'Have you heard back from her yet?'

Dub was pale. 'Oh, err, not yet.' His knee was bouncing up and down. 'Not really a surprise. Probably doesn't want to talk to me.' He stood up. 'Can you pour me a cuppa, too? I need the toilet.'

Trent watched him leave the room. He didn't like confrontation but Dub clearly wasn't going to volunteer the truth. He'd have to challenge him when he was back. He glanced at the worktop and saw Dub's phone charging. He made a quick decision and picked it up. It was unlocked. He didn't have long.

He opened his text messages. Dub had allegedly sent the message to his ex within the last hour and he'd been watching Oli for most of the time since then. There was a text to someone called Andy, which simply said *Alright mate. Fancy a drink some time?* There was nothing else. Trent checked Dub's direct messages on Facebook, Twitter, and Instagram. Flicked into WhatsApp. Nothing apart from the messages from Paddy. He searched for other messaging apps but couldn't see any.

He heard the toilet flush. A knot formed in his stomach. Why would Dub have lied to him? He couldn't think of a single positive reason whilst negative reasons flooded his brain. He switched into Dub's emails and scanned the sent folder. Again, nothing. Footsteps. He was too slow.

'Hey, what're you doing with my phone?' Dub reached out for it.

Trent weighed it in his hand, brain scrambling. 'I've been wondering whether I should upgrade. I think it's too big for me though.' He held it out to Dub who took it in one of his massive hands.

'It works for me.'

Trent shrugged and hoped that Dub couldn't hear his heart beating. Dub still had a woman shaped secret. It seemed unlikely that she was behind the game. Hell, she might not even exist but why would Dub lie about it? And did whoever *was* behind the game know who was really in the missing video? 'Why are you lying, Dub?'

'What?' Dub's voice was slightly too loud.

'I spoke to your old landlord.'

'You spoke to my landlord?' Dub moved closer to Trent, his extra height more menacing than ever before. 'Why the hell did you do that, mate?'

'I was trying to find out who's behind this game.'

'Yeah, right. You're not interested in the game. You just want to find the video.' Dub was pushing back hard.

'I don't care about the videos. What you do in your own

time is none of my business. Anyhow, it doesn't seem like your work colleague is involved in the game, does it?'

Dub turned away but immediately spun back round, his dark eyes staring at Trent. 'Just leave it. Please.' There was something new in Dub's tone. And his eyes. It was a plea. But why would Dub be begging to be left alone? He'd already faced his round. What was he afraid of?

Dub slumped into a chair and stared at his phone. He stayed like that for a few seconds before his head jerked up. He put his finger in front of his lips. What was he doing? He tapped his finger against his mouth a couple of times as if quietening an infant. Then he stood up and very deliberately opened a drawer in one of the kitchen units before making a show of turning off his phone. He pointed to Trent and then at the drawer. Confused, Trent switched off his phone and placed it next to Dub's. Dub tapped his lips again and nodded his head towards the garden. Trent narrowed his eyes and moved to the back door and opened it. Dub stepped outside and waited for Trent to follow him. They walked to the end of the garden and then stopped, standing together in the rain.

'What are you doing, Dub?'

'Shush. Keep your voice down. Listen.' He bowed his head down towards Trent. 'This game? I'm scared, mate. It knows everything. I don't know how. Maybe it's bugged my phone.' He paused and took a deep breath. 'Look, I made the woman up, my ex. I thought this whole thing would go away after the videos were released. The damage had been done, but then I got a message.'

'From the game?' Trent asked. Dub nodded. So Trent wasn't the only one to receive individual messages. 'What did it say?' A trickle of rain crawled down his back.

'It said it has the final video and it will release it if I don't do what it says.'

Christ. So there *was* a final video. What or who the hell was on it? 'What has it asked you to do?' Trent swallowed and his temples started to throb. What on earth was this thing?

'Nothing, yet.' Dub was still talking. 'So, I don't know what this thing is but I'd be careful about investigating anything. I never thought you'd go and track down my landlord. Jesus, Trent,' he wiped his hand through his hair. 'Is it you?'

Trent took a step back. 'What?'

'The game. Is it you?' His hair was splayed down across his face. He looked young. Young, and afraid.

'No. Why would you even–' Trent stopped. He'd been riding Dub hard. Pushing him for the truth about the videos. And he hadn't told his friend about the messages that he himself had received. 'It's not me, Dub,' he said.

His friend stared at him for a long time. The rain was getting harder, and Dub had to brush the water from his face. Eventually he nodded. 'I believe you.'

Trent pulled his thoughts back to his friend. 'Have you thought about going to the police?'

'No.' The word cracked though the air like a gun shot. 'I'm not risking it. I'm just going to wait and see what it wants me to do.'

Trent's own messages from the game flashed through his mind. He didn't trust Dub enough to divulge them and yet he had so many questions he wanted to ask him. But Dub's whole posture shouted conversation over and so all Trent could do was watch his friend trudge back down the garden to the house.

29

TUESDAY, 10:50AM

Oli was walking through a park when her phone buzzed. She stopped and brushed her hair from her face. There was a notification for a new message on the app. Her knuckles whitened as she gripped the phone. She looked around and spotted an empty park bench. She forced herself to move towards it and lowered herself down.

She'd thought the worst was over. She'd told the truth and was prepared to face the judgement of her friends. She'd be preparing herself for that, for some time. She tried telling herself that it didn't matter that much if they disowned her. She was pretty sure none of them actually liked her. Even when they were at school she'd never felt any one of them was comfortable being with just her. She just about fitted in as part of the wider group, but she was a fringe member. If she'd stood alone, none of them would gravitate towards her over any of the others. She was the friendship equivalent of the last pick for the sports team.

And that had continued over the last few years. She'd tried to deepen the individual relationships. But it had been like when she stopped switching her shade of lipstick. No one noticed. Would a single one of them call her a friend? Not really. Not beyond social media and hanging out. Well, friendship only worked if it was a two-way street and by removing herself from their chat groups she was planting a one-way sign. She'd have to deal with the future in the only way she knew how. Alone.

She clicked to access the message. It was written in red text on the black background, the same as the other group messages. But unlike those, this message had been sent just to her.

I know all about your first love.

Her body started to shake. Maybe if she hadn't been reliving her secret over and over, it wouldn't have felt so threatening. She'd survived this long without anyone knowing. Or so she'd thought. But someone else did know. Knew the secret that had changed her. Knew the secret which, if shared with the world, would change her again. A change she wasn't sure she would survive.

The fracturing of her friendships over her five yes-or-no questions was nothing compared to what would happen if her real secret came out. Her whole life would be shattered.

She pushed herself up, absentmindedly brushing the creases out of her dress. She needed to get to work. Jesus how was she going to face her parents? It was certainly possible that her parents had been aware of her flirtation with right-wing politics. Vince had turned up on their doorstep more than once, and he wore his heart inked on his tattoo sleeve. But she was sure they had no idea about the blackmail or the married man. And then there was the message. The promise of worse to come. She shook her head, brushing away the tears that were pooling in her eyes.

Her parents had always been able to tell when she'd been

crying. They'd quiz her. Question after question, concern etched on both their faces. Her knees buckled as she started to walk, her limbs making her feel like Bambi on ice.

Her phone buzzed with the arrival of a second message. She ran her hand over her mouth as she read it.

You will have one chance to tell the truth. Only if you do that will the information be permanently deleted.

It was clear that her round was far from over. Oli twisted a strand of hair around her little finger and wound it tight. Who would she have to tell the truth to? Because once the secret was out, it couldn't be put back in the box.

Was it too much to hope for? That whoever it was that was behind this thing, they'd be prepared to bury her darkest secret if she confessed to them, and only them. Her very own confession box. *Bless me father, for I have sinned.*

She lifted her chin and forced herself to continue walking across the park. Slowly she recovered some sort of rhythm, placing one foot in front of the other. Living her life, one step at a time. She'd have to face up to what she'd done, to what had happened. Yes, there was a possibility that her secret would remain private, but there'd have to be a price to pay, wouldn't there?

In Oli's experience, there always was.

30

TUESDAY 11:32AM

Frances slumped into her favourite armchair, and carefully lifted her feet so that they rested on the stool. Her legs felt heavy and she was going to take her opportunity to rest. The twins were at nursey and Jake was in his office, no doubt 'wired in.' That's what he called it. Man and machine, in perfect harmony.

The last six months had been a rollercoaster. Partly because of the pregnancy. Jake had said that he was happy when she broke the news to him. But his face had told a different story. Eventually she got the truth out of him. He wanted to quit his job with Microsoft to join a start-up with a couple of mates. Normally, Frances would've been on board. She understood, well tried to, the technology industry. It moved fast. What was the Facebook mantra? *Move fast and break things* – which also seemed to what her boys heard when she told them to be careful. And maybe that's what how leaps in technology were made. Big kids playing, without parental supervision.

But a start-up? With two kids in pre-school and number three on the way. Out of the frying pan, and into the fire of long hours and an uncertain financial future. She could see the conflict in his face, she knew he'd pass on his dream if she asked him to. But that was the problem. Then it would be her decision. He would choose to do it, regardless. And the truth was, he'd tried hard. Was still trying hard. Made sure he did his share of the chores, seemed happy when he was with her, or the boys, or the whole family together. It made it easier that he spent most of his time at home. When they had a 'sprint,' their term for working to a deadline, he'd go into the office. Basically, he'd be away until the deadline. They'd work round the clock. Takeaways. No exercise. No downtime. Little sleep. Totally focused on work. But sprints were few and far between, and they could plan around them. So, all in all, it had been alright. So far.

She heard the door open and Jake walked into the lounge. 'Fancy a cup of tea?' he said.

'That'd be perfect.' Frances picked up her phone. She looked again at the Honesty Index group chat and shook her head. There'd been no follow up since Oli had left. She'd seen Oli's round. Had seen her secrets.

In a sense she'd been shocked, but the revelations hadn't really surprised her. Perhaps she wouldn't have guessed the correct three offences but she would have pitched it at around that level. She and Olivia had never been close. Partly because Frances followed the rules that Oli ignored. It wasn't even as if Oli was a rebel, looking to take a walk on the wild side. It was more that she didn't think rules applied to her. Frances had seen first-hand Oli's confused expression when someone explained to her she'd just done something that wasn't considered right. What had surprised Frances had been Oli's honestly. But perhaps that went hand in hand with her view of rules.

Jake was back with her mug of tea. She enjoyed the

warmth of the cup against her hands and blew on the liquid. 'Can I show you something on my phone?' She wanted his take on the game. She nodded for him to pick it up. 'It's that app. The red and black one.'

'What is it? A new game?'

'Not exactly. I was sent a link to download it, on Sunday. After Nicholas Samson's wake.'

'Okay.' Jake drew out the word.

'It was sent to us all. Me, Trent, Lila, Dub, Oli, and Paddy. I don't know who from.'

'And you downloaded it?' Jake sounded incredulous.

'I didn't, at first. Paddy did. He was drunk. He thought it would be fun. It was addressed to Hayden Road leavers 2011. We thought it was something to do with Nicholas Samson.'

'But he's dead.' Jake was shaking his head. 'I can't believe you downloaded it.'

'Can you skip the morality lesson, Jake.' Her tone was clipped. 'I'm asking for your help. We were sent some videos.'

She could see Jake forcing himself to move on. 'Okay. Huh. What the–' Jake's finger scrolled over the screen. 'That's Dub. Are these...?' He looked at her.

'Yes. They're sex tapes.'

'What the hell is this thing?' He was tapping on the screen. 'Why have you got sex tapes of one of your friends?'

'I told you. We were sent them. Dub refused to play the game and when it timed out it sent us all these videos.'

Jake was silent for a few seconds. 'Jesus, Fran. You should have told me about this before.' He was frowning. 'The last message is from this morning.' He read it out. '*Honest answers will not be shared more widely. The only people who will know these truths are all of you. You are the judge and jury. What decisions you each make are for you alone.* What on earth does that mean?'

'There was a second round this morning.' She ignored his point about not telling him earlier. 'Olivia Pearson. She was asked five questions. She gave five honesty answers.'

'And then what?' Jake was no longer looking at the phone, he was staring at his wife.

'Nothing. Just that message.'

'You saw the questions? And the answers?' He scratched his forehead. Frances simply nodded. 'What were they?'

Frances had already decided that she wasn't going to share Olivia's secrets. Not even with Jake. 'They were things that she wouldn't want widely shared. And that she would've preferred us all not to know.'

He held her gaze for a while, his eyes narrowing. 'Okay,' he said. 'Right, but this is...' He trailed off again. 'So what, there've been two rounds so far. Dub, and Oli, right?' Frances nodded again. 'Do you know who's next?' he asked.

'No. But I don't imagine we'll have to wait long.'

'And what about Dub and Oli?'

Frances shrugged. 'I don't know. I guess they're done. It will move on.'

'Aren't you worried?' There was a catch in her husband's voice. What was that about?

'No.' Frances took a sip of tea. 'I haven't got any secrets.' She studied him over the top of her mug.

'It's not fun, though. I mean, these days even accusations can be enough to hurt people.'

'Wait. You think I *should* be worried?' She stared intently at her husband.

'No. What? No.' He shook his head to emphasis the point. 'Of course not.' He put her phone down on the arm of the chair. 'It's creepy though.'

'You know what, I'd hoped you might be able to help find out who's behind it. But if all you're going to do is make veiled accusations that I have secrets from you, then don't bother.'

'That's not what I meant, Frances.'

Frances. Not Fran. Argument territory.

She shrugged. 'Forget it. I'll let you know what happens next.' Jake's expression was hard to read. 'Pass me the remote would you? I think I'll watch some telly.'

He handed her the TV remote and then he placed her phone on the arm of the chair. Perhaps he thought taking it with him would have been affirmation that he wanted to snoop for her secrets.

He bent down and kissed the top of her head, no doubt hoping to rebuild the peace. 'Well, I'd better get back to work. Maybe I can finish early tonight. Spend some time with you and the kids.'

Frances managed a half-smile. Jake said that nearly every day which is how she knew she and the kids would be fast asleep before he switched off work for the day.

31

TUESDAY 6:32PM

Someone was hammering on the front door, but Paddy had no intention of opening it. He slipped off his bed and crawled over to the bedroom window. There were no lights on in his house but was he safe to look out? The last thing he wanted was anyone to see him. He leant against the wall, trying to slow his breathing. He raked his fingers through his hair.

Thud, thud, thud.

Everything about it felt violent. They hadn't rung on the doorbell, or used the knocker. They'd simply thumped on the door itself.

Could it be them? Could they have found out that he'd called the tip-line? He closed his eyes and buried his face in his knees. Why had he done it? He hadn't needed to. He could've just left it well alone. And they'd made it easy for him to turn a blind eye by making the decision to call the tip-line even harder. They probably thought they'd made it impossible. Which is what he was counting on. Because no one would be stupid enough to accuse someone of fraud when the evidence suggested they were involved themselves.

Paddy heard the letterbox in the front door swing open, and after a few seconds swing closed again. He started to look around for a makeshift weapon, as he braced himself for the sound of shattered glass. He swallowed and flexed his hands. He crawled over towards the metal bin. It wasn't much, but it was better than something. He pushed out another breath.

He realised that he was counting. Twenty-seven seconds since they'd looked through the letter box. He kept going. At what point would he believe they'd gone. One hundred? Two hundred? No idea. The longer the better. He flinched as a car door slammed shut. Could that be them? Had they given up?

He listened to the sound of the car start up and drive away. He counted another one hundred and then pulled himself up to peer out of the window. It was pitch black but he couldn't see anyone in his drive or on his doorstep. They'd gone.

He picked up his phone. There'd been nothing from the Honesty Index since the message to them all after Oli's round. The only new messages on his phone were from his work colleagues.

Where are you, Paddy? The boss is asking about you.

You alright, mate?

And one from the boss.

Paddy, please can me when you get this message. I hope everything is okay, but you know the protocol is to call in before ten if for any reason you can't make it into work.

His mouth was dry and he felt stretched and hollow. He'd been worried about being unveiled before the game arrived. From the moment he'd ended the call with the tip-line he'd been looking over his shoulder. He threw his phone onto the bed and the climbed back under the covers. He buried his face into the mattress and pulled the pillow over his head.

The night would be long, but he knew he'd make it through to tomorrow. He just wasn't certain that he wanted to.

32

TUESDAY 9:32PM

Trent could hear Dub moving about in the spare room as he walked down the landing to his home office. He shut the door behind him. He used to think of the room as being like an old friend, comfortable with no surprises. He still liked the room but that analogy had been shattered.

His desk sat under the window that looked out over the back garden and was flanked with shelves lined with books. Opposite the table was an alcove - it was almost as if the space had been designed to hang a corkboard. Trent had purchased the largest one that would fit in the space and had hung it up a couple of months ago. He'd intended to fill it with details of the file, to build up a visual representation of everything he knew in the hope that it would lead him to learn the things he didn't know. But it had been blank cork ever since.

He flicked the light switch next to the door and lowered himself into the chair before turning on the Anglepoise lamp and taking out a blank piece of A3 paper and a pencil from the drawer.

He wrote the words Honesty Index in the middle. That seemed to be the best name for the mysterious game. To the right he printed the name Nicholas Samson. This had all started after his wake and the same school friends who had attended, the exact same group of people who were invited to Samson's sixteenth birthday party, had been included in the game. Samson's mother had explicitly stated how particular her Nicky was; how he planned everything down to the least detail. He'd even left her notes on the six of them. Could that bizarre behaviour extend to things that happen after he died? Trent shook his head. Surely he was crazy to even consider it.

He jotted down some prompts on the left-hand side of the page: means, motive and opportunity. Next, he wrote down the name of each of his friends caught up in the Honesty Index. He moved his hand back up to Dub, his pencil poised over his name. He sketched out the spokes of a wheel and added some key words. *Journalist. Sex tapes. Leaked to employer. Leaked to landlord. Who had access? Still hiding something. What is the missing video?*

He moved on to Oli. *Politics.* He shuddered. Oli had been born, if not with a silver spoon in her mouth, then with it at least in reach on the table. So much privilege and yet so much anger. How did that happen? Next up. *Blackmail.* Christ, what a list of character traits. He pushed on. *Affair.* The hits just kept on coming. *Needs money.* He drew one line from Oli's money to *family job* and another to Paddy. Trent stopped, his eyes tracing from word to word. Money. Blackmail. Paddy had been clear in his WhatsApp message that he'd made Oli a loan but maybe there was more to it.

Trent tapped his pencil on Paddy's name. His friend had changed over recent months. He started to scribble a list. *Accountant. Money. Where from? What is he scared of?* He thought of his own reaction when he saw Paddy at the wake;

the first time he'd seen him for a few months. Perhaps it was nothing but he needed to keep an open mind right now. He added a further question. *Is he unwell?*

Next was Lila. *Left to go to Cali. Why did she leave? Why is she back?* So many questions. Some of which he wasn't going to write down.

Frances was the last name. *Psych degree. Part-time teacher of oriental studies. Children. Married.* Trent's eyes jerked up to *Affair.* Could it be? Frances and Oli were yin and yang but maybe that was Oli's motivation. But it was a stretch. Oli had many friends and there was no reason to assume that she'd slept with the partner of anyone on his list.

All the names on the page circled around Nicholas Samson. He was at the centre of this. But why? And the killer question, how?

There was one player's name missing. He picked up the pencil and printed out his own name. Above that he wrote *Freddy.* Pain twisted in his guts and the skin underneath his eyes pulled taught. God, Freddy. His little brother. It was rare to have someone worship the ground you walked on but Freddy's face would switch to full beam whenever he saw Trent. And if Trent loaded Mario Kart on the Wii and handed him a controller, Freddy looked like he was about to ride shotgun all the way to heaven.

The horror show was readily available on instant playback and, without wanting to be, Trent was back there once again, with his brother, in the last moments of his life. Watching him die. Trent's body started to jerk even before the tears reached his eyes. He rested his head in his hands as the picture from the local paper seared back into his memory. He knew the words of the article by heart because that's where he kept them and yet he always heard them spoken by his mother, for reasons he didn't understand.

A couple and one of their children have died after a fire engulfed their home this morning, while two surviving children are fighting for their lives.

Firefighters found the parents and their three children – aged 15, 12 and 5 – at their home just after 1am.

The parents, David Ryder, 36, and his wife, Sally Ryder, 38, were pronounced dead shortly after arriving at hospital.

The couple's 5-year-old son was pronounced dead at hospital, where his two siblings — a 15-year-old boy and a 12-year-old girl — remained in serious condition late Saturday afternoon.

The coroner had recorded the three deaths as accidental. Faulty electrical wiring and a smoke alarm that didn't work.

It was difficult to see the problem with the wiring on account of the wires being buried in the walls and not having been touched for over twenty years, but the guess was that the wires were old and no longer had the capacity to take the load.

The problem with the smoke alarm was easier to identify: there were no batteries in it. No batteries, no alarm. No alarm, no Mum, no Dad, no Freddy. That was the critical path.

Trent pushed the pencil hard against the paper. How many times would he go down the same dark path? All he had left were the memories. And guilt. And the guilt always shouted the loudest.

He hadn't protected his baby brother. He hadn't done the one thing that older brothers are there for. He hadn't saved him. The lead snapped and his hand jerked leaving a scrawl after Freddy's name.

Trent closed his eyes and tried to quieten his mind. After a few seconds he was composed enough to draw a line from his own name to another. Lila. She knew what it was like to have someone who was dazzled by your halo. He'd felt their connection start to fuse back together at her flat two nights ago, or possibly even before that, back to the moment when they'd first laid eyes on each other outside Samson's house. He'd begun to open up to her and he knew he needed to keep going. He had to make things right between them both.

In the space to the right of his own name he wrote *Pen.* He was still close to his sister but as they had grown up they'd grown apart a little. Was he please she'd found happiness with Bobby? On balance, yes he was.

He tapped his pencil on the table. He was better than this. He needed to get a grip. His hand glided left. *Dad.* More spokes covered the page. *Medal. Rejection. How does the game know? Link to the fire? Aunt Jo.*

Trent pushed his feet hard to the floor to stop his knees shaking. He still hadn't heard from his aunt. It had only been a couple of days so maybe she was having difficulty accessing her voicemail from overseas. He grabbed his phone, pulled up her contact details and clicked on the text button.

Aunt Jo, I need to speak with you urgently. Please can you call me. Trent.

He unlocked the middle drawer beneath the desk, took out his laptop and booted it up. Waiting for technology to respond had taken on a sinister vibe over the last two days but once the multi-coloured wheel stopped spinning, he opened the search engine, typed in Nicholas Samson's name, and scanned the results. It took him a while but after some refinements and scratching around there was a hit that looked promising.

An article in a computer science journal, authored by Samson a year ago. He was shown as being an employee of a company called Analytic Systems. The title was, *Thinking machines are already here*.

Trent started to read the introductory remarks about how a computer could be left to take its own actions independent of human interaction. Trent's mouth was dry and he leant in closer to the screen, reading as quickly as he could.

Within a few paragraphs he was drowning in neural nets and deep learning but his thoughts about how Samson could be behind the Honesty Index started to coalesce. It was clear that Samson had been working as a computer scientist in the emerging field of Artificial Intelligence.

The Honesty Index seemed to react to players actions. Could Samson have programmed it so that it ran by itself even after he was dead? Trent could imagine how it could set answers or actions to players' responses. But what if it went further? What if Samson had programmed it so that, even though he was dead, the programme could not only run, but it could make its own decisions. What if Nicholas Samson had built the Honesty Index to live on after his death so that it still felt as if there was a live human behind it. What did they call it? Something to do with the guy who designed the enigma machine in the war. Alan Turning. A few seconds later, Trent was reading Wikipedia.

'*The* ***Turing test****, originally called the* ***imitation game*** *by Alan Turing in 1950, is a test of a machine's ability to exhibit intelligent behaviour equivalent to, or indistinguishable from, that of a human.*'

Trent's mouth was dry. Surely Samson couldn't have done that. Could he?

33

TUESDAY 10:00PM

Trent pushed his laptop away and tapped his fingers on the desk. He'd signed up with Public Record Search and checked the online record. Everything certainly seemed to tally with Samson being dead. There was no way that his wake could've been a hoax to give him cover for the game. No, Samson was as dead as Friends Reunited.

Trent had an hour and a half before his meeting with Dylan. A message appeared on his screen. It was Lila.

You free for a video call?

Trent needed no second invitation and a few seconds later Lila's face appeared on his laptop, her music playing in the background.

'Hey, Trent.' The angel inside the machine. 'Just give me a minute.' She disappeared off screen and the music faded. Then the picture was moving as she carried her laptop across the room. She came back into shot, lying on a bed with her head resting on a couple of pillows.

'Right. I'm all yours,' Lila said. Trent forced himself to ignore that. 'I'm still pretty shaken up by what happened to Oli.'

Trent nodded. 'Yeah. She was here when it happened.'

'What do you mean?' She frowned. 'She was at your house?' He'd forgotten that the others wouldn't have known where Oli was and there was an edge to Lila's voice that he hadn't expected.

'Yeah. She called early this morning.'

'What for?' The edge had softened slightly and she leaned a little closer to the screen.

'I'm guessing she was going to ask me for money, like she asked Paddy, but we didn't get that far. She'd only just calmed down enough to come inside when her round started.'

'Calmed down?'

'Oh, yeah. Dub's staying here for a few nights.' He caught her look. 'Sorry. He needed somewhere to stay.' He bit his lip whilst waiting for her response.

Lila nodded slowly. 'Oli asked me for money, too. Early this morning.' Trent took a sharp breath. Oli had done the rounds. 'How was she after it was over?' Lila asked, clearly having decided to avoid the topic of Dub, at least for now.

'She left without saying anything. She looked dazed but also, I don't know,' Trent searched for the right word to describe Oli with her chin up and looking forward, 'resolute.'

Lila fell silent. 'What's going on, Trent? Who do you think is behind it?'

'Well, I have a theory.'

'Spill.'

'Okay. Well, originally I thought it was someone out to humiliate Dub, like an ex-girlfriend. He let slip that there was another video, one that wasn't included with the ones we were sent. So, I thought that made sense. Except now I know that the woman he said was in it, doesn't exist. He made her up.' He watched Lila carefully. Anything involving Dub was weighed down by their history.

'What?' she asked, furrowing her brow as though the idea of a made-up woman was baffling, which seemed to cover any deeper feelings she was repressing nicely. She was staring intently into the screen.

'I know. Really odd.' Trent considered mentioning what Dub had said to him, the warning about the final video, but Lila already looked on edge.

'You said 'originally.' You've got another idea?' She shuffled her shoulders on the pillow.

'Yes.' He paused, knowing it would sound ridiculous. 'I think it's Nicholas Samson.'

'Samson, but–' Lila was frowning.

Trent sighed and rolled his eyes. 'I know what you're going to say.'

'He's dead,' Lila said anyway. 'It seems like an important point.' She pushed her hair back behind her ears whilst trying out her most earnest expression.

'Let's agree that you're very funny,' Trent said, and Lila laughed as confirmation. 'Okay, good,' he said, 'So, what if Samson used computer coding, like AI?'

'What if he what?' Lila asked.

'AI. Artificial intelligence. I'm no expert but in essence he could have coded it all so that this game responds depending on what answers people give.' Trent could practically feel Lila's scepticism bursting through the screen and so he pressed on. 'I've found some research Samson published. It looks like he worked in that area.' Trent clicked on his laptop to split his screen between the Google search and Lila.

Lila was quiet for a moment. 'So, you're saying you think he programmed this whole thing before he died?'

'I don't know.' It sounded far-fetched but Trent wasn't yet ready to rule it out. 'Maybe.'

'Do you think we could hack it?' At least Lila was trying to sound as though she thought Trent's theory was a possibility.

Trent smiled. 'You want to give it a go?'

'Very funny. Video calls and Google are about my limit.'

'It's a good idea though. I've asked a friend of mine for some help. Her contact does that sort of thing.'

'Her?' Lila said it as if there should only be one *her* in his life.

'My boss, Tina. She has her own software company. She's put me in touch with one of her tech guys.' He clicked on to the next page of search results.

'Your boss is your friend?' The lightness in Lila's voice only served to stress the question.

'Yeah, I guess.' He hesitated. 'I didn't mean...' What didn't he mean?

'I think that's sweet.'

What did *that* mean? Trent cleared his throat and tried to reboot his mind by studying the Google searches, his eyes tracing down the screen. He stopped and reread a hit. 'Hold on. There's something here about his father's death.'

Trent clicked through to an obituary for Christopher Samson. He had died when his private jet – *yes, private jet* - crashed after getting into difficulty in heavy fog in 2013. That was three years after they'd all left school. The article confirmed that Christopher Samson was the founder and CEO of the 'secretive technology firm, Analytic Systems.' That was the same company that Nicholas Samson was working for.

'Are you reading this, Lila? Samson worked for his dad's firm which specialised in data brokerage and data analysis.'

'What does that mean?' Lila asked whilst she twisted and reached for something off screen.

'I don't know exactly, but it sounds like the sort of technology that might be useful if you wanted to develop something like this game.' He paused, trying to pull back a distant memory. 'Hey, do you remember Samson's secret from the night of his bonfire party?'

He could see Lila thinking as she took a sip of water from a plastic bottle. 'From his party? Wow. Sort of. I can recall the gist of it.'

'I don't remember it well. I wasn't really listening.' He'd been caught up in thinking about the fire.

'It was about his father,' Lila said. 'Some suggestion that he'd interfered in a local election, I think. All unfounded, at least according to Nicholas. But there was some media coverage about it. He told us that someone published their home address and they had protestors wearing balaclavas camped outside their home. Some of them threatened his mum. And then Nicholas started to get messages about it on Facebook.'

'That last bit rings a bell.' Trent was tapping on his keyboard. 'Didn't he say that's why he had to change schools?'

'Yes. They had to move to a new house. In a new area.'

'And he made a whole new group of friends,' Trent said, wondering whether Lila was thinking the same thing as him.

'I don't get it. Let's just say it is Samson. We've just been to his wake. His mother, his family and his friends were all there. I mean, he is *definitely* dead. In which case he programmed something to attack us *after* he died. Why would he do that?'

'I don't know.' Trent pulled his eyes away from the screen. 'I said I had an idea. I didn't say it was a good one.'

'Maybe he thinks one of us betrayed him or something?'

'Betrayed him? What do you mean?'

'Well, the only real link between all of us, those of us that he's got playing this game and him, is that weird discussion at his party.' Lila was blinking.

Trent crawled through his memory but came up with nothing. 'I can't think of anything obvious. Maybe we upset him by not taking it seriously?'

Lila's arms were tightly crossed over her chest. 'Whoever it is, they're more than just upset. Do you think we should go to the police now?'

'I don't know.' Trent brushed his mouth with his hand and bit on his thumb. 'If it *is* Samson, then what can they even do? I think our best bet is to get someone to hack the technology.' He glanced at the time. If Dylan was as good as Tina said she was then he might have the answer, all the answers later that night.

'What's wrong, Trent?'

He pulled his focus back to Lila who was yawning. 'Nothing, sorry.' He tried out a smile. 'Let me see how I get on with the technology. Anyway, it's late and you look tired.'

'Are you worried I won't get my beauty sleep?' She had moved closer to the screen again.

'I just don't want you to be grumpy tomorrow.'

'Love you too,' she laughed and blew him a kiss. 'Okay. Well, sweet dreams. Come and see me soon.'

Trent stared at the screen after she'd gone and tried to make sense of the world. It was almost as if they hadn't been apart. Almost. He still owed her the truth about how and why he'd acted like he did after she left for the US. He resolved, once more, to tell her everything. Soon.

Another message from Lila flicked up on his laptop.

I found this. And now I really must go to bed if I'm going to be able to speak to anyone tomorrow. Lx.

34

TUESDAY 10:23PM

Trent followed the link to a blog and started to read. He hadn't heard of the author but he appeared to be a political journalist.

You've probably never heard of Analytic Systems, the private company based in the UK, or indeed the company's founder, Christopher Samson. No reason why you would have and I'm sure Mr. Samson prefers it that way. Because Analytic Systems is a highly secretive company. It is incorporated in a tax haven and public details of its ownership and indeed its true purpose are scarce. Its employees are reluctant to speak on the record, certainly to me, but there are rumors of firmwide NDA's and hints at a culture of secrecy. Fair enough, you might think. It isn't, after all, a public company. And the British Government hasn't designated it as a high-risk company. But here's the thing – maybe a company that specializes in data poisoning should be.

Data poisoning – what's that, I hear you ask?

Trent's breathing became shallow as he digested the words.

What if I said you could run a script that can scan your various electronic posts and infuse them with random characters to scorch your digital earth to prevent others from mining your data. Sounds good? Guerrilla warfare, fighting back against the man, right?

Maybe. But get this. Analytic Systems was retained by one successful party in our recent mayoral elections. That's right. A tiny company, that you've never heard of, based all the way over in England, played a role in OUR 2005 Orange County election. IT MAY HAVE SHAPED THE OUTCOME OF THE ELECTION. This is electoral fraud. We need answers.

Unfortunately, Christopher Samson died last week and so we may never get the answers we deserve. But the risk to our democracy didn't die with Christopher Samson. There will be another Analytic Systems, there will be other elections and there will always be someone who is prepared to do anything to win. YOU HAVE BEEN WARNED.

Trent blinked. Then he read it a second time before he scribbled down the name, Christopher Samson, on his paper and drew a line to link father and son. He circled Christopher Samson and sketched out comments around the ring. *Data company. Analytic Systems. Election scandal. Death. Wealth.*

He pushed his chair back. The rumours of electoral fraud were real. And data poisoning sounded dark. Could Nicholas Samson have planned the Honesty Index before he died? He knew he had cancer, so he would've had time to organise it. Trent sighed. He had more information but still no answers. He banged his fist on the table. He was nowhere.

He needed to find out more about the Samsons. And there was only one family member still alive. He drummed his fingers on the laptop. Would speaking to Mrs Samson help? It was hard to see how it could make things worse. He clicked off the lamp, closed the computer and carefully locked it away in the drawer, leaving the piece of paper on the desk. He'd switched off the main light and was reaching for the office door when his phone buzzed with a new message. His pulse quickened. *No, it couldn't be. Not yet.* He needed more time.

But it wasn't from the game. It was from Oli. To him, Dub, Lila, Paddy, and Frances. He relaxed his jaw; aware his teeth had been tightly clenched.

I know you will all have seen my round. It's the truth but not the whole truth. I've been warned to stay away from you and I'm not prepared to take any risks merely to put my side of the story. But there is one. Olivia.

Trent stood in the dark, trying to keep his breathing even. *Not the whole truth.* Did she simply mean that there was more to the questions and answers that they had seen or was there another, deeper secret missing? Something equivalent to Dub's final video? He walked across the room and stared out the window at the night sky.

Was it Nicholas Samson? His eyes scanned over the fence at the back of his garden, taking in the neighbours' houses and the fields beyond. Who was out there? Who was playing them? And why?

The Honesty Index had launched its first attack on Sunday night. Oli's round had been that morning, approximately thirty-six hours later. If it was consistent then round three would be tomorrow night. He sighed, knowing that he wasn't moving fast enough to keep up, let alone move ahead.

He messaged Frances to ask her to contact Samson's mother. She'd built some rapport when they had met and was the best chance of securing an audience. That one at least was easy. Then he picked up the A3 sheet of paper from the desk and turned and pinned it to the centre of the cork-board. He didn't have much time before he needed to leave but this was important. That was the nature of truth. He walked over to the desk and opened the bottom drawer and took out some drawing pins together with a buff-coloured folder that contained his research into the fire. He turned to face the corkboard and started work. He divided the board into different areas: the data on deaths from house fires, research on smoke alarms, and the different obituaries and newspaper reports of the fire. Then he moved on to his research on gallantry awards. He repeatedly reorganised the board, trying to reflect the mental map that he held in his mind.

He'd lost track of time but finally, standing in front of the corkboard, he was nearly happy. He just had one more addition. He swallowed as he added a family photograph.

He stood there, trying to set his mind to receive mode. Connections couldn't always be forced but he felt sure that there had to be something there.

Just then, he heard Dub's footsteps, walking down the corridor and stopping outside the office. Then nothing for a few seconds. Trent pulled his attention away from the corkboard. It was time for him to leave. 'I'm going to bed, mate,' Dub shouted through the door.

'Okay,' Trent said as he stepped out into the hallway. He locked the office door behind him, ignoring the raised eyebrows from Dub. 'I'm heading out. I'll see you tomorrow morning.' Without waiting for a reply, Trent headed towards the stairs.

'Have fun,' Dub called after him.

But Trent wasn't expecting it to be fun; he was meeting Dylan Steele.

35

TUESDAY 11:28PM

Trent was only a few yards away from the tube station and it was two minutes before the appointed time. There were a few people standing around. He had no idea what Dylan looked like but he was happy to have a guess. A woman with bright red hair that came down to her waist caught his eye. She was standing next to the Evening Standard newspaper stand, clearly waiting for someone. Her glance washed over him and she turned to look the other way.

His phone buzzed as three new messages arrived and his breath caught in his throat. But none of the messages were from the game. Neither were any of them from his aunt. Why hadn't she replied?

Two were from Frances. One just to him, confirming that they were meeting with Mrs Samson tomorrow morning. The other was her WhatsApp group message confirming the same thing to the others. Trent wasn't sure how Frances found the time to be so organised but he was grateful that she was.

The final message was from Pen.

Any news from Aunt Jo?

He fired her a quick reply – *nothing yet, have texted her* – and then took up his post standing directly outside the main entrance, just a few awkward yards away from the red-haired, cursory-glancer. He walked over and grabbed a paper and studiously started to catch up with the day's world events. He checked the time on his phone. Dylan should be there by now. He had just returned his attention to the newspaper when someone grabbed his phone out of his hand.

'Thanks. I'll get it back to you in a few hours.'

Trent didn't even have time to answer before the woman was heading away from the tube station. He'd barely even got a look at her. She appeared to be bald under a heavy green hooded jacket, boyish looking, with blue eyes.

'Pleasure to meet you, Dylan,' Trent muttered to himself. And then he shouted, 'Pass code's one, two, three, four by the way.'

It wasn't but he thought she might return and ask him what his actual password was. She didn't even glance back and five seconds later she was out of sight.

TRENT LOOKED at the newspaper in his hand. He folded it over and was about to drop it back in the display box when he caught sight of the photograph below the fold in the page. His body fizzed. It was Freddy. Blinking he peered again at the photo. His breathing slowly returned to normal as he realised that it wasn't his brother, although there was a strong resemblance. This kid had raised over a million pounds for the NHS. This kid was alive; and changing the world.

Trent dropped the paper into the box and wiped his hand over his face. Would it ever stop?

36

WEDNESDAY 2:27AM

Trent's doorbell rang. He'd been expecting to hear from Dylan but he didn't know how she'd get in touch with him. She hadn't asked for any details and all she had to go on was his phone. He almost slapped himself. His *phone*. On which he stored his entire life's data. He smiled as he walked downstairs. She now probably knew as much about his life as he did. He tried not to think about that too much as he opened the door.

She was still wearing the green coat but this time she had the hood down. Her hair was cut short, blonde and unstyled – which may have been a style of its own, he wasn't sure. Trent left the door open and turned towards the kitchen. He needed coffee.

'Aren't you going to invite me in?' she asked.

'Oh, yeah. Sure. I forgot that you like to stand on ceremony. Come in and make yourself at home.' He led her into the kitchen. 'Tea, coffee?'

She shook her head and passed him his phone. 'The security on your phone is shocking. You should be glad I didn't have any interest in your bank accounts or your browser history.'

He let that slide. 'What did you find out about the Honesty Index?' He flicked the switch on the kettle. He'd need caffeine for a middle of the night computing class.

'That application had the most robust security of anything on your phone.' She paused and he wondered whether she was paying her silent respects to its programmer. 'I've found out everything that it's possible to find out from what we have so far.'

'So, who's behind it?'

'I don't know.' Which was definitive but not helpful.

'Any clues?'

'Not many. The server that hosts the app is based in Panama and all the updates, such as the messages, are routed through a network that also starts in Panama.'

'So the person behind this is based in Panama?'

'Of course not.' Nothing like breaking it to him gently. 'Probably a paid service. There's no way to trace it back beyond Panama.'

'Who owns it?' Trent added the milk to his cup of coffee and took a sip.

'An LLC.'

Trent raised his eyebrows. 'Which is what?'

'A limited liability corporation. This one is registered in the secrecy capital of the world.'

'Switzerland?' Trent guessed.

'Close. Delaware.'

He shrugged. 'What's this LLC called?'

'Nameless.'

Trent tried to get his mind around that. 'Can you even do that?'

Dylan looked at him and spoke very slowly. 'No, it's actually called Nameless LLC.' Trent let that soak in. Dylan was staring at him. 'I hope you haven't got any secrets.'

He met her gaze. 'We all have secrets.'

'In which case I suggest you work out how you're going to feel when this thing shares them for you. From everything I've seen you're dealing with someone who's driven and smart. They've gone to a great deal of effort. I don't think they'll stop at your friends Dubnyk and Pearson.'

Trent shivered. His limbs felt heavy and his mind was racing. He probably shouldn't have had the coffee. 'What if we just delete it?' he asked.

'It might save you from watching things unfold but my guess is that when you don't play your round the game will release the information it holds to people you really don't want it to be sent to.'

Damned if you do, damned if you delete. Which was no choice at all. 'Could you write that software? I mean, could you programme the game and then just leave it so it sends fixed answers to questions.' He paused. 'Using AI?'

Dylan stared at Trent without blinking. 'That's not how AI works.'

'Okay.' Bluffing his tech know-how clearly wasn't going to work with Dylan. 'Well, with or without AI, could you do it?'

A subtle tilt of the head. 'Yes.'

'And how about other people?' he asked. 'Someone less...' He grasped for the word but failed to find one.

'Not many, but yes, it's possible. Someone,' she paused, '*less* could also do it.'

Arrogance or comedy genius? Too close to call. 'Well, thanks for your help. I wouldn't have the first clue how to do any of that stuff.'

'I know.' Dylan clearly hadn't been to charm school

although to be fair she was also just stating the obvious. 'I could do with seeing the app in action to find out more.'

'It hasn't given much notice for either round so far.' Trent wondered whether Oli had been given an early warning. She had certainly moved fast to try and arrange some funding.

'You can call me again if you want,' Dylan said.

Which caught Trent off guard. 'You mean, like, call me, call me? Because I–'

Dylan replied before he could finish. 'No. I mean I like solving puzzles and I don't like dead ends.' Her eyes seemed distant. Even more distant. 'I *really* don't like dead ends.'

Trent smiled, despite himself. 'Thank you for clearing that up. I wouldn't want to be left with the impression that you liked me.'

'Nor would I.' She stood silently in front of him.

For a second Trent could have sworn that Dylan smiled but, to be fair, her lips didn't move. And then she turned on the spot and walked out of his house, shutting the door softly behind her.

Trent shook his head as he picked up his phone. Tina wasn't wrong, Dylan Steele was an unusual woman.

37

MANIFESTO EXTRACT 6

t some point they will consider going to the police. They will need encouragement not to do so.

#TRIGGER FOR SEARCH for police by Player_List

IF SEARCH_TERM='POLICE' then exe.msg017

BACKGROUND COLOUR: Black

FONT COLOUR: Red

MSG017 TEXT:

. . .

Do not go to the police. Do not speak to anyone about this. Await instructions.

38

WEDNESDAY 4:29AM

Trent opened his eyes and looked around his bedroom. The clock showed half past four in the morning. What had woken him? He could have sworn that he had heard the sound of a door closing. Maybe Dub had used the toilet. He lay still in bed, listening. But there was no creaking stair and no voices. He swung his legs out of bed, blinking to find his focus, and crept over to the bedroom door. Still nothing. He took a breath, opened the door, and hit the landing light switch immediately. Light bathed the hallway. Nothing. Moving quickly now, he ran down the stairs again flicking on the light switch. But there was no sign of anyone. His heartrate was slowing as he finished his search of downstairs. Everything was as it should be. He went to look out of the front door. His stomach knotted. The door chain was off and yet he remembered clearly sliding it into place after Dylan had left.

He turned, running upstairs. 'Dub' he shouted. He reached the spare bedroom and flung open the door. Two suitcases were padlocked shut, next to the bed. But there was no rucksack. And no one asleep in the bed. Dub was gone.

. . .

TRENT no longer felt like sleeping. Dub's middle of the night departure had unsettled him. Why would he just up and leave? And where would he go?

Trent sat downstairs on the leather sofa waiting for sunrise. He'd been over and over everything but until he could speak to Samson's mother, there was nothing more he could do and he still had another thirty minutes before it was time to ride over to Frances' house. Just then his house phone started to ring. He looked at the caller display. The digits were displayed alongside the message, *number unknown.* His heart started thumping and there was a tingle at the base of his spine. He picked up the phone and waited.

'Trent, this is Dub. Don't hang up.' He sounded breathless. And it was a strange way to open the call. 'I need to talk to you.' His words were running into each other.

'Okay.' Trent managed to stop himself from pointing out that it was easy to have a discussion when two people were in the same house.

'Look, I've had another message warning me not to talk to anyone.' Trent tightened his attention to focus on what Dub was saying. 'I'm on a burner phone.'

Where the hell had Dub sourced a burner phone? And why was he using one? Trent picked up a pen and scribbled down the mobile number on the pad next to the telephone.

'What's going on, Dub?'

'Not ... the risk...' The line crackled.

'What?' Trent strained to hear. 'I didn't hear what you said.'

'...just going to do what I'm told from...' The line faded out again.

'Dub? Dub, can you hear me?'

The signal cut back in again. '...sorry. Good luck, Trent. I hope it doesn't–'

'Dub? Dub.'

Trent glared at the handset. *Call ended.* He grabbed the paper and punched in the number. A recorded message kicked in.

This number is not currently available.

What the hell was going on? Oli had messaged everyone to say she would have nothing more to do with them. Now Dub had called to say he was out, after slipping away in the middle of the night. Not only that but he'd called Trent's landline, not his mobile, and on a *burner phone*.

There was only one conclusion. Dub must think that he was being bugged. And if Dub was being bugged, the likelihood was, that they all were.

39

WEDNESDAY 7:28AM

Although Frances had moved into the house shortly before she and Jake had had the twins, Trent hadn't visited before. In fact, Trent couldn't recall having even seen Frances' husband other than at their wedding six or so years ago.

Jake opened the door and nodded. 'Hi, Trent. Come in.'

He wasn't tall but he was lean with a tanned face with a hint of stubble. He looked like the type who rose at five in the morning to run a marathon or to swim around a lake before being at his desk in work by seven with a triple expresso to power him through his inbox. His physique, dress sense and even the way he moved seemed to have been modelled on a minimalist philosophy.

'How's things, Jake?'

Would Oli have slept with him, Trent wondered as he followed Jake into the hallway? Probably, if he'd made himself available. Would he have done that? Impossible to tell but Trent wouldn't rule it out. Not just yet.

'Fine. Fran's just seeing to the kids.' Jake called upstairs to let his wife know Trent had arrived. There was a waist height, white gate across the bottom of the stairs and a cluster of mini coats hanging on the hooks on the wall. They were neatly arranged in size order. Jake showed Trent into the kitchen.

'Well, I've got to join a conference call. No rest for the wicked.' Jake walked out before Trent could reply, leaving Trent alone looking at the kids' colourful art gallery displayed on the fridge door. Even that was neatly arranged with the corners of each picture secured with colour co-ordinated magnets.

Jake had been slightly brusque. What was that about? Trent heard a door close upstairs and then the sound of muffled voices. Frances' footsteps on the stairs announced her arrival. Her frizzy hair was pulled back in a bun.

'Sorry to keep you. Did Jake offer you a drink?' she asked.

'I'm fine, thanks.' Trent had already had two coffees. 'You know I think that's the first time I've seen Jake since your wedding,' he said.

'Really?' Frances' forehead creased. 'Wow. He's been asking about you all with this whole Honesty Index thing.' She nodded towards the kitchen door and dropped her voice. 'He's partly intrigued by the technology.' She pulled a face. 'That's what his new start up does. Like DeepMind. Using data, apps, that sort of thing. But I think he's also suspicious of you all.'

'Suspicious?' Trent echoed, wondering whether that explained the slightly terse exchange. 'Why?'

'Because he thinks one of you must be behind it.'

Trent nodded. He couldn't blame Jake for that.

Frances had picked up her car keys and was looking at him. 'Ready?'

'As I'll ever be,' he said.

He hadn't managed to eat any breakfast and he wondered

whether he would get his appetite back after the meeting with Samson's mother. He followed Frances along the hall. She knocked on a closed door, presumably Jake's study and shouted, 'don't forget to take the boys in half an hour. I've packed their stuff.' On receiving a muffled acknowledgment, she waved Trent out the house.

He walked round to the front passenger seat of the hatchback. It had family car written all over it; car seats in the back and some fluffy toys lying in the passenger footwell. Trent froze. The sight of the small fluffy dragon ripped a memory from his heart. Freddy had loved Puff the magic dragon. Christ, it hit him at the most unexpected time. Sometimes it was too much to bear and yet he was expected to carry on. And mostly, he did. But sometimes it was enough to stop him; to stop time. His little brother had ceased his own fearless roar.

'Are you okay, Trent?' Frances was already behind the wheel with her seatbelt on. She was leaning over and peering up at him as he stood with the passenger door open.

Feeling numb, he sat down and swung his legs round, nudging the dragon as he made room for his feet. The toy rolled over, but rather than fire breathing retribution it waved its padded feet helplessly in the air. 'Yeah, sorry. Just trying to process everything.' Including the impossible.

Frances nodded. Mirror, signal, manoeuvre, and they were flowing smoothly with the early morning traffic.

40

WEDNESDAY 8:31AM

Mrs Samson opened the door and smiled at them. She was as immaculately attired as she had been at the wake. Today she'd opted for a dark green twin set and pearls.

'How lovely of you both to make the time to come round. It means so much to me.' Trent's guilt ratcheted up a couple of notches. 'Do come through.' She led them into a formal sitting room and directed them to sit in the high-backed chairs. 'Now, I've made a pot of tea. How do you like it?'

Trent tried to characterise her tone. She was polite but he sensed there was a brittleness to it.

'No milk, no sugar, please,' said Frances.

'Same for me, please,' Trent added. Best to keep things simple.

Mrs Samson disappeared through the door and Trent sat up, taking in the room. Everything seemed to be precisely displayed. Religious paintings illuminated by dedicated wall lights, model boats in display cases and ornaments carefully placed on the shelves and on the mantlepiece. In the corner, and slightly out of keeping with the rest of the room, was a huge tropical fish tank. Trent watched the bright colours blur as the fish darted around. There was a small mahogany table, placed against the wall.

Mrs Samson was back, carrying a tray with the drinks. There was a folded piece of white paper tucked underneath the sugar bowl. They each took the cup and saucer offered to them and sat back in their chairs. Mrs Samson placed the tray on the table, picked up the piece of paper and lowered herself very deliberately onto the chair opposite them. Trent noticed the silver cross dangling on the chain around her neck alongside the pearls.

'So,' she said before taking a sip of tea, 'why don't you tell me why you're here?'

A chill brushed his heart. Her expression gave nothing away but had there been a shift in her tone? He shuffled on his chair and looked at his friend.

'Yes, of course.' Frances dropped smoothly into gear. 'We were talking after the wake. It was a lovely occasion and we were reminiscing about school. It's the first time that all of us have been back together since then.' She lowered her gaze. 'I'm sorry. Not all of us.' It was perfectly pitched. Just the right amount of apology. Mrs Samson nodded with the hint of a smile. 'And we realised that we hadn't been good at staying in touch. All of us. With each other. Including with Nicholas.' She paused. A portrait of wistful regret. 'I guess you think that there'll always be time.' A tightness crept into her voice. 'I wish I'd made more effort to keep in touch properly. We wanted to come to tell you that, to see how you are doing and express our condolences more privately.'

Mrs Samson didn't reply immediately but let the sentiment hang in the air. She smoothed her hands over her skirt. 'Thank you, Frances. I mentioned to Trent that Nicky had written notes to me about each of you.' Frances nodded but said nothing. Mrs Samson unfolded the paper she was holding and peered at it. 'I printed a copy. There's only a line or two on each of you.'

'He gave you those notes shortly before...' Frances trailed off. Trent was holding his breath. They'd wanted to discover what Samson had written about them all, to understand his motivation in inviting them to the wake. And it looked as though Mrs Samson was going to deliver for them.

'I guess one of the blessings of a terminal illness is that it gives you time to plan.' She half-smiled. 'He wanted me to know who you all were.'

'We were pleased to have been invited, of course,' Frances replied. 'I think we knew Nicholas better than most.'

'Yes. He told me that you were the only friends he had at school.' Mrs Samson paused. 'He found it difficult, the move. It wasn't the easiest age to have to make new friends, and Nicky wasn't a confident boy. You accepted him, and I think that meant a great deal to him.'

Trent thought it sounded genuine. Samson had really wanted them to be at his wake. But it didn't sound as though he'd want to punish them through a posthumous game.

Mrs Samson returned her attention to the paper. 'Let's see, what do we have here. Frances Churchill.' She cleared her throat and began to read Samson's notes. '*Copper coloured, frizzy hair. Her nickname used to be Copper, but I think she goes by Frances now. She's married and has twin boys. She's always been good to me.*' Trent exchanged a glance with Frances, his eyes wide. '*Trent Ryder. I've lost touch with Trent a little. His family were in a tragic accident before I got to know him. He's quite private, claims to have no secrets and he's hard to read. But he was one of the few kids at school who would even talk to me.*'

Trent bowed his head. He'd cleared the friendship bar but only because Samson had set the level at people who would talk to him. Trent felt the guilt spread into his chest. Nicholas Samson sounded lonely. He'd asked his mother to invite six friends from school. Six people who hardly knew him, but the only six people who would talk to him. A lump formed in Trent's throat.

Mrs Samson folded up the piece of paper and handed it to Trent. 'It's a copy but I thought you might like to share it with the others.'

'Thank you,' Trent replied, fighting the urge to read the notes on the others there and then.

'Nicky was, as I'm sure you know, a private man. Did he tell any of you about his cancer.'

Trent and Frances shook their heads. 'The first we heard of it was your email,' Frances confirmed.

Mrs Samson nodded. 'That doesn't surprise me. As far as I know, he only told me, and his fiancé.' She looked at them, confusion on her face. 'You didn't know Nicholas was engaged?'

No. We didn't know he was engaged, screamed Trent. Silently. They shook their heads in unison, once again. Mrs Samson sighed. 'They hadn't been engaged for long. Nicholas told me that they were planning to tell people one by one, you know, in person, rather than making an announcement.'

'I'm afraid I hadn't seen him for a while,' Frances said. And for a while read, since leaving school.

'How about you Trent?' Mrs Samson's turned to face him.

'I had no idea. I'm sorry. She must have been devastated.' Playing defence, with a flat bat and his foot thrust forward.

'I rather doubt it.' She was pulling up her emotional drawbridge. 'She finished with him.' Her tone was clipped. 'One month before his death.'

'I'm so sorry,' said Frances, her hand covering her mouth. There it was again. Not the hardest, but the easiest word.

Mrs Samson paused, looking as though she was weighing something up. 'I don't know why.' Her voice cracked very slightly. She straightened her back and waited before continuing. 'Nicky had told me how happy they were together. He'd arranged to bring her over for dinner. I'd not met her and I was so looking forward to it. Unfortunately she cancelled at the last minute. And then, not long after that, she called off their engagement. She, Annabelle, sent me some flowers for the funeral but that apart, she hasn't been in touch. I guess she thought it would upset me.' She dabbed at her face. 'I'm sorry. I shouldn't let it bother me.'

Had he heard that correctly? Mrs Samson had never even met her son's fiancée.

'It must be heart-breaking, Mrs Samson.' Frances leaned forward, seemingly on the verge of stretching out a hand. 'I wish there was something we could do.' The offer dangled, twisting on a line, waiting for a bite.

'Well, maybe there is. I'd like to know why they split up.' She sniffed. 'I couldn't ask her myself but perhaps you could speak to Annabelle?' She looked at Trent. Her eyes were wet, her defences breaking down. 'That might help.' She raised her cup to take another sip. When she continued she was looking down at the floor. 'It's just me, now, you see. First, my husband. And now, my son. I'm all alone.'

Trent felt a hole open inside him. He had some experience of dealing with what she was going through. He could say that he knew how she felt but he didn't believe other people when they told him that they understood his pain; they couldn't and, he guessed, neither could he. Mrs Samson was holding the silver cross in her fingers as she closed her eyes.

'Of course we'll see if Annabelle will speak to one of us,'

Trent said. Frances was nodding her support. It seemed to be what Mrs Samson was looking for.

'Thank you. Do excuse me for one moment.' She stood up and left the room but returned a few seconds later holding her phone. She carefully prodded at her screen as if concerned she might break it. 'Here we are. This is her mobile number. Annabelle Jackson. She works in London so she might agree to meet you. She's in computing, like Nicholas.' She paused. 'Like Nicholas used to be.'

Frances recorded the number on her phone before standing up. 'We'll try, Mrs Samson,' she said. 'I'll call you and let you know how we get on.' The two of them hugged before Mrs Samson held her hand out for Trent.

'Thank you both for coming,' she said.

Trent opted for a handshake. 'Thank you for seeing us. And thank you for this, too.' He held the piece of paper in the air.

FRANCES RECLINED BACK into the driver's seat and let out a deep breath. 'Well, let's hear it then,' she said.

Trent was leaning forward in the passenger's seat, already focusing on Samson's notes. He cleared his throat.

'Andrew Dubnyk. You'll recognise him because he'll be the tallest person there. Everyone calls him Dub. He worked hard at school and followed the rules. Always seemed happy enough to talk to me. He didn't always hang around in the group in the sixth form because he was going out with various girls.'

'Various girls?' Frances asked. 'Was there anyone other than Lila?'

Trent hesitated. 'Not that I know about.' He racked his memory. 'I did wonder whether there was something going on between Oli and Dub, before he got together with Lila, but he always denied it.'

Frances simply laughed. 'Who's next on the list?'

'Talking of the devil. Olivia Pearson. *Oli was always the one the boys swarmed around. I liked her although she wasn't my type. She used to be the life and soul of the party, kind of impulsive. But she really withdrew in the sixth form.*' Trent paused. It was true. Some of Oli's shine had faded and her fire had dimmed even further over the last few years. He carried on reading. '*I don't know why, and we weren't close enough for her to ever tell me. She always seemed somewhat sad.*'

'Oof,' Frances said. 'I never knew Samson paid that much attention to us all.'

Trent let that sentiment hang in the air as he moved onto the notes on Paddy. '*Patrick Wilding. He's funny. Spends most of his time making people laugh. He's the most easy-going of all of them. I hope he comes along.*'

'Samson might have been surprised by the version of Paddy that turned up,' Frances said. Which Trent had to admit, was spot on.

'What did he write about Lila?' Frances asked.

'*Lila Jain. One day she might understand the choice I made.*' Trent's mouth was dry. What did that mean?

'Read that again,' Frances said. Trent obliged and waited to see what Frances would say. She scrunched her nose. 'Do you think he liked Lila? He said Oli wasn't his type, maybe Lila was.'

'Maybe,' Trent replied. But he'd never been aware of it if that had been the case. He rubbed his temples. *The choice I made.* What choice? Trent didn't have a clue. He pulled out his camera and took a photo of the notes. 'I think I should share it with everyone. Maybe it will make sense to Lila.'

'Hold on,' Frances said. 'Do you think that's a good idea?

We don't know who's behind the Honesty Index.' She clipped in her seatbelt and switched on the engine.

'You think it could be one of us?' Trent asked, as Frances rolled the car back down the driveway.

'I don't know.' She sighed. 'I think we should wait to speak with Annabelle Jackson. She might be the key to unlocking everything. We can find out whether Samson's behind it.' Frances reversed into the empty road and slipped the car into gear.

'His notes didn't give me that impression.' He tapped his fingers on his legs. 'Although I guess he wouldn't set it all out for his mother if the Honesty Index was his secret masterplan.'

'Exactly.' She stopped at the T-junction and then pulled out into a gap in the traffic. 'But if he is behind the game, he would almost certainly use those notes to misdirect us.'

Trent was silent. He'd felt that they were getting closer to the truth with both Samson's notes and a possible discussion with Annabelle Jackson. And maybe they were. But Frances was right. He didn't know who to trust, and so it made sense not to share the notes. Not yet.

Trent settled back into the seat, watching Frances flick her gaze up to the rear-view mirror as she swung out to overtake the car in front of them. Samson's notes on Frances hadn't given anything away. He sighed to himself. Frances had suggested not sharing the notes, and he'd agreed with her. But he didn't even know whether he could trust her.

41

MANIFESTO EXTRACT 7

Some players will need more reminders than others.

#Time lapse message to Player_3

#Time to send: Round[Player_3] - 07:00

Background colour: Black

Font colour: Red

Text:

. . .

Look within yourself to find the courage to acknowledge the truth. You're next. Ready to play?

42

WEDNESDAY 10:15AM

Trent's phone started to ring as Frances was parking the car in her drive.

'It's Paddy,' Trent said. 'Do you mind if I get this?'

'Go ahead,' Frances said, putting on the hand-break and switching off the ignition.

'Hi, Paddy. I'm just getting out the car. Frances and I've just been to see Samson's mum.' With his free hand he unclipped the seatbelt and opened the door, swinging his legs out, onto the drive. Frances was opening the front door, and indicated for Trent to follow her in.

'I need to meet you.' Paddy was whispering. 'In a couple of hours.'

Trent frowned. 'Okay. Is everything okay, Paddy?'

'I'll text you the address.'

'Fine. I think we ... Hello? Hello? Paddy?'

Trent looked at the screen to see that his friend had already ended the call. Shrugging he pushed his phone into his jeans' pocket and walked into Frances' house. Paddy had seemed permanently on edge in recent weeks. In fact, the only moments that Trent could recall his friend being his old self was when they first received the invite to play the game.

Frances was wiping down the kitchen work surfaces. 'Shall I message Annabelle? See if she'll meet us this evening?' She didn't look up as she squirted the spray onto the granite.

'Don't worry. I'll do it. I've got a few days off from work,' Trent said.

'I want to meet her. Jake can look after the kids once they're back. I could make any time from five.'

Trent watched her methodically work her way around the kitchen. 'You don't need to. I'll report back.'

'She's more likely to agree to meet if I'm there, too. Single bloke, friend of Samson, probably not going to do it.'

'I wouldn't say I was his friend,' Trent said.

'Sure. Why don't you lead with that.' She moved over to clean the kitchen table.

'It might be a positive, by the sounds of things.'

Frances laughed. 'Fair enough. Still, we both met his mum, I think it makes sense for us both to meet Annabelle.'

'Sure.' Trent didn't mind Frances coming along. She was probably right, and in any event, it took some of the focus away from him. 'I'll let you know what she says.' He glanced at his watch. 'Right, I'd better get going. Paddy wants to meet.'

Frances stopped wiping and looked up at him. 'Now?'

'Yeah. He sounded stressed.'

Frances blinked a couple of times before returning to her cleaning. She was moving the cloth more vigorously and her jaw was clenched.

'I'll see myself out,' he said. He was rewarded with a perfunctory nod, as Frances rinsed the cloth in the sink, and started cleaning the hob.

As he walked towards the front door, her voice carried

from the kitchen. 'Don't forget to let me know about Annabelle.'

43

WEDNESDAY 1:05PM

The café Paddy had suggested appeared to be a popular destination with the locals and was already filling up when Trent slid onto a chair at a table for two in the back corner. A light drizzle was pushing the customers indoors notwithstanding the awning and heaters that were working hard to make the outside more appealing. He ordered himself a coffee and scanned the room. Maybe some of the customers were there for work meetings; there were as many suits as not and the three staff were flat out bringing the orders through from the kitchen out the back of the café.

Trent sipped the black coffee, savouring the bitter taste. As he drained the last mouthful he checked his phone. He'd messaged Annabelle Jackson. They needed to meet with her quickly, but he hadn't had a reply yet. Every time he heard the buzz of a notification it tore him in two. It could be Aunt Jo, Lila, or, right now, Annabelle confirming a time and a place. They were the potential positives. But the sum total of that hope was eclipsed by his fear of receiving a fresh anonymous threat. The Honesty Index wasn't going to simply fade away. It had taken less than two days from Dub's round to Oli's. Which suggested that the bell would soon be sounding for round three. Either later that day or tomorrow.

He signalled to the waiter for another cup of coffee and poured himself a glass of iced water from the jug on the table. He didn't immediately recognise Paddy when he came in. It wasn't his newfound slim line clothing range so much as the woolly hat that was pulled down low and the collar of his coat turned up. Trent watched him step into the café, glancing around like a malfunctioning radar. He sat down with his back to the entrance.

'You alright?' Trent asked, studying Paddy, trying to make sense of what he was seeing.

'Yeah,' Paddy replied as the waiter put Trent's second mug of coffee on the table. 'Ah, could I have the same please?' he asked.

'Sure thing. You guys want food?' The waiter was a young lad, holding his pad and pen and waiting for something interesting to happen. Trent ordered the café's famous number seven all day breakfast. The waiter looked at Paddy.

'Just the coffee. Thanks.' He glanced over his shoulder as if he was expecting trouble to have followed him through the door.

'What's up, Paddy?' Trent asked.

Paddy looked at him and then ducked his head down. His breathing was rapid, as if he'd run to the café. He flinched as a woman parked her pram next to their table and started to organise her stuff to sit down.

Trent's phone buzzed and Paddy stared at him, eyes wide. It was a response from Annabelle. She was happy to meet Trent and Frances. Six o'clock, that evening.

'What is it?' The tendons in Paddy's neck were stretched.

'It's nothing.' Trent bit his lip, tried to focus back on his friend. Pushed his phone back into his pocket.

'Let's go outside.' Paddy was already up and moving.

'Okay,' said Trent, as much to himself as to Paddy. He grabbed the coffee and waved to the waiter to indicate they were switching tables. There was no one else sitting outside which Trent assumed was the main attraction for Paddy. Trent had never seen him like this. Normally he'd have gone for the full English with extra laughter which he would share with the crowd. But not today.

'Better?' asked Trent once he thought that Paddy was happy with where they were sitting.

'Yeah. Sorry. I'm just, you know.' He was blinking rapidly.

'No. I don't know. What's going on.' He started to scout around. Strange how you could catch fear like a virus.

'Shit.' Paddy's shoulders were rigid.

Trent looked back towards the café and it was only then that he saw a man staring at him. The man was leaning against a post that was part of the entrance porch to the pub next door. He was squat with a mop of dark hair. There was nothing remarkable about him except that his entire focus seemed to be on Trent. And Trent had no idea who he was. The man dropped his cigarette and ground it out with his foot, his eyes still not leaving Trent. Trent looked away trying to ignore the chill between his shoulder blades. He turned back. Still looking. Damn.

There was no smile to suggest the man's interest was friendly. He pointed at Trent with one hand, two fingers stretched out and his thumb pulled back. A hand gun. Locked and loaded. And trained on Trent. And then he shifted his aim. It was subtle but the intent was clear. The crosshairs weren't focused on Trent. No, the target was painted, clear and present, on Paddy's back. The man pulled the trigger, even played out the recoil. Only then did he smile, balling his fist before exploding it high into the air. His mouth mimed the detonation. Silent. But deadly.

Paddy had opened his eyes and shifted his weight to lean on the table. 'What are you looking at?'

The man sauntered away from the pub, only averting his gaze as he started to turn the corner before disappearing out of sight. Trent's mouth was dry and he could feel his blood pumping. What the hell had that been about? 'There was a guy, over there,' he pointed towards the pub. 'He was looking at us. I think he just threatened you.'

'What did he look like?' There was an urgency in Paddy's voice as he craned his neck round to look. 'Skinhead?'

'No. He had a full head of hair.' So, Paddy knew someone was after him. Although now it seemed as though there were at least two of them.

Paddy seemed to relax slightly. But only slightly. 'Jesus.' He pulled his hat even more tightly on his head. 'I can't do this.'

'Do what, Paddy? What's going on.' Trent tried to keep part of his attention on the teenager who was now walking past, strutting along as if he owned the place. Trent didn't trust anyone right then.

'I've done something. Something stupid,' Paddy said. He placed his phone on the table, resting his hand on top of it.

The kid moved past without incident and Trent saw Paddy momentarily relax. 'Tell me, Paddy. I can help.'

'Not with this.'

'Is it the Honesty Index?'

Paddy looked as though he was concentrating on his breathing. He shrugged. 'Yes. And no.' He leant forward. His voice dropped to a whisper. 'Okay.' Another deep breath. 'Okay. One of my clients, I think they're running a scam.'

Trent stared at his friend. 'Have you told your boss?'

The vein in Paddy's temple was throbbing. 'No.' A glance over his shoulder, a pull down on his beanie hat. 'Not exactly.'

'Why not? Surely your firm has a whole procedure for dealing with that. My old law-firm did.'

Paddy said nothing but for a few seconds. When he finally spoke the words came out in a rush. 'The client employs this guy. The skinhead. He gave me the third degree when I was last on site.'

'You think he knows that you've uncovered something?'

Paddy's eyes were dark. 'No. I didn't at the time. And if he did, I think he'd have tried to deny it. To explain that they're a legitimate business. I asked some colleagues about him, back at the office. People who'd worked on the account before.' He swallowed. 'He's got a reputation. I heard a couple of things that worried me.' His voice was almost robotic, as if his soul had already left him for dead. He kept his head down.

'You haven't said anything though.'

Paddy shook his head. 'What about the game?'

Trent glanced down at his friend's phone on the table. 'You think it knows?' he asked, keeping his voice low.

'I don't know. Jesus, Trent. It knows everything. You saw what it said about Oli. And there was all that stuff for Dub. Stuff we didn't even get to see.' His voice was rising as he shuffled on his chair, his shoes scuffing the ground. 'How the hell –'

'Paddy,' Trent cut in, 'try and stay calm.' He was trying to reassure his friend but, at the same time, he was trying to make sense of what Paddy he'd just heard.

Paddy had uncovered a scam, but he hadn't followed the

usual reporting lines. He hadn't raised his suspicion at all. So why was he so on edge. It didn't make sense. Only a handful of seconds earlier a man had mimed shooting Paddy dead with a gun. A man who'd been waiting and watching. A message without words. But the message had been received. Not loud, but crystal clear.

'Is it something that the police could help with?' Trent asked.

Paddy was shaking his head. 'No. But I'm scared, Trent.' The joking, layabout schoolboy was gone, maybe forever. His face looked hollow as he scrunched his hair through his hat with his hands. 'Oh sweet Jesus.' He gestured at his phone. 'If this game...'

'Maybe it doesn't know, Paddy.' He said it softly, but Trent couldn't hear any conviction in his own voice.

'Yeah. Maybe.' He pivoted round. 'I shouldn't have come.'

Paddy seemed trapped; back where he'd made a decision and taken a wrong turn. He was far away with no way back. Trent's best friend was opposite him, sitting on death row, and Trent didn't know how to help.

'You've got to go to the police, Paddy. I'll go with you. Right now.' He locked Paddy with his gaze, tried to urge him with his tone.

But he knew his friend wouldn't do it. 'No. You can't tell anyone. I'm serious, Trent.' Paddy was starting to hyperventi-late. 'I'm going. Don't try and contact me. Shit. This was a mistake.'

The sizzle of the eggs and the smell of toast reached Trent before the waiter did, but Paddy was already standing up. The boy slid the loaded plate onto the table and placed down the cutlery wrapped in a white serviette. A breakfast Trent no longer wanted.

'Come on, Paddy. This is way too dangerous. You need help.'

But Paddy was already walking away and Trent wasn't even sure that his friend had heard him. First Dub, and now Paddy. Choosing to run, rather than face the truth.

44

WEDNESDAY 5:54PM

Trent ordered himself a beer and then found a table to seat four people. The pub was a typical weekday refuge for the suited and booted. Chatter danced around the high-ceilinged room as salacious stories of corporate London began their pandemic spread. No doubt a few more events would claim folklore status tonight. He was sitting opposite the door and was keeping track of the new arrivals.

Annabelle would be looking for a man and a woman, not a single man. He scanned the crowd. A woman stood awkwardly at the bar, glancing between her phone and the entrance as she sipped a white wine. She was wearing a black suit with matching trainers, hair in a ponytail. Average height, average build. He saw her turn towards the door before taking another sip of her drink. Definitely waiting for someone. Odds on, she was Annabelle Jackson.

'Hey, Trent.'

He'd been so intent on trying to identify Annabelle that he hadn't noticed Frances arrive. He stood up to give her a hug.

'No sign of Annabelle?' she asked.

'I think that might be her, standing at the bar.' He was about to point but the woman was already looking at them. He smiled which seemed to be the cue she was looking for.

She picked up her glass and walked over towards them. 'Frances?' She held out her hand as Frances nodded in reply. Then she turned and shook hands with Trent. 'Hello. Can I get either of you a drink?' Posh and polite.

'Oh no, I'll go. Do you want another wine?' Frances was already pulling her purse out of her bag.

'Thank you.' A smile. 'Sauvignon Blanc, please.'

She wasn't wearing any jewellery or make up. Unusual. Trent wondered whether that had attracted Samson. The unvarnished truth. She was looking directly at him, unblinking. He gestured towards the free seats and she shuffled in tight to the table as if she was about to chair a meeting.

'How was the wake?' Her dark eyes waited for his response.

'I've not been to many. Which is a good thing, I guess. There were lots of people there.' Which was about as neutral as he was able to be. 'It's good of you to meet us,' he said.

She smiled again and sipped her wine. The wait for Frances to return with the drinks was ticked off by a brief chat about her journey to the pub that evening. Frances chose the seat next to Annabelle. Solidarity sister.

'I guess we might as well get straight to the point,' Annabelle said. Frances flicked her eyes to Trent, eyebrows slightly raised as Annabelle continued. 'You said in your message that you wanted to talk about Nick.' She drained her first glass and picked up the second. 'So, what do you want to know?'

Frances cleared her throat. 'Thank you, Annabelle.' A hesitation. 'May I call you Annabelle?'

'Of course.'

'Great. I know this will be difficult but we–'

'It won't be difficult for me.' No anger. Just a matter of fact.

'Oh, right.' Frances recoiled slightly. 'That's good.'

Trent lent forward. 'Mrs Samson told us that you were engaged to Nicholas, to Nick. And that you called it off shortly before he died.' Annabelle rolled her eyes. Trent pushed on. 'His mother's obviously upset about his death. It might be helpful for her to understand what happened between you two.'

'It won't be helpful.' A slight shake of the head.

'Sorry?'

'What I'm about to tell you will make Mrs Samson feel worse, not better.' She was staring at Trent with the occasional glance sideways to Frances. 'That's why I haven't told her myself. But I'll tell you. I don't have any agenda and I've nothing to hide but it didn't seem right to tell her something that could only upset her. I imagine you'll make the same decision but,' she shrugged, 'that's up to you.'

Frances was frowning whilst Trent was trying to keep his countenance neutral.

'Nick and I were never engaged.' Trent said nothing. 'I didn't even know him that well. A friend of mine worked with him. She set us up on a blind date.' She spoke fluently, no hesitation, almost scripted. She took another sip of wine. 'The date was fine. I thought he was a little weird but he was bright and interesting and so I agreed to see him again. That was, with hindsight, a mistake.' Trent was absorbing every word. Annabelle paused and appeared to study him. 'Is there something you wanted to say?' she asked.

So, so many things. But Trent managed to shake his head. 'No. Please carry on.'

Annabelle pulled out her phone from her handbag. Trent

could see a message but couldn't read what it said. Wordlessly she slid her phone back into her bag and very deliberately reached for her wine glass to take another drink. As though she was facing an interview and needed time before answering a challenging question. She nodded before continuing. 'The second date was conclusive for me. It wasn't going to work out and I was debating how best to tell him when he announced that he was terminally ill.' She blinked and gave another slight shake of her head. 'We were in a restaurant. They'd just served the main course. He told me he had only a few more months to live. Cancer.' She shrugged. 'Turns out he was being truthful about *that.*'

Trent leant forward, unable to hold fire any longer. 'What was he lying about?'

'I'm coming to that. I agreed to a third date. I needed to give myself time, to decide what to do.' She turned towards Frances. 'I'm direct but I have a heart. On the third date I told him that I didn't want to take things any further. We could be friends but that was it. He went very quiet before telling me that he'd told his mother all about me. He said she was looking forward to meeting me. He wouldn't even look at me when he was telling me this.'

Nicholas Samson; experiences in social awkwardness. So far, so familiar. Trent waited for her to continue.

'We left the restaurant that evening. Went our separate ways. Later that night my social media accounts started going crazy.' Ice water pumped through Trent's veins. 'I was receiving all these messages of congratulations. Things like *wishing you both a very happy future together* and *can't wait to meet the lucky man.*'

'He announced your engagement online?' Frances' eyes were wide.

'Oh, he did more than that. He hacked into my Facebook

account. Changed my status to engaged. Then he posted a message from my account announcing our engagement along with a picture of the two of us, which he also posted on Instagram. That photo was a selfie that I'd taken on my phone on our first date. I hadn't even shared a copy with him.'

Frances was staring at Trent. The approach and the method were the same. Annabelle had rejected Samson and he'd punished her. And he'd used data and technology to do it.

'He hacked into your phone.' A statement, not a question. Frances was shaking her head.

'Yes, and my laptop. I've no idea how he did it.'

For the first time her head dropped, and Trent decided to push. 'The Nicholas Samson we know, we knew, liked to...' he tried to catch her gaze, '...expose people's secrets.' A pause. 'Did he threaten you, Annabelle?'

She lifted her head. 'His final message said, *you will regret it. I know people, bad people, who owe me.*' The bastard had done it to her, too. Trent took a long drink as Annabelle continued. 'Look, I'm sure Mrs Samson is a good woman but I've never met her. I barely knew her son and what I do know about him I don't like. I decided to break off all contact. Blocked him, deleted his contact details, and hoped never to hear from him again.'

You got that wish, Trent thought, but he said, 'You sent some flowers to his mother.'

'What?' She was scowling and shaking her head. 'No, I didn't. I only heard that he'd died a few days ago.'

'You didn't send flowers?' Frances asked, her brow furrowed.

'No.' Annabelle shook her head. 'This is crazy.' She pushed her chair back and stood up. 'You know, I'd hoped that meeting you would give me some level of closure on a very weird episode of my life.' She twisted a strand of hair in her fingers. 'But I wish I hadn't come.' She shivered. 'I don't ever want to have to think about him again.' And with that, she turned and walked towards the exit.

45

WEDNESDAY 6:33PM

'Bloody hell,' said Frances. Which summed it up nicely. 'Samson even ordered flowers for his own funeral and pretended to his mum that they'd been sent by his fiancée.'

'Who wasn't even his fiancée,' added Trent. 'Ironic, isn't it?'

'What do you mean?' asked Frances.

'The Honesty Index forces you to confront the truth. Do you think Samson wants us to apply the same philosophy to his mum?'

Frances exhaled loudly. 'I don't know. We should let the others know. See what they think.' She checked the time and stood up. 'Well, I'd better get going too.'

'Hey, Frances?' She stopped buttoning her coat and looked at him. 'Are you scared about your turn?' Trent wanted the comfort of hearing Frances dismiss it. He caught a flicker of sadness in her expression and then she nodded. 'Oh, sorry. I was expecting ... maybe...' He trailed off. Expecting what? Perfect marriage. Perfect children. Perfect life. He wasn't particularly close to her, but he liked her and he sure as hell respected her.

'Not because I've got anything to hide.' She smiled. 'Although I'm sure that's what we all say.'

'I intend to use it when my turn rolls around,' Trent said.

'It's just that, well, it's hard not to be scared when you look at what's happened already. I don't think I've any skeletons in my closet but...' She ran her hand over her face before continuing. 'There could be something about my husband.' She winced as she spoke the last few words.

Christ. Jake. Oli's adultery confession flashed through Trent's mind. 'You think there *is* something?' he asked, trying to keep his voice neutral.

'I don't know of anything. Not specifically.' She sighed. 'I feel bad even mentioning it. It's ridiculous.' She rubbed her eyes. Suddenly Trent could see the dark shows under her eyes, and the creases on her forehead. 'A week ago, I wouldn't have even entertained it but all this stuff makes you think.' She shrugged. 'How well do you really know anyone?'

'You've been together a long time.' Trent was treading lightly. A Chinese Shaolin monk walking on rice paper had nothing on him. 'You know him better than anyone.'

'Yeah, I know. And I do trust him, completely.' Which is where those sentences should end. But she carried on. 'It's just that everything that's happened has been so deliberate. The game knew about Dub's videos, it knew everything about Oli.' She paused, her eyes distant. 'So, I think, what's the worst that could happen to me? I haven't done anything. Not really. My kids are too young to have done anything. So, the worst thing that could happen to me is to discover that there's something involving Jake.'

'Have you spoken to him about it?'

'I've tried to, but he's very distracted with work right now and I underplayed it.' She was balling her hands now. 'I haven't really told him how I feel and I'm hesitant to. He'll think I'm accusing him of something.'

Which, Trent had to admit, was likely to be right on point. But if Frances didn't make the accusation, the game would. There was no way out unless the Honesty Index had nothing. Which the first two rounds suggested wasn't likely to be the case.

'Dub disappeared,' Trent said.

'What?' Frances did a double take.

'Dub's gone. In the middle of the night. Packed some of his stuff and vanished.'

'Did he say where's he was going.' Trent shook his head. He was about to mention Dub's theory about being bugged, but something made him hold back. 'Perhaps he has more to hide that we know about.'

'Maybe.' Trent shrugged. Would Dub feel different if he knew that Samson was behind it? It was impossible to know. Except that Dub wasn't running from anyone, he was trying to outpace the truth. 'I'm sure it'll be okay.' Why the hell had he said that? He was meant to be a friend not a wannabe relate counsellor.

'It'll be what it'll be.' Frances shrugged and turned away to end the discussion. They walked outside and Trent squinted into the dark. There was a light drizzle in the air. He reached out to hug Frances. She hesitated momentarily before resting her hand on his arm and brushing his cheek with hers. 'Speak soon, Trent,' she said.

He watched her for a few seconds, her outward composure belying the doubts she'd shared with him, before walking in the opposite direction. He turned off Fleet Street towards Embankment pulling his phone out of his pocket. He fired off a text to Dylan, asking if they could meet. His phone beeped two seconds later.

Dylan hadn't said yes or no, but she had sent an address. And it was only a fifteen-minute ride away.

46

MANIFESTO EXTRACT 8

They must choose the truth. The pain revealed by the truth is nothing as compared to being denied the freedom to choose.

#TIME LAPSE for message one of two to Trent Ryder

#TIME TO SEND: Round1 + 48:00

BACKGROUND COLOUR: black

FONT COLOUR: Red

TEXT FOR MESSAGE:

. . .

YOU MUST BE ready to burn yourself in your own flame.

47

WEDNESDAY 6:50PM

Trent stood in front of the building which had three stories and probably, given the gunmetal stairs leading down from road level, a basement. The house was faced with white stucco and thick pillars framed the vast, black front door. There was a balcony at the front of the first floor with columns reaching up to support the floor above. And it was slap bang in the middle of one of the most expensive roads in London. Totally not what he was expecting.

He double checked the address before he pressed on the doorbell and heard a chime resonate deep within the building. After a few seconds during which he visualised himself on Dylan's CCTV screen there was a buzz, followed by a click and the door swung open. He stepped into the entrance hall and reached out to touch the wooden door, pushing it gently closed behind him. The inside reflected the outside but was totally at odds with what Trent had expected of Dylan. The whole set-up dripped with opulence. He walked along the corridor staring at the artwork on the walls. He was no expert but the collection reminded him of the last Impressionist exhibition he'd seen at the National Gallery. Surely they couldn't be originals. He peered more closely before catching himself. Who was he trying to kid? Two feet or two inches distance made no difference to his appraisal – he would only ever be guessing. But whatever they were, they were way out of his price range. How could Dylan afford to live in a place like this?

'Down here.' Dylan's voice floated up from the staircase that was waiting for him at the end of the entrance hall.

He moved towards the stairs, conscious that the squeak of his trainers on the polished floor was echoing around the house. Hopefully sound couldn't damage original Old Masters. He felt for the solid wood banister that curved its way down to the basement and saw Dylan standing at the bottom. She was wearing a t-shirt, cardigan and what he was sure couldn't be, but certainly looked like, gym shorts.

'This is your house?' He could hear the shock in his own voice.

'It was my dad's.' No emotion. No expectation of any in return. 'Follow me. You'll like it downstairs.' Yeah, because the upstairs was just bricks and mortar. And the artwork was merely paint on canvas. Move right along. Nothing to see here.

He tracked along the basement corridor and followed Dylan into a room. He stopped in the doorway to take everything in. After the museum feel of the upstairs he wasn't expecting what looked like the command centre for NASA. There were multiple screens scattered around the room along with a stack of computers and similar pieces of kit.

'Jesus, what is this?' Less shock now, more awe.

Dylan didn't answer. Instead, she sat on a chair which looked oddly out of place, pulled herself towards one of the keyboards and started to type.

Trent indicated towards a seat and Dylan nodded. 'I met a woman tonight,' he said, lowering himself down.

'I don't do dating advice,' Dylan said, looking at her screen.

'Good to know,' said Trent. 'But it's relevant to the Honesty Index.' When she didn't ask why, he decided to tell her anyway. 'This whole thing started immediately after we all attended a gathering organised by a former classmate, a guy called Nicholas Samson. The woman I met tonight, Annabelle Jackson, told me that Nicholas Samson announced their fake engagement by hacking into her Facebook page.'

Dylan turned away from the computer to face him. 'Go on.' She listened intently as Trent relayed the details of Annabelle's relationship with Samson. 'And you think this friend of yours could be behind the Honesty Index?'

'Not a friend but, yes. Maybe. Although there's a problem. The gathering was his wake.' He paused before adding, 'He's dead.'

'Which is why you asked me whether the game could've been pre-programmed.' Dylan tilted her head. 'Did he hate you all that much?'

Trent had been asking himself the same question, but he still didn't have a good answer. 'I don't think he liked anyone that much.'

'The game isn't attacking just anyone.' It didn't quite sting like a rebuke, but it was close.

'No, that's true.' Trent decided to go with the only thing he had. 'The exact same group of us were invited to his sixteenth birthday party and he made us all share a secret but promise not to share them beyond the group. It was all rather awkward and teenage. But we were never really close friends. He'd hang around with us, but he never got to know any of us. Not properly' Was it that way around? Trent certainly hadn't approached Samson to strike up conversation after that night. 'But we were the only ones from school that he invited. He even made notes on us all for his mother.'

'Okay. Let's assume he had a reason to create this programme, although I'd think harder about that if I were you. Did he have the ability to do something like this? It's not hard if you're around to update it but if you're dead...' She trailed off. 'Some firms are working on large language models but we're probably still a couple of years away from the game responding appropriately without any human input.' She was talking more to herself now. 'But it doesn't permit free form inputs. It's a decision tree.' She looked at Trent.

'His mother said he worked in computers and he published some articles about data and programming.' Trent leant forward, resting his elbows on his knees. 'And his father founded a tech company called Analytic Systems. There was some scandal about its involvement in a US county election. There's a blog about it that talks about data poisoning.' He shrugged. 'It didn't mean much to me.'

'Could his father be involved?' Dylan asked, tapping on her keyboard.

Trent shook his head. 'Also dead. He died in 2013.' He sat quietly whilst Dylan flicked through different search results. She didn't stay on any page for more than a few seconds and after three minutes she delivered her verdict.

'It's possible.'

'Samson could've done all this before he died?'

'From what I've seen of the game, so far, and looking at his coding background, yes.'

Trent sat back in his seat, chewing his lip. It was progress. But even if Samson was behind the game he still needed to work out how to make it go away. He took a moment to take in the room, although computer lab would be a better description. So much expensive equipment but he was prepared to wager that Dylan was the secret weapon that money couldn't buy.

'Do you think you can hack into the game?' he asked.

She didn't immediately answer, but Trent wasn't worried. He wasn't anywhere close to being as smart as Dylan, but he did know which button to push. Because she'd as good as told him when she'd said that she *really* didn't like dead ends.

He cleared his throat. 'It's just that we appear to have reached a ... dead end.'

Dylan gave him a look that made him feel as though he was in a police interview. 'You shouldn't try and play me, Trent.'

'Sorry.' He dropped his eyes to the ground. What now?

'Yes, given time,' Dylan said.

It took Trent a second to realise that she wasn't only confirming her belief that she could hack the game but that she was offering to help him.

'Really? Are you sure? Samson was pretty smart.' The excitement had scrambled his brain. What had he said that for?

Dylan scratched her nose and looked at him hard. 'Who was the brightest kid in your school?'

Trent didn't so much as pause. 'Alexander Maton-Hill. He was a genius. Two surnames, one for each brain.'

'Well, there's Samson, there's your man, Alexander two-brains, and then there's me. Even genius has its own ranking.' Pithy. And confident. Dylan turned round in her chair. 'But are you sure you want me to? We'll discover everything the game knows. Are you sure you're ready for that?'

She hadn't explicitly mentioned his father, but Trent was sure that that was why she was asking him. He swallowed. It wouldn't just reveal his secrets. The whole Pandora's box would be opened. He sighed and thought of Paddy. He wasn't sure that he wanted to know the detail of what he was involved in but if it helped his friend then that's what he would do.

He pushed his chair back. 'Yes, I'm sure.'

His confirmation was interrupted by his phone vibrating with a new message. He blinked rapidly as his eyes registered the notification of a new message on the red and black icon. He opened the message, his breath catching in his throat. But it wasn't the announcement of the start of the next round, not yet. This was another message just to him.

48

WEDNESDAY 7:14PM

You must be ready to burn yourself in your own flame.

Trent's mind warped into slow motion. What did that mean? Was it a threat or a direct reference to his family's death? It didn't make sense and yet he knew that those words were designed to prompt a response. His face started to flush with heat.

Dylan was looking at him with concern on her face. He handed her the phone.

'It's another Nietzsche quote,' she said, passing the phone back. 'It's from Thus Spoke Zarathustra. You look very pale. Are you okay?'

'I was just thinking about the game. Isn't that enough?' And in truth, it was enough. It just wasn't the truth.

'You were thinking of the game before that message arrived. There's something else.'

Did he want to tell Dylan about the fire? He barely knew her and he guessed he would never truly know her, and yet he realised that he already trusted her implicitly. His phone buzzed for the second time. The Honesty Index hadn't finished with him yet.

Don't you want to know why your father wasn't awarded his medal?

The words were like a spark spitting at tinder and a wave of heat flooded his body. The game knew everything. Fear began to scratch inside his stomach.

But it just wasn't possible; it couldn't know. He tried to slow his thoughts, to set things out, point by point.

There was no record that it could access. Even if Nicholas Samson was behind the game he couldn't have known. He slowed his breathing. In. Hold. Out. Repeat. It took him a moment to become aware of Dylan looking at him, unblinking.

'I know about the fire,' Dylan said.

Like a punch to the face. The old one, two. The Honesty Index. *I see you.* Dylan. *I see you, too.*

He'd given her access to his phone with an instruction to learn as much about his father as she could. He shouldn't be surprised that she'd discovered something whilst doing that. Or she could have done her own search. It'd be easy enough to find the news report about the fire. So, yes, of course she'd know about the fire.

He hadn't explicitly mentioned it to her and so perhaps she was simply letting him know that he could talk about it if he wanted to. His thoughts were kaleidoscoping again.

'It must be very hard for you,' Dylan said. He hadn't been expecting that. 'I lost someone too. A few years ago, now,' she added.

Trent shook himself back into reality, opening his eyes and blinking slowly. 'Your father?' He needed to catch up. She'd never shown any sign of vulnerability before. He tried to shift his perspective to focus on Dylan rather than himself.

'No, someone who I was close to.' There was something in her eyes. Sadness, perhaps. Or regret. And also a challenge.

She hadn't been close to her father. 'Anyway. I don't know what it must be like for you but I can perhaps imagine. I will help you, Trent, but I can't control what I find.' She didn't spell out what she might discover that could hurt him but she didn't need to. Guardian Angels were like that.

He pushed out a breath and started to talk. 'I just want to know the truth. I've been trying to find out myself, but I haven't got very far.'

'Do you think that the fire was an accident?' Dylan asked.

Trent swallowed. 'I don't know. Probably. I was only thirteen when it happened and so no one told me much. Most of the discussions were with my aunt. But there was a Fire Safety Officer working alongside the police. That suggests to me that there was something unusual about it.'

'What was the Coroner's finding about the fire?' She was like a barrister cross-examining him in court.

'Accidental death.' His voice cracked as he spoke.

Two words. One a shrug, the other inescapable. Trent's atheism had been born when those two words were forced together and changed his worldview forever.

'Based on the report of the Fire Safety Officer?'

'I don't know,' he said – which was the short answer to the question.

'You must have read the report?' she asked.

'All that I could. They wouldn't release the police report.' The email denying access had been official, cold. The memory of his tears brushed his eyes. 'There must be something in it, something that they can't tell me.' And somehow the Honesty Index had uncovered it.

Dylan looked at him as if she was trying to weigh his soul. 'I'll try and hack the game. I'm not promising anything, but I'll try.'

Trent thought of his corkboard, the distillation of the

hours he'd spent pouring over what he knew about the fire. Possible reasons for being denied access to the police report. He thought of Pen, his parents, and of Freddy. Yes, he wanted to know. And he wanted to find out in his own time and on his own terms.

'Do you really think that you can do it?' he asked.

'Yes.'

Trent was getting used to her by now. If Dylan thought she could do it, then that was enough for Trent. A dull buzz forced its way into his thoughts. Dylan stared at his phone. Trent shook his head and swallowed as he lifted the screen. Please, no more Honesty Index messages. His body relaxed as he saw that the message was from Lila.

How did it go with Mrs Samson? Can you come over tonight? Lx

Trent looked up to find Dylan watching him. 'Girlfriend.' Her tone was detached, like a computer announcing a test result.

'No. She's not my girlfriend. It's not like that between us.'

Dylan frowned. 'Do you know *anything* about what you really want in life?'

Christ, what was she like? 'What happened to you not giving dating advice?' Trent thought he heard her sigh.

'Be yourself; everyone else is taken,' she said, by way of reply.

'Nietzsche?' he asked.

'No, this is a higher authority on life.' He waited for her answer.

'Oscar Wilde.'

'And it means what, exactly?'

'You know what it means.' She stood up. 'You just need to decide whether or not you want to take the advice.'

Trent was about to push for some level of clarity when his phone chimed again.

'Your not-girlfriend seems very keen to see you,' Dylan said.

Trent smiled. But the notification wasn't for a text from Lila. It was the Honesty Index and his breath caught in his throat as clicked on it and stared at the pictures swarming around his screen.

Rounds three was starting. And the name in the spotlight this time was Patrick Wilding.

49

WEDNESDAY 7:30PM

The memory of his discussion with Paddy fizzed through Trent's mind.

'It's the game,' he said to Dylan. A slight tremor pulsed in his legs. 'Paddy's turn is starting.'

Dylan reached over her desk, grabbed a cable, and threw it to him. 'Plug your phone in so we can see it on this screen,' she said.

She twisted the display slightly towards Trent and for a second the screen was black and then the Honesty Index logo filled the screen. Seconds later it had been replaced by the gallery of evidence against Paddy.

Trent caught an image of a bank statement, headed notepaper of the accountancy firm where Paddy worked and a mugshot of a male suspect. Trent didn't recognise the man but one detail sucked all the air from his body. He was bald. The guy who worked for Paddy's client; the man who Paddy's colleagues had warned him about.

Perhaps none of the evidence in isolation would be explicit in exposing any secrets but Trent now knew how the game worked. Paddy would be seeing a series of promises, each one whispering to him that the game knew the truth, that the game knew everything about him. Trent's stomach churned as he read the extract from the school report.

'Patrick would do well to not leave things so much to chance. One day his luck may change.'

Trent could believe that it was a genuine extract from Paddy's school report but out of context the words sounded like an alarm bell. Red text appeared across the top of the screen.

Whoever fights monsters should see to it that in the process he does not become a monster.

No doubt Nietzsche again. For Trent it was quotes about fire, for Paddy, the game had chosen monsters and the message was clear. Paddy was at risk of becoming whatever it was that he was fighting.

The familiar digital countdown and the 'waiting for player' message were on the screen. But then the screen shimmered, and they were looking at another document.

'He's playing,' Trent said softly. Tension crept up his back and cramped his shoulders. They were looking at what appeared to be a close up of the statement from Paddy's bank account.

10.09
Cash deposit £1,950

13.09
DD Sky Digital £27.70
Card Payment to Tesco £89.34
Cash Machine Withdrawal £500
Deposit GoPoshWash Ltd £15,750

And then the first question was appearing.

Did you use the cash withdrawal to purchase class A drugs?

Jesus. Paddy had told him he'd done something stupid. 13th of the month. Unlucky for some. If the Honesty Index had proof of that, Paddy could be looking at prison. Dylan was typing on her keyboard, but her eyes were fixed on the screen.

'Huh,' she said.

What did that mean? But Trent would have to ask her later because the second question was already visible.

Have you ever asked a client to pay your accountancy fees in cash to avoid declaring the payment in your tax return?

Was that suggestion linked to the cash deposit on the bank statement? Trent's nails dug into his palms. Paddy, what have you done? The next question blazed across the screen.

Have you slept with Olivia Pearson?

Some of the tension lifted from Trent's shoulders. Not a crime, and not exactly a secret. Trent knew that there had been a phase a few years ago. Perhaps the worst of the round was over. Paddy must have answered immediately because the next question flashed up.

Have you discovered a corporate fraud?

Trent swallowed. The game knew, just as Paddy had feared. He was clearly taking his time over deciding how to answer. Which wasn't a good sign.

'Just tell the truth, Paddy, please,' Trent muttered to himself as the next question appeared.

Have you extorted money from a client?

Was that the payment disclosed on the statement from GoPoshWash Limited. Nearly sixteen thousand pounds. GoPoshWash had to be one of his clients. The one he'd suspected of fraud. Trent froze. Paddy hadn't reported the suspected scam.

'I've done something. Something stupid.'

That's what Paddy had said. Had he tried to exploit, or steal from, his client? Was that why he was being threatened? Trent swallowed. What the hell had Paddy done?

And what would he do now? If he lied then every indication so far was that the game would expose the truth to the people who cared the most. A cast list that could feasibly include the police, Paddy's family, his employer, his professional regulator, and his client.

The red radar started tracking its way round the screen. Which meant that Paddy had rolled the dice. Trent caught himself holding his breath and gulped in some air.

The score board flicked into view.

HONESTY INDEX

80%

One incorrect answer.

The hairs on his neck stood up. Dub hadn't even played, and Oli had scored one hundred percent. Whereas Paddy had played. And lied. Which meant Trent had no idea what would happen next.

The radar didn't reappear. Instead there was more text.

REVISED HONESTY INDEX

100%.

Trent looked at Dylan, but she was focused on the screen. He turned back to see another message. Two words that chilled his soul.

Information dispatched.

50

MANIFESTO EXTRACT 9

If they can't find their way to telling the truth, the truth must find its way to them.

You reap what you sow.

#Macro to dispatch information for player 3

IF [Score<100%, P3_answers=P3_truth,null]

IF [P3_Q(x)=FALSE, exe.p3_Q(x).data,null]

#DELIVERY ADDRESS

. . .

P3_Q(4)DELIVERY_ADDRESS=1658329@LINE.COM

51

WEDNESDAY 7:42PM

Trent's shout echoed around the room. 'What information? What's happening?'

As if in response, the screen updated to reveal the answers that Paddy had given. Every question along with his answer was on display. The same as had happened with Oli.

Paddy had denied the Class A drug allegation, rejected accusations of tax fraud and, in a minor surprise, denied that he'd slept with Oli. He'd also confirmed that he had discovered a corporate fraud. All those answers had been accepted as correct.

The last question, have you extorted money from a client, he had answered no. But the answer had been revised. As Trent tried to order the information in his brain, the screen reverted to his home screen. The Honesty Index, its work done, had closed itself down.

His phone beeped. He grabbed his phone and pulled out the cable. The text was from Paddy.

I didn't lie.

Paddy was claiming that he'd told the truth, that the

Honesty Index was wrong. But Paddy had also told Trent that he'd done something stupid. And the bank statement had revealed that there was an unexplained transfer of a significant amount of money into his personal account.

Another beep announced a second text.

TeeQ.

What, or who, the hell was TeeQ? Trent had never heard the name before, either from Paddy, or from anyone else. But he was guessing it was the name of someone who you wouldn't want to be associated with. Someone like the skinhead in the mugshot.

He fumbled for Paddy's number and hit the call button. He heard the click immediately before he heard Paddy's message.

Here comes the beep you know what to do.

'Paddy. It's Trent. Call me. Let me know you're okay.' He ended the call and raked his fingers through his hair. 'Have you heard of TeeQ?' he asked Dylan.

She shook her head, her fingers dancing on her keyboard. 'Looking now.'

Trent tried Paddy's number again. He cut off the answerphone message. 'Answer your phone, Paddy,' he muttered to himself.

This must've been why he'd sounded so scared earlier. But he'd refused to say anything much to Trent. And he still hadn't confessed to the theft.

The Honesty Index hadn't done anything after Oli had correctly answered her questions, other than confirming the answers to the rest of them. She'd told the truth, and the game had left her alone. As if admitting the truth to the rest of them was punishment enough. Is that how it worked? It only cared about people telling the truth, that same truth didn't have to be broadcast to the world.

'Do you think TeeQ is linked to GoPoshWash?' he asked.

Dylan merely shrugged.

If Paddy had answered the final question truthfully the game would've left him alone. Trent was sure of that. Instead, it had punished him for lying. *Information dispatched* could only mean one thing – the client now knew that Paddy had stolen from them.

And yet, Paddy was still protesting his innocence.

Trent hit redial. Same result. He stuffed his phone in his pocket. 'I have to go,' he said. It would take him the best part of an hour to get to Paddy's house.

'Take this.' Dylan had opened a cupboard and taken something from the shelf. She handed him a slim disk the size of a five pence piece. 'It's a tracking device. Slip it under the innersole in your shoe. You won't even feel it and at least that way I can see where you are.'

'Why not just use my phone?' he asked as he slipped off his shoe and pushed the disk in place.

'If trouble is waiting for you then they'll take your phone.' Trent didn't much like the easy assumption that he might be heading towards trouble, but he knew it was a realistic assessment. 'Do you want me to come with you?' Dylan asked.

Trent looked at her small fame swamped by the cardigan. He'd never make the mistake of underestimating Dylan Steele but he couldn't help but feel that she was most powerful when she was hooked up to technology. 'Thanks, but it might be better to have you here. I'll stay in touch. Hopefully he's safely locked up at home.'

And keeping that thought close, Trent set off to Paddy's house.

52

WEDNESDAY 8:00PM

Lila dried herself with the towel and wrapped it round her body. She slipped on a fluffy dressing gown and reached for the cup of hot chocolate that she'd left next to the shower. She took a sip. Still warm. Just about. She rolled her neck and walked through to the bedroom. She grown used to her new place. Amazing how quickly a place could feel like home.

She sat on the side of her bed and picked up her phone from the chest of drawers where it was charging. Her arms tensed as she saw the notification. She opened the app but there was no new message. Which meant that a new round had been played.

Her arms were shaking as she plugged in her headphones and clicked on the missed call from Trent.

'Lila? Are you okay?' Trent was speaking fast. It was a bad line and it sounded as though he was on his motorbike.

'Yes. I've just seen it. Who was it? What happened?' she asked.

'Paddy. He lied about ... don't know where he is. I'm on my...' His words faded out. '...information dispatched...'

She listened intently, trying to decipher the response. Paddy had lied and the game had released details of Paddy's secrets. Her mouth was dry. 'I can't hear you very well. Trent?' She waited. 'Trent?' She sighed and looked at her phone. The call had dropped. She immediately hit redial but the call didn't connect.

She tried Dub. *This number is not reachable or is switched off. Please try later.*

She flicked through her contacts and called Frances.

The answer was immediate. 'Hi, Lila.'

'Hey. I was just talking to Trent, but we got cut off. Did you see–'

'Yes. I've saw it.' Frances sounded composed. 'I've tried calling Paddy, but he's not answering.'

'Trent's on his way over there, now, I think. I tried Dub, too. But his phone is switched off.'

'Dub disappeared,' Frances said. 'Packed his stuff and left Trent's house in the middle of the night.'

Lila didn't say anything for a moment. Then she swallowed and took a breath. 'Trent didn't tell me.' She could hear a slight note of petulance in her own voice. 'Not that he needs too,' she added. 'It's just, well, I thought he might've mentioned it. Considering we're all involved in this thing.' Frances didn't offer any comment and Lila pulled the belt on her dressing gown tight. 'What happened, in Paddy's round?' she asked. 'I missed it.'

'It looks like he extorted money from a client. He denied it, but the game corrected his answer. Then it said *information dispatched.*'

'Jesus.'

'Yeah. I'm guessing the police or his employer will have been sent the details.'

'What should we do?' There was a pause, and for a moment Lila wasn't sure that Frances was going to answer.

'I think we should wait and see whether Trent finds him. I'll let you know if I hear anything.'

There was a soft click as Frances ended the call.

53

WEDNESDAY 8:38PM

The rain had stopped but the pavements were still wet and water was dripping off the shop awnings. Headlights danced amongst the puddles as cars made their way along the road. Trent locked up his motorbike and then took a left into a smaller road – quiet, dark and one way. He pushed away the hollow laughter of the metaphor. None of the cars followed him and he walked on. He looked around again to check if he was being watched. But there was no one. His phone buzzed in his pocket.

'Hi, Dylan.'

'I've got something on TeeQ.' There was a pause just long enough for fear to squeeze itself into his chest before she carried on. 'I think you should call the police.'

Trent moved the phone away from his ear. He peered into the darkness and flinched as a nearby car blasted its horn. He wiped his mouth with his hand before re-engaging with the conversation. 'Why?' The question came out as a croak.

'He's involved in organised crime. There's nothing explicit about who he is or what he's done but I've seen enough to know that he's dangerous.'

Trent's heart rate edged up. Paddy had heard disturbing stories of the man connected with his client. And Paddy had been scared. Very scared. 'I'm already here,' he said, keeping his voice low. 'Call the police and give them the address. But if Paddy's in danger. I can't wait.'

He ended the call and stood still. The silence closed in on him and he caught the whiff of a cigarette before he spotted the spiral of smoke. A young woman was smoking whilst sitting on her front step. Her free hand flicked like a metronome on her phone. Trent crossed over to the right-hand-side of the road and stopped in front of Paddy's house. There were no lights on inside the semi-detached building. Either Paddy wasn't home, or he was hiding.

Trent took a short, sharp breath and then stepped forward and pushed the front door. It swung open. Odd. Trent zipped up his leather jacket and turned around, eyes scanning the street. The smoker had gone back inside and he couldn't see anyone else but someone could easily be standing in the dark watching him. He shivered. His head started to throb as if beating out a warning but he made himself move. He stepped into the house and heard a subtle click. He froze, listening intently.

'Hello.' The word stuck in his throat; caught between a shout and a more casual enquiry. He tried again. 'Anyone there? Paddy? It's Trent.'

There was no response. He thought the sound had come from the back of the house and so he edged along the hall-way, body tensed. He hadn't been here for a few months. It always surprised him how clean Paddy's house was. Every-thing had its place and every room had a sense of being finished. Trent peered into the lounge off to the right bracing himself to come face to face with an assailant. There was no one there. Same story with the dining room. The door up ahead led into the kitchen. It was ajar and Trent crept towards it. He nudged the door open with his foot and flinched as the hinges creaked. He moved into the room, looking around. Nothing.

He could hear blood pulsing in his ears. He turned to go upstairs when a scuffing sound made him twist back. He ran over to the back door. It was open. *Jesus*. Either Paddy had slipped out or someone else had. He spun round and sprinted to the stairs, calling out Paddy's name as he took two steps at a time. He powered left into the office. No luck. He moved the other way, trying the main bedroom next. Where the hell was he? He checked in the spare room and then he pushed the bathroom door. It juddered to a halt. Something was blocking it.

'Paddy? Is that you?' Trent called as he pushed the door again. His heart was pounding. He was sure there was a body lying on the floor of the bathroom. 'Paddy,' his voice cracked as he shouted. He heard a groan. A good sign. A groan meant life.

He craned his head around the door to see Paddy's feet blocking the door. Trent grabbed the handle and with a shove he succeeded in shifting Paddy's legs enough for him to be able to squeeze through into the bathroom. Paddy was slumped against the bath, eyes open but unfocused. There was blood on his face next to his left ear.

'Jesus, Paddy. What the hell happened?' Trent was next to him within seconds. Close enough then to hear a soft moan. 'What happened?' Trent whispered again.

Paddy's eyes closed as Trent grabbed his wrist and felt for a pulse. It was faint and slow. But reassuringly regular. He checked over his friend's head, neck, and chest, but there were no visible wounds to explain the blood under the ear. All in all, he didn't seem in a bad way, other than he didn't look to be in a good way. Trent pulled a hand towel from the radiator and turned to the wash basin. 'I've got a wet towel, Paddy. I'm just going to wipe your face. It'll make you feel better.'

Paddy's spaced-out eyes seemed to struggle to register where he was or what was going on.

'Talk to me, Paddy.'

Paddy pulled himself into a more upright sitting position, still using the bath for support and began to gently rotate his neck. 'Where are we?' His words were slurred.

'In your bathroom,' Trent answered.

'What time is it?' Paddy asked. He focused his eyes at Trent, blinking rapidly. 'I feel very strange. What happened to me?'

'It's Wednesday night.' Trent chose to answer the easy question. Paddy was talking but Trent couldn't make any sense of what he was trying to say. Paddy started to scratch his neck. 'We need to get you to a hospital,' said Trent. 'The police should be on their way.'

Paddy didn't react other than to close his eyes and to redouble his efforts at scratching. He clawed with his hand and Trent could see the red and white tracks on his skin as his nails dug in. Backwards and forwards. Backwards and forwards. Trent gently pulled his friend's hand off his neck. 'Steady on, Paddy.'

Paddy's head lolled before snapping up again with his eyes wide open. 'I need to make a call.' Paddy fumbled in his pocket but only succeeded in dropping his phone on the floor.

Trent reached down to pick it up and then he very deliberately held on to it. Paddy had downloaded the Honesty Index in a moment of drunken enthusiasm, and now he was a target for organised crime gang. Trent's eyes darted around. Were they being watched? Did they know that he was here?

He stood up and looked out of the bathroom window. Paddy's rear garden was small and it was also pitch black. They needed to get out. Now. He reached out to grab Paddy's hand and froze. His brain switched to long play mode. He knew what he was looking at but there was something wrong.

A hand should have five fingers.

Trent's skin stretched tight under his eyes. Two of Paddy's fingers were missing.

54

WEDNESDAY 8:49PM

Trent gagged, turning to lean over the wash basin. He closed his eyes as he retched again, the image of the two stubs taunting him. His heart was hammering. Paddy had slumped back against the bath, his eyes starting to close. *Jesus, no.* Paddy was totally out of it, oblivious to having had two of his fingers hacked off.

Trent calmed himself sufficiently to call for an ambulance before he prepared to get Paddy downstairs. Something on the floor, near the toilet cistern, caught his eye. Trent squatted down to take a closer look and then spun away, gasping for air. Paddy's severed fingers. *Christ.* Averting his eyes he used the damp towel to pick up the two fingers. He left Paddy resting against the bath as he ran downstairs to the kitchen. He snatched open the freezer door. In the second drawer he found a bag of peas. He ripped them open, pouring some into the sink to make some room in the packet. Gritting his teeth he pushed the severed fingers into the centre of the frozen bag and twisted the top round as he moved into the hall. He grabbed Paddy's coat from the hook it was hanging on in the hallway and stuffed the package into the coat pocket.

When he was back in the bathroom, he set his jaw and pulled the coat around his friend before sliding his shoulder under Paddy's arm, being careful not to touch the hand with severed fingers and walked him towards the door. It was hard work with Paddy barely able to keep himself upright but a few grunts later they were at the front door.

The blue flashing lights had caught the attention of some of Paddy's neighbours who were standing watching from their driveways as the paramedics moved quickly to take over from Trent in getting Paddy to the ambulance.

'What happened?' asked a paramedic with a round face that was fringed with a neat, dark beard.

'I don't know,' Trent said. 'I found him in the bathroom with two fingers missing.' He climbed into the ambulance and clicked in his seatbelt. Paddy's phone buzzed in his pocket. He took it out but the screen lock had kicked in. Trent turned to ask Paddy to unlock it but his friend was asleep. All he needed was Paddy's finger to release the phone.

Trent closed his eyes and counted to ten.

55

WEDNESDAY 11:10PM

Trent studied the scene through the window of the ward door. Visiting time was over but two uniformed police officers were standing next to the last bed, currently occupied by Patrick Wilding. Trent was on the phone to Lila.

Time had crawled since they'd arrived at the hospital. Close to two hours after being seen by the triage nurse the doctor had finally examined Paddy, using a microscope to examine the severed fingers and his hand.

'They've operated to try and reattach his fingers,' Trent said. 'They sounded hopeful that it'd work. Right now he's drugged up to the eyeballs.' Trent could no longer see Paddy due to the police wall. He felt hollow, as if the adrenaline had mined out his body.

'I can't believe they did that to him.' Lila's voice sounded brittle. 'That someone is capable of doing that.'

'Yeah, I know,' Trent agreed. 'I think the client he stole from has connections to organised crime. A guy called TeeQ.'

Lila was silent for a moment. 'How do you know that?'

Trent relayed Paddy telling him that he'd discovered his

client running a fraud and the client's enforcer's reputation. 'And he texted me, immediately after his round ended. He said he didn't lie.'

'About extorting money from his client?'

'I guess so,' Trent replied. 'That was the only answer that the game changed. His second text just said, TeeQ.'

'Do you think the game could be wrong?' she asked.

'I don't know. Maybe.' He thought for a moment. 'After Oli's round, I expected Paddy to tell the truth. Logically, that was the safest thing to do. And I think he did tell the truth.'

'But why would the game think he was lying?'

'Good question.' Trent sighed. 'There must be another reason for that transfer to Paddy's account. It looks bad, but perhaps there's more to it.'

'Or, Paddy was lying. And he still is,' Lila said. But she didn't sound convinced, and it was, Trent had to admit, definitely a possibility. 'Has he said anything to you?'

'No. I couldn't get any sense out of him.' He took a deep breath. A nurse caught his eye through the glass door and he turned so he was facing away from the ward. 'The police are here now but I imagine they'll have to come back tomorrow to interview Paddy. They've already spoken to me.' He winced slightly as he pushed on. He hadn't mentioned the Honesty Index to the police. 'Paddy was totally out of it when I found him. I think they drugged him before slicing his fingers off.'

Lila said something but Trent was staring at Paddy. Trent doubted that the police would be getting anything at all from his friend. He'd already challenged to tell the truth by the Honesty Index and frankly, right now, the police were looking like a much less scary proposition.

'Trent?' Lila asked.

'Sorry. I was miles away.'

‘I asked whether you can you come over, after you leave the hospital? I won’t be able to sleep. I feel really unsettled.’

One of the nurses was heading over towards him. It had been a very long day but Trent’s brain was fizzing. There was no way he could simply go home and sleep right now either. ‘Sure. I need to go now but I’ll be over as soon as I can.’ Ending the call, he pushed his phone into his pocket and looked at the nurse.

‘I’m afraid visiting time ended a while ago.’

The nurse looked shattered, and she was probably just starting her shift. She smiled at him and Trent couldn’t help but think that if it wasn’t for the fact that empathy was her second nature, even smiling would have been too much effort. She turned away to face whatever challenges God would choose to throw at her that night. The police had stepped away from the bed and were chatting with the Sister. Paddy still had his eyes closed. Perhaps the world looked better that way.

Trent made his way out of the hospital. His motorbike was still at Paddy’s house and he didn’t fancy leaving it overnight so he tapped on his phone to order an Uber to take him to collect it. He slipped his hands into the pockets of his leather jacket. It was cold and there was still a drizzle in the air. It’d be a while before he’d make it to Lila’s.

Information dispatched.

That’d been the instantaneous response from the game to Paddy lying. Samson had coded an algorithm and there was no room for reflection. It was as simple as, if he lies, release the truth. There was no appeal process, no ability to provide further context. It was a blunt instrument.

If Samson was still alive, they could argue and maybe even reason with him. But that wasn’t available to them. Because he was dead, there was, ironically, no one to flick the kill switch. The game would just do what it had been programmed to do.

Trent was now increasingly certain that Nicholas Samson was behind it, although he didn't know what he'd planned next. But he was sure of one thing. They were each going to have to face the game.

Six players.

Three down, three still to face the music.

Including him.

56

WEDNESDAY, 11:27PM

Pen answered the phone with a yawn. 'I was asleep, Trent. I hope it's important. My Thursdays are always intense.'

'I'm sorry.' Trent checked his watch. 'I lost track of time. I hadn't realised it was so late. I'll call you tomorrow.'

'You heard what I just said about Thursdays, right?' More of a tease than a rebuke.

'Sorry. Yeah. Tomorrow evening?'

He heard her yawn again down the phone. 'It's okay. I'm awake now. So, fire away.' They both paused. 'Sorry, poor choice of words. What's up?'

'I still haven't heard from Aunt Jo.'

'That's odd. What about the app. Have you had any more messages?'

Trent shivered. He was conscious that he'd already asked her to carry a heavy burden. 'No,' he heard himself say. 'But I've got someone who's helping me.' He paused. 'I think it might have something to do with Nicholas Samson.' Trent sighed. 'I know it doesn't make much sense. But he was a weird kid. Into secrets and, I don't know, manipulation I guess.'

'And what, he sent you a delayed message before he died?'

Trent massaged his temple. 'Yes. Effectively.'

'Pretty hard to ask him straight up, I guess.' She sounded distracted, as if she was still processing. 'There was something strange about him. I can't remember what it was. Something about computers.'

Trent's shoulders tensed. 'He worked for his dad's technology firm. His dad died in a plane crash, three years after he left school.'

'I remember that.' She paused. 'Oh, hold on. That's it. A teacher at school was subjected to a trolling campaign. All sorts of allegations were anonymously posted on social media. Spying on the changing rooms, taking inappropriate pictures.' Trent felt a tingle at the base of his neck. He waited for Pen to carry on. 'Samson was interviewed by the police. No action was taken against him, but everyone knew he was a suspect.'

'Was it him?'

'No one knows. The police didn't charge him. But in the court of the school yard, yes, he was guilty. But then his dad died, and it all went quiet.' Trent was silent for a moment. 'Are you still there?' Pen asked.

'Yeah, I'm still here.' He swallowed. 'Thanks, Pen. I'll call you again, soon.'

Nicholas Samson had form. Back then it was social media. And he'd done the same with Annabelle Jackson.

The weight of evidence was building. Nicholas Samson had to be behind the Honesty Index. Now Trent just had to work out how to stop it.

57

THURSDAY 12:33AM

Lila was dressed in pale blue pyjama trousers and a baggy white t-shirt. She took a step towards Trent and embraced him. Her hair was damp and he could still feel the water on his skin after she released him. He followed her to the living room where he settled on one of the sofas as she poured them both a glass of wine before sitting next to him. Music was playing in the background. He recognised the hypnotic guitar riff. One of their shared favourite songs, Teenage Riot.

'I can't believe it,' Lila said. 'Poor Paddy. I guess...' she trailed off.

Trent knew what she was going to say. *It could have been worse.* Was that where they had got to? He remembered their laughter when Paddy had downloaded the game and given Dub a hard time for not joining in. Now Paddy was in hospital having suffered a brutal assault. And Dub was in the wind. 'I don't know,' he sighed. 'I never thought that Samson would escalate things to this level.'

'Samson?' Lila asked.

'Yeah.' He'd dropped his theory without thinking.

'There's a lot I need to tell you.' He recounted the meeting with Annabelle Jackson, her tale of Nicholas Samson's one-sided engagement and finished with Samson's vow of revenge.

'You think he set this all up before he died?' Lila asked. 'Is that even possible?'

'Yeah, I think it is.' But Trent didn't know why Samson had waited until after his death to release the app. A thought wormed its way into his mind. He raked his fingers through his hair as he tried to recall Paddy's round. He played it back in his mind. The first question.

Did you use the cash withdrawal to purchase class A drugs?

Dylan had reacted with 'huh' the moment she'd read it. It was as if the question had changed her view. Or, perhaps not the question, but Paddy's bank statement.

'What's wrong, Trent?' Lila rubbed her fingers against her temples.

Trent tried to visualise the statement. He was missing something. Transactions. Amounts. Dates. And then it hit him. 'Damn.'

'What?' Lila asked.

'Paddy's first question included a copy of his bank statement.' He was spelling it out for himself as much as for Lila.

'Yes, you told me that before.'

'Okay, well, there was a cash withdraw of five hundred pounds.' He blinked.

'Which is unusual, but not incriminating,' Lila replied.

Trent was trying to remember the details. What the hell had the date been? He thought it was September. Yes. He was sure that was right. But what day? And then he remembered – unlucky for some. The 13th.' He felt a weight crush down on him. 'I'm not sure, but I think the date of the cash withdrawal was after Samson's death.'

Lila hesitated. 'But that ... Could the game do that by itself?' she asked.

Trent was already following that line of thought. Samson couldn't possibly have foreseen that and arranged for the game to access a bank statement of Paddy's that was issued after his death. Trent leant back into the sofa. If he'd understood Dylan's tech lesson properly, the game couldn't react to unforeseen events. It was all pre-programmed. His image of Samson in the dock began to crumble.

Everything he'd learnt had put Samson in the frame. The prosecution had rested. And then this. It couldn't be Samson, because whoever had arranged Paddy's round had to be alive after the final date on the bank statement.

But there was so much that pointed towards Samson. An idea began to spin its web in Trent's mind.

He blew out a breath. 'If Samson was still alive, I'd be convinced it was him.' He shuffled forward. 'Do you think he could have organised it and arranged for someone to help him?'

'I guess it's possible.' Lila replied. 'Everything you've told me points to him being behind it. But who would want to help him?'

Trent let the idea soak in. It did seem like the most likely answer albeit one that felt like sliding all the way down a snake after having scrambled up some ladders. 'I don't know. Do you have anyone in mind because I'm back to square one on this.'

Lila shook her head. 'Perhaps we need to go back to why they might be doing this. That has to be the key. If it's Samson's idea then it must be something to do with the night of his birthday party. It has to be. That's the only thing that really connects us all to him.'

'Maybe, but I've been through that before and there's

nothing obvious.' Trent thought of his list of motives and the names of all his friends. Plenty of potential ammunition but nothing obvious as to why anyone would have the group in their crosshairs.

Lila reached out and grabbed his arm. 'Let's go through the secrets together. Most likely it was Samson's secret. Perhaps someone broke his trust about the story he told about his father. Or maybe there was more to it than that and someone shared the secret without realising the impact it would have on him.'

Trent sighed. 'I just don't see what it could be.'

Lila rubbed her hand up and down his arm. 'Just keep an open mind. The answer has to be there somewhere.'

She was right. Dylan had also told him to think harder about the reason why Samson would go to all this trouble. Lila released his arm and topped up her wine glass. 'Let's run through them. Maybe we'll spot something that you've missed.'

'Okay.' He drained the last of his wine and reached forward to put down the glass. He twisted to face Lila. 'Let's start with your secret. The *not very much* older man. Maybe Dub was so upset that you split up with him that he framed himself,' he paused, 'no pun intended, and he's working up to punishing you.'

Lila raised her eyebrows, just not in the way Trent often dreamt about.

'We can rule that one out.'

'Why?'

Lila pushed back her hair and took a second to compose herself. 'Dub finished with me.'

A jolt of electricity shot through Trent. *Jesus, Dub had been the one to end it.* Lila caught his expression and folded her legs up in front of her. Her hair fell over her face as she rested her head on her knees. 'I know. Neither of us ever told anyone. It was generous of him really. People assumed I'd finished with him.'

'Okay.' Trent coughed. *Guilty as charged.* 'So, it's not your secret. Who's next? How about Paddy?' he said.

Lila laughed. 'Yeah, I don't think so.'

She was right. Hard to imagine Paddy would have minded his favourite story of his private time being interrupted by his dad spreading more widely. Trent wasn't even sure it was true. He'd probably only said it to make people laugh in the first place. A stark contrast with the current Paddy.

Trent pushed on. 'Frances' story was about her dad's secret stash of adult magazines but I can't see it being that either. On the face of it, Dub's story is the most likely. A dead body by the river. Certainly, if it really was a murder. But there's no evidence of that.'

'We should check it,' said Lila. 'We could check on the internet. Do another trawl for any local newspaper articles around that time.'

'Nah,' Trent said, shaking his head. 'It's most likely that the dead body he thought he saw was just someone sleeping off a hangover. Even if it was something more serious than that, he hadn't actually revealed anyone's secret. As far as we know.' Trent just couldn't see how it could've resulted in Dub feeling he'd been betrayed. 'I can't remember Oli's secret,' he added.

'What was Oli's?' Lila stared at the floor for inspiration which must have done the trick as she immediately jerked her head back up. 'Oh yes. She told us her best birthday present was the sex she'd had.'

There was something in Lila's tone that was off. She hadn't always been Olivia's greatest fan. Maybe that was all it was. The silence stretched.

The only secret that they hadn't discussed was Trent's because he hadn't shared one. The knot in his stomach pulled tighter making it hard to breathe. He tried to fight it but it was hopeless. He was already travelling back in time to the day of the fire.

His skin sears as the blasts of heat push him backwards. Flames dance around the door frame. Smoke stings his eyes and invades his lungs. He stumbles forward and falls as the stairs behind him crash to the floor. His head jars and his vision blurs. He starts to lift himself from the carpet, fixing his eyes on his brother's bedroom door. Please Freddy. Wake up. Get out. Live. *Pushes himself up to his knees. Just a few more metres. Energy seeping away. Another half step.*

He lunges at the door, falls again. He drags himself into Freddy's room. The smoke is thick. He can't see. Only a small shape. On the bed. Asleep. Flames kissing his baby brother. And then he feel weightless. So light. Is this it? Is he being taken by heaven? He closes his eyes...

'Trent?' The heat receded as if Lila's voice had doused the flames.

He opened his eyes, but he didn't trust himself to speak.

Lila was staring at him, scanning his face. 'Sometimes it helps to talk about things.' She tilted her head. 'It's something I'm working on myself. Trying to be better at facing up to things. Decisions I've made.' She leant towards him. 'I know it's hard. Especially for you.'

Trent forced out a breath.

'Look, it's fine if you don't want to share it with me,' Lila said. 'But it's clear that something is eating you inside. Have you tried speaking to Pen about it?'

He shook his head. 'We don't share everything like we use to.' He saw Lila's eyebrows rise but it was true. In their discussions in the park, after the fire, Trent and Pen had spoken for hours about everything and nothing. But a slight distance had grown between them with age. Of course, he'd told her about the anonymous messages about their father but, even then, he'd held back the full details. He sighed. Maybe Lila was right; he should talk to Pen about the night of the fire, about the batteries.

'I'm sorry I didn't reply to your messages.' He almost caught himself off balance with the abrupt change of topic. Perhaps his subconscious knew that was the only way he'd ever be able to talk about the reason he froze her out. It was like rolling the stone away from the entrance to the tomb. Who the hell knew what they'd find inside but maybe something would be born again. He tensed as she stretched out her hand, laced it with his and squeezed.

Lila blinked. Twice. Maybe the first was in response to him not talking about the night of the fire. And the second, for finally opening up about their transatlantic relationship.

'I won't pretend that it didn't hurt,' Lila said.

Her words sliced at his heart. At the time it'd felt like the only way to protect himself. Lila had been his world. Even when she was with Dub, their relationship had an importance all of its own. Unassailable. Until she told him she was leaving.

Only with the clarity that distance brought could he now see that she'd been holding back, and yet needing him to step forward. At the time her rejection had smacked him around the face, turned him around and pushed him away. And his immaturity had turned it into a narrative all about him. The belated realisation that she'd needed him more than ever when she'd chosen to be apart from him, and that he had spurned her, burnt him deeply.

'I assumed that it was because of the fire.' Her hand was cool, her skin soft.

He shook his head because he didn't trust himself to speak. He sucked a breath in slowly, trying to keep it smooth. Counted to four. Now to let it flow out. Jag. Jag. Jag. Lila's hand brushed against his cheek.

Before she'd left he'd wanted to confide everything in her. Lock, stock, and two smoke-alarm batteries. And then she'd moved abroad, without the time to explain. For either of them. All their conversations – their *big* conversations – had been face to face, and so their relationship, starved of the physical presence it needed, had hermetically sealed. But without proper care the seal of a vacuum can crack and things seep inside. Things such as fear, uncertainty, and doubt. Especially after his transitory girlfriend had vetoed him from messaging Lila. So their silence had ceased to act as a pause button and had become something in its own right. Their shared silence became their long-distance relationship. And Trent knew that the only thing that could reverse that was for them to be back together.

'I'm sorry.' His voice was scratchy. 'I was angry. I felt as though you were rejecting me by leaving.' Lila rested her head on his shoulder as he continued. 'I behaved so poorly, and the longer I left it, the harder it became to make contact. I wish I'd been more mature.'

It made it easier not to be looking at her as he spoke, but his body jerked when Lila whispered, 'It's okay.'

He wanted to stay there forever, breathing in the scent of her hair with their fingers entwined. The playlist kicked round to the next track and the electro beat of The KLF's

What Time Is Love? pounded into the room. Neither said anything. It was enough, for the moment, just to be together. They stayed sitting there, reborn in the silence, until Trent felt himself starting to drift off. He fought to rouse himself.

'It's late. I'd better get going home,' he said but he didn't move. He didn't want to.

Lila paused before she replied. 'You can stay.' He waited for her to continue. 'I've only got one bed, but it's a double.'

'I'll sleep on the floor,' he heard himself reply. *So, he was staying.*

'Let's both sleep in the bed. We've done it before.'

He remembered that night, all those years ago, when he hadn't wanted to be alone, and Pen was staying with a friend for a sleepover. Lila had slipped out of her own home late that evening and had come over to stay the night with him, curled up in his bed with her arms around him. They were fifteen. She'd climbed out of his bedroom window early in the morning and was back in her own bed before Trent's aunt or Lila's parents had a chance to suspect anything.

Trent never told anyone, because he knew he wouldn't be able to control his anger if anyone, and of course at fifteen it would've been everyone, made a sly suggestion that they'd only spend the night together for one reason. Nudge, nudge. Wink, wink. Smack. Smack. Smack.

He knew it would be the same tonight. Knew he'd tell nobody.

'Okay,' he said quietly.

HE HEARD the latch on the bathroom and caught his breath as Lila Jain walked into the bedroom. She was wearing ... well, it didn't matter. She'd removed her makeup. He looked at her.

Doing nothing, other than proving that heaven was a place on earth.

'You alright, Trent?' He was sliding further. Falling harder. 'I'm cold,' she said as she pulled back the cover from the bed and shuffled under the duvet, pulling the pillow down so she could rest her head. She was lying on her back, looking at the ceiling, whilst he was standing on the edge of the universe, staring at the sun.

'Trent,' Lila said softly, 'come to bed.'

58

THURSDAY 7:21AM

Trent and Lila hadn't spoken since they'd woken up that morning. Nothing about what'd happened the previous night. Or more accurately, not happened. Not one word about the fact that they'd simply slept beside each other, and that it had felt like the most natural thing in the world.

Trent pulled on his clothes as Lila watched him from the bed.

'Hey, I hope Pen manages to get Bobby G to change his plans for tomorrow,' Lila said.

Trent nodded. 'Yeah, me too.'

Bobby, Bobby, Bobby G. I don't much like him; he don't much like me.

He walked over to sit on the edge of the bed, reaching out to stroke her hair and she took his hand and kissed it before resting her head back on the pillow. If this was to be the way that it would always be then he'd have no complaints. 'Thank you,' he whispered as her eyes closed.

He wanted to stay. For a few short hours he had sheltered

from the storm but the Honesty Index was still out there and it was coming for him. And for Lila. He was going to do whatever he had to to stop it, starting with a visit to Oli.

59

THURSDAY 8:35AM

The crisp morning air had chilled Trent's face on the ride over to Oli's. He worked his jaw to try and recover some feeling. He could do with a hot drink but he wasn't even sure Oli was still living at this address and she certainly hadn't invited him over. Which might explain why she wasn't answering the doorbell.

He leant on it again, keeping an eye on the windows to see whether she would peer out. After a few seconds he let go and bent down to look through the letter box. He poked his fingers through to move the brushes that blocked his view on the other side but even so he couldn't see any sign of anyone being in. He turned and sat down on the step. It was cold but he had no choice. He'd wait.

It was twenty minutes later when he saw Oli walking along the road. She had headphones on, with her head hunched down over her phone as she autopiloted into her drive. Trent stared. Her usually flowing hair was pulled back in a severe bun. She was pale but not in her usual alabaster model skin type way. Her eyes were sunken. But the real break with Oli's reality was her clothes. Not that Trent cared but he knew Oli did. That's part of what made Oli, Oli. Well, no longer it seemed. Her jeans were an ode to baggy and she must have chosen the t-shirt based on its windsock properties. It swamped her and left Trent feeling that she had pivoted from wanting to be constantly noticed and admired to wishing she could simply disappear.

Her eyes narrowed and her jaw tightened when she spotted him. She pulled on the white cables and the earbuds fell from her ears. She already had the key in her hand as she stepped past him and went to open the door. 'Didn't I make myself clear?'

'I wanted to talk to you.' Trent stood up, ready to block the door from closing on him if he had to.

The hinges creaked as Oli stepped into her hall and turned to face Trent with her hand on the door. She shook her head and, this time, it wasn't to allow people to admire the shimmer in her hair. 'There's nothing to say, Trent. I've made my mistakes. Now I'm trying to get on with my life. I can do that without your help.'

'Just talk to me, Oli. Please,' he said.

Emotions flicked over her face as if Trent had pulled the handle on a one-armed bandit. He waited for the final display and was rewarded with a slight nod of the head. She checked up and down her road and then reached out to take his phone. Puzzled he watched as she switched it off and handed it back to him before walking into her house, leaving the door open behind her. He recalled Dub putting their phones in the kitchen drawer before talking about the Honesty Index. Oli was following a similar game plan.

He'd never been inside Oli's house. He stepped over a pile of unopened post and the collection of shoes strewn on the floor. He'd expected her home to be immaculate – like Oli herself – but it wasn't. Had it always been like that or was that too a recent shift?

It was dark inside because the curtains were pulled shut and the blinds were down. He followed her into the kitchen. Unwashed plates, bowls, cutlery, and pans sat on the side and had spilled over to the small table where he assumed she must sit to eat. One bowl was still full of snap, crackle and pop, the spoon ready and waiting to go. A collection of unemptied shopping bags stood bunched together between the wall and the fridge.

'Skip breakfast this morning?' he asked.

Oli shrugged. 'Wasn't hungry.'

She didn't offer him a drink. Just as well. It would have taken all morning to find a clean cup.

'I want to talk about the Honesty Index,' said Trent.

'Well, I don't.'

'Look, I'm not interested in your secrets, your politics, your shopping habits or your sex life.'

'And yet you list those specific things,' she replied, turning to look out of the kitchen window.

Touché. 'I want to find out who's behind this. I want to stop them before...' he trailed off, already too far down the wrong path.

'Before what, Trent? Before someone you like gets hurt? Like you. Or the lovely Lila. Give me a break. Why should I help?' Before he could answer she spun back round. 'And have you considered that it could still get worse for me?'

He balled his hands. 'What do you mean?'

'I mean, this thing is just warming up.'

Trent forced his jaws shut. Oli was staring at him. Daring him to ask. *You've got worse secrets?* He dropped her gaze. Dub had told him straight out that he still had a hidden secret and Oli had now hinted at the same thing.

'I'm on my own, Trent. My secret is going to be visible to everyone in a few months in any event and so I decided to tell my parents.' She was blinking rapidly. 'They disowned me, even the–' She stopped, pushed out a deep breath. 'I'm on my own now.' She bowed her head.

Right then she *looked* alone, standing in oversized clothes in a bomb-site kitchen. And then his brain caught up with her words. *Visible in a few months*. She was pregnant.

'Oli, I don't know what to say. Congratulations.' The final word hesitated on his lips before tumbling out.

She continued as if she hadn't heard him. 'Dad fired me. I'm a slut, apparently.' She shrugged. 'One of the downsides of working in the family business. No employment rights.'

Trent saw Oli catch his glance towards the collection of shopping bags and her eyes hardened. She paused, weighing something up. 'I don't regret it,' she said.

'Don't regret what?' Where was she going with this?

'I slept with someone I shouldn't have. It only happened once.' And yet once was all it took. Oli was staring out the window.

'But you want the baby, right?' he asked.

She turned to face him. 'Yes.' It was a whisper. 'Yes, I do.'

'Well, that's great, then.'

'It's not exactly how I imagined it to be, Trent.' Her eyes dulled and she returned to staring out of the window. And then she walked over to the table and switched on the radio before standing next to Trent and whispering in his ear.

'I thought it would be over once I'd played the game.' Her voice was dull now too. 'But it isn't. It's worse. It knows everything. It probably knows you're here because it'll have tracked you. It listens to conversations.' Her breath was warm against his ear. 'But the game doesn't force you to reveal your darkest secret. That's its sick twist. You think the stuff you admit to is the worst it knows and then it taunts you with the one thing that you were so relieved that it hadn't revealed.'

Trent turned to face her. Tears were gathering in the corners of her eyes and at the same time a ball of fear began to spin in Trent's stomach.

'But now it's made it clear that it'll tell everyone that secret if and when it decides to. And if I think things are bad enough now, bad enough with what will happen,' she ran her hand over her belly, 'they're as nothing compared to what will happen if that comes out. That's a secret you *really* don't want to know.' She started to cry. 'But it knows. This game knows *everything*. And there's nothing, nothing that I can do to stop it.'

Trent was frozen. Who would want to do this to her? He reached out towards her, but she flinched from him.

'All I can do is wait, do what it says and hope that's enough.' She sucked in air as she carried on. 'It's awful to say it, but I'm hoping there's something else, some other final secret, that it really wants. That that is what this is all about.' She rubbed the tears from her face, but a strand of hair was stuck to her cheek.

'Another secret?' Trent asked, trying to keep up.

'Not mine. Someone else's.' Her stare was intense. 'And if I'm right, God help whoever's the last one to play.'

And it was as if the ice had cracked and Trent was falling into freezing water. His body was closing down. Everything was turning grey. And he was falling. Down. Down.

The crackle of the radio seeped into his brain. A mournful synth rumbled through the room with a staccato drum beat morphing into a more insistent rhythm. The vocal refrain on the radio swirled around him like a haunting requiem. *Don't walk away, in silence.*

Oli wrapped her arms around her torso, the t-shirt

twisting around her like a straight jacket. 'You should go,' she said. 'There's nothing you can do for me. There's nothing anyone can do.'

Trent didn't want to accept that truth, but he merely nodded. And then he turned and made his way out of her house.

60

THURSDAY 10:40AM

Trent stepped out of his shower, dug out some clothes that he hadn't worn for a couple of years and pulled them on. He slipped on his trainers making sure that Dylan's tracker was still fixed inside. He'd messaged her a meeting time from Oli's driveway and he knew that she'd be able to find him, wherever he was.

In the kitchen, he picked up the two empty crisp packets that he'd left on the draining board and pulled out his phone. He switched it off and then slid it into one of the packets before then dropping the covered phone into the second empty packet and securing it with an elastic band. Hopefully Terminator was a reliable guide for avoiding phone-tracking. He packed some food, a notebook, and a pencil and filled his travel cup with steaming hot coffee and then let himself out the house.

Trent headed off on foot. Thoughts crowded into his head, squeezing and blocking each other. He needed to try and think clearly and he wanted to use his walk to try and unclutter his mind. The park was nearly deserted, just a couple throwing a ball for their spaniel to retrieve. The bin was overflowing and the litter that had escaped tumbled around in the breeze. The grass was dull and the bench he sat on was in need of a paint job.

He thought back to his conversation with Oli. The game had held back a secret. For Oli it was the identity of the father of her baby. Who could the father be to cause her such distress? A public figure or the partner of a close personal friend? A revelation that would destroy a reputation or a relationship. Possibly both.

For Dub, there was the missing video. Perhaps a recording that wasn't consensual. Or maybe it wasn't a sex tape at all. Trent scratched his jaw.

Dub and Oli had both played the game and yet for each of them a final secret had stayed buried. Which meant it was likely to be true for Paddy too. And everyone else who still had their turn to come.

He turned around as he heard someone call out his name and his head jerked in a double take. Dylan, outdoors in daylight and wearing a dress. Trent paused, wondering how he would ever know if the world had stopped turning. 'Hi,' he said.

'Have you got your phone on you?' she asked.

'Yes, but –'

Dylan rolled her eyes but stopped as Trent held out his crisp packet encased parcel. 'Perhaps there's hope for you yet. Double bagged. Nice. I didn't imagine you'd know what a Faraday cage was.'

'A what?' he asked, aware that he was proving her point. 'I just copied it from Terminator.' The reference appeared to slide past Dylan as if she'd never heard of Hollywood. 'By the way, Samson can't be the one running the game.'

Dylan nodded. 'Yes. We've known that since Paddy's first question.' She tilted her head and then carried on. 'I've found

TeeQ.' Dylan sat down next to him. 'His real name is Todd Line. He owns several local businesses. Considers himself to be quite the self-made entrepreneur.' She paused so Trent could let that information sink in. 'I took a look at the accounts for one of his businesses, Gosh Posh Wash.'

'That was the name of the company that made the payment into Paddy's account,' Trent said.

'Yes. And their auditors are none other than Wilkinson & Carter LLP.'

Trent ran his hand over his face. 'The firm Paddy works for. Do you think that's who Paddy suspects of fraud?'

'It's a car wash,' Dylan said by way of reply.

'Meaning?'

'Meaning, yes, I think that's who Paddy suspects of fraud.'

Trent digested the information, watching the spaniel dip its nose to the grass and zigzag across the park like an out-of-control leaf blower. There were still some data gaps which he hoped to fill in that day but TeeQ's real name would be a great help. 'I need to know how I can check some things online without being traced or tracked,' he said.

'Come round to mine.' Never had those words sounded less like a come on.

He shook his head. 'I'll come over later but I want to use somewhere I've never been before to do this. And I need a bit of space.' He hesitated. 'No offence.'

'I understand the need for space,' she said. 'Okay, nothing's perfect but what I'm about to tell you should be good enough.'

Trent listened intently for the next five minutes, making some handwritten notes before agreeing to call round later. He needed time to get everything in focus and he wanted to do it securely, without using any of his own electronic devices. He stood up to leave. Dylan was looking at him, her head tilted. 'What?' he asked.

'You *do* know what that the most likely answer is, don't you?'

He did. But he didn't want to say it. So he shrugged, knowing she would say it instead.

'One of your friends is behind the Honesty Index.'

61

THURSDAY 11:15AM

Trent stepped off the bus in Kentish Town. He found what he was looking for in the first newsagents he entered, paid by cash, and then walked on down the road. It only took a few minutes to find a suitable internet café. Small but quiet enough even in the late morning. Most people inside had their heads down at their terminal although a couple of older men were chatting to each other in the furthest corner of the room.

Trent headed to the counter and waited for the young man behind it to finish whatever he was doing. The guy had a shaven head, bright blue rectangular framed glasses, and a full ginger beard. His t-shirt bore the slogan, *While you were partying I studied the blade.* 'Hi mate, how can I help?' the guy said without looking up.

'I need internet access for a couple of hours.'

The man waved a hand towards the room. 'There are some terminals free. Help yourself.'

'Can I pay upfront?' Trent opened up his wallet.

'You put in your credit card details.'

'I haven't got a credit card.'

The man finally looked at him and narrowed his eyes. Trent hoped he wasn't thinking about his blade. 'Okay. If you've got cash, go and use terminal twelve and I'll set you up. Two hours you said?' Trent nodded and handed over the money. 'You're all set. Clock's running. Come back if you need more time.'

Trent carried his bag over to the terminal and sat down. He was in a corner, with the seat to his right currently vacant. He twisted the screen to give himself some more privacy and then pulled the keyboard towards him and used it to navigate his way to a virtual keyboard application. Dylan had advised him that it would offer some protection should the internet café have hardware designed to record his physical keystrokes. He selected the log in screen for webmail. He'd memorised the new account details that Dylan had said she'd set up for him and typed them in. It was a nondescript name, nothing that would easily lead back to him.

He had one new message. He didn't recognise the sender but Dylan was the only person in the world who knew this email address for him. He opened the email and clicked on the link. A password prompt blinked at him. Again from memory he carefully typed on the virtual keyboard and a few seconds later he was given access.

He settled in for his first deep dive. He had decided to work through his friends in the order that they had played the game which meant that he was kicking off with Andrew Dubnyk. His first search was rewarded with numerous articles about ice hockey players. He refined the search and hit a rich seam of articles that Dub had written after joining his first media outlet.

Trent jotted some details down in his notebook without having any sense of having found anything useful. He turned his attention to nine years ago. Dub had told them that he had seen a body lying motionless next to the neighbourhood river. He'd claimed that he'd checked for any reports in the local news but hadn't found anything about a dead body. Trent spent the next forty minutes reading accounts of deaths that matched either the timing or the general location of Dub's report but none of them tallied with the details of Dub's sighting.

He turned to a fresh page in his notebook and then typed the name Olivia Pearson into Google. He found a link to her parents' business and an online article about young entrepreneurship featuring a perfectly posed photo of Oli under the title, *Olivia Pearson, raver turned bookkeeper*. He smiled. How'd she kept *that* quiet? He remembered the fallout from her parents' discovery of her glow stick party lifestyle and their actions to bring her back under control, but he'd no idea that the transformation had been immortalised online. Still grinning, he tried a search for both Pearson and Samson. Nothing. Sighing and gritting his teeth, he delved into some right-wing propaganda sites, but if Oli did lean that way she'd done a good job of tucking her elbows in. Maybe it had been nothing more than a passing dalliance; classic Oli.

Paddy was next. His promotion at work to assistant director was recorded for posterity in a short press release from Wilkinson & Carter LLP. The photograph captured a larger, and on the face of it, happier and healthier, Patrick Wilding. Trent spent some time clicking through the Wilkinson & Carter website and making a few notes. He methodically worked through his searches but his checks on Zoopla and Companies House threw up no surprises.

He stopped and poured himself a coffee from his flask, gulping it down in a few seconds. Even though he was sure he wasn't being watched Trent still checked on the people near him before typing in the name Todd Line and tabbing through the hits. On the next page he saw Line's LinkedIn profile and clicked on the link. The site was asking him to log in but he wasn't about to do that. He started to move down the list when his hands jerked up as if the mouse had short-circuited. He ran his hand through his hair. The summary profile he could see without logging in to the LinkedIn site told him everything he needed to know.

Todd Line. Previous jobs. Head of security, Analytic Systems.

He felt a tremor in his hands. He'd hit pay dirt. A link between Nicholas Samson and Todd Line, aka TeeQ. He jotted the details down in shaky handwriting before changing tack and searching on TeeQ. Dylan had been able to find information on TeeQ, but Trent found nothing. Eventually he reverted to searching Todd Line and Analytic Systems.

The third hit sucked the air from his body; an article with the headline *Assault charges against security guard dropped.* Todd Line had been arrested following a fight with another man, after a night out. The other guy had to be taken to hospital and Line was charged with battery but released on bail.

There'd been no witnesses although the argument had been captured on CCTV and a prosecution had looked likely. Two months later the case was dropped after a software engineer analysed the CCTV and noted several interruptions, where periods of up to eight minutes were not able to be viewed. The police made a statement about the CCTV footage. Trent shivered as he re-read it. *Evidence suggests that the CCTV tape was deliberately corrupted by some type of data scrambling technology.*

And who did Line know who had the skills to poison the police data? Step onto the podium, the Samson family. Trent moved to write in his book but his hand froze as the memory of Nicholas Samson's last threat to Annabelle Jackson slithered into his mind. What had it been? *I know bad people, who owe me.*

Trent tapped his pencil on the pad, his foot also bouncing up and down on the floor. Todd Line was a bad man. A bad mad who owed his very freedom to Nicholas Samson. Tick, tick, boom.

Could he have found the man who was keeping the Honesty Index alive after its founder's death? He blew out the air from his lungs. He still had more work to do but his whole body was tingling. He had Lila and Frances left. He navigated to Airbnb and scrolled through their properties, looking for Lila's flat. It wasn't there. He widened the search parameters and looked again. No record at all.

Changing tack, he flicked into Zoopla and used the map to narrow results down to her street. Seconds later her flat appeared and he clicked the listing. Scrolling through the photographs, he soon saw the distinctive orange sofas. Trent peered at the image. He couldn't make out the pictures on the wall but he could tell that they weren't the Escher prints that hung on the walls now. The property was showing as having been sold just a few weeks ago and yet Lila had told him that she was renting it. Was it possible that it had been purchased a few weeks ago and the rental details hadn't been updated by Airbnb? The other explanation was that Lila had bought it herself.

Frowning Trent made his way through the searches relating to Lila's time at college in the US. She'd been a student at the University of California – Berkeley, he knew that much. He was dotting about. There were so many other Lila's and Jain's who'd been or were currently at Berkeley. He couldn't find Lila Jain in the publicly available online alumni directory, but it looked as though people registered for that voluntarily. She might not have wanted to register, or perhaps she'd dropped out from college.

He worked through the remaining search categories. There was nothing on Companies House but then she'd been in the US for years. Trent scratched his nose and shrugged before pulling up a final website. An open-source database of offshore entities exposed by journalists with the help of various data leaks.

He typed in Nameless LLC. Nothing. But then he hadn't expected to find anything. Dylan would have already tracked it down if it was possible. An idea crawled into his brain. He typed Lila Jain's name into the company director field. Trent's body went rigid when he saw a hit. She was the registered owner and director of Demeter Inc, a Cayman Islands entity. There were no accounts and no other information. It wasn't Nameless LLC but, if it was Lila's, what was it for and why hadn't she mentioned it?

There was no website when he searched on the company name other than for a US perfume business with the same name. Wikipedia told him that Demeter was the Greek Goddess of agriculture. Frowning, Trent scribbled some notes in his book and moved on to the final friend on his list.

Frances had her own website advertising her tutoring services for Japanese language lessons but other than that she was largely invisible online. He only had one other avenue to explore and that was Frances' husband. He found some coverage of Jake's start up and also some results for the iron man competitions he had competed in. At least that wasn't a surprise. After a fruitless twenty minutes of searching, he turned back to his notebook.

He sunk back into the chair, chewing on the end of the pencil. The revelations about Todd Line kept reeling him in like a needle in the groove of a record. He took a minute to flick through the manual notes he'd made and paused as he looked again at the details. The more he thought about it the more certain he was that he'd found a critical link. Samson was the brain and Line was the brawn. A chill crept down his spine as he recalled Paddy's severed fingers. Any hope that TeeQ had only been interested in Paddy had evaporated with the discovery of the connection to Samson. The game had moved on. Created by Samson, refined by TeeQ. Except that refined wasn't a word to describe someone who hacked off fingers.

Trent shut down his online session, following the instructions that Dylan had given him, before leaving the internet café. He found a park bench where he pulled out one of the mobile phones that he had purchased that morning. Carefully he logged himself back in to the webmail account using the phone and changed the password before logging back out, switching off the phone and removing the SIM card. Then he slipped the SIM card into a nearby bin. If he was hunting down Todd Line, he wasn't going to risk giving himself away.

62

THURSDAY 1:20PM

Trent's energy quickly drained as he made his way into the computer room and lowered himself into a chair. Dylan didn't say anything, or even look at him, preferring instead to tinker with a soldering iron and some circuit boards.

Trent took a deep breath and started to share what he'd discovered. As he spoke she secured the soldering iron in its stand only to then move to inspect her work through a microscope. Trent sighed loudly.

'You don't have to stop talking,' she said.

Trent couldn't help himself. He needed her help. And to start with that meant he needed her attention. 'You haven't listened to a word I've said. If you're not prepared–'

Dylan started to talk whilst adjusting the focus of the microscope. And she didn't stop until she had repeated, word for word, Trent's entire summary of his investigation. When she'd finished she placed the circuit board on a shelf, next to some others, and sat down in front of her keyboard. 'The information about the assault charge is very helpful,' she said.

Which, after the lesson in never doubting the teacher, was perhaps the closest thing to praise that Trent was going to get. Dylan was quiet for a while. Apparently even geniuses needed time to think.

'I assume you have a plan,' she said.

He nodded. It had come to him on the bus and the more he'd considered it, the more he'd liked it. 'At the moment the game is totally in charge. It drives everything, controls everything. And now we know Line has taken over from Samson we can reasonably expect the level of sophistication to decline considerably. Meaning now is the perfect time to upset the equilibrium. We need to force the game to respond.'

'Exactly.'

Great minds think alike. But lesser ones have to be told the details.

'How do we do it?' Trent asked.

'I've got some ideas. Why don't you leave it with me. If we can neutralise TeeQ without involving any of you, then so much the better.'

Amen to that. He grinned at Dylan. 'Did you just say *neutralise?*'

She replied by asking another question. 'Leave me your notebook. I want to see everything that you've found.'

'To check I haven't missed anything?'

'To check that *I* haven't missed anything.'

Trent smiled. She might be awkward but he was glad that she had his back. 'Should I tell the others our plan?' he asked.

'No.' It was fired back as if he had thrown his question at a wall.

'Did you even consider it?' Surely his question was worthy of at least some thought?

'Sure, I considered it.' Dylan was now busy pulling some cables towards her.

'It's just that, well, it seems like you didn't consider it for very long.'

'And what do you base that on?' she asked.

He frowned. 'You answered immediately. You must have weighed things up *very* quickly.'

Dylan actually laughed. And it wasn't even in response to a line. 'Reasonably quickly,' she said. Trent scowled as she turned to look at him. 'Trent, is just now the first time you've thought about whether or not to share your thinking with the others?'

'Yes.' Doing his best impression of an algorithm. Two could play at that game.

'Oh.' Dylan laughed again. That was twice within a minute. Trent bowed his head. 'You should tell them about Todd Line. They deserve to know who they're dealing with but we can't trust anyone right now. Okay, I'm going to switch on your phone,' she said. 'Be careful what you say from now on. You have to assume that the game is listening to everything and also that it knows where you are.'

'Are you worried about messing with TeeQ?' he asked.

Dylan didn't even look up. 'No. But he should be worried, because his life is about to take a sudden change of direction.'

Trent watched Dylan unwrap his phone and switch it on. He was about to give her his passcode but he hesitated. He congratulated himself on learning some lessons as Dylan tapped on his phone. His phone beeped and Trent shivered. Surely it couldn't be another round already.

Dylan was nonplussed. 'Frances has invited you and Lila over to her house. Tonight, seven o'clock.'

Frances, Lila, and Trent. The three players who hadn't yet faced their round.

He craned his neck to scan the notifications. Still no message from his aunt. Why hadn't she replied? She was never quick to respond but at this rate it might have been quicker to approach the Government directly about the medal.

Dylan connected her cable to his phone and after a few seconds the Honesty Index app opened on the screen in front of her. Trent stared at it. What did it have in store for him? The image of Paddy's severed fingers pushed to the front of his mind. TeeQ had done that.

The same TeeQ that, to use Dylan's phrase, they wanted to force to respond.

63

THURSDAY 7PM

They were sitting in Frances' living room, with Trent and Lila at either end of a long sofa and Frances in an armchair opposite them. There was a serving hatch through to the kitchen but it had been pulled closed and Trent could hear dull thuds as Jake moved around. The kids were, he guessed, already in bed. Trent cradled a glass of water whilst Lila and Frances had opted for wine.

Trent had taken them through his findings about Todd Line. Frances' knee was bouncing up and down and Lila was twisting her hair in her fingers.

'Shouldn't we go to the police now?' Lila asked.

Frances spoke before Trent could respond. 'I asked a friend about that. He's a policeman. Jake actually suggested it.' Frances sounded calm. She pushed away a stray lock of frizzy hair from in front of her eyes. It was no surprise to learn that Frances was friends with a policeman. It was more interesting to hear that it had been Jake who had suggested it as a way forward. 'I didn't go into any detail and it was obviously before I knew about this Todd Line character. I described the game as being like a stalker. Someone making it clear that they know a lot about you. And demanding that you answer questions.'

'What did he say?' Trent asked, wondering when she'd had this discussion. She hadn't mentioned it before.

'He spent a long time asking me to clarify what I meant. Asked me if I was being coerced into doing anything, or whether someone had threatened me.' She paused to take a sip of wine. 'I'm pretty sure he thought I was crazy. I told him that one of us receives a message and then we're asked to answer some questions.'

'And?' Lila asked.

'Well, he said that that it didn't sound like anything illegal but he thought I might want to get some new friends.' She smiled.

'Okay. Probably good advice, but did he say anything helpful?' Trent asked.

'Not really. He mentioned online harassment but he also said, off the record, that the police would find it hard to investigate it. We'd need to provide evidence.'

'Which we don't currently have,' said Trent.

'Right. He couldn't really get beyond why I wouldn't just walk away. I tried to explain that if I did that then I risked certain truths being made public.' Frances hesitated again. 'And then he started to question me again. Had I done something that I shouldn't have? Was that why I'd really asked him to come around? I could trust him. He would treat what I told him in confidence. Mate to mate. I could see in his eyes that he was desperate for me to confess something to him.'

Trent stayed silent. Clearly the way that Frances had framed the discussion with the policeman had brought his focus onto her own life. But that was the problem. You'd walk away if you were confident that the game had both nothing on you and nothing to promise you.

'Okay.' He sighed. 'So, a dead end.'

'But it's changed, hasn't it?' Lila said. 'I mean, Paddy was viciously assaulted.'

'Yes and no,' Frances replied. After a pause, she continued. 'It was his secret that pushed things to the next level. He tried to extort money from a criminal. He was playing with fire.'

Which might have been true, but still sounded harsh to Trent. 'He's still in hospital,' he said. 'We can ask him if he wants to tell the police about the Honesty Index but my bet is that he'll refuse. They haven't been in touch with any of us after they interviewed him so he can't have told them about the game.' He remembered his conversations with Dub and Oli. 'No one who's played their round wants to go to the police. I don't think we have much choice other than to respect their choice.' He saw Frances shiver. She'd called the meeting to discuss what they should do and they seemed to be concluding that there was nothing that they could do.

Lila was frowning at him, looking as though she was deciding whether or not to say something. Or was she thinking that his reasoning was a little too convenient. He'd argued against the police at every turn so far. 'Are you okay, Lila?' he asked.

'I'm worried,' she replied. She flashed him an embarrassed smile. 'And I can't decide whether or not involving the police would make things better or worse.'

'I can't see how it would help,' Frances said and Trent felt the tension in his shoulders ease slightly. For once it wasn't him making the argument. 'If we went to them with what we now know they'd have to question Todd Line. And we haven't got much evidence, so my guess is that they'd have to release him.' Frances filled her glass as she spoke and Trent could see the wine wobbling even once she had finished pouring. 'So, my guess is that it'd be worse.'

Lila nodded in response to Frances' analysis but there was a tension in her body that Trent hadn't seen before. Was it simply that the hit list was now so short that the time for facing up to the truth was charging towards her? She'd told him that she was working on trying to face up to things. Did that include telling the truth about dropping out of college, buying property back in England and setting up an offshore shell company?

An uneasy silence crept over them. It appeared that they had reached a tentative conclusion. They wouldn't go to the police. Trent felt rather than heard the alert on his phone as it vibrated in his pocket but the chimes that came from the other two phones in the room were as clear as a maniac firing a starting gun.

It was time for round four. The only question was who had been chosen.

64

THURSDAY 7:12PM

Trent swallowed hard as he slid out his phone. His heart was racing. He didn't want it to be Lila or Frances. But he really didn't want it to be him. He placed his thumb on the home button and his screen sprang into life but he heard the gasp before he could open the app. He looked up to see Lila's face was pale and her arms were shaking.

Trent's screen teemed with snapshots of data: what looked like a text conversation with Dub, a freeze frame of Lila twisting to face the camera with a pale blue 'play' triangle superimposed on her naked back and a copy of her US Green Card as a permanent resident of the USA. Trent tried to absorb the patchwork that the game had stitched together of Lila's secrets. There were legal documents that looked like the incorporation details for Demeter Inc, her mysterious company, and a letter from the University of California – Berkeley, addressed to Lila Jain with the heading *Report of Conduct Hearing.*

The images lost definition as he stared at the screen. Edges blurred and colours bled as tears gathered in Trent's eyes. Numb, he waited for the round to begin. But this time there was no school report. Maybe the game didn't have one for Lila. Or perhaps it had moved beyond it. Trent tried to focus. There was a quotation.

Love is blind; friendship closes its eyes.

And on some level the words resonated with him. He couldn't say what it meant and yet he knew it to be true. Lila's hand was covering her mouth, her fingers brushing her lips. Trent's eyes flicked back to the quotation. *Friendship closes its eyes.* What had Samson written about Lila in his notes to his mother? *One day she might understand the choice I made.* Samson had known something about Lila and the choice he'd made was to stay silent. Was the secret something to do with Lila's relationship with Dub? Or perhaps some broken romance in the US?

Lila was centre stage; the bell was ringing, and Trent was powerless to do anything. All he could do right then was watch. And pray.

The text of the first question appeared on his screen.

Was it Dub that ended your relationship?

Trent jerked back as if he'd been slapped. Not because of the shock of the question but rather the realisation that the game knew so much. Lila had confided that truth to him only a few days ago. And yet the game knew.

Lila wasn't looking at her screen she was staring at him, her eyes wet with tears, her lips pursed. *What? No.* She couldn't think that he was behind it. The game must have been bugging them. Listening in to their conversation. But that's what her expression was saying, why has my best friend betrayed me.

Lila jabbed at the screen and the next question scorched the screen with its blood red text.

Were you made to go to the US against your will?

Trent massaged his forehead. What could possibly have *forced* her to go to the US? She'd always had college in the US as an option. Originally it was an outside bet and it'd stayed that way until the last moment. His head was spinning and he squinted hard to be able to read the next question.

Have you ever killed someone?

The air emptied from his body and he heard a gasp. The floor tilted and Trent closed his eyes. His hand squeezed the arm of the sofa. He couldn't see her answer but it *had* to be no. It just had to be.

He swallowed. His breathing was ragged and yet Lila now looked as though she'd reached a state of calmness. Trent forced himself to breathe. Part of his brain told him not to accept the premise of the question. A question could be designed simply to shock. The answer would be no. Next question. But Trent couldn't move on from the word *killed* until his eyes absorbed the next question and loaded it unvarnished into his brain.

Have you ever made a sex tape?

That question twisted deep inside him. They'd all seen the still shot when the app opened. Lila had denied being videoed by Dub and he'd believed her – but now this. Could she have made one with someone else? But there was no time to dwell on the disturbing images that were assailing him as the final question appeared.

Did you reveal anyone's secret from Nicholas Samson's party?

A very different question but one that finally struck at the heart of the game's motivation. The Honesty Index was finally showing its hand. It all led back to that night.

Trent studied Lila's face. A flicker. A narrowing of the eyes. A hesitation. Why? Why not the same calm resolve as before? She finally tapped on her phone to respond and then he was looking once more at the red radar sweeping round the screen.

Breathe in. One. Breathe out. Two. The screen shimmered and the scoreboard revealed itself.

HONESTY INDEX

100%

No incorrect answers.

There were tears in Lila's eyes. She knew, as they all now did, what was coming next. She'd known as she'd answered. All the different scenarios had been exhausted by the previous players. She was the first to know the full extent of her options. And she'd chosen for her secrets to be revealed, not to the world, but only to their group.

More text had appeared on the screen. All her answers were on display. Trent's brain scrambled to try and process everything. He chalked them off.

Not a murderer.

No sex tape.

Not a snitch.

His pulse started to drop towards a normal rate as he checked the first two answers. Yes, Dub had ended it with her. And yes, she had been forced to leave for the US against her will.

Frances already had her arm around Lila who was sucking in air, tears steaking her face.

'I'm sorry.' Lila was pushing her words out in between breaths. 'I don't know why I'm crying.'

'You're okay.' Frances rubbed Lila's back. 'It's over.'

Except it wasn't, thought Trent. Yes, Lila had answered all the questions. But there would be a secret, a final secret, that the game was holding on to. And it had tipped its hand. Lila had been forced to go to America and Trent was pretty sure that the reason for that would be her final secret.

'It's so scary,' said Lila. 'When it asked me whether I had killed someone, I felt sick. I thought ... I'm so relieved that it...' she trailed away as Frances pulled her back into a hug. Eventually she eased herself free. 'I think I should go home.'

'Do you want someone to take you?' Frances asked, glancing at Trent.

'No, I'm fine.' But her voice faltered. 'I'm fine, really. I just need to be by myself.'

Trent felt another twist in his guts and hated himself for feeling rejected. This wasn't about him. He'd made that mistake before. 'I'll come and see you tomorrow, Lila,' he said.

She smiled at him. 'Thank you. That'd be great.' She looked around for her coat, locating it discarded on another chair and slipped it on, flicking her hair out from under the collar.

Trent pulled his gaze away after she gave a half-hearted wave and walked out. He understood that she needed time, but he felt a part of him leave with her.

Frances stared at Trent as she walked back in from shadowing Lila to the door. 'Poor Lila.' She paused, frowning. 'I assume you don't know why she had to leave for the US?'

'Nope. Not really. She said it had something to do with her parents.' He shrugged as he spoke. Trent was still thinking about Lila's departure for the States. Their farewell had been unsatisfactory. And back then Trent had been upset about that. There'd been a distance that had never been there before. He'd expected to be able to unlock her reasons for leaving but she'd kept the door closed. Or more accurately, he hadn't knocked. Would she have told him if he'd asked?

Frances shuffled forward on her seat. 'We're the last two, Trent.'

Oli's whispered warning echoed in his head. *God help*

whoever's the last one to play. Frances topped up his drink from the pitcher of water but he couldn't stand this anymore. It wasn't as simple as it all being over after two more rounds. No, these rounds were just the foundations for a final challenge, when everyone's darkest secrets would hang over them.

And he still didn't know what the game really wanted. Why had Samson set the damn-thing up in the first place?

He had to shut it down. He pushed his drink away and stood up. 'Sorry, Frances. I'm going to go, too,' he said.

He needed to speak to Dylan, and she'd better be ready because it was now or never. And Trent wasn't settling for never.

65

MANIFESTO EXTRACT 10

There is only the truth. Whether they embrace it is their choice. A choice that was denied to me.

#Time lapse message to Lila Jain

#Time to send: Round[Lila_Jain] + 00:30

Background colour: Black

Font colour: Red

Text:

. . .

I KNOW why you had to leave. Do as I say or the world will know too.

66

THURSDAY 8:35PM

The rain trickled down Trent's face as he took a step back from Dylan's front door and peered into the windows. She hadn't answered when he'd rung the doorbell. She hadn't responded to his texts or calls. *Where the hell was she?*

He spun round and walked back towards his motorbike. He needed her help and she'd committed to continuing to work on their plan when he'd left her earlier that afternoon. She'd always been so responsive. Until now.

He slipped his helmet on and swung his leg over the motorbike. A flash of light caught his eye. He spotted a silhouette of a man looking out of his front room window from the house opposite. The man stared for a few seconds and then the curtain swung back and he disappeared. Shaking his head, Trent turned back to his motorbike. A blur of movement knocked him off balance and he shuffled his feet to stay upright. A tabby cat arched its back and hissed at him, its green eyes focused and accusatory. Trent wiped his hand over his face and gritted his teeth.

The feeling that he was being watched stayed with him

through the journey and even after he arrived home. He locked the garage and then checked that the security chain was fixed on the front door. Even when he was in his study he turned the key and listened to the reassuring sound of the bolt sliding into place.

He dropped his bag by the desk, took out his laptop from the drawer and fired it up, resting his phone next to it. He'd locked himself away but he knew that none of it made him safe. The Honesty Index was hunting him down and no bricks and mortar or chains and mortis locks could protect him.

TRENT DIDN'T KNOW how long he'd been sitting in his office in near silence. The only sounds had been the clicking of the keyboard and the occasional creak of his chair. So the sound of the doorbell smashed into his world like a Molotov cocktail crashing through the window.

He spun round, blood rushing to his head. He stopped at the office door and waited, his breathing heavy. He was tensed for the sound of the door crashing down or the subtle click of a picklock in action when he heard the buzz of his phone over on his desk. Biting his lip he rushed over and grabbed it. His heart was hammering now but there was no message on his phone. Then he heard a second alert. Once again his phone showed no new message. Then the doorbell rang again. A short, shrill burst this time.

Trent swivelled and his foot nudged against his bag on the floor. *His bag*. Of course. He hurried to kneel down and unfastened the bag. He pulled out the two burner phones he had bought earlier that day. One of them was showing two new messages. His hands shook as he navigated the menu system. Read Message.

I know you're inside.

The unknown caller had sent a second message.

Let me in.

Trent closed his laptop and headed downstairs, rubbing the back of his neck. He peered through the opaque window and a sense of relief hit him. He pulled back the door and saw Dylan standing on his doorstep.

'You need to come with me,' Dylan said.

'What?'

'We need to go now. Believe me this is something that you're going to want to see.'

Trent shook his head, but turned back inside to grab his keys and a few minutes later they were on his motorbike turning out of the road. Dylan was riding pillion, wearing his spare helmet, her hands on his waist.

She'd given him the directions to Todd Line's carwash business, which wasn't exactly Trent's first choice of venue. They secured his bike a few streets away and he followed Dylan as she set off towards the premises. She turned into the forecourt of the restaurant opposite the carwash. Trent looked around but the building and grounds were deserted. 'What are we doing?' he whispered.

'Finding a good viewing point.' She squeezed past an outdoor table into a space where she was largely hidden by the restaurant's shrubs but with a view over the road into the carwash. She beckoned for Trent to join her, moving along to make some room for him.

'Isn't this dangerous?' Trent asked. There were four carports with red signage next to a couple of buildings and a BMW was parked outside with a light on inside.

Dylan smiled. 'Just wait.'

Trent began to get a cramp in his leg as he squatted behind the shrubs. 'What are we waiting for?' This time

Dylan didn't answer but passed Trent an earpiece which was plugged into her phone. The static on the line faded and a voice kicked in. '*...you don't deserve a second chance, Donny.*' The voice oozed with menace. There was a cold click of metal sliding against metal. Someone grunted in response. Trent's stomach twisted. 'Jesus,' he whispered, 'is that Todd Line?' She nodded. 'We shouldn't be here.' His heart was racing and his breathing was shallow. Dylan glanced at her watch and held up her hand. Trent could hear a car driving up the road, then another one, and then a third.

'But I'm going to give you one.' Line must have been too busy dishing out his own form of justice to hear the marked police cars pull into the carwash. Trent stared at Dylan. The headphones exploded with the noise of the front door being smashed in.

'Armed police. Don't move.' Trent heard it in stereo through the earpiece and from across the road. *'Get on the ground. Now.'* He flinched in response.

It was impossible to unpick the detail of what happened over the next few minutes, but the headline was clear. Authorised Firearms Officers had raided the carwash and arrested Todd Line. Dylan and Trent listened as Line was read his rights. His accomplice was also arrested. Not a good night for him but perhaps not as bad as he'd feared moments earlier when Line had a gun to his head.

Trent watched as the police forced the two men into the back of the police cars and five minutes later, drove away, silent but with their blue lights flashing.

'It's over,' Dylan said. Trent took a step towards Dylan. He was light-headed. 'Don't try and hug me,' she said.

Trent caught himself. 'Okay. High five?' Dylan raised an eyebrow and kept her hands by her sides. He stretched his legs as they walked back towards his bike. He laughed. 'So, it really is over.' Dylan nodded but when Trent stopped next to his bike she walked on towards a footpath that started a few yards beyond it. 'Where are you going?' Trent called after her.

She stopped and turned back, looking puzzled. 'Home.'

'Don't you want to stay to, I don't know, chat about it a bit?' he asked. Dylan stared at him. *Blink once for yes, don't blink at all for no.* 'Please, stay,' Trent said.

'Why?'

'Because I still need your help, Dylan.'

'I've done what you asked me to do.' She still hadn't moved.

Trent searched around for a reason which would convince her to stay but he wouldn't have long. 'It was the police who arrested Todd Line. I appreciate all your help and everything but technically, you didn't actually stop the game, the police did.'

Dylan took a step towards him as he finished his sentence, and he felt his conviction drain away. 'If you say so, Trent.' Never had those words sounded so effortlessly withering.

'What? It's not me saying so. That's what happened.' Each word felt more precariously balanced on the last.

'So, take me through it. Explain to me exactly what happened.' Her head tilted and Trent felt a deep conviction that he was going to look really stupid in less than two minutes.

He scratched his head. 'The police arrested Todd Line,' he said, doubling down. He had seen it with his own eyes. Unarguable fact.

'A remarkable coincidence. No sooner does he appear in your life, than the police arrest him, a man who has been breaking the law for years. It's almost as if the corrupted video evidence of his assault had been restored.' Trent just stared at Dylan. 'Or perhaps they received an anonymous tip off that his business was money laundering together with a report that outlined the obvious fraud that was taking place at his car wash business.'

It was the longest that Trent could remember Dylan talking for. 'So, you're saying that –'

'I'm saying that I've done what you asked me to do. I ended the game.'

'I don't know what to say, Dylan. Thank you.' Dylan shrugged. 'Did you manage to hack into the app?' He saw her twitch in response to his question. *No, she hadn't.* And he knew he had her because she hadn't fully defeated the Honesty Index, not yet. She'd shut it down but she hadn't opened it up. 'I really do still need your help.'

She looked at him for a long time. 'And you're sure you want to go there?' she asked.

'I'm sure,' he said. Matching her no blink for no blink.

She nodded once. 'Okay, then. I'm in.' And then she turned and walked down the footpath.

'Don't you want a lift home?' he shouted after her, but she carried on walking.

He shook his head, smiling as he watched her until she had disappeared from view. Samson dead, Line in prison. The Honesty Index was history.

What a night.

67

FRIDAY 1:01AM

The sound pushed its way into his conscience. Persistent and loud. A burst every few seconds. Trent's head throbbed but he dragged himself up from the sofa and lurched for the light switch. Someone was ringing the doorbell. He groaned and rubbed his forehead. The whisky bottle was close to being fully drained although the glass was half full. The Honesty Index was over. He smiled as he shuffled towards the front door. Who could it be at his hour? Maybe Dylan had returned to celebrate.

He swung open his front door and saw his sister standing on the step, concern etched on her face. She reached forward and embraced him but she didn't say anything. Trent tried to recover his thoughts. Why was Pen here in the middle of the night? He released himself from her arms and wrestled for some composure. He cleared his throat. 'What are you doing here?'

Pen ignored his question and guided him back into his living room. 'Wait here,' she said heading towards the kitchen.

Trent lowered himself onto the sofa and some minutes

later Pen reappeared. Trent had no idea how long she had been away but he did know that she hadn't brought the second whisky bottle. 'Where's my drink?' He could hear his own slurring.

'The kettle's boiling.'

'Want a whisky,' he said. Pen just nodded. Nothing more. 'Whisky helps,' he added.

'What's happened, Trent?' Her tone was gentle. How was she able to do that? To control her emotions. Hard to believe that he was the older sibling. 'You texted me to say you needed to talk. Tonight. About the fire.' Pen blinked several times.

Had he? A vague memory fought to crystallise in his head. Trent shuffled forward on the sofa although it was harder than usual to maintain his balance. He fumbled for his phone and checked his messages.

Need to takl. Tonight. Wan 2 tell u abot the fire. X

Guilty as charged. He had messaged Pen. At 12:07am. She must have left her house as soon as she got his distress call and rushed across London to be with him.

Pen itched her nose. 'Has this got something to do with the message you received about the medal?' She tucked her hair behind her ears. 'Have you heard back from Aunt Jo?'

He took a gulp of air. He owed it to her to tell her the whole story. 'Can you get me that coffee and then help me upstairs?'

'You might as well sleep on the sofa.'

'I don't want to sleep. I want to show you something.'

68

FRIDAY 1:52AM

Pen said nothing as she stood in front of the corkboard. She reached out to touch the photo of herself, Freddy, and Trent on the beach, sitting in a sand car. Trent had dug out the sand and constructed the vehicle, sending Pen with the bucket to collect the sea water. Freddy had decorated the car with flags. They were all laughing. Trent's heart twisted as Pen's fingers brushed the family portrait.

'I remember Dad taking that photo,' she said. 'We had to wait until Freddy finished decorating the car.'

Trent said nothing as Pen moved to looking at the cuttings. Articles dense with statistics about domestic fires, deaths, and the importance of a smoke alarm. He watched her frown as she scanned the headlines and freeze when she saw the article about their fire. When she finally turned away, he could see tears in her eyes. She wiped her eyes. 'I had no idea how much it still haunts you.'

Trent swallowed. Hard. Pen seemed to be grasping for the right direction to turn. He gestured towards the corkboard. 'I've had all this stuff going round in my head for years. About the fire.' He was looking at his information hub, blinking hard to try and refresh his eyes. Right then it looked like the work of a crazy man. Perhaps it was. 'There's something there, Pen. It might not be good but I can't stop thinking about it. I *can't* just switch it off.'

She walked over to him and rested her head on his shoulder. 'Then let me help you.'

Her words almost broke him. He tilted his head to rest on hers and felt his body judder. It was time. Finally. 'I need to tell you something first,' he said.

Perhaps it helped that he hadn't prepared. Maybe it was better that he was still drunk. Because he did need to tell her and it was never going to be easy. Pen said nothing as she slid his laptop to one side and perched on the edge of the desk. He hated that she had to go through this; he wanted her to know what had happened but without her having to listen to the story. But he knew that saying it out loud to someone was the first step. He could, he should, share his secret.

He cleared his throat and started to speak. 'That day, the day of the fire, I'd been playing Mario Kart with Freddy. You know how he loved that game.'

'Yeah, I remember,' said Pen. Trent was lost in memories of their baby brother and he hadn't realised that he'd stopped speaking. 'Go on,' his sister prompted him.

'The batteries in Freddy's remote died and he started to cry.' Trent felt a scratch at the back of his throat. 'So I took the batteries from the smoke alarm.' Trent swallowed.

After the fire he'd read all the stats about smoke alarms and their effectiveness in preventing death. He still didn't know what to believe. It was fifty/fifty.

Anger surged through him. Even after all those years.

Yeah, sure. He wasn't even born when the electrics in the house were wired but of course he should've known they'd cause a fire.

But he *had* taken away the protection. Freddy had no chance. He died from the smoke. The same smoke that would've set the alarm off, the alarm that would've woken him up, would've woken them all up. Those batteries would have saved all their lives.

Would've, could've, should've. Take your pick.

And the truth, Trent's truth, was that he'd spent every day since the night of the fire wanting to believe that the batteries made no difference. That they wouldn't have saved Freddy or his parents.

Sometimes, in the dead of night, when he lay awake thinking about Freddy, the guilt would sweep over him. He tried to let it. He should feel guilty. He'd taken the batteries and so the reason that they weren't in the alarm was one hundred percent down to him.

Except.

Except that he was only fifteen years old at the time.

And he *had* asked his parents if he could go to the shop to buy new batteries.

But they were in no mood to talk to their children that night. They'd been arguing, and his mother had been drinking. Trent could still have snuck out late at night and put the original ones back. He could even have done it in full view of his parents – they wouldn't have stopped him, would they?

But he didn't. Because the risk was one in a million.

But then again, so was Freddy.

TRENT PUSHED out the hardest words to say. 'If I hadn't taken those batteries out, Freddy would still be alive.' He bowed his head. Time stretched but in truth it wasn't long before he heard her reply.

'You can't know that.' Pen's voice was a whisper. 'No one could ever know that.'

Trent cracked. He'd told her the hardest part. His mea culpa. His hail Mary for forgiveness. He wanted it so much. He knew Pen would forgive him unconditionally if he told her the rest, the full truth; that he went downstairs that night, with his money in his pocket, and asked to go and buy new batteries; and that their mum, slurred and screamed at him to go back to bed. But that was too easy. Because then Pen wouldn't judge *him*, she'd judge their mother. Which wasn't what he wanted. And so he stayed quiet.

Pen was shaking her head and her eyes were wet. 'Why have you never told me this before? How have you kept it a secret for so long?'

Trent couldn't speak. Not only did he not trust his voice he also didn't have an answer. And then, when Pen put her arms around him, he knew. Because he was scared that she would judge him as he had judged himself.

Pen was talking but her words were buried into his neck and he had to strain to hear her.

'Do you remember when we went on holiday to Cornwell?' Trent tried to catch up. 'Dad had set the alarm for four in the morning. I still shared a room with Freddy back then. The alarm went off and I jumped out of bed.' Pen wiped tears from her face.

Trent clawed his way through his thoughts. He'd heard the story before but he couldn't recall the punch line. Why was Pen telling him this now?

'Freddy slept through the alarm,' she said. 'It took all of us to wake him up.'

The memory rolled back into view. Trent had tickled his

brother's feet to try to get him up. Eventually Pen had blown a raspberry on his belly. Only then had Freddy opened his eyes.

Pen was rubbing his back. 'It wasn't your fault, Trent. It wasn't anyone's fault. It was a tragedy.'

His sister's arms began to shake and it took a moment for him to realise it was because his body was jerking. It came in waves. And Pen just stood with him and absorbed it all and each time he started to drag himself away she would hold him tighter.

69

FRIDAY 5:35PM

Most of the post-work crowd flocked to the local pubs and bars, so the café wasn't too busy. Trent let the coffee cup warm his hands and stared at this phone. He allowed himself a sense of calm as he realised his last two messages were ones he had sent to others: one telling his boss he planned to return to work on Monday and another chaser to his aunt. Then he turned his mind to wondered how much longer Lila would stay in England.

Since the events of yesterday the world was finally turning more slowly. But he welcomed the quieter pace. Tomorrow was the anniversary of the fire and, now that Pen had convinced Bobby to defer the start of their Mills and Boon adventure until the evening, Trent was able to look forward to it. The previous evening had been a high watermark in his relationship with his sister and he felt lighter.

Lila walked into the café and smiled at him. He waved to her across the room and stood to wait for her. She slipped her arms around him and kissed him on the cheek.

'I'm going to order a coffee. You want another one?'

Trent shook his head and sat back down to watch Lila

whilst she queued. It may have been easier when she wasn't in his life but easy wasn't his choice. Well, not any longer. He was facing up to fundamental truths. One by one. Time paused until Lila placed her coffee cup down on the table and sat in the chair opposite.

'How's Paddy?' she asked.

'I still haven't heard from him. I don't think they'll have discharged him from hospital yet.'

He made it sound unremarkable but in fact Paddy hadn't replied to any of his messages or calls. Even the one telling him it was all over. Paddy was definitely avoiding him. He'd tried not to dwell on the fact that systematically each of Dub, Oli and Paddy had cut off contact with him. He'd understood it when the game was active. He knew that they each had a final secret hanging over them. But now? It was over. They were free.

'He'll be in touch when he's ready.' She sipped her coffee. 'You all set for tomorrow?'

Trent smiled. 'Yes. Breakfast is booked. And the weather forecast is good so we should stay dry.' He hesitated and Lila gave him a searching look.

'What, what is it?' Lila asked.

How much did he want to say? 'Pen and I had a good discussion, last night.'

'Okay,' she said, encouraging him to continue. Her eyes peered at him over her cup.

'We talked about the fire. Properly. For the first time in forever.' Trent saw a flicker cross her face. 'Thank you.' She deserved more but it would do as a start. 'You know, and I feel bad saying this, but I'm almost sorry that the Honesty Index is finished.'

'Because you still don't know the truth about that medal?'

She knew him better than he knew himself. Trent nodded.

Lila took her time before continuing. 'I don't think it can have known everything.' She leant forward and rested her hand on his. 'It was ten years ago, Trent. I know it's hard but maybe it's time to let it go.'

He said nothing. The people in the coffee shop, their conversations, the music, phones ringing and Lila talking began to crowd in on him. Everything blurred as if he was falling and yet he knew he was sitting down. He closed his eyes, trying to centre himself. He suddenly felt tired. Exhausted. After a moment he became aware that Lila had again reached over to hold his hand. She was speaking to him. He blinked his eyes open. Locked onto her. Tried to block everything else out. Tried to focus.

'...some fresh air. Come on.' Lila was standing. Helping him up. Leading him to the exit. 'Let's walk back to my place.'

The chill of outdoors stung his face and his eyes started to water. Lila's fingers laced through his and she leaned in close to him. Still talking. Even though it was cold Trent could feel the warmth of sunshine on his face. Step by step, everything began to separate back out until he was once again aware of individual sounds – birdsong, a passing police siren, and Lila's voice. He could feel the ground underneath his feet and smell the musky leaf piles as they cut through the park.

Before long Lila was closing her front door and guiding him to the living room. He couldn't remember why she'd suggested coming back but he wasn't complaining. Once he was sitting down on the sofa Lila slid down next to him. She kicked off her trainers and twisted so that her feet rested on his lap. They used to sit like that, all those years ago. She tipped her head against the back of the sofa. 'We should celebrate,' she said.

Trent ran through a number of events in his life and wondered which one she was thinking of. 'Sure,' he said.

'I've got some champagne in the fridge.' She swung her feet round and stood up. 'Don't go away.'

Trent sighed and stretched out his arms. The Honesty Index was history. He'd told Pen the truth about removing the batteries from the smoke alarm. Lila was back. All in all, things were good.

He stood to look at one of the framed pictures hanging on the wall when Lila walked in with the drinks. She handed him a glass and returned to her previous position.

'You like them?' she asked, following his gaze.

'It's very you.' He turned to face her. 'Hey, back in the café you said you didn't think the game could know everything.' She nodded. 'I know you were talking about me, and my dad and the medal, but how about you? Do you think it knew everything about you?'

Lila paused, wrapping a strand of hair around her finger. She took a sip of champagne, but Trent could see the light in her eyes had dulled. She pulled out her phone, tapped on it and then handed it to him. 'I had a message from the game. Shortly after my round.'

Trent felt a familiar chill run up his spine as he read the message. The Honesty Index was dead but it had left a legacy.

I know why you had to leave. Do as I say or the world will know too.

He was acutely aware of Lila studying him as he passed her phone back. 'I think it did the same thing to everyone,' he said.

He knew it was a cop-out. By showing him the message she was all but telling him to ask her the question. But if she wanted to tell him, she would tell him. Trent swallowed and ventured in another direction. 'What did it ask you to do?'

'Nothing,' said Lila. 'That was the last message I received.' She brushed her hair away from her face. 'You know, and this is going to sound silly, but I sort of respect what the game was trying to do.'

'Okay.' Trent drew out the word as if it had three syllables. 'So, I miss it and you respect it.' And then he laughed. 'Listen to us both, eulogising a game that set out to destroy us.'

Lila sighed. 'Obviously I don't like what happened to Paddy, or any of the others, but the philosophy, I get it.'

'You're going to have to help me with that one,' Trent said.

'Okay, imagine you had a secret, like maybe you knew exactly what happened on the night of the fire, and as far as you were aware, no one else knew it.' Trent flinched as he absorbed her words. 'And then one morning, you get a call from a reporter. They know your secret and they're going to run the story. Wouldn't you wish that you'd been the one to tell everyone the truth?'

'Yes, I guess.' He paused, focusing on the explicit question. 'But I'm not sure that it's right to compare the Honesty Index to a tabloid. Most newspapers are focused on maximising their sales.'

'Fair point.'

But Trent was still thinking. Maybe Lila was right. Could that be the raison d'être of the game – to reward those who fronted up and told the truth, and to punish those who ran or lied? Like some type of moral authority. Perhaps if Paddy had told the truth he wouldn't have been attacked and tortured. Was Oli the only one so far to have played it right? What would he have done? He could only guess.

'But what if I don't want *anyone* to know? Why should the game have the right to force people to reveal things they want to keep to themselves.' His mouth was dry. 'Like the reason why you had to leave for the US.' They were staring at each other now. She was seeing his secret and he was raising hers. He pushed on. 'Do you think it's right that someone else can force you to tell people that?' Trent felt a shift as Lila's eyes sparkled.

'Do you want to know –' Lila's whispered words fingertipped down his spine. She shuffled closer and leant into him. '– why I left?' Her lips were wet from the champagne. Just inches away.

There was so much that he wanted, but right then he'd lost all sense of what he believed. Now wasn't the time to kick-start a physical relationship with Lila. Or was it? A part of him died as he turned away, but not before he caught a flicker of her disappointment. 'I'm sorry,' he said under his breath and her smile cracked his heart. *What was wrong with him?*

His thoughts were interrupted by their phones beeping in stereo. Trent knew the game was over but any alert still kicked his nervous system into overdrive. He balled his fists so as not to reach for his phone. The Honesty Index was the past and Lila was his future. And he could jump start it right then.

'Trent.' Lila's hand was over her mouth and all the glitter in her eyes had vanished. She was holding her phone out in front of her. 'Oh my God.'

It couldn't be. It was over. The two operators were out of the picture. The Honesty Index was finished. But he knew the precise words that he would read. Because Lila's reaction could mean only one thing.

70

FRIDAY 6:27PM

Trent Ryder – ready to play?

Lila's mouth was gaping, and her fingers were rubbing her temples. Tightness crushed Trent's forehead as a countdown started on his phone. It made no sense. Everything had pointed to Samson and TeeQ. It was so neat.

And then it hit him. It had been too neat. Someone had pushed him to the edge of the cliff. He hadn't needed the final push; he had jumped, headfirst.

'Jesus Christ. I can't believe this,' he said.

He tried to control the shakes that were traversing his body. There was a cache of his personal data. A photo of Trent and Lila from their time at school. A picture he'd never seen before. But they weren't together. Lila was a little in the distance, laughing as she walked away, her face half turned so you would only know it was her if you knew her well. Trent was in the foreground and the shot was taken from off to the side and slightly behind him. His expression was impassive but his focus was clear. Trent was staring at Lila. The sun was setting, and Trent's shadow stretched out over the field as if reaching for her.

He pulled his gaze away and scanned the rest of the page. Everywhere he looked triggered silent alarms: contact details for Dylan Steele, the photo of the Queen's Gallantry Medal and then his eyes rested on the final taunt. It was the photograph of Trent, Pen and Freddy on the beach that was pinned to his corkboard. And the edges of the picture were smouldering.

Jesus.

He stared at the countdown at the bottom of his screen.

Nineteen, eighteen, seventeen...

He understood then why Dub had refused to play. Some of the data made no sense but the overarching effect was as if he was facing charges for crimes he hadn't committed. And he felt violated. But if he'd learnt anything from the earlier rounds, it was that it was better to play. His hand trembled as he hit the button. He heard Lila gasp and then the red radar was spinning round, like the Devil's tail. And then the radar faded leaving only a black background until blood red words washed over his screen.

How could you rise anew if you have not first become ashes?

Trent's jaw tightened. He wanted to find out who was behind this thing and shove their sanctimonious philosophy back down their throat and then keep on pushing. But the game was already moving on and the first question was appearing.

Are you sleeping with Dylan Steele?

Trent flashed a look at Lila. The answer was easy enough but the question was a taunt. *Of course* the game knew about Dylan. It left no room for doubt. He didn't think he'd explicitly mentioned her by name to anyone but the game had already showed him that it had access to his contacts. He'd been to her house and if the game had been tracking him perhaps it could have worked out who owned it and matched it to his contacts. Or they could have been watching or bugging him at his house. Or simply reading his texts.

He swallowed, reminding himself to answer with the truth, that he had nothing to hide. He could feel Lila studying him. She'd be wondering who on earth Dylan Steele was, and whether or not Trent was sleeping with her.

He swallowed and hit 'no' on his phone.

Do you love Lila Jain?

Five words that spun around to weave the truth. Lila bowed her head, her hair covering her face. How could anyone but Trent himself truly know the answer to that? Except that it was plain for all to see. The game had moved from taunting to mocking. The photograph of the two of them that it had chosen confirmed that. Not, are you and Lila in love? No, this was one-sided and with the silent emphasis on unrequited. He clicked 'yes' and was rewarded with the next question.

Do you know where Pen was on the evening of the fire?

Even before he'd finished reading the question, a heat burned through his chest and his fingers started to tingle. He had never even asked himself that question.

'What?'

He realised he had said it out loud. He didn't know where Pen was on the evening of the fire but his brain screamed, why does that matter? And yet even as he selected his answer, he felt the game pulling his strings. It knew what he didn't know, and it was making that clear. Power shifted irrevocably to the game. Not only did it have all the answers, but it was also telling him the questions he'd never known to ask.

The third question faded away and was replaced by a document. The first few lines were clearly legible. The writing started to scroll up the screen. Trent strained his eyes to read it.

Civilian Gallantry Medal: Nomination

On 21 September 2006 shortly before midnight, the Fire Service received a report that a fire had broken out at a residential address. On arrival, the Fire Service could see that the ground floor was completely engulfed in fire, and flames were licking up the first floor. Nominee David Ryder had contacted the fire service via a 999 call when he had arrived home to find the family home ablaze.

Trent's pulse quickened and then he realised what was happening. No. It couldn't be. The text was fading.

His wife and three children were in the house, asleep. Mr Ryder entered the building to attempt to rescue his family. He was able to drag his daughter to safety and she was found alive and well when the fire service arrived.

He tried to refocus. The words were now slightly blurred. Fainter. *No.* He shook his head and rubbed his eyes but the text remained out of focus.

Mr Ryder then re-entered the building and battled his way upstairs.

And then Trent could read no more. But it was clear that the game had the full letter. It knew the truth about his father. The text of the next question was superimposed over the report.

Do you know why your father's gallantry medal nomination was refused?

This was no longer a test of his honesty; this was the game letting Trent know that it controlled him. It had the answers, it wanted him to know it had them and, for now, it was keeping them just out of his reach.

His hand was shaking as he hit the button for 'no.' And then he held his breath. Because it was the last question. And he knew what was coming next.

Did you take the batteries out of the smoke alarm on the night of the fire?

Trent had only reached the word batteries when Lila gasped. And then he was shouting. *How the hell did it know?* He'd been over and over it in his mind. No matter how powerful the game was, no matter how incredible its ability to scrape data from electronic devices and files, there were limits on what it could know. Until he had told Pen, no one else knew. Not a single living person. There was no secret record or file that revealed it. Trent's head was spinning.

The words of the question burned into his brain. He needed to answer. He fought the urge to throw his phone down, to walk away, because if he did that then the game would release information. Would it tell the world about Trent removing the batteries? What if it was something else, something about his father? His stomach lurched. What did it know? No, he couldn't risk it. He needed as much control as he was allowed. And then he remembered the quote.

How could you rise anew if you have not first become ashes?

Was it true? Was this his time? He took a deep breath. Not rising anew yet, but at least he was still breathing. He felt Lila tense beside him as he answered yes to the final question.

He shook his head.

Pen was the only person who knew about him removing the batteries. Why had the game asked him about where she'd been on the evening of the fire? He tried to imagine his sister being behind the whole thing but it was impossible. It couldn't be her. But could she have told someone? He couldn't believe that either – it wasn't a casual conversation piece. Maybe she would've told Bobby? Trent's heart smacked against his chest. No. No, surely not. Okay, they were head over heels, but no. No.

Trent lowered his phone. He couldn't bring himself to

meet Lila's gaze. The Honesty Index was alive and well. Which had to mean that one of his friends was behind it and they had used Samson as a screen. One of them was responsible for invading each of their lives and ripping their secrets into the world. But who? It didn't seem possible to Trent, not least because whoever it was had subjected themselves to playing the same game.

Except for one. Frances. The psych grad.

Which was a tick in the box not only for Nietzsche but also the training needed for screwing with everyone's mind. He barely noticed the game awarding him his mark.

HONESTY INDEX

100%.

No incorrect answers.

'Trent?' Lila's voice sounded as though it was coming from far away.

He felt something snap deep inside of him. His body juddered and he sucked in a gulp of air. His chest was tight. Lila slid close to him and wrapped her arms around him, pulling his head to her neck. Sobs racked his body and he felt her absorb the energy as her fingers tangled tight in his hair.

'It's okay, Trent,' she whispered.

He didn't understand what she could mean but he took the words and held on to them. She stroked his hair and wiped his tears from his face. Slowly, his body quietened. He became aware of his face pressing into Lila's collarbone. His mouth touching her skin. He felt her kiss the top of his head.

He tilted his head to look at her. 'I asked my parents to let me go out and buy more batteries.' He could feel his tears streaking down his face. He wasn't even clear to whom he was offering his plea. 'But they wouldn't let me.' His words were pushed out between sobs.

'You don't need to explain, Trent.'

Random thoughts sparked through his mind, but no connections formed. Dylan. Lila. Pen. Freddy. Mum. Dad. And yet through everything there was one constant question. How the hell did it know *everything* when he didn't even know the truth himself.

71

MANIFESTO EXTRACT 11

Some people are hiding their secrets. Other secrets are hidden from them. Freedom only comes when all secrets are revealed.

#Time lapse message to Trent_Ryder

#Time to send: Round[Trent_Ryder] + 00:30

Background colour: Black

Font colour: Red

Text:

. . .

SECRETS WORK BOTH WAYS. Play by the rules or you will never know the truth about your father.

72

FRIDAY 6:48PM

The silence was broken by Trent's phone ringing. It was Frances. Trent took a deep breath and hit the button to activate the speakerphone. 'Hi, Frances. I'm here with Lila.'

'Trent, are you okay? I can't believe it's back. I thought you said it was all over.' Her veiled accusation skewered her sympathetic opening. Frances. The only one of them who hadn't been made to play. Trent caught Lila's expression.

'I'm fine.' Trent said it without warmth.

'Do you think it's over now?' she asked.

What? He'd never had Frances down as self-centred. How could she possibly think it would be over now? Unless...

'I imagine your turn will come, Frances, don't you?' He could hear the edge in his voice.

'What are you talking about?'

Trent looked at Lila but her gaze was unfocused. 'Isn't it obvious? You're the only one who hasn't had to face it yet,' he said. Even if she was behind the whole thing surely she was dumb enough to suggest that.

'But my turn was immediately before yours.'

Trent felt as though he'd been punched in the gut. Lila was tapping on her phone. 'I can't see any notification apart from the one for Trent's round. There's nothing else at all.'

Frances cleared her throat. 'I played my round. The same as everyone else. I assumed that you'd all seen it.'

Trent switched into the Honesty Index app. 'I can't see anything either.' Which all felt a touch too convenient. 'What happened?' he said.

'Well, nothing really. There were no dramatic revelations.'

Something inside Trent stretched. 'You were asked questions though, right?' he asked.

'Yes, of course.' He listened as she spoke, trying to decide whether he believed her. Instinctively, he'd always trusted Frances. But this was pushing him to the edge. 'Firstly there was another Nietzsche quote. *There is always some madness in love. But there is also always some reason in madness.*'

There was always a quote. Dangled at the start, hinting at some weakness in the life of the player. And it was always a quote that Frances knew by heart.

Frances was still talking. 'The first question was whether I'd committed benefit fraud. My answer, no.' She sounded confident but then she would do if she was answering her own questions or not answering real questions at all. 'The second one was odd. Did you have any contact with Anthony Wilson after you left school? Given that I didn't know anyone called Anthony at school, I went with no for that one, too.'

Lila was looking at Trent, eyes quizzical. He strained his memory. Ant, Tony, Tone? He shook his head and shrugged. He was trying to focus on what Frances was saying but he couldn't stop himself from wondering why her round hadn't been broadcast to the entire group as had been the case with all the others.

'The third question was whether I had told anyone any of the secrets revealed at Samson's sixteenth birthday party.'

'The same question as me,' Lila said.

But not me, thought Trent. Why hadn't the game asked him the question it seemed to be most focused on? Frances confirmed that she had answered no to the question and Trent instantly knew that she would be corroborated by the game. He swallowed. Two more questions.

'Four was, is your husband the father of your children?' Trent forced himself to breathe. If Frances was behind this whole thing then her answer would be the simple truth. She wouldn't be feeling any sense of shock. But if she wasn't... 'My answer, yes. Which brings us to the final question.' She paused. This one must have been harder. Her voice was quieter when she continued. 'The final question was whether I trust my husband.'

Trent remembered the conversation he'd had with Frances about her fear of what the game might reveal about Jake. But could she have been setting Trent up for this moment. If she was, there was no way she could answer this with a yes.

'I went with *no* for that one.'

Trent sucked in air.

'What was your result?' Lila asked.

'100%,' replied Frances. Every single answer, God's honest truth.

Trent felt empty, as if life had drained away from his body. Maybe the game did what it said on the tin. If you had nothing to hide, you could emerge from the star chamber blinking into the light and life could carry on. Each of Oli, Lila, Trent, and Frances had answered truthfully at the first time of asking. Oli had suffered but in reality only because she had chosen to tell her parents that she was pregnant, a secret not revealed by the game. Dub had refused to face up to the truth, and Paddy had lied, and they were both now living with the consequences.

Trent, himself, had been forced to expose a secret that he'd kept to himself for ten years and yet he'd already confessed to the person who would care the most. Revealing the truth to Lila, and any of the others who were watching, hadn't been easy but now he was through to the other side, did he regret it? No. No, he didn't. He wasn't exactly reborn but he did feel free.

So, what if whoever was behind it all was helping them to live better lives? Or if not better, then more honest lives. Maybe that was the same thing. Trent was sure there must be a Nietzsche quote for that.

Frances broke the silence. 'So, I repeat my earlier question. 'Do you think it is over now?'

Trent replied automatically. 'No.'

Lila's eyes narrowed.

'No?' echoed Frances. 'Why not? We've all had our turn.' He could hear the stress in her voice.

'It's building up to something. These individual rounds have been a test. And for each one of us the game has dangled a final secret.' The fading words of the letter teased his memory. 'Even you, Frances. The game knows something about you. Possibly about Jake. And it wants you to know that it knows.' But as he said it he wondered whether Frances knew that, already.

'So, what do you think will happen next?' Lila asked.

There would be a final round, he was sure of it. And he was equally convinced that they'd all be there. Brought together for the final inquisition. The game would demand it and it would use the final secrets, the threats, and the promises, to force a confession.

'Trent?' Lila said.

He struggled to recall her question as he looked at her. His relationship with Lila Jain had been the signature score to his life from the day he started secondary school. And where were they now? Moments ago he was inches away from a kiss that would have kickstarted their future. And then the game had resurrected and now he was forced to wonder who was behind it.

Frances? Or could Lila possibly be behind it? And how he would feel if she was.

They were in her flat. A property that he suspected that she owned and yet she had told him that she'd rented it. She'd left suddenly for the US and now, almost as impulsively, she was back. Why?

'Trent?' Lila said again.

'I don't know,' he said.

'Well, I hope it's over,' Frances said. 'In the nicest possible way I'd be happy not to see either of you for quite a while.' Trent stared at the phone. Could he read anything into that? Reverse psychology? 'I'll leave you both to it.'

Trent slipped his phone into his pocket. The world had shifted. He needed to leave, to try and clear his head. Not what his money would have been on only a few minutes ago.

Lila reached for his hand. Was the magic still there? Lila smiled at him and he was aware of something happening for the first time he could remember. He felt nothing.

Did he love Lila Jain? Yes.

Did he trust her? Right then, he didn't trust anyone.

'I'm okay,' he said, pushing himself up. 'But I'm going to head home.'

She was standing next to him and she reached up and hugged him, leaning into him. Instinctively he stroked her hair. He could smell her perfume, feel her warmth and he felt empty. He tightened his grip, pulling her close. As they uncoupled her hair brushed against his cheek. There they were again, at that inflexion point. Moving close enough to kiss, or far enough away to be saying goodbye. He saw tears in Lila's eyes.

'Do you want me to stay?' he asked, almost a reflex action.

She shook her head and smiled through the tears. 'No, I'm fine. You go. Just promise me you'll come and see me soon.' Her hands were still on his arms.

He kissed her on the cheek and then he turned and walked out of the flat. Trent held on to the banister as he descended the stairs to the ground floor. So many thoughts jostled in his mind but he didn't want to think. What he really wanted to do was drink. He pushed open the front door to the block of flats and headed out to the road where his motorbike was locked up. It would take him twenty minutes at this time of night to get home. He could be drunk within the hour.

Then he remembered that he was meeting Pen tomorrow. It was the anniversary of the fire and they were booked to go for breakfast to start their day. Trent didn't want a hangover. He sat astride the engine, stifling a yawn as he pulled on his helmet. He looked up at Lila's flat. The light was still on and he imagined her, sitting alone with the bottle of champagne. It could all have been so different. And maybe it still could. Just not tonight.

His phone buzzed. He knew what it would be. There was a pattern that the game followed. After each round, there was a warning that it wasn't over. He unlocked the screen, read the message, and then pocketed his phone with the words still echoing in his head.

Secrets work both ways. Play by the rules or you will never know the truth about your father.

He kicked down, adjusted the throttle, and pulled out into

the road. He rolled up to the junction at the end of the street and waited whilst a pedestrian crossed the road.

Only the final group round was left, and history suggested he would have at most two days before the endgame. He needed help and there was only one person he trusted right now. He hit his indicator and turned left.

73

FRIDAY 7:31PM

Twenty minutes later, Dylan opened her front door.

'It's back,' he said by way of explaining his presence.

'I know.' She turned and walked down the corridor. He knew the drill by now, so he closed the door behind him and switched off his phone before making his way to her computer room. Should he be surprised that she knew about the game's return? He was getting used to others knowing more than he did.

'I've made some progress in hacking the game,' she said. 'I don't know who's behind it yet but I was able to see what was going on.'

'Jesus, really?' His heartrate ticked up. 'You saw my round?'

'Yes.'

When it was clear that that was her total response he pushed on. 'How about Frances? Did you see her round? Neither Lila nor I saw it. And there wasn't a notification.'

'Yes.'

They both sat down and Dylan pointed to a screen which

showed Frances' questions and answers. Trent whistled. 'I thought that maybe she was making it up.'

'It looks to me as though it was done that way to make you think that Frances is behind this whole thing.'

In which case, it had worked pretty well, Trent thought.

'Can any of your friends code?' Dylan was trying a different angle.

Trent considered the question. 'I doubt it. Dub's a journalist so I guess he's good at researching online – but not coding.' He grimaced to himself. 'Frances tutors in Japanese. She's no computer geek but her husband works in computers. Some start-up that's going to rival DeepMind, apparently.'

Dylan perked up at this. 'What's his name?'

Trent was still following his thoughts. He shook his head, replaying her question. 'His name? Jake. Jake Churchill.'

He heard keys click as Dylan set to work. 'Got him. Interesting. Wow, can just anyone start their own tech firm these days? What's happening to the world.' She paged through his CV in a few seconds. 'Okay, here are some papers he's published.' She fell silent as she scanned through what was, presumably, some of Jake's finest work. 'It's not Jake,' she said.

'No?' Trent was scanning the papers on Dylan's screen but none of it made any sense to him.

'No. If he was behind the programming of the app, I'd have found him already.'

'Maybe he used a friend,' Trent suggested.

'His friends don't look all that either.' She had his company's website open on another screen. It appeared that she'd already taken the time to 'Meet the team' and, at a guess, there'd be no second date.

'You know, I think I'd actually prefer it to be Jake.' Trent didn't want to reject the idea too quickly. 'It's not as painful as it being one of the others.'

'It's not Jake. I just told you that.' Dylan gave him a look that offered him a cap to wear whilst he sat in the corner. 'What about motive?' she asked.

Trent scratched his head. 'It has to be connected to the secrets that were shared at Samson's sixteenth birthday party.'

'I agree.'

'But there's nothing obvious. Lila talked about her crush. Dub had, on the face of it, the most troubling secret. He thought he'd spotted a dead body at the river near to where he lived but it'd gone by the time he'd made his way back there with his father. Frances told us that she had discovered her father's collection of porn mags. Paddy, well,' he stole a look at Dylan, 'Paddy told us a story about his dad walking in on him when he was measuring the length of his penis.' He rubbed his chin. 'And Oli told us that she'd had sex on her sixteenth birthday. Something like that.'

Dylan tapped again on her keyboard. 'Okay. Well, let's review the clues the game has given us.' Trent just looked at her. 'You want me to spell it out,' she asked.

'Yes,' he answered.

'I've made a start.' She clicked on the screen and Trent shuffled forward. 'Every question that's been asked by the game is here in the order they were asked. Anything strike you about the questions as the rounds play out?'

Trent stared at the list. Oli's round felt much longer than three days ago. He read through them all. There was something there but it was as if his mind couldn't sharpen his thoughts into focus. What exactly was it?

'I think we're dealing with someone who's smart but emotional,' Dylan said. 'The first round encouraged everyone else to play. For the next two rounds it's clear the game had some very specific, objective knowledge and they wanted Oli and Paddy to know they'd use it. But it changes for Lila's round.'

Trent looked again at Lila's first question. *Was it Dub that ended your relationship?* He shrugged.

'Presumably only Dub and Lila knew the answer to that?' Dylan asked.

'She told me about the breakup,' Trent said.

'I was ruling *you* out.'

'Yeah, I mean, she told me. She could have told others.'

'And the answer was a surprise?' Dylan looked at him for confirmation before continuing. 'So, designed to throw people off balance in their assumptions about everyone else. But the most important question was Lila's final one. *Did you reveal anyone's secret from the party?* That is *the* question for the game. If it knew who'd revealed the secret, I'm not sure the game would even exist.'

'Meaning what?' asked Trent.

Dylan tilted her head. 'The whole purpose of the game seems to be focused on outing the person who gave up a secret. We don't know who gave up what secret and we don't know who cares so much but it's the crux of this whole thing.'

'But the game knows it wasn't Lila?' Trent asked.

'Yes. And Frances was asked the same question.'

'So it also knows it wasn't Frances.' Trent stopped as the thought slid into view. 'But it didn't ask me.' Dylan didn't say anything. 'Because it doesn't know whether it was me or not. So, I'm still a suspect.'

'Who's Anthony Wilson?' Dylan asked by way of response.

Trent frowned. 'I don't know.'

'That's a shame.' She moved on to the next point. 'Frances' final question is also odd. *Do you trust your husband?* Not, is your husband having an affair or, is your husband fiddling his expenses. It's just preying on her insecurity. It's the question that keeps her in line even if she doesn't have a final secret.' Dylan pushed on. 'The structure of the rounds also broke up for Frances. It was done in a hurry. No glimpses of private information, no school report.' She stared at Trent. 'I think something happened to bring her timing forward.'

Trent was silent. He'd thought the game was dead and yet the minute he'd told Pen about the batteries the game had roared back into life. And forced him to play his round.

'Let's look at your questions,' said Dylan.

The words of his first question were easy to recall. *Are you sleeping with Dylan Steele?* He swallowed. 'What do you make of that?'

'There's no way anyone apart from you and me could know that we haven't slept together.' Her delivery was textbook. From the clinical guide to discussing sexual relationships with people you barely know.

'I still don't –'

'The point is that the game didn't know the answer to that question. Same for the second question.' *Do you love Lila Jain?*

'What about the others?' His voice cracked.

'It wants you to push Pen about the night of the fire. It also knows about your father's medal nomination.' Trent jutted his jaw as Dylan continued. 'It wants you to think that it has what you want and for you to believe that it'll give it to you.' Trent felt his world tilt. Whichever way he took his thoughts he couldn't escape the fact that Pen had been thrust into the centre of everything. 'And that was confirmed in the message that you were sent after your round,' Dylan added.

'How did you know about that?' Trent lifted his head, recalling the message.

Secrets work both ways. Play by the rules or you will never know the truth about your father.

'I've been able to access all the messages it's sent. Group and individual.'

Trent's heart slammed against his chest. Surely Dylan would've been able to see who hadn't received a message. 'In which case –'

'If one of your friends is behind this, they've been smart enough to include themselves in the same way as everyone else.' She paused. 'Unless it's Paddy. He's the only one not to have received a final message.'

'Seriously?' Trent's eyes narrowed. 'Can you put them on the screen?'

Dylan was already typing. 'Here you go.'

Trent stepped forward. Dub's message was first up.

Six videos have been released. I have not yet released the final video. Or more accurately, the first video. You will have one chance to tell the truth. Only if you do that will the remaining video be permanently deleted.

The *first* video. That meant it could be old. Very old. But beyond that it told him nothing more.

Oli's was next.

I know all about your first love.

Again, too cryptic to be useful. But it pointed to something that had happened years ago. Trent had no idea who Oli would consider as her first love.

'Why do you think Paddy didn't get a message?' he asked.

'It's possible there wasn't another secret. But my guess,' she tilted her head, 'is that the game got it wrong with Paddy and had to abort.'

'He said he didn't lie.' Trent nodded. 'And if he didn't extort money from his client, something else entirely could have been going on with his client and TeeQ.'

He continued to read down the screen. Lila's he already knew as she'd shared it with him.

I know why you had to leave. Do as I say or the world will know too.

The final revelation was the message to Frances.

You were right not to trust your husband.

Trent slumped back on his chair. 'There's nothing there that helps.' But the pattern of final messages re-enforced his belief that there was going to be a final round. An idea was beginning to form. If there was to be a last round, perhaps they could turn the tables.

'Could you make a replica of the game?' he asked.

'Yes.' Dylan's expression clouded as if she was confused by the question. 'But if your plan is what I think it is, wouldn't it be better to just take over the existing game?'

Trent looked at Dylan and smiled.

74

SATURDAY 11:12AM

Trent and Pen walked, arms linked, towards the grounds where their family was buried.

'I'm glad you managed to sort things out with Bobby,' Trent said.

She smiled. 'He was fine, in the end. He's got this romantic trip sorted for this evening. He's taking me away to a surprise destination. I imagine it will be champagne and great food. He's told me he's confiscating my phone.' She smirked at him. 'So we don't have any interruptions.'

'Spare me.' He didn't need any more details. She was still his younger sister, after all. 'How's school going?'

She laughed before she proceeded to update him on the latest playground scandals and staff room fights, changing the names to protect the underage and the clueless. As he listened Trent forced himself to stay grounded. Today was not a day for anything but remembering their family and for being there for each other. They turned into the cemetery. It should have been raining, as they stood together, with the sky a foreboding grey and the clouds massing. A setting for tragedy. Instead, the sun skidded between the sparse clouds, and the sky was an iridescent blue, sometimes deep, sometimes pale.

Despite the sun, Trent shivered in his hoodie. The modern church where the funeral had taken place was a couple of hundred yards away from where they were standing, the expanse of glass, the wooden frame and the sloping roof looking no different to how it had been all those years earlier. A slight breeze played across his face as he felt in his pocket and pulled out the bright green plastic watch. Yoshi, Super Mario's friendliest dinosaur and Freddy's favourite.

The watch battery had lasted for a few months after Freddy's death and Trent remembered the day he'd looked at it and realised that it'd stopped. A dead battery. The end of time. The symbolism had crushed him. But Freddy had loved Yoshi and there was no way Trent would do anything other than treasure his brother's prized possession. He wrapped his fingers around the watch and pushed it deep into his pocket. He blew out the air from his lungs and took a deep breath. Pen took his hand and squeezed it. He glanced at her. Tears on her face, love in her heart. They interlaced their fingers and stood together, in silence, in memory of their baby brother and their parents.

'How are you doing?' she asked. 'You look troubled.'

Clearly, vowing not to think about something wasn't the same as not thinking about it. 'The Honesty Index. It knows all about me.' His voice cracked as he spoke. And perhaps more than his voice.

Pen let go of his hand. 'What happened?' she whispered.

Trent tried a shrug. 'It asked me five questions. Very specific questions. It knows I removed the batteries from the smoke alarm.' The last word caught in his throat. He'd tried to sound disinterested. But it was a forlorn hope because the statement was too heavily loaded. He still didn't truly believe that Pen had told anyone about it. But the fact remained that no one else knew.

Her eyes widened. 'Oh my God. How did it...' She turned to face him, frowning. 'You don't think I told anyone?' Her words carried a pain that crushed down on him.

'No. No, Pen. I don't. I know you wouldn't.' He paused before adding, 'I know you didn't,' but he could see the tension in her jaw.

'I haven't told anyone.' She stood quietly for a moment. 'Have *you* ever told anyone else? The police? Lila?' Her questioning was tentative, and he was grateful for that.

'No. Nobody. Not even Lila. I kept that secret to myself for ten years,' Trent said. 'They must've been listening when I told you the other day. The Honesty Index has been spying on me, and my friends too. Whoever's behind it knows everything about us.'

'Jesus,' Pen said.

Trent thought back to that night. An intensely private exchange between the two of them. A night when after carrying a burden for almost half of his life, he had confessed his sins. And all the time, someone else was listening. Someone who was planning to use it for their own twisted purposes. His round had taken place almost exactly twenty-four hours after his conversation with Pen. He'd nearly told Lila before he'd told Pen. Was the game listening then too? Of course it was. The game had been listening from before any of them had even heard of the Honesty Index.

'Why don't you tell me all about it?' Pen managed to make the question sound like a recommendation. 'Properly, and right from the beginning. We've got all day.'

Trent felt something unlock inside him. He hadn't wanted to think about it today out of respect for his family but Pen had given him permission. He paused to gather his thoughts and then he started talking about the events that had unwound in the park when they'd all received the invitation. It was almost impossible to believe that it was less than a week earlier.

Pen's hand flew to her mouth when he told her about Dub's videos and stayed there as she listened with just the occasional shake of her head as the story unfolded. Trent talked through each round before showing her the full suite of messages that he'd received about their father, the medal nomination, and the fire. Pen scratched her head. 'Whoever's doing this has access to really personal stuff.'

'Yeah. They must've hacked our phones, laptops, everything you can think of to scrape all this information.'

'Is that even possible? To access so much without any of you knowing?' she asked.

'Yeah, apparently. A friend of mine is into all this stuff, and she thinks so.'

'She? Lila?'

Trent laughed. 'No, she's called Dylan and she specialises in this type of thing.'

Pen raised her eyebrows, but Trent shook his head. 'No. It's not her. I didn't even know her when this started. And, believe me, she'd have zero interest in anyone's personal life.'

'And this all started after Samson's wake, and it's focussed on the six of you?' She paused. 'Samson had experience of manipulating data through his time working for his dad's company. What did you call it, data poisoning? It sounds so creepy.'

Trent nodded his head. 'I know, and Samson had some form of his own.' He told her about Annabelle Jackson. And TeeQ, and how he thought someone had carried on with Samson's plan after his death. Pen's frown hardened as he approached the end of the story and then she looked off into the distance.

'What is it?' he asked.

Pen tapped her fingers against her mouth. 'I'll ask Nicola whether anyone else was ever mentioned along with Samson in connection with the trolling of the teacher.' Trent looked blankly at his sister. 'Nicky, my best mate from school.'

'Red Knickers Nicky,' Trent said before he could stop himself. The story of Matthew Allenby walking into the girls' changing room at school and finding one of the girls standing almost naked had spread around the playground faster than she was able to pull her school dress back on. Red Knickers Nicky. A legend in her own underwear.

'Yeah.' Pen rolled her eyes. 'Nicola Wilson.'

A jolt fizzed through Trent. He was turning to face Pen when his phone rang and Lila's name lit up his screen. She'd messaged him every year without fail on the anniversary. And this year, she was calling. His hand hesitated above the *answer call* button. Had he heard Pen correctly? 'What did you just say? Nicola *Wilson*?' He hit the button to direct the call to voicemail.

'Yeah,' she said.

'Didn't she have a brother?' Trent asked. His heartbeat was tapping out its own SOS message.

'Yes.' Pen was looking at Trent, frowning.

'What was his name?'

'Oh, let me think. He was a couple of years older than you.' She pulled at her earlobe. 'Richard.'

Trent's shoulders slumped. He'd been certain that he'd found Anthony Wilson. 'Are you sure? Not Anthony?'

Pen shook her head. 'Definitely Richard. We used to laugh at their parents for calling them Ricky and Nicky.' Could the game have got the name wrong, Trent was wondering when his sister's words jolted. '*Anthony* Wilson is Nicola's *dad*. Mr Wilson. The teacher who was trolled.'

Trent stood in silence. *My God.* Pen rolled her eyes as Trent's phone rang again. He held his hand up to Pen as he answered. 'Hi Lila.'

'Hey, Trent. Oh, I wasn't expecting you to answer. I was calling back to leave you a message. I just wanted to let you know I'm thinking of you, and of Pen.'

'Thanks Lila, we appreciate it.' He paused, still processing what his sister had just told him. 'Hey, you know Frances' question about Anthony Wilson?'

There was a delay before she replied. 'From the game? Yes.'

'Well, Pen just told me who he is. She knew his daughter. He was a teacher.' There was a silence whilst Lila absorbed the information. Trent continued. 'I'd assumed it was another pupil. I didn't even think about teachers.'

'I can't believe I didn't make the connection either. He taught English.' There was another pause. 'But why would the game want to know about Frances and her teacher? It doesn't make sense.' Lila spoke slowly, as if feeling her way into the possibilities the new information opened up.

'Wilson was trolled by a student.'

Lila took a second to absorb Trent's word. 'Jesus,' she whispered. 'I can't imagine Frances would've done that.'

'Yeah. I know.' Trent caught a glance from Pen, a subtle reminder that today wasn't the day for long chats with anyone but her.

'Did Pen share anything else?' Lila asked. 'Anything that might explain what was going on?'

'No. That was it. Look, I'd better go, Lila,' he said.

'Yes, of course. Enjoy the rest of the day.'

'Pen says hi,' he added, catching Pen waving at him.

'Tell her I hope she enjoys her date with Bobby G. In the meantime give her a hug from me and take care of yourself.'

'Will do. Thanks, Lila. Bye.'

THE SUN DRIFTED behind a cloud and Trent reached for his flask. He poured coffee for both of them and handed one to Pen, who warmed her hands around the cup.

'People really thought that Samson was behind the trolling?'

'It was school playground stuff mostly. He wasn't popular and he was into computers. People thought he had the ability to do it. It was never anything more than that. The noise sort of faded away. He'd left the school and so had most of the people who knew him.'

'And nobody was ever charged?'

'No. Nicola still doesn't know who it was.' She took a sip of her coffee. 'She visited me when I was at teacher training college. We'd been drinking and she started talking about her father. I just let her talk because it felt like it was cathartic for her. That was when she told me about the trolling campaign.' Trent's mouth was dry. 'It sounded awful. Her dad denied all the allegations. He was interviewed by the police, and the school conducted an investigation. He was cleared, but Nicola blames it for her parents' separation.' She had no idea why anyone would want to attack her father.' Pen looked distant for a moment. 'And if her dad knows who it was, he's never told her.'

Jesus. Trent's head was spinning. Frances had been asked about her contact with Mr Wilson. But what had the precise question been? He tapped on his phone. *Did you have any contact with Anthony Wilson after you left school?* She'd answered no. But the campaign had taken place when she was still at school. And Frances had studied English at A level. As had Lila, Dub and Oli.

But why would any of them troll Mr Wilson?

'Can you do me a favour, Pen? Can you get me Mr Wilson's contact details. I need to speak with him.'

'Sure. He still works at the school, though. I bet all their emails have the same format. They do at my school.'

'Good point,' he said. He pulled out his burner phone and saw Pen's eyes widen. 'It's complicated,' he said whilst tapping out his message to Dylan. He'd found Anthony Wilson and now he needed Dylan to convince him to meet with Trent later that evening.

'Is everything okay?' Pen asked.

'I think whoever trolled Mr Wilson is also behind the Honesty Index. All I have to do is to get him to tell me who it was.'

TRENT AND PEN stayed at the grounds until the last of the sunlight had faded. They hugged each other tightly.

'Back to the real world,' Pen said.

Trent almost laughed. There'd been nothing normal about life over the last week. He was pleased for his sister though. Bobby was parked around the corner and was ready when she was. She was about to leave for her date and, if Dylan had worked her magic, Trent would soon be sitting down with Mr Wilson.

'Yeah. Have fun with Bobby,' he said. And as he spoke his mind rhymed.

Bobby, Bobby, Bobby G, if he's good for you, he's good for me.

75

SATURDAY 8:20PM

The pub used to be called the Three Pigeons, or the Three Pigs to Trent and his school friends, but no longer. The three pigs had met their maker and the pub had been renamed, The Butcher's Arms. Apart from the name, it hadn't changed much since Trent was last there. Less smoke, but similar gatherings of underage drinkers. He took a sip from his half pint glass. The beer hadn't improved any either.

He'd chosen a table out of the way of most of the teenagers and he was at the end of his drink when the pub door swung open and a man sporting a bright blue waterproof jacket walked in. Trent's suspicions were confirmed when a number of the boys at one of the tables visibly wished themselves into a hole in the ground as their teacher walked by. He had ginger hair, a full beard, and grey blue eyes. Trent was sure that he'd never been taught by Mr Wilson but he recalled having seen him around the school. And it appeared that Mr Wilson recognised him because he was striding directly towards him.

Trent stood up and offered him his hand. 'Hi. I'm Trent.

Thanks for coming on such short notice. Can I get you a pint?' he asked.

The teacher shook his head. 'Just a coke, please. I'm driving.'

Trent thought of his motorbike as he headed back to the bar and returned with two cokes. Mr Wilson had taken off his jacket and placed it on a spare seat.

'I don't get approached by reporters very often.' So, that's how Dylan had got him to turn up. His eyes locked onto Trent, flecks of steel in amongst the cornflower blue. 'Ever, actually.'

'Well, I should explain.' Trent had decided to be upfront from the get-go.

'I think so, Trent. You went into the law if I recall. Your friend, Andrew Dubnyk, he went into journalism.'

It was becoming a problem. Everyone knew everything nowadays. 'Yeah. Look, I'm sorry. I should've been honest with you.' He tried a shrug. 'I thought you might not come.'

'How reassuring. I assume there's nothing to stop me leaving?'

'No.' Which, unfortunately for Trent, was the truth. He cleared his throat. 'I wanted to ask you about something that happened years ago.'

It was a while before the teacher responded. 'You're Penny Ryder's brother, correct?' His expression soften slightly and Trent nodded. 'It must've been very difficult for you both. I taught her in the sixth form. I liked her. She had talent.'

'She'd be pleased to hear that but there's no way I'm quoting you.' Trent half smiled and shuffled in his chair. 'She's a teacher now. English.' He stopped himself adding, *like you.*

'Well, I hope she's got resilience.' He put a heavy emphasis on the last word. Was that a reference to his own troubles? Mr Wilson took a sip of his coke and glanced around the pub.

'I'll get to the point,' Trent said. 'Recently, I heard about a scandal involving a teacher. It would've been when I was in year thirteen, but it didn't come out until later.'

Mr Wilson sighed heavily. 'That was a long time ago.'

'Right. And I'm not here to make any problems.' Trent pushed on. 'But the pattern of behaviour, of attack, that was described to me sounds very similar to something that is happening to me and my friends now.' He'd decided that he wasn't going to mention that the teacher had himself been namechecked by the Honesty Index.

Mr Wilson took another sip of his drink. 'Then you have my sympathy. What happened all those years ago was very challenging.'

Trent didn't speak immediately. Sympathy was a start but he needed more than that. He crunched on a small ice-cube as he worked out how best to phrase things. 'And all the time it was going on, you didn't know who was behind it?'

Mr Wilson smiled but his eyes were dull; a smile to drain away any joy. 'They only used one name online. PokerFace.' He shook his head. 'Even now I can't listen to that song.'

'What did they do?' Trent asked, noting that the teacher hadn't answered the question.

Mr Wilson leaned forward and dropped his voice. 'You have to understand that teachers are very vulnerable online. I'm not on any social media now but back then I was. It all happened so suddenly. Posts saying things like *stop creeping around the swimming pool changing rooms*. Comments on other people's posts calling for the school to *find the paedo scum*. Replicated across various sites and forums. Nowadays we would identify them as trolls and block them, but back then I didn't know what to do. I was shocked. They hacked into my then wife's social media accounts too. Posted the same comments there.' His tone was robotic, like an economics student reading Shakespeare out loud to the class.

'And you never found out who it was?' Trent asked. And held his breath.

'People reveal themselves through their actions,' he replied.

'It might save some people from a great deal of pain if you tell me who it was.'

Mr Wilson put his glass down on the table and scratched his chin. For a moment Trent felt as though he was about to have his homework returned to him. Finally the teacher started to talk. 'If it's the same person then...' he trailed off.

'Please, tell me.' Trent shuffled forward on his seat.

'This person was,' he paused, searching for the right word, 'troubled. They caused terrible harm but they were also very young.' His eyes flicked towards Trent. 'Do you know your bible, Trent?' He didn't wait for an answer. 'Luke, Chapter 23, Verse 34. *Father, forgive them, for they know not what they do.*'

But Trent wasn't interested in forgiveness. Why did teachers always had to make everything a life lesson? He just wanted the answer. 'They're old enough now to know precisely what they're doing,' Trent replied.

He pulled out a piece of paper from his pocket and unfolded it before sliding it across the table. 'Did you teach all of these people?'

He'd printed three names: Lila Jain, Olivia Pearson, and Andrew Dubnyk. He'd selected them with care. Equally he'd been deliberate in leaving Frances off the list.

Mr Wilson didn't reach for the list, but Trent saw him look at it. He was watching the teacher's face intently and there it was. The tell. An involuntary twitch of his jaw before he folded the piece of paper back up and held it out towards Trent.

Trent took back the piece of paper. He was sure that the name of the protagonist was one of the three on that list, which meant that Frances was no longer under suspicion.

The teacher cleared his throat before speaking. 'I have no desire to revisit the past. There was an agreement and they've paid their price. It's over.'

Mr Wilson picked up his coat and stood up, pursing his lips. 'We're all protecting people, in our own way.' He took a step towards the exit before hesitating and turning back. 'When I received your invitation to meet this evening I was worried that you might be contacting me on behalf of the person behind it. I'm still not totally sure that isn't the case.'

The teacher's breathing was heavy as he stood opposite Trent, seemingly caught between the possible actions available to him. Whether to break the deal and reveal the name with the consequential pain of reliving those historical allegations, or simply walking away and protecting their identity. Time stretched and Trent held his breath.

'But the deal was that I would say nothing and she'd leave me alone,' he said. 'And a deal's a deal.' Trent stared at him, his heart thumping. 'Goodnight, Trent,' Mr Wilson said, and he shuffled his way to the door, nodding his head at a couple of teenagers who were on their way to the bar.

'Night, Sir,' Trent replied. Because old habits die hard.

And some tunes just stick in the mind. *Poker face. Poker face.* Repeat to fade.

76

SATURDAY 8:40PM

Trent tapped his fingers on the table. He hadn't got what he wanted. Mr Wilson had refused to divulge the name, but he had given him the next best thing. He'd narrowed the list down to two when he'd said that the deal was that *she* would leave him alone, forever. Which meant it had to be either Oli or Lila.

Nicholas Samson had been the original suspect for the campaign waged against Mr Wilson. Trent pulled out his phone and scrolled through the photographs until he found the copy of the notes Mrs Samson had given him. What had Samson said about Oli? One phrase jumped out at him.

We weren't close.

He scanned down to the comment about Lila.

One day she might understand the choice I made.

The choice not to give her up when everyone thought it was him. Could that be what it meant? Had Samson known it was Lila all along.

Trent didn't want to believe it, but the scales were beginning to tip inexorably towards Lila being behind everything.

He reached into his pocket and pulled out his burner

phone. He punched in Pen's number and waited. The call clicked through to voicemail. He cursed. He'd try again later. And then he remembered what Pen had told him earlier that day. She was giving Bobby her phone.

Bobby.

Bobby G.

A nickname Pen hated, and never used.

His breath caught in his throat. *Jesus Christ.* Lila had referred to Pen's boyfriend as Bobby G and yet Trent was sure that he hadn't ever used the nickname when speaking to Lila.

So, how did Lila know Bobby's nickname? There was only one possible answer. She knew Bobby already, and independently of his sister. But Lila hadn't mentioned it.

'Pen,' Trent said out loud as he grabbed his leather jacket and pulled it on.

He ran through the bar, almost knocking over one of the kids who'd waved at Mr Wilson. Once outside Trent sprinted across the carpark and unlocked his bike. As he stowed away the lock and chain he felt his phone buzz in his pocket. *Pen.* He scrambled in his pocket and raised the screen so he could read it.

A wave of nausea swept over him. It wasn't Pen. It was a notification of a new message from the Honesty Index.

That which does not kill us, makes us stronger.

Tonight at 10pm.

12 Gracechurch Lane.

As he read the text, Trent realised he was hearing it spoken by Lila. His subconscious was willing to accept the verdict before he'd rationally been able to come to terms with it.

He stared at the address. He'd been there three times before: Samson's sixteenth birthday party, the wake, and a few days ago to talk to Samson's mother.

Trent had expected a final round, but he'd hoped for more time. Why had Lila activated the final round now? It hit Trent straight from leftfield. Mr Wilson had left their meeting with a cold determination that a deal's a deal. He'd kept his word that he would never reveal that she was behind the smear campaign. Had he messaged Lila to tell her to back off, an ultimatum that could have triggered Lila to accelerate the final round.

Because Trent now knew the betrayal. Lila had been the anonymous troll. And she believed that one of them had known and had given her name to Mr Wilson. That the grass was therefore responsible for turning her life upside down.

Another thought hit Trent.. None of them had confessed, despite the pressure brought to bear by the game. Maybe Lila would be casting her net wider. If Mr Wilson had also mentioned Pen to Lila, perhaps disclosed that Pen was best friends with his daughter, she might now think his sister had been the one to betray her. Pen, who was currently with Bobby, Lila's secret friend.

Please, God, no. Don't harm my sister.

Trent dialled Pen's number again, this time using his usual phone. He was beyond caring who heard their conversation. He just needed her to answer. He had to warn her. But the call diverted to voicemail. *Damn.* He checked the time. Nearly nine o'clock. It would take him an hour to get to Samson's house.

He switched back phones to call Dylan. He had a plan in mind but as he tried to sharpen it, thoughts of his sister overwhelmed him.

That which does not kill us.

He was so tired of all the psychological bullshit but what if it wasn't an idle threat?

Until he knew Pen was safe he had no choice but to take it

seriously. A drip of sweat trickled down his back. And then he heard the click as Dylan answered his call.

'I know who's behind the game,' he said.

'Good.' She didn't ask for the name. Which meant that she was on the same page, or possibly the one ahead and waiting for him to catch up. 'Tell me what to write.'

Trent took a deep breath and started to dictate.

77

SATURDAY 8:59PM

Lila sat on the floor of her bedroom, the metal fireproof box resting on her bed, in front of her. She chewed her lip as she relived her first mistake. She hadn't even needed to include the bank statement. She just wanted to add a certain punch. A strong visual. And she'd been too tied up in that to spot the date. She'd played it to near perfection until Paddy's round. She sighed.

She'd misread the situation with Paddy. And she'd also misjudged him. As far as she could tell, Paddy had raised some concerns with his client's finance team about accounting irregularities. No doubt he hadn't been explicit, but evidently they'd been sufficiently worried that he was close to uncovering their fraud to do something about it. And what they'd done was to pay him a bung. They'd no doubt worked on the basis that he wouldn't call them out for fraud because he'd be wrapped up in it himself.

Paddy had told the truth. He wasn't extorting money. But the game had sent details to Todd Lane, information that suggested that Paddy might be talking to someone. And they'd shut him down. Lila hadn't known that Todd Lane was TeeQ. Didn't know his background. Wasn't familiar with his chosen methods of persuasion. She'd never imagined Paddy would be physically assaulted. And the shock of his mutilation had been enough to make her considered stopping.

But she was tired, so tired, of being who she was. She'd carried too many secrets for too long. Maybe she should even confess to what she'd done to Anthony Wilson. After all, that's where it had all started.

I'M the only one in the classroom, apart from him. Anthony's reading my essay, his brow furrowed as he turns to the last page. He hasn't looked up, not once. But I take that as a complement. He's totally absorbed by my words. I study his face as he reads. His frown deepens and I know he's aware that I'm watching him.

My story is about a teacher who falls hard for his student. It's not subtle.

I push back my chair and walk towards his desk. Anthony always smiles at me. He offered to spend the extra time with me 'for a final push' for my exams. He looks up at the sound of my shoes on the classroom floor. I can't read his expression. His eyes are more grey than blue. More experienced than youthful. But right then he looks uncertain. Almost vulnerable. I've never seen him like that.

I perch on the edge of his desk, aware that I'm closer than normal convention would permit. But then that's my whole plan. To push the boundaries until they wrap around us.

'What do you think?' I ask. I tilt my head, sparkle my eyes.

He clears his throat. Glances up at me and then his eyes dart away. 'I think the writing is strong.'

'I'm glad,' I say.

He pushes his chair back and stands up. But he's moving away from me. 'The subject matter is somewhat challenging.' He's left the essay on his desk.

'Really?' I keep my voice neutral. I'm not sure which way this will go.

'A touch too adolescent.' The word adolescent reverberates through my skull. 'And, I'm afraid, somewhat inappropriate.' He takes another step away. His voice is harsh, his smile nowhere to be seen. 'If you've got the wrong idea about–'

'It was a joke,' I say. But the words practically burn my tongue. 'My God, you didn't think ... you thought that I...' I force a laugh. But it sounds cold. Devoid of humour.

'Ah, yes. Of course. Well, even for a joke, I think it's inappropriate.'

I snatch the essay up of the desk. 'Fine. I get it. F grade for Lila. Must do better. Must try not to be inappropriate.'

I storm towards the door, the pieces of paper scrunched up in my hand. I glance at the metal bin and move to throw the essay away. But I stop myself. I don't want anyone reading it. So, I yank open the door and walk out into the corridor. The hinge creaks as the door slams shut behind me.

I make it to the toilets before I start crying. I bang my head against the wall. Not hard, but repeatedly.

WHEN SHE LOOKED BACK she knew that was the moment. The moment she stopped hitting her head and stared at herself in the bathroom mirror.

Maybe if she hadn't seen with her own eyes what he'd made her, the damage he'd wrought, maybe she would have got beyond it. But as she'd looked at herself in the mirror, she saw a hollowed out, shallower version of who she'd been only moments earlier.

Humiliation had burnt inside her.

And she'd known, right there and right then, that she'd make him pay.

The move to America was meant to be the great re-set. She'd thrown herself into college and pulled herself out of her downward spiral. For a while at least. And then, slowly at first, she found herself gravitating to internet chatrooms, learning about coding, technology, and the powerful lure of data. She was digging deeply in that hole when, three years ago, she'd met Nicholas Samson, by accident, at a technology conference in San Francisco.

Well, by accident on her part. She'd got the impression that he knew she'd be there. More generally, she'd had the sense that, back then, he knew most things about her. She'd even suspected that he knew the truth about Anthony Wilson.

One day she might understand the choice I made.

That's what he'd written about her in his notes to his mother. So, it turned out, he did know about Anthony Wilson. He knew and he'd said nothing, when the easiest route would have been for him to tell the world.

They'd had a drink together that night in San Fran. Then another. And another. And Samson had begun to relax.

NICHOLAS SAMSON'S eyes are struggling to focus as he finishes his latest vodka and coke.

'I had this idea a while back,' he says. 'It was sort of an online version of the secrets game we played that night, on my birthday.'

I say nothing, nursing my own drink.

'Five questions. Five pleas. Nice and clean.' He pauses and leans forward to put down his empty glass. I signal to the waiter for another round. 'I coded it so that it marks the answers. Then it corrects them.'

I think of everything I know. Of the burden. And my intense desire to feel weightlessness.

Samson's still talking about his game. 'I used to imagine all your faces.' He laughs. 'It sounds silly now.'

I crunch the ice cube between my teeth. 'How would you know if we were telling the truth?' I keep my tone casual, but an idea is beginning to form. My snooping became a habit during the sixth form. Hanging round with the others made it easy to pick up information, to hack passwords, to find things out. None of them had been careful. Paddy still uses the same online banking passwords he had at school. But my casual habit has morphed into a full-blown, paying-money-to-access-information, addiction.

He shrugged. 'I didn't finish it. I was close but I stopped.' He shrugged. 'I guess I moved on. Grew up. Whatever.' Samson looked at me. 'You know, I think you were the only one who told us a proper secret that night.' His eyes dart over my face as if he's running his own facial-recognition software.

I concentrate on keeping my face neutral. Could he know about Anthony Wilson? 'I'd like to see it,' I say. 'The game.'

He laughs and leans over to pull his phone out of his pocket. 'I'll send it to you.' He tapped on his screen and a few seconds later I felt my phone buzz.

'You know my email?'

His eyes clouded. 'Yes. I send you my newsletter every year.'

'Yes, sorry. Of course.'

'I bet none of you read it.' He holds out a hand. 'It's okay. You don't need to tell me you do.' He stretches for the fresh vodka and coke that's been delivered to our table and takes a mouthful. 'It doesn't really matter.'

'I'm sure–'

'Really,' he says quickly, 'I don't mind. The five of you, you probably don't realise, but you were the only friends I had at Hayden Road. And I know that 'friends' is stretching it. I think the

whole secrets game, it was my way of trying to integrate myself into the group.'

'I'm not sure that was the best approach.' I smile as I speak.

He laughs. 'Yeah.' Shakes his head. 'You're right about that. Still, in my own way, I'll always be grateful.'

His words twist inside me. He's being genuine. I had no idea that we were ever that important to him.

NICHOLAS SAMSON HAD GIVEN her the scaffolding for the Honesty Index. She'd supplied the content and some final flourishes and some misdirection.

Lila blinked away the memory. She'd been genuinely upset to learn that he was dying from cancer. Did he suspect that she was working on his game? Was that why he brought the six of them together? She sighed. She'd never know whether it was partly for her benefit that he'd invited them all to his wake, but it was the perfect time to bring everything to an end. To remove the burden of knowing more than she had any right to know.

She still didn't want to be the one to expose other people's secrets. But she needed them to step up. To take responsibility for what they'd done and what had happened to them. She wanted them to tell the truth. To reveal the secret that tied Trent, Pen, Oli, and Dub together. Everything would be better for it; she was still sure of that.

She unlocked the case and opened the lid. She'd opted for the security of a cold storage copy of the final secrets. She looked at the two recordings. The first an audio recording on an USB stick which was both Frances' and Oli's secret wrapped into one neat package. She held the USB stick in her hand.

She knew the dialogue by heart. The build-up of Oli

ringing the doorbell at Frances' house. The click as the door opened. The pause. And then, a man's voice. Angry. Rough.

'What are you doing here?'

'I need to talk to you, Jake.' Oli's voice wavering.

'You can't come in.' Pulling down the shutters.

'I know she's away for a few days. We need to talk.'

'I told you that it's over. We can't–'

'I'm pregnant, Jake.' The shot. And then the chaser. 'And the baby's yours.'

It evidently took Jake quite a while to get his head around that simple concept, but he must've decided it was better to continue the conversation indoors. He rambled before he eventually came out and said what he'd no doubt been thinking almost from the outset. 'You should have a termination.'

'You don't get to tell *me to have an abortion, Jake.' Oli was practically screaming. 'I didn't come here to ask you. I've had an abortion before. And I've had to live with that every day. I'm not doing that again. I'm having this baby. That's what I came to tell you.'*

And that was Oli's secret. Well, half of it, anyway.

The other half was stored on the CD. Dub's missing video. His penchant for dirty videos dated all the way back to school. He'd asked Lila several times and she'd said always said no.

One time, he'd snapped. 'Why can't you be more like Oli? She likes a good time.'

It hadn't been hard to find the recording and to make a copy. She'd accidentally deleted the original but she'd still returned the original tape to Olivia's original hiding place.

Oli's parents must have been away the day they shot the video. Dub started videoing, with Oli pirouetting for the camera. He'd brought a tripod and the camera swings wildly around Oli's bedroom before fixing its view on the bed.

Most people wouldn't have noticed anything remarkable beyond the act itself. But Lila wasn't most people. And once she'd copied the tape, she'd rewatched it over and over. Trying to understand Dub. Or Olivia. And during those viewings she noticed two details.

The first was simply the date. Which could be very useful should anyone, such as the police, want to establish people's age. Certainly Oli had used it to blackmail Dub on and off over the years, right up until Dub discovered that Oli had slept with Jake. From then on they were equal.

Lila's second observation was more subtle, but much darker. She'd seen a red and blue striped tie on the floor next to the bed. Which was remarkable for two reasons. Firstly, because Oli wouldn't have been seen dead wearing a tie. And secondly because Lila had recognised the tie and knew immediately who it belonged to.

She placed both recordings back in the box, closed the lid and punched in the code to lock it.

She didn't have long to wait. She felt calm. After all, whether any of the secrets would emerge, wasn't ultimately up to her.

She could only hope they would make the right choices.

And then she'd finally be free.

78

SATURDAY 9:44PM

Trent tried to concentrate on the traffic as he made his way to the Samsons' family home but thoughts of Lila constantly assailed him. He'd never acted on his feelings for her because whilst they were at school she'd been in other relationships. And now, having reconnected over the last week, he'd held back, keeping that distance. There was a natural hesitancy, and then there was the Honesty Index. Everything was in flux.

Instead, he'd stuck with what he had, even if it was like worshipping a priceless work of art. Everyone could see not only how much you loved it, but also that it could never be yours.

And what now, now that he knew that she was behind the Honesty Index?

She'd been playing them all, playing him, this whole time. Was that why she'd come back? Because she believed that she'd been wronged. He couldn't help but hope that it was more than that; that it was bigger than that. Even with what he now knew he couldn't think of Lila as being so small. What had she said to him during their conversations?

It's something I'm working on myself.

Trying to be better at facing up to things.

Decisions I've made.

Had she been signalling to him that it was her? That the game was her way of making her face up to the truth. That she too had a final secret and she wanted that to be revealed. Although perhaps *wanted* wasn't the right word.

He pulled away from a green light and wondered how the others would react. He couldn't imagine Oli, Dub, or Paddy having any sympathy. And why should they? Frances was harder to call but Lila had hinted strongly that Frances' husband was having or had already had an affair. Surely, she'd gone too far to repair her relationships with any of them.

He turned into the Samsons' road and parked a few houses away. He felt his phone buzz in his jacket pocket and his stomach churned. He pulled out his phone. Reading the message was like being plunged into ice cold water.

Pen Ryder has been added to the group.

79

SATURDAY 9:53PM

Trent stuffed the phone into his jacket pocket and ran along the road to the Samsons' house. There was no one else in sight as he approached the driveway. The gate was open and Trent didn't hesitate as he turned in and headed for the front door. The first thing that struck him was that there were no lights on in the house. It looked uninhabited. He noticed the 'for sale' sign that was staked into the garden. It had only been three days since he'd been there and Mrs Samson had already moved out. He heard the crunch of footsteps on the gravel path. His heart was thumping against his chest.

Frances appeared from round the side of the house.

'I thought I heard someone,' she said, using one hand to push her hair away from her face whilst the other rested on her belly. Hard to fathom that on top of everything else Frances was pregnant. 'There was no answer when I rang the doorbell. The side gate's open, though.'

There was no warmth in her words but then Trent didn't expect any. Everyone would be on edge. Exactly as the game wanted.

The invitation, if that was the right word, hadn't been explicit but he knew they'd be meeting at the clearing in the woodlands at the end of the Samsons' garden. Where they'd all sworn to keep each other's secrets over nine years ago. There was a symmetry to it that was too neat. Too obvious. And it had taken Trent too long to work everything out but finally, he knew. Knew who, and knew why. But as to precisely what was going to happen, that was still anyone's guess.

A motion sensor light flicked on as he led the way along the path that ran down the side of the house. He stepped onto the decking before they dropped down to the lawn. As they walked through the garden towards the darkness of the woodlands Trent wondered about Nicholas Samson. He wasn't ultimately behind the Honesty Index but if he hadn't invited them all to his party, encouraged them to share secrets, none of this would have happened. Or would it?

Samson was just a decoy. Everything that was relevant was independent of Samson but Lila had seen the opportunity to build everything around him. Had she even recruited Annabelle Jackson to her cause, putting things in place as soon as she knew Samson was terminally ill? Annabelle had been almost perfect. Trent recalled the text message that she'd received part way through their meeting. He had no way of knowing what it had said but had that been from Lila, had she been ring-mastering the whole exchange?

He climbed over a low fence that he didn't remember from before, waited to help Frances over and then followed the path into the woods. Frances was using her phone to light the way and didn't seem to be in the mood for talking, both of which suited Trent just fine. There would be plenty of time for talking when everyone was together. He ploughed on, scanning ahead for his sister. Minutes later he came out into the clearing. There were a few logs pulled round in a rough circle. Improvised seating that was so familiar.

The others were already there. He wasn't surprised they'd turned up; he knew the power that the game held over them all. But there was no sign of Pen. Lila and Oli were sitting whilst Paddy and Dub were standing behind them.

Trent tried not to stare at everyone. He had actively worked through analysing each of them, challenging himself to be as objective as he could and it'd made him feel awful. Even for those who he now knew to be innocent he'd forced himself to look for the worst in each of them and it was hard to un-see those human failings.

Lila was wearing a denim jacket and had her arms wrapped tightly around her body. Did she know that Trent was seeing her properly for the first time? He had spent nearly half his life loving her. And he knew that in her own way, she loved him back. But people could still hurt the ones they love; sign the confession and then add, P.S. I love you.

Lila was looking back at him. She had summoned him here and she held all the secrets of his life in her heart. He lowered his head. It was instinctive and natural. To wither under a searing light.

Paddy looked a mess. He couldn't have been out of hospital for more than a day but the bandage on his hand was dirty and there was grime on his face. His eyes were wild and he was twitching on the spot.

Dub was leaning against one of the trees. Trent wasn't sure where he'd been sleeping for the last few nights and from the state of him it was possible that he hadn't slept anywhere. Faded jeans, black trainers and a red adidas long sleeved t-shirt. His normally neat hair was unkempt and he was sporting the beginnings of a beard. Dub, uncharacteristically, was also smoking. Trent recalled a memory from a previous lifetime and shook his head. He wouldn't be smoking for Lila Jain tonight.

Oli glanced at him. She wasn't wearing any make up and her hair was pulled back. Oddly Trent thought she looked better for it, as though she had ditched her shield. She was wearing jogging bottoms, another XL t-shirt, and yellow crocs. She didn't say anything, didn't wave, just sat their chewing gum, waiting for destiny to come calling.

Trent sat down and watched the others join the circle of seats. He took a slow breath. What doesn't kill you might well make you stronger but first of all you had to survive.

It was Frances who broke the silence. 'This really isn't funny. Whichever one of you is behind this sick joke, Jesus Christ, so help me God, will you please stop.'

He understood her pain. She knew one of them was behind the game; that one of them had set out to destroy people who regarded them as a friend. She couldn't have expected anyone to come forward. Not then. But there was movement from the trees. Trent strained his eyes to look into the woodlands. Two people emerged into the clearing.

'Jesus, Pen.' Trent was on his feet. His sister had changed into a floral cocktail dress but that wasn't what shocked him. She was wearing a blindfold and Bobby was guiding her forward and her boyfriend's hand was behind Pen's back. *What was happening?* 'What the hell are you doing, Bobby?' Trent shouted.

'Trent? Is that you? Bobby, is that Trent? Is he part of the surprise?' Pen didn't sound concerned.

Christ. She thinks that this is all part of her mystery date. 'Let her go, Bobby,' Trent said, starting to walk over towards them.

'Wait there, Trent. Now, relax man. No drama. Hey, Penny-pooch, I'm just going to take off your blindfold.' Bobby's eyes flicked around and he held out a palm towards Trent.

'What's Pen doing here?' Paddy asked. His tone was aggressive and carried some unspecified accusation against Trent.

Trent didn't blame him. Some of them would no doubt be thinking that he was behind the whole thing.

Pen shook her head as the blindfold dropped away and confusion flooded her face.

'Where are we, Bobby? Why are we here with Trent?' She looked around. 'And...' The realisation hit her. She'd been brought to the group who were being played by the Honesty Index.

Bobby passed her a phone. 'You're going to need this,' he said. 'It's part of the surprise.'

Pen looked at her brother. 'Trent?' Her voice waivered as she said his name.

'It's okay, Pen,' Trent said. But he was lying. And praying like hell.

Everyone was there. And as if in a modern-day séance, they all held their phones. Trent knew they were all looking at the same screen.

Ready to play?

It was time for the last dance.

80

SATURDAY 9:59PM

Dylan was locked in. She was deep into the code of the game. She'd read the notes that peppered the coding, a monologue that formed Lila's personal manifesto. Quite the eye opener.

Dylan stared at the notes for the final round.

BACKGROUND COLOUR: Black

FONT COLOUR: Red

And then she had an idea. She flexed her fingers and returned to the coding. Her fingers danced over the keyboard until the code was finished. Then she updated the notes.

BACKGROUND COLOUR: Black

. . .

FONT COLOUR: White.

She smiled. She was done.

81

SATURDAY 10PM

Trent hit the *play* button.

Four out of seven people have joined.

Waiting.

A few more seconds.

Five.

Six.

Bobby was standing behind Pen, peering over her shoulder at her phone. He didn't look like a man who knew what was about to happen.

Selection complete.

The red radar began its sweep around the screen. This time there was an instruction to turn up the volume on the phone and then a mechanical voice started to speak; all the phones were broadcasting simultaneously.

Nine years ago one of you betrayed me. You didn't have the courage to face me and so you denied me the right to confess to my own truth.

There was a pause. Everyone's eyes looked hollow. Trent knew it had been coming but his stomach still dropped and he felt his pulse quicken.

You have seen what happens when you lie. For each of you there is a final secret. A secret that you prayed that I would not know or, for some of you, a secret that you are desperate to learn.

Trent swallowed as the voice continued.

This time you all get to play. All that is needed is for the right person to confess and that confession will release all the others. But a false confession will trigger the revelation of your final secret or deny you learning the truth forever.

Over the next minute you will each see your own individual information that I will share when the minute elapse unless the right person does the right thing. So now it comes to this. Tell me which one of you gave my name to Anthony Wilson.

And for the first time it was explicit. *This* was what it was all about. Lila believed that someone had told Mr Wilson that she was behind the smear campaign.

But Trent knew that that wasn't true. Mr Wilson hadn't needed anyone to tell him that it was Lila. He'd told Trent that '*people reveal themselves through their actions.*' Which meant that the whole game had been built on a lie.

In the top left corner of Trent's display there was the usual red digital countdown.

59, 58, 57...

It had given up its place to a new button on the top right of the screen emblazoned with a blood red confession.

It was me.

'Who the hell is Anthony Wilson?' Dub shouted.

'Mr Wilson was our English teacher from school.' Lila sounded calm but then again, she'd had more time than the others to process the news about Mr Wilson. Nine years more.

'Jesus. Trent?' Pen said, taking a step forward. Bobby's face was clouded with confusion. 'You said you didn't even know about it. And now you're saying not only that you knew, but that told Mr Wilson who it was.' She stared at him. 'Who the hell was it?'

It took all Trent's strength not to answer his sister and he felt a twinge of guilt at misleading her. Instead he focussed his attention on the image now displayed on the screen of his phone. It was a screenshot of the letter about the medal. He squeezed the phone and reached out with his fingers to scroll down the screen. The final paragraphs were still blurred. A tremor started in his hands and began to crawl up his arms. Pressure crushed down on his head and shoulders. He wanted the truth. But what would he discover?

Trent managed a glance around the group. Everyone was staring at their own personal nightmare. The numbers in the corner of the screen started to flash.

20, 19, 18.

'Will whoever did it, own the hell up.' Oli's voice was stretched.

But nobody moved. Trent shook his head. Think. Deal with Dad another time. Stick to the plan. His knuckled were white from gripping his phone.

10, 9.

The others were looking round the group.

'It wasn't me. Come on.' Oli pleaded.

Six seconds left.

None of them had betrayed Lila to Mr Wilson. So none of them would risk their final secret to protect the others. Which meant Lila had miscalculated. Everyone's secrets would be revealed. For nothing.

The screen shimmered.

'Jesus. Who hit the button?' Paddy was breathless. 'My screen just says *information deleted.*'

'Mine, too,' said Dub.

'And mine,' added Oli.

Trent cleared his throat. 'I did,' he said. 'It was me.'

Trent looked at his friends. He couldn't read the different emotions; he didn't have the space to process them right now. He settled his gaze on Lila who, as if on cue, stood up and walked over to sit next to him. She slipped her hand into his just as the Honesty Index's next voice message broke the silence.

Trent Ryder, you must stay and play the final round of the Honesty Index.

Nobody moved at first. There was no convention to follow. And then Oli stood up. She looked as though she was going to say something to Trent but then she turned and started to walk back towards the house. Away from Trent. Away from the Honesty Index.

'Guys. It's fine. I need to do this.' He smiled. At least he thought he had. 'I'll see you all on the other side.'

Paddy and Dub were standing a few yards away, hesitation in their eyes, unsure what to do. Dub started to move but Paddy loitered for a few seconds, until Trent nodded to him. Frances was moving too. She didn't say anything but her look was enough. Lila was biting her lip. Frances, Dub and Paddy clustered together as they made their way from the clearing.

'You should go too, Pen,' Trent said.

'I'm not going anywhere.' There must have been something in her voice because all the others stopped.

'Me neither,' added Lila.

'Okay. I'm staying, too,' Paddy said.

Trent turned to face Lila. Her face was strained and her shoulders slumped. They weren't exactly in this together but Trent couldn't go through with it without Lila. He lifted her hand and held it against his cheek. He needed this to be one secret that he could keep from her. For at least a few more minutes. Her eyes were dark, switched to dipped rather than dazzle. His father's image crashed into his brain, but he pushed the memory away.

One by one Paddy, Dub, Frances, and even Oli sat back down.

'Okay, let's get this over with,' Trent said.

Lila pulled on his hand. 'Are you sure? We could just walk away. Forget all about it.'

Was this her final test? She guided his hand up to her face and brushed his fingers against her skin. Mirroring his earlier action. There was a question in her eyes. She leaned a fraction forward as a self-conscious smile danced over her face. What would happen if Trent turned off his phone, if he said he would never be ready to play? The Honesty Index had already released the others, but it still had a hold over Trent.

'I can't. I need to know the truth.' His voice cracked as he spoke and he lowered his eyes.

'I know, Trent,' she whispered. 'I know.' She stood up and he released her hand. It was as if she couldn't bear to watch. Strange to think that they were each playing each other. Both believing that what they were about to do was for the best, not for themselves but for the other. A love that burned for the truth.

Trent couldn't afford to feel tired but more than anything right then all he wanted was to disappear. But it was so nearly all over. He'd known from the outset that this round of the Honesty Index would be different.

Lila's phone buzzed. Her forehead creased as she read the message. And then her eyes widened.

As if she had been messaged directly by God.

But it wasn't God.

It was the Honesty Index.

With a three-word question for Lila.

Ready to play?

82

SATURDAY 10:12PM

'What? No. This can't...' Lila looked at Trent. 'It's not possible. It's over.'

'Not quite,' he said. He stared at the screen. The switch to a white radar was a nice touch.

'What's going on, Trent? Why is it asking Lila to play again?' Frances' voice was strained.

And then Trent was looking at the first of Lila's five questions. He didn't have to read it to know what it said. Because he'd written it.

Did you know Bobby before he met Pen?

He studied her as she looked at the question. The real test was not what answers she would give, she must've known then that Trent had uncovered the truth, but rather whether she would answer at all.

At first, he thought that she was wrestling with her conscience but then he began to wonder whether it was something else. Looking back he could see that Lila had almost explicitly outlined the philosophy behind the Honesty Index, behind her creation. People should tell the truth but they should also be given the chance to confess to the truth.

Only if they refused should the truth be revealed, and then it should be released without constraint, without filter and without exception. And if it didn't kill you, you would be stronger for it.

Trent looked at his friends. Were they better off now than before the game announced itself? Maybe over time they would tell him. Or perhaps time itself would change their perspective. Pain fades. Guilt festers. Was that the choice?

'Who the hell is Bobby?' Dub asked.

Bobby himself had taken a couple of steps back into the woods as Pen turned to face him. 'Bobby? What's going on?' Pen asked.

Bobby paused before continuing to edge away. His face was crumpled with confusion. 'I'm sorry, babe. Look, I'd better bounce. I'll call you, yeah?'

'Bobby?' Pen said but Bobby turned and started to jog through the woods. 'Bobby,' she called after him. 'Come back.'

It hurt Trent to see his sister's pain but he was glad Bobby could no longer cause Pen any harm – intentional or otherwise. 'Pen, let him go,' he said.

Pen spun round, open mouthed, staring at her phone. 'Jesus. What *is* this?'

Lila twirled a stand of hair around her finger and that was when Trent knew that she was going to answer. He saw her click and her answer, *yes,* appeared on their screens.

'Lila?' Pen was incredulous. 'You knew Bobby? How did you–' She stopped mid-sentence and turned to face Trent. 'What's going on?'

But Trent's attention was already on the second question.

Was the secret you revealed at Samson's party that you had a crush on Mr Wilson?

Dub whistled and Oli turned to stare at Lila. 'Jesus, Mr Wilson was the older man you had a crush on?'

'What did he do to you, Lila? What could possibly make you attack him in the way you did?' Frances asked.

Trent was minded to think that Lila would've been unaware of the true impact her campaign would have, that she hadn't set out to destroy her teacher's life. It was easy to be a keyboard warrior and for things to escalate. She'd cloaked herself in anonymity but Mr Wilson had known that it was her and he had confronted her or her parents. There'd been an agreement between them. *A deal is a deal.* Trent was guessing but he'd put money on the fact that Mr Wilson approached Lila's parents and they'd sent her to America whilst they themselves moved to India. They'd sent her out into the world to make her own way. Dismissed. Disgraced. Disowned.

Lila again selected yes.

The third question appeared.

Did you anonymously troll Mr Wilson leading to an investigation by the school and emotional damage to him and his wife?

Lila swept back her hair and stared at Trent. Tears began to well in her eyes. There was something in her look. She was crying but Trent wasn't at all sure that she wasn't in some way relieved. She tapped her screen, pleading guilty to the third charge.

Trent wished he didn't have to watch. It was so hard to separate the Lila who'd done this from, well, Lila. His Lila. The soundtrack to his teenage and young adult life. As he watched her silently crying, his theory crystallised into conviction. This was what she'd wanted all along; this was the confession she was denied all those years ago.

But why bother with the game at all? He thought of their conversations. A question here, a comment there. Pushing

Trent to investigate his father, the insistence that they go back to Samson's party to uncover the truth.

The thought twisted. She had used Samson as her puppet. He'd wager that she'd had more contact with him over recent years than she'd let on. What had Samson said about her in his note to his mother?

One day she might understand the choice I made.

Samson had been accused on the smear campaign against Mr Wilson. Was that the choice? He knew it was Lila, but he chose not to expose her, even though it would've cleared his name. Whatever the truth, Lila had exploited Samson's history brilliantly, the connection with Todd Line, the blog about Samson's father's company. She had consciously tried to misdirect them all, first with Samson and latterly with Frances, to give herself time to build up the game's ability to coerce them all.

But when she was with Trent, when she was the *ideal* Lila, she would struggle to suppress the truth. She believed her philosophy. And, on some level, she knew it must apply to her as it applied to everyone else. No matter how painful. And so it had ended, as she had no doubt planned all along, with her sitting with Trent as he asked her to confess her secrets and admit to the truth.

Once he'd discovered that she was behind it, he'd thought that he could play her; make her endure her own final round. And yet right then he knew that it was him that was being played. Still. There was still something to come. Something she wanted him to know.

But the game was like a bullet that had already been fired. The next question was on the screen.

Did your parents force you to go to California after Mr Wilson confronted them?

Another yes.

Are you the Honesty Index?

Lila lifted her tear-streaked face. His every instinct was to go to her, to hug and to comfort her. But he fought to stay where he was. Even as she selected the final answer.

Yes.

He saw her shoulders jerk and heard her sobs but still he didn't move. Every synapse of his brain urged him to tell her that it was okay, that things could be worked out, but he forced his mouth closed and his heart to harden.

HONESTY INDEX

100%

No incorrect answers.

Was he a monster, to watch someone he loved break down and to not help them? There was no game to answer that for him.

None of the group had moved and every single one of them was staring at Lila. Trent doubted that any one of them had seriously thought that she could be behind it and now they were facing yet another truth. She had played them and, whether she had explicitly intended to or not, she had most definitely hurt them.

Oli took a couple of steps towards Lila, her face tilted down towards her. 'You total bitch.' Lila said nothing. 'What makes you so special?' Oli was spitting her words out.

'I'm not special.'

'I nearly lost my fingers because of you.' Paddy waved his bandaged hand towards her. 'And all because you had a crush on a teacher who had no interest in you.' He shook his head. 'You're unbelievable.' He began pacing around, seemingly unsure of what to do.

'You've all still got a secret.' Lila said it quietly but everyone heard. And everyone understood exactly what she meant.

It wasn't over.

A convulsion racked Trent's body. He was expecting a further revelation for him but not for his friends. 'I confessed, Lila,' Trent said. 'You've already released the others.'

She met his gaze. She must have heard the tension in his voice, a stress that told her that she could still win. 'That was on the basis that you were prepared to learn the truth.'

He nodded. 'I know.' He knew Dylan could hear everything. 'And I am. So let's do it.'

He waited for a second. From here on in, Dylan would cede control back to Lila. And that was the biggest risk. Dylan hadn't been able to access the link to Trent's final secret. It required fingerprint authorisation to access the file. So, it was a gamble.

Lila had promised that the others would be free, but the price was for Trent's final secret to be revealed. She knew about his obsession with the fire. And Trent believed that she knew the truth. A truth that was now only seconds away.

The screen in front of him shimmered. Lila's questions and her score disappeared. The original game was back. Trent's screen now showed his picture next to a button.

Click here for the truth.

Trent lined his finger up carefully next to his photo.

Lila was typing on her phone. What was her final reveal? He knew Lila was behind the game. He believed that on some level, she just wanted him to know the truth because the truth would make him stronger.

One click and the letter would be there and he would be able to read it in its entirety.

He swallowed. And then he hit the button.

No letter appeared. Just a statement. A statement that made no sense to Trent.

Ask your sister what happened on the night of the fire.

83

SATURDAY 10:31PM

Trent stared at the words, and then at Lila, and finally at Pen. Surely his sister couldn't have been keeping a secret all these years.

'What are you doing, Lila?' Pen took a step towards her. 'What game are you playing? I don't know anything more about the fire than Trent.' Her arms were folded over her chest.

'It's not about him.' Lila didn't say anything more.

What? *Not about him.* Trent felt his grip on reality loosen. His sister and his best friend. And he didn't recognise either of them. How had he got this so wrong?

'I thought I'd find out the truth,' he said, 'not play more games.' He could barely get the words out.

Lila spun towards Pen with an energy that surprised him. 'Tell him where you were that evening.'

Trent scanned his sister's face. Why did it matter where she'd been that evening? He thought she'd spent the afternoon with her friend, Hazel. He remembered sitting outside his bedroom door as he listened to their mum talk to their dad on the telephone. He'd only heard one side of the conversation but he'd felt the tension. Their mother was slurring and was talking unnaturally loudly and their father had returned home later that evening, his face flushed and his eyes dark and sunken. Why was Lila fixated on where Pen had been? Nothing was making any sense.

'You know where I was, Lila. But I don't see–'

'Tell him where you were.' Lila pointed at Trent as she delivered each word like a punch.

He fixed his gaze on his sister. 'Where were you, Pen?' Trent said the words as if he feared they could break her. Or break them.

Pen pinched the bridge of her nose and shook her head. And then she started to speak. 'I was out with Lila.' Trent took a step back as if he'd been hit. *With Lila?* 'I'd told Mum and Dad that I was going round to Hazel's house. And I did. But I got bored and so I came home via the park, where I bumped into Lila.' Pen looked as though she was in a trance. Her voice was monotone, her face impassive. 'We hung out for a bit and I lost track of time. Dad and Hazel's father found me in the park.' She glanced away. 'I was smoking. Dad hit the roof.'

Trent's legs wobbled. That's why their mother was in a mess. Because Pen had been missing. The phone call from their dad was to say she'd been found. And then Dad had come home with the disgraced daughter. Trent could remember his parents screaming. Snatches of his mother shouting came back to him.

'She's a teenage girl, for Christ's sake.'

'And you think that makes everything okay?'

Followed by the front door slamming closed.

He recalled Freddy creeping into his room, his eyes wide, asking what was going on. He'd given his brother a hug, told him not to worry and sent him back to his own bedroom to sleep. As it turned out, forever.

All those years. Every single night since the fire Trent's guilt had been waiting for him as he fell asleep. Yes, he'd taken out the batteries. But he'd also asked to put them back. His parents, drunk and angry, had been in no mode to drive to the shop.

Trent saw a narrowing of Pen's eyes. He hadn't told his sister that he'd asked to replace the batteries. When he told her that he'd removed them, he didn't want to shift blame in any way onto their parents. He'd wanted to own his actions.

But he could see clearly now. She'd never told him where she'd been when she should've been at Hazel's house.

Because there'd been no reason to.

Pen was next to him reaching for his hand, tears welling in her eyes. 'Trent, I don't understand. What have I said? What did I do?' Her bottom lip was trembling.

Trent wiped his own face. His words sounded scratchy. 'I asked Mum and Dad, later that evening. I said I wanted to sort out the smoke alarm before we went to bed. But Mum was drunk and Dad was emotionally wrung-out. Mum shouted at me and Dad told me he'd sort it out the next day.'

He could hear Pen still talking but couldn't make out the words. The fine drizzle had hardened to rain and he could feel water seeping through his hair. He shook his head and tried to focus.

'I didn't know,' she was saying. 'I had no idea. My God, Trent. Why didn't you tell me?' He put his arms around his sister and pulled her close. 'I'm sorry.' Pen sniffled into his neck.

'You've nothing to apologise for.' He squeezed her. 'Except smoking,' he whispered. She shuddered. Laughing? Crying? Probably both.

The others were standing together. The rain was heavier now but Trent didn't care.

Lila smiled at him and for the briefest time he forgot everything. But he knew it was an illusion. They could never go back. And then she turned and walked away from him. The others parted as she moved between them.

But Trent couldn't watch her go. So, he tipped his head up, rested his chin on his sister's head and closed his eyes.

84

SATURDAY 11:15PM

Trent, Pen, and Paddy were sitting on the logs. Oli, Frances, and Dub had left not long after Lila, exhausted and no doubt relieved. Paddy was still there although he'd checked that he wasn't crashing family time.

'How did she do it?' Paddy asked.

'She hacked us. She's been doing it for years. Our social media, email, web browser, databases.' He blew out a deep breath. 'She pretended she could barely manage email and internet searches but she learnt how to code in the US.'

Dylan had told Trent earlier that evening that she'd discovered a series of blog entries amongst the code for the game. Lila had dropped out of college to focus on data technology. Trent glanced at his sister. 'I'm pretty sure she even recorded us talking through my laptop.'

Paddy whistled. 'Unbelievable.'

'I found a record of a company she set up, Demeter Inc. I had no idea what it was for but it turns out that she used it for payments to access data.' He shrugged. Dylan's voice recounting Lila's recorded fascination with the dark web echoed through his head.

'Demeter is the Greek Goddess of harvest,' said Pen. Trent raised his eyebrows. His sister had never studied classics. She grinned at him. 'I remember her from the Percy Jackson books.'

'Huh. Well, that makes sense, I guess.' Data. The food of social media.

'So, Pen, that American guy's your boyfriend?' Paddy asked, scratching his head with his good hand.

'Yeah. Well, he was,' replied Pen. 'I'm not sure what he is now. Today was meant to be our six-month celebration.' She ran her hands over her face. 'Not quite the night I'd imagined.'

'For what it's worth, I'm sure he likes you, Pen,' Trent said. 'He wouldn't have known about all of this. Lila will have just told him she had a surprise arranged for you.'

She sighed. 'He didn't hang around though, did he? His car's gone from round the front.' She tipped her head back and screamed into the night air. No one said anything for a moment. Pen's next statement was a whisper. 'I really liked him, Trent.'

Trent forced himself to his feet. His wet clothes clung to him as he walked over to Pen and offered his hand. 'Come on, Pen, you're coming home with me. Oh, hold on, there's something I need to do.' He pulled out his burner phone. 'Dylan, you still there?'

'Yes.'

Of course she was. She always was. 'Thank you. For everything.'

Paddy and Pen started to walk up the garden and Trent dropped behind a couple of paces as he followed them.

'Are you okay?' Dylan asked.

'Probably not,' he said, glancing at Pen, 'but I think I will be.'

'I think so too.' And although he'd never tell her so, that reassured him more than almost anything. 'I've got some other news for you.' Trent felt a tremor travel through his body. He was sick of news. Dylan carried on. 'I know why your Aunt hasn't replied.'

Trent caught his breath. He hadn't yet reconciled himself to the game not revealing the truth about his father. He recalled Lila's words sometime from the days before.

I don't think it could ever have known everything.

Was that her way of preparing him? Had the source of his parents' argument been the big reveal?

Dylan was still talking. 'Lila changed her contact details on your phone. Every time you were calling or texting her, it connected you to a number that Lila had set up. If you check your text messages, you should see that the first message you sent didn't continue from the previous message history.'

Trent was almost too tired to process what Dylan was telling him. He forced himself to think. 'So Aunt Jo wasn't ignoring me.' Lila must have changed the number in his contacts when he was at her flat. He'd left his phone with her for a few minutes. Right after he'd received the message about the medal. 'But if there was no medal, no nomination, if that was all fabricated why would Lila need to do that? Aunt Jo wouldn't know anything about it.'

'Correct.'

'Whereas, if it was true, she'd have confirmed it. Aunt Jo would already know everything that the game was promising me.' He stopped walking. 'The game would have lost its control over me.'

Dylan didn't speak which Trent knew meant that she was waiting for him to catch up. And his brain finally fused the connection. *Jesus.* The Honesty Index might be finished and Trent still didn't know the truth. But Aunt Jo did, and now he assumed, so did Dylan.

'I haven't read it,' she said.

And there it was. The game knew why his father hadn't received the gallantry medal. Trent was too tired to process his feelings. He sighed. 'Thanks, Dylan.'

Trent started walking after Paddy and Pen. All the energy and all the hope that he'd directed into learning about his father had drained away when he'd unmasked Lila as the Honesty Index. He didn't know how he felt about anything, right then.

'Trent?' Dylan asked.

'Yeah?' They were all back out on the road now. He waved to Paddy who was heading off towards the tube and Pen was waiting for Trent to finish his call.

'I just want to be clear with you, I have no interest in having sex with you.'

He smiled to himself. 'Okay. Thanks for clarifying that.'

'But a drink sometime could be acceptable.'

He laughed. 'Yeah. I'd like that too, Dylan.'

ONE WEEK LATER

85

SATURDAY 2:52PM

Earlier that afternoon Pen had led Trent into his private study and together they'd dismantled everything on his corkboard.

Pen hadn't said anything about it – what was there to say? – but she had carefully removed the drawing pins, folded the paper into the recycling bin and slipped the family photo into a frame which she'd placed on his desk. And when the corkboard was empty she had gone downstairs and returned to the room with the printed email from Aunt Jo and pinned it in the heart of the board.

Pen had rested her head on Trent's shoulder as he had stood rereading the known facts about the application on behalf of their father for the gallantry medal.

Dear Sirs,

Civilian Gallantry Medal: Posthumous nomination for David Simon Ryder

On 21 September 2008 shortly before midnight, the Fire Service received a report that a fire had broken out at a residential address. On arrival, the Fire Service could see that the ground floor was completely engulfed in fire, and flames were licking up the first floor. Nominee David Ryder, my brother, had contacted the fire service via a 999 call when he had arrived home to find the family home ablaze.

His wife and three children were in the house, asleep. Mr Ryder entered the building to attempt to rescue his family. He was able to drag his daughter to safety and she was found alive and well when the fire service arrived. Mr Ryder then re-entered the building and battled his way upstairs to try to save his wife and sons whilst the fire was taking hold on the first floor where they were sleeping. His carried his eldest son down the stairs and through the flames and placed him in the garden. His son was taken to hospital having inhaled some smoke and lost consciousness. He later made a full recovery. The fire service found Mr Ryder by the side of the bed of his youngest son. Sadly both of them, and Mrs Ryder, were dead by the time the fire service discovered them.

The actions of David Ryder were courageous, utterly selfless and displayed extreme bravery in the face of such immediate danger. The actions of David Ryder saved the lives of two of his children.

Yours faithfully,
Mrs Josephine Carter

RECORD OF NOTIFICATION OF OUTCOME:

To: jcarter1245@hotmail.com
From: honours@cabinetoffice.gov.uk
Date: 12 July 2011

. . .

Dear Madam,

Thank you for submitting your nomination for your recently deceased brother, David Simon Ryder, for a Civilian Gallantry Award.

The nomination has been duly considered by the George Cross Committee and we have concluded that whilst the circumstance around the death of your brother and his family were tragic, the evidence did not suggest that the criteria of any gallantry award were met.

Yours faithfully

Sir G. O'Flaherty, Cabinet Secretary,
Chairman of The Cabinet Office's George Cross Committee.

Aunt Jo hadn't told them simply because there was nothing to tell.

But Trent simply couldn't believe that there was nothing more. On the face of the application, the award should have been granted – that had long puzzled him. The publicly available information on cases where the award had been made didn't seem disproportionate to their father's actions.

Trent sat on the chair in his kitchen, a cup of cold coffee in his hand. He was staring at the screen of his phone. He swallowed and tried telling himself that it'd be okay. There was a picture of each of his friends. His mouth was dry and a chill worked its way down his spine. Because next to each picture was a link with a five-word invitation.

Click here for the truth.

He'd had enough truth for the rest of his life.

What even was truth? He no longer knew.

He scanned the faces of those who'd be forever bound by

the experience of playing the Honesty Index. They each deserved to share their own truths on their own terms or not at all. That was *his* philosophy. His eyes fell on Lila's photograph. She still made his heart stop.

Click here for the truth.

He blew out air, emptying his lungs. His finger hovered over the link. Had she always known he'd get to here and, if so, what message had she left for him? He caught himself. No, that wasn't right. The real question was whether or not he wanted to hear what she had to say.

He looked up to see Pen watching him. She came over and wrapped her arms around him. 'You've tortured yourself enough already.' She had a point. It had been on a loop in his mind. How it'd begun and how it'd ended. Each round of the Honesty Index had been a means to an end, a clearing of the board until the final two pieces were left, exposed and waiting. Trent and Lila. 'I'm going to make another coffee.' She prised the mug out from his fingers. 'You want a fresh one?'

He nodded. Pen had moved in to his house a few days ago, just a couple of days after the final round of the Honesty Index. It had helped him having his sister around and he hoped that he was helping her too. Together they'd started to pull everything they knew apart and they'd begun to rebuild their lives, together.

Trent's eyes were drawn to the invitation next to his own photo.

Click here for the truth.

And then, before he could stop to reconsider, he pressed on the button and his screen filled with the text of a memo.

GEORGE CROSS COMMITTEE DECISIONS – JULY 2011(page 4)

. . .

NOMINEE: DAVID SIMON RYDER (deceased)
NOMINATOR: JOSEPHINE CARTER (sister of nominee)
DECISION: NO AWARD

CONFIDENTIAL NOTE OF DECISION:

WHILST THE INITIAL evidence was supportive of the nomination, citing the bravery of David Simon Ryder in returning to the burning building and risking his own life to save the lives of his children, the committee concluded that the additional evidence made it impossible to conclude that the criteria for any gallantry award was met.

The Fire Safety Office's full, unredacted report made it clear that the door to the main bedroom, where Sally Charlotte Ryder was found dead, was locked at the estimated time of her death.

Although it was impossible to conclude exactly what had happened, there was a report of a domestic incident at the property earlier that evening. It is unclear whether the bedroom door was locked from inside or outside the room. It was therefore felt inappropriate, with regard to all the circumstances, for a civilian gallantry medal to be awarded.

TRENT SAT in silence until Pen brought in the coffee. He waited until she placed both cups down on the table.

'I know why Dad wasn't awarded the medal.' His voice sounded robotic.

Pen's eyes widened and she slowly lowered herself down to the chair. 'Why?' It came out as a whisper.

He went to pass his phone to her but Pen waved her hand. 'No. I'd rather you told me.'

Trent swallowed. 'Their bedroom door was locked. Mum was inside.' The words rasped in his throat. 'Dad was outside.' He blew out a breath. 'They didn't, they couldn't, conclude on what had happened.'

Tears filled his sister's eyes. Trent stood up and took a step towards her, his arms outstretched. They held each other and he stroked her hair. The image of the locked door swamped his thoughts. Who locked it? And why? He thought he'd find the truth. But the absolute truth was unknowable.

'My mind keeps running these scenarios,' Pen said, her words muffled in his jumper. 'Mum did this. Dad did that. I don't know what to think.'

'I know,' Trent said. He sighed heavily. 'There aren't any good conclusions. There's just pain.'

Pen sniffed and lifted her head from his shoulder. 'I love you, Trent.'

Trent squeezed his sister as tightly as he could. 'I love you, too, Pen.'

86

SATURDAY 4:12PM

Pen's phone beeped and Trent pulled the lounge back into focus. How long would it be before phone alerts no longer sent his central nervous system into spasm? He'd turned all his own notification off.

'Dylan's invited us round to hers for dinner. C'mon, let's go.' She pulled Trent out of the chair. 'We need to get out of here.'

'Yeah, okay,' he said. 'There's something I need to do. It'll only take a second.'

He held his finger down on the Honesty Index icon until it started to shake with a small cross hovering over it.

Do you want to delete this app?

Jesus, yes. Yes, I do.

He hit delete.

He received a message by return. This time it wasn't the app resurrecting itself. It was an email. From Lila. He hesitated.

The rest of them had discussed reporting her to the police. Perhaps one of them still would but Trent just wasn't sure what her crime had been. Hacking and invasion of privacy, for sure. But none of their secrets were protected by law. Nor was it libel or slander because she was sharing the truth. She hadn't tried to extort them. Even Todd Line seemed to have Paddy marked out before he played his round; Trent himself had seen the warning shot fired.

He thought back to Lila's rationale. She saw herself as nothing more than a tabloid journalist asking for a comment before launching an exclusive. Perhaps she felt a higher calling, but it was a good enough analogy.

His thoughts were interrupted by someone ringing the doorbell. He closed his phone and pushed himself up. He opened the door to find Oli standing on the doorstep.

'Hi, Trent. May I come in?' Trent hesitated. Pen was hovering behind him. 'I need to talk to you. Both of you.'

Trent took a step back, indicating for her to go through to the lounge, and followed her in. He exchanged a glance with Pen. Oli perched on the edge of the sofa; her hands clasped together.

'I've been thinking about this since the game started. Well, longer than that. I've decided that you should both know the truth. I don't need you to do anything with it. I just think ... I think you should know what happened.'

Trent's whole body tingled. He'd just deleted the app. He'd thought this was all over. 'I'm not sure I want to–'

Oli closed her eyes. 'I know. Look, I'm telling you both this because it concerns you. I think it's important. I've kept the secret for so long. I'd thought that was for the best. But if the last couple of weeks has taught me anything, it's that I'm not built for keeping secrets.'

She blew out a breath. Trent was balling his hands, his nails digging into his palms. He swallowed. And waited.

'I lost my virginity before I was sixteen.' Trent remembered Oli revealing that secret the night of Samson's party. Oli bowed her head. 'The guy was...' She was hyperventilating now. 'I'm just going to say it.' She bowed her head. 'It was your father.' The world slowed. What had she said? Their father. That couldn't be true. 'I was pregnant. And shortly after my sixteenth birthday, I had an abortion.' Trent couldn't speak. He stared at Oli. Then at Pen. Thank back at Oli. 'That's it. That's my truth.'

TRENT CLOSED the door behind Oli and watched her walk down the drive. She'd stayed for nearly an hour. He shuffled back into the lounge. Pen was lying on her back, on the sofa.

'I just can't get my head round that,' Pen said.

Trent lowered himself to the floor. 'The night of the fire, Mum and Dad were arguing.' His sister nodded. 'After what Lila made you tell me, I'd thought they were arguing about you. But they weren't.' Tears pooled in his eyes. If Lila had known Oli's truth she'd tried to bury it in the end. At least until Oil herself decided to dig it up.

'No,' Pen said. 'I don't think it was about me either.' She swung her legs round and slipped off the sofa onto the floor. She reached for Trent's hands.

'The things I heard Mum say...' He trailed off, replaying the words in his mind. 'I think Dad must've told her. And she threw him out. But he came back and the house was on fire.' He sniffed and swallowed, trying to keep control of his voice.

'Do you think he...? Do you think Mum...?' Pen couldn't finish either question.

'I don't know,' he replied. He squeezed his sister's hands. 'We'll never know the truth.'

. . .

TRENT HAD no idea how long the two of them had been lying on the floor. Pen rolled over and pushed herself up.

'Come on. Let's go to Dylan's.'

He watched her walk out the room, heard her getting her coat from the cupboard. With a sigh, he picked up his phone and opened Lila's email.

I leave tomorrow to fly back to California. Can I see you before I leave? X.

He knew what the others would do in his place. Block sender. Delete message. But he wasn't the same as the others. And this was Lila. He'd cut her off once before. And he knew he should do so again given what she'd done.

He raised his eyes to the ceiling, shaking his head, before he typed *yes* and hit send. Then he switched off his phone, slid it in the table drawer, and followed his sister out into the evening.

ONE YEAR LATER

The evening sky was tinged with orange and red; a bewitching combination of the angle of the sun and particles in the atmosphere unweaving the pure white sunlight to paint the clouds with a golden hue.

As they turned out of the graveyard onto the road, Trent felt Pen nudge him in the ribs. She was pointing down the street.

'Look. Dylan's waiting for us.'

Trent still wasn't quite sure how to describe his relationship with Dylan. She was a decade or more older than him, and they didn't have anything in common. But she seemed to have taken an interest in him. In his well-being. They didn't spend much time together and yet every so often she would appear. Never for long. Never with a suggestion to do anything. But they'd talk. And then, after a while, typically on some unspecified cue, Dylan would leave again.

Yes, she was outside, which was unusual. And she was, of all things, leaning against a lamppost. But he wasn't surprised to see her. Not today. Because it was the anniversary of Freddy's death. Of the day that the fire claimed his little brother, and his mother. And ... his father.

He swallowed. Had the truth set him free? Were things better now, than had his father's secret remained buried? Trent still didn't know. All he did know was that, day by day, the hardest things, unimaginable realities, blurred just a little more out of focus, and all he could hope for was to continue down that route.

'Hi,' Pen said as they approached Dylan.

Dylan pushed herself upright. 'I just wanted to check on you both.' A pause. 'Today being the anniversary.' Trent nodded. 'How are you doing?'

How was he? He couldn't answer that. Not easily. What about his sister? In truth, they hadn't chatted much that day.

Maybe they were out of words. Or perhaps they'd reached an equilibrium. Whatever the reason, they'd passed much of the day in companiable silence. It was unusual for Dylan to ask a question. Particularly one with such resonance. Trent felt a lump form in his throat. Why was that? He'd been fine all day. Even looking at his brother's grave. He felt Pen reach for his hand and give it a squeeze.

'We're doing okay, Dylan,' Pen said.

Dylan nodded, her gaze flicking between the two of them. 'I'm glad you have each other.'

'Yeah, we're doing okay,' Trent echoed eventually because anything else was too hard. He opted to switch tack into calmer waters. 'Hey, I'm just heading off to meet some of the others. Paddy, Frances. Maybe Dub.'

'Yes.' Pen was bouncing with enthusiasm at the idea. 'You should go along. I'm sure they'd all like to see you.'

'Well, that would be a hard no,' Dylan said, glancing down the road.

Trent didn't even try to hide his grin. Same old Dylan. 'Paddy been giving evidence in the trial against Todd Line.' He studied Dylan carefully. Surely she had to be interested in the case, given she'd provided much of the evidence that was being used to prosecute Lines.

'I've been following it,' was all she said.

Trent eyes narrowed. Had she been in the court, sitting in the audience? He wouldn't put it passed her. Either that, or she'd bugged the judge. 'Then you know it's a murder trial, too. Paddy was lucky to get out of that alive.'

'I still can't believe he's giving evidence,' Pen said. She brushed her cheek as if to wipe away a speck of dirt. 'It's like he's been reborn. I don't know what he's going to do when it's all over.'

Pen was right. The transformation in Paddy had been

both miraculous and heart-warming; as if the real Paddy had been on sabbatical for a couple of years. And now he was back. Louder and buzzing with more energy than ever. Trent had spoken to him about the change but he hadn't plucked up the courage to tell him that he was still in touch with Lila Jain. He had broached the aftershock of the Honesty Index and he could remember every word of his friend's answer.

'I don't think I'll ever forgive her for what she did to us. But, at the same time, part of me admires her for doing it. It's crazy, I know. She had the courage ... no that's not the right word ... but if she hadn't done what she did, I'd still be living a nightmare. Maybe we all would. I don't know what that means. But I think it must mean something.'

Trent took a deep breath. Paddy's analysis wasn't so far away from his own. Except Trent's worldview was twisted. Filtered. Distorted. Call it what you will. He'd wrestled for a long time, probably always would, with why that was.

His most frequent conclusion was that it was because he loved Lila Jain. And that love seemed to exist independently of what she'd done. Perhaps you love people for who they are rather than what they did. Or he did, at least.

Which allowed him to then view her actions from the point of view of loving her. So, whilst his view was in some ways similar to Paddy's, it was also very different. Because, whilst he hadn't told anyone else, he knew in his heart, he *had* forgiven her.

And ultimately it wasn't because love conquers all, it wasn't even because of who she was, in isolation. No, it came down to one simple thing. Because of whom he was when he was with her.

He concentrated on trying to catch up with the conversation between the two women.

'What about you, Dylan. You ever killed anyone?' Pen

grinned as she asked the question.

Dylan cocked her head. 'What's this? My round of the Honesty Index?'

Pen laughed. Dylan didn't. Situation normal. 'I still can't get my head round everything that happened.' Pen sighed and tapped Dylan on the arm. 'I bet you didn't have all this drama when you were younger.'

Dylan flinched at the rare direct contact but said nothing. She'd been born trademarked as hard-to-read, but right then Trent knew she was thinking about Pen's question and reliving a personal drama all of her own.

'What was your life like, growing up?' he asked. 'You never talk about your past.'

She looked at him, her trademark unblinking stare in full effect. 'That,' she said, her voice flat, 'is a whole other story.'

'We've got plenty of time,' Trent said.

Dylan titled her head. 'Today's about the two of you. Besides I've got somewhere else I need to be. I just wanted to check on you.'

'Love interest?' Trent asked.

Dylan stepped towards him, her face just inches away from his. 'There's no love interest in my life,' she said, before touching her finger to his lips. 'Except you,' she whispered.

Trent couldn't swear to it, but he thought he caught the beginnings of a smile as she turned and walked away from them down the road.

'Same old Dylan,' Pen said.

'Yeah. Same old Dylan.'

Pen grabbed her brother's hands. 'Well, I'd better be going, too.'

'You sure you won't come?'

'Yeah. I need to finish the job application.' She squeezed his hands. 'I really want this, Trent.'

He nodded. Pen had adjusted remarkably well. To Bobby. To the truth about their father. To everything. 'They'd be crazy not to offer you the job.'

She kissed him on the cheek. 'Well, let's hope they're not crazy, then.'

TRENT SETTLED back into his chair and wrapped his hands around the pint glass. His phone vibrated in his pocket. He pulled out his phone and smiled as he saw who the message was from.

It's tonight you're meeting the guys, isn't it?

He started to type a reply when the pub door swung open and Paddy and Frances walked in. Trent locked his phone screen and place the phone on the table, face down, next to his pint. He stood up and waved his friends over.

Paddy cracked open a grin, and Frances wiggled her fingers in the air, as if waving to a five-year-old. Which was fine with Trent. He hugged them both before Frances sat down and Paddy headed to the bar.

'I'm afraid I can't stay long,' she said, pushing her frizzy mop from her eyes. 'A friend's looking after the kids but I need to be home by eight.'

'A rare night out, hey,' Trent said.

Frances shrugged. She and Jake were on a trial separation. They'd stayed together at first, after the news exploded into her life. It was as easy as one, two three. Jake had slept with Oli. Oli was pregnant. And Jake was the father. Simple facts that spawned an emotional nightmare. Trent had no idea how a relationship survived that, or whether it ever could. Frances and Jake had two children together, and at the time of the revelation, Frances was heavily pregnant with their third.

'How are you coping?' he asked. He wanted to drop his head, but he managed to keep eye contact.

Another shrug. 'Somehow,' she replied. Frances was strong. She always had been. There was brief pause, and she twitched her nose. 'She messaged me. The other day.' Frances didn't say who. But then again, she didn't need to. Trent tapped his fingers against his mouth. 'She said she was in touch with you.'

Trent cleared his throat. Glanced towards the bar to see Paddy on his way back, holding a tray with two drinks and peering at his phone. 'We text.' His voice was scratchy.

Paddy placed the drinks on the table and sat down. He looked at them both, a crease appearing across his forehead. 'Have I interrupted something?'

Frances raised her eyebrows. 'Now, that's a good question.'

Paddy shuffled on his seat. 'Okay. Well, I don't know what's going on between you two.' He took a sip of larger. 'Dub just messaged. He'll be here in five.'

'All the boys. And me,' Frances said, 'the only girl.'

Trent's neck was tight. He hadn't been sure how the evening would go, but it sure as hell wasn't starting off on the best path. He leant forward. 'I need to tell you something, Paddy.' Neither of them said anything, so Trent swallowed and pushed on. 'I've been in touch with Lila.' He whispered, hoping that would soften the impact of his words.

Paddy pushed his chair back. 'Jesus.' He shook his head. 'Really?'

Trent nodded. 'She's been seeing a counsellor.' A pause. 'A psychiatrist.'

'You know what she did to us, Trent. How could you...' Paddy trailed off.

'I think...' He sucked in some air and tried again. 'She did it because she wanted me to know something.'

'Yeah. About Pen, on the night of the fire. We know. We were there. Played the game. Attended the court case.'

Trent shook his head. 'No, not that. Something else.'

'Jesus. Another secret. Will this thing never end?' Paddy asked. But he hadn't stood up to leave. Not yet. The jury was waiting to hear the evidence for the defence.

'What's the secret?' Frances asked.

Trent flinched. 'I can't tell you.'

'Well, that's not good enough. After what we've been through together, we can't have secrets from each other.' Paddy jabbed his finger at Trent as he spoke.

And maybe he was right. Trent's mind was spinning. He knew the secret. As did Pen. And Lila. And Oli. But of all of them, it was Oli's secret to share. And hers alone.

'Paddy's right, Trent. Look at what happened to the two of us.' Frances gestured between her and Paddy.

'But...' Trent bit his tongue. Wasn't Paddy glad that Todd Line was facing jail? And wouldn't Frances rather know that her husband was the father of another woman's baby? He shook his head and blew out another breath. Wasn't he glad he knew the truth about his father? He still couldn't answer that question.

'Just tell us, Trent. Better out than in,' said Paddy.

Maybe if he told them his father had raped an under-age girl, but didn't say who. No. Too risky. They might work it out. They'd shout out names, and he wouldn't be able to hide his reaction. His hurt and anger at what his father had done to Oli. No. 'I can't.' The tension in his jaw almost locked his mouth shut.

A shadow fell over the table. 'Evening all.' The Canadian twang, dropped down from on high.

They all stood to greet Dub and Trent offered to get the next round. Without waiting for agreement, he headed to the bar. He rested his elbows on the bar, careful to avoid the puddles of spilt beer. His heart was thumping and his mouth was dry. He wanted to tell them, but knew he couldn't. He pulled his phone out and hit dial.

'Hi.' Oli's voice was quiet.

'Hey. Sorry to call.'

'It's okay. Sophia's asleep. How's the evening going?'

Trent sighed. 'They know I'm in touch with Lila.'

There was a silence and then Oli spoke. 'And how's that gone down?'

'Badly and getting worse.' His hand was shaking.

'Yeah.' The word was drawn out. Trent could practically hear her thinking. 'Trent?'

'Yes?'

'Tell them. About me. About your dad. Tell them.'

'But I...' His voice rasped. He coughed to clear his throat. 'That's not right,' he said.

'Who's to say what's right and what's wrong?' There was a sound in the background, and she paused, as if to see whether it would develop into something more than a murmur. 'I've been thinking about it a lot over the last year. And I've decided. I want you to tell them, Trent. And not just for you, but for me, too.'

Trent sniffed. 'Are you sure, Oli?'

'Yes. I'm sure.' Another pause. 'I need to go. I'll see you later.'

Trent stood with his phone against his ear for a few seconds. The barman was looking at him.

'You alright, mate?'

Trent wiped his hand over his face and nodded. In tapping his phone against the card machine to pay he caught sight of Lila's message. He typed his reply.

Yes. I'm going to tell them everything.

He pocketed his phone and then picked up the tray to carry the drinks back to the others. The three of them were sitting in silence. Trent could see the tremor in the drinks as he handed them over, and could feel the tightness in his chest. It was clear that Dub had been brought up to speed. Trent cleared his throat.

'Okay. I've checked. And I've been cleared to tell you the secret.'

'By Lila?' The scorn in Dub's voice could have started a fire.

'By Oli,' Trent replied.

Dub's eyes bulged. 'That's not your secret to tell,' Dub said. He was twitching, and massaging his chin. 'Is that why you invited me here?'

'Dub, hold on. This has nothing to do with you.' Trent scanned the group. 'None of you.' He swallowed. 'It's about my dad.'

'Your dad?' Paddy was frowning. 'Why would Oli need to give you permission–'

Trent fired the words out, as if they were coated with poison. 'My father got Oli pregnant just before she turned sixteen. She had an abortion.'

Dub's bug-eyes were back and Paddy's mouth was hanging open.

'That's statutory rape,' Frances said.

Trent hung his head. 'Sexual activity with a child.' His voice cracked.

'My God,' Paddy said.

Dub was pale, and rocking slightly on his chair.

'Poor Oli,' Frances said. 'I guess that puts various things into some sort of perspective.' She was frowning, her moral code no doubt being crushed through a mangler. How the hell was she going to make any sense of that, Trent wondered? Frances blinked. 'Oli told you?'

Trent nodded again. 'Lila knew. She wanted me to know, but in the end she knew that Oli had to be the one to tell me. Oli came to see me after the Honesty Index was over. She told me and Pen.' He sniffed. 'The night of the fire, that's what my parents were arguing about. My dad must have told Mum. Or Mum guessed and accused him.'

'Christ, you don't think the fire...' Paddy didn't finish the question.

Trent tried to speak, but he had no words. He shuffled on his seat. Frances reached over and stroked his back.

'Don't answer that,' she said.

'How the hell did Lila know?' Paddy asked. Maybe because it had just occurred to him. Or maybe to pivot away from the fire.

Trent took a moment to compose himself. 'She's never told me.' He paused and tried a half-smile. 'I think she's trying to do things differently now.'

'Huh.' Paddy buried his head in his hands for a few seconds. Then he looked up, picked up his pint and drained it. 'Well, I for one, am going to need another drink. Anyone else?'

TRENT TURNED the key and pushed open his front door. He closed it behind him, being careful not to make too much noise. He slipped off his coat and hung it over the banister at the foot of the stairs, before steadying himself, and then walking into the kitchen and pouring himself a drink of water.

He didn't hear his houseguest follow him in.

'Did you have a good evening?'

Trent almost dropped his glass. He turned round. 'Sorry, did I wake you? I thought you'd be asleep.'

Oli smiled. 'Sophia went down a couple of hours ago. I should've gone to bed but I've been snoozing on the sofa.' She peered closely at him. 'How did it go? Did you tell them?'

'I did.' He took another mouthful of water. 'Thank you.'

Oli shrugged. It'd been one of the few good things over the last year to see how Oli had flourished. Her parents had kicked her out, and Trent hadn't hesitated to invite her to move in with him and Pen. They'd tried their best to keep it under wraps, although they'd agreed it wasn't a secret, as such. And against the odds, it was working. Somehow.

He put the glass down and made his way over to Oli.

'You're drunk,' she said. But she was smiling.

Trent pulled her into a hug. 'I think they might forgive me for staying in touch with Lila.' His words were slurred.

'I'm not sure *I've* forgiven you for being in touch with her.'

Trent staggered back. 'But I thought...'

'Trent, I'm joking. Come here.' She pulled him back into the embrace.

He felt the warmth of her body against his. There was nothing between them, and yet now their lives were entwined in a way that was complex and nuanced. 'Hey, Oli?'

'Yes?'

'How did Lila know about what happened?' He vaguely remembered someone asking that question earlier that evening.

Oli was silent for a minute before speaking. 'I don't know. But I'll tell you what I do know.'

'What's that?'

'I don't care.'

Trent nodded into her shoulder. He rubbed her back. 'Neither do I, Oli. Neither do I.'

ACKNOWLEDGMENTS

I hope you enjoyed reading *The Honesty Index.*

This story will always have a special place in my heart. I vividly remember writing the opening chapter when Trent was waiting for Lila Jain. I had no real idea how the novel would turn out, just a loose concept and a cast of characters. And whilst the final version is very different from that initial draft, the first chapter is virtually the same (I added the prologue later), and the opening lines are *exactly* the same. I remember how I felt when I wrote that opening. It was the moment I knew what writing meant to me. Pure joy.

So, I'm thrilled to see *The Honesty Index* in print. It's the story that hooked my agent, Jo Bell, and was so, so close to securing a publishing deal.

It would be unusual I think, to get this far without the support and help of a collection of fantastic people. In no particular order, my heartfelt thanks:

To special agent Jo, who was been a champion of my writing these last few years, super reader Sarah, and all at Bell Lomax Moreton.

To the Faber crew: Emma, Siobhan, Tonks, Zo, Vania, Robyn, Nicole and Alison - it's no exaggeration to say that I wouldn't have got this far without you.

To my A* grade, beta-readers, Susie, Lucia, Helen, Kay, Aunt Mel, Mike, Elizabeth and Alison.

To the 'Premier book club in Limehouse' and their very generous hosts, Mike and Paula.

To Kathryn Price, for her early editorial advice and enthusiasm.

To the course tutors at Faber and Jericho - Richard Kelly, Rowan Coleman, and Debi Alper - for their guidance and support.

To all the great editors at publishing houses who read an earlier version of the manuscript and provided feedback and hope, even if they didn't eventually make an offer.

To Jason Anscomb, for my stunning cover.

To Billy Angel, for my wonderful book trailer video.

To the powerhouse that is Sara Naidine Cox, for helping me kick the manuscript into its final form.

To Claire, and to James, for everything that I can't adequately put into words.

Finally my thanks to each and every one of you for reading my book. I'm forever grateful to you all.

THE GENIUS CLUB

READ ON FOR AN EXTRACT FROM THE NEXT ELECTRIFYING THRILLER FROM NJ BARKER...

They were intelligent enough to be selected, but are they smart enough to survive?

17-year-old Matthew Stanford's life changed the moment he was invited to join the Genius Club, a group of gifted children handpicked for patronage by the mysterious polymath Benjamin Caesar.

Nearly two decades later, Matthew returns from work one day to discover that Lucy, his wife and fellow Genius Club member, has apparently taken her own life.

Convinced that Lucy's death wasn't suicide, he begins to dig. He uncovers Lucy's regular secret meetings with an ex-member of the Genius Club who Matthew thought had broken off all contact, and records of private daily electrotherapy.

When Matthew learns that Lucy's doctor has not only treated other members, but also that he and Caesar had formed an elite society at college, Matthew suspects there is something sinister behind the Genius Club.

The future feels very different, but so does the past.

And if Matthew is right, then Lucy was murdered and Matthew, his teenage son, and his Genius Club friends are now all targets of the killer.

Desperate to save everything that remains dear to him, Matthew must race against time to uncover the true evil that lies at the heart of the Genius Club.

TUESDAY, 11 JUNE 2019

5:05pm

Professor Matthew Stanford cursed under his breath. The bus edged along through the rush-hour London traffic, barely outpacing the pedestrians. Should he get off and run? It was only another mile until his home stop opposite the train station.

He hit redial and waited. Counted the rings until it flipped to his son's voicemail.

'This is Alfie. Knock yourself out.'

Matthew had already left one message. *I'm on my way home. Call me.* He'd sent the same text. But he hadn't heard from Alfie since the first messages that had arrived as Matthew had been climbing aboard the bus.

You nearly home?

I can't go in.

Matthew stared at his phone. There was a missed call from the school, but he couldn't worry about that now. He tried Alfie again.

'Hi, Dad,' Alfie's voice sounded hesitant.

'Hey, Alfie, are you okay? I'm only a few minutes away now.' No reply. 'Alfie?' Matthew's shoulders tensed and fear began to scratch inside his stomach. He heard Alfie swallowing. 'Alfie?' His voice was slightly terse. He knew it was anxiety, but he worried his son might think it was anger.

'I...' Alfie started.

Matthew forced himself to wait, glancing out the window and silently swearing at the car that has stranded itself across the roundabout, blocking the bus.

'I...'

'It's alright, Alfie. Whatever it is.' Matthew was trying to sound calm. 'Are you at home?'

'Yes.' Still sounding unsure. Sounding younger than his sixteen years. 'I'm inside the building but I haven't gone into our flat.' There was a hesitation before Alfie answered the unspoken question. 'Mum's left a note on our door.'

Matthew's heart began to thump. Alfie must have read the note. But what the hell could Lucy write that would throw Alfie like this?

'Well, just hold on, I'm nearly at the bus stop now.'

The car had finally driven off and the bus was moving again. Rain began to sweep down against the window.

'Dad?'

'Yes, Alfie?' Keep your voice even. Don't rush him.

'I'm worried, Dad.'

His son's voice was stretched. Not far from tears. Heat burnt down Matthew's chest.

'It's okay.' What else could he say? He started to walk down the bus as it slowed towards the stop. Less than five minutes away from home. He needed to keep Alfie talking. 'What does the note say?'

'It's addressed to you.' Matthew heard Alfie take a deep

breath. 'But I read it.' Alfie paused, leaving a gap for his dad to slip in an admonishment.

Matthew stepped off the bus and started to jog along the road, twisting to see the traffic so he could dart across to the other side.

'That's okay.' He heard his own voice; the cold air, asthma and physical activity triggering a wheeze already.

Alfie was a good kid, a bright kid, a very bright kid, and it was unlike him to be upset.

'I think I ... I should tell you ... tell you when you get home.' He forced out a few words at a time.

Matthew was sprinting now. He flew by the parade of shops and the group of teenagers hanging around on their bikes, spun up the road, his feet splashing through the shallow puddles, until he reached the front door to the flats. He fumbled for the keys, knowing his son was the other side. The entrance hall was bare and unloved. There were two doors, theirs and the downstairs neighbour's. Home was on the other side of their door, but this was no man's land.

Alfie was sitting on the floor, his back against their front door, hugging his knees. His son. All the hope in his heart. All the fear in his stomach.

A piece of paper was pinned on the door. Matthew's name was neatly printed in his wife's handwriting. Alfie must have read it and then placed it back. As you did when you didn't want someone to know that you'd read it. Or perhaps because you wished you hadn't, and it felt like turning back time.

Matthew moved to hug him, but his son buried his face into his knees. Matthew straightened himself up and reached out. He blinked and read the words that Lucy had written to him.

My dearest Matthew,

I'm sorry.

I love you both.

Lucy x

The world slowed and sharpened. Alfie's gentle sniffs echoed around the lobby and then Matthew's phone's ringtone burst into life. But Matthew could only focus on the note. The words *I'm sorry* reverberated in his mind. His heart was thumping, and his mouth was dry. Oh Lucy. What had she done?

He pushed away the obvious assumption that assailed him. His phone stopped ringing and he put his ear against the door. Silence. Jesus Christ. He glanced at his phone's screen to see if the call had been from Lucy. No. It was a missed call from Alastair, and a text. He'd forgotten that he had been due to meet Alastair for a drink at the local pub.

Matthew shoved his phone into his pocket and squatted down to face Alfie. 'I don't know what's going on, Alfie.' His swallow caught in his throat. He glanced at the note in his hand. Knew he couldn't wait any longer. He looked at Alfie. 'I'm going to go in, okay. You stay here. I'll be back down in a minute.'

There was a barely imperceptible nod from Alfie. Matthew blinked rapidly and then unlocked the front door, walked through, and pushed it to behind him. Then he turned and sprinted up the stairs.

'Lucy.' His shout died against the walls of their hallway. His wife's red duffle coat was hanging on the peg but her black trainers that always rested on the shoe-rack next to Matthew's slippers had gone.

He called out again as he moved forward. No answer. He spun round in the empty kitchen and moved into the bathroom. Nothing. The bedroom door creaked as he pushed it open. He swallowed. No Lucy. He turned into the living room, sweat now dripping down his back. She wasn't there.

There was only one room left to look in. Lucy's study. Breathing heavily, he reached out towards the chipped brass handle. He gripped it expecting resistance, but it turned smoothly. His chest squeezed in, and he could hear the blood rushing in his ears. The door swung open.

The floor tilted and Matthew reached out to the wall to steady himself. Lucy was lying on the floor stretched out on her back. She was dressed in the jeans and the yellow tunic top he had watched her pull on that morning. He could tell immediately that she was dead. Yet seeing her there, devoid of life, made no sense. No sense at all.

For a moment it was as if he was watching himself looking at her and waiting to see how he would react. He was dimly aware of his knees smashing into the wood effect laminate on the floor as he reached for her, knowing though that it wasn't her any longer. Knowing that she was gone.

His cry reverberated around the room. His fingers fumbled towards her neck. Please God let there be a pulse. Please. Hot tears streaked his face, and the room began to swim. Her skin was cold. There was no pulse except his own which was thumping against his temples. A convulsion threw his body forward so his head was on her chest. But her arms didn't comfort him, her fingers didn't tangle in his hair. Already, those memories belonged to a different lifetime.

One of Lucy's arms was folded so that her hand supported her head on the floor whilst the other was flung backwards as if she was mid-stretch. Matthew pushed himself back into a sitting position and pulled out his phone to call an ambulance. The conversation was a blur. He heard himself say the words *Sierra Whiskey*. On some level his brain was working normally. Or was that abnormal?

'No, she's not breathing.'

He moved her arm, and then the palm and heel of his hand were on her chest. One, two, three, four. He was tilting her head, pinching her nose, and sealing her mouth with his. Breath. Breath. Back to compressions.

Lucy's eyes were closed and her expression - was it still her expression when there was no emotion to show? - was calm. But there was no shudder of life rebooting, no flinch as her heart restarted. There was nothing.

It was then that Matthew spotted it. His body tensed. His instinct was to reach towards it, but he forced himself to continue to beat out the compressions whilst staring at a cheap plastic tube with the plunger hammered all the way down to the bottom. He knew he shouldn't touch it. That there were rules about that. But what force did rules have in a situation like this? He wanted to lean forward. He wanted to smash it; to destroy what had taken his wife.

Just then he heard a loud banging from outside the room.

God, Alfie. Alfie. Oh no. Jesus.

Footsteps hammered up the stairs and voices called out. The ambulance had arrived.

'In here,' Matthew called.

He moved aside as the paramedics took over. What should he do? He staggered out of the room to find Alfie standing with another paramedic at the top of the stairs. Nothing could have prepared Matthew for that moment.

Lucy was gone and now he and Alfie were alone. As he

stared at his son, one truth swamped him. If it'd had to be one of them it should have been him.

And yet he had no choice. That decision had already been made.

He swallowed and walked towards his son.

THE GENIUS CLUB - AVAILABLE EARLY 2024

ABOUT THE AUTHOR

NJ Barker started writing books when he was eight, but he took his time before completing a draft of his first thriller, some forty years later. He studied Pure Mathematics (truly a branch of the arts) at Warwick University, and law at The College of Law, before building a career in personal tax.

In 2019 he retired to focus on his passion. As it turned out, this wasn't maths (surprised?) or tax (shocked?) but writing fiction.

He is a graduate of the Faber Academy where he began writing stories in which people are forced to follow someone else's rules or face the consequences. He is currently editing his next standalone thriller, *The Genius Club,* which will be published later in 2024, whilst also working hard on writing more standalone thrillers.

NJ Barker also writes the Kennedy Logan Thrillers. His short story, *The Catastrophe Test*, is an introduction to Kennedy Logan. *The Moral Authority*, book one in the series, was published in December 2023, and book two will follow in 20024.

NJ Barker lives in Kent together with his wife, son, and their two cocker spaniels.

Printed in Great Britain
by Amazon